Praise for Karen Witemeyer's Previous Novels

A Tailor-Made Bride

"Witemeyer's debut will grab fans in the historical romance crowd. She blends lively writing, storytelling prowess, and enough romance to keep readers satisfied. . . . Thought-provoking and entertaining faith-based fiction for sure."

Publishers Weekly

"In *A Tailor-Made Bride*, Karen Witemeyer presents a well-paced story of evolving insight, loving acceptance, and a humor that takes the reader from knowing chuckles to out-and-out laughter."

lovewesternromances.com

"Readers of historical romance will be delighted to discover a new author who writes like a seasoned veteran of the genre yet with a freshness that is uniquely her own. Karen Witemeyer has penned a novel as fun and feisty as the cover suggests, with an innovative heroine determined to make the most of the blessings bestowed upon her and a hero who is as surly as he is good looking."

Novel Reviews

Head in the Clouds

"Readers won't be disappointed . . . in the strong, lovable Adelaide and her ultimate Prince Charming."

Publishers Weekly

"Witemeyer writes a powerful novel about deceit, betrayal and love. The main character is a combination of strength and vulnerability, with a fierce desire to protect Isabella. The love that develops between Adelaide and Gideon is fast, but believable."

Romantic Times—4-star review

"Joyful outlook and wit in the face of hardships and sacrifice blends with the story's other strengths to make *Head in the Clouds* a satisfying read."

lovewesternromances.com

Books by
Karen Witemeyer

A Tailor-Made Bride
Head in the Clouds
To Win Her Heart

KAREN WITEMEYER

DOUBLEDAY LARGE PRINT HOME LIBRARY EDITION

This Large Print Edition, prepared especially for Doubleday Large Print Home Library, contains the complete, unabridged text of the original Publisher's Edition.

Cover design by Dan Thornberg, Design Source Creative Services

Scripture quotations are from the King James Version of the Bible.

Published by Bethany House Publishers
11400 Hampshire Avenue South
Bloomington, Minnesota 55438

Bethany House Publishers is a division of
Baker Publishing Group, Grand Rapids, Michigan.

Printed in the United States of America

ISBN 978-1-61129-895-6

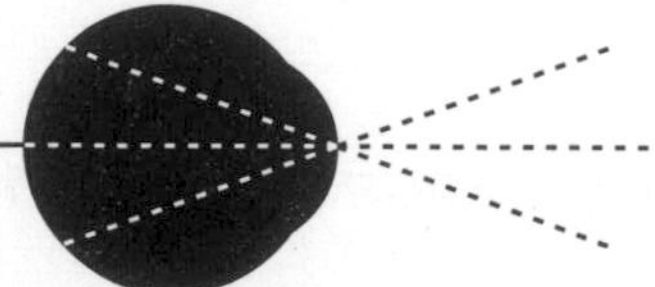

This Large Print Book carries the
Seal of Approval of N.A.V.H.

To my dad.

I knew you for only sixteen years before Jesus called you home, but in that time, you taught me to laugh, to sing, and to give my best in every endeavor. Because of you, it is easy to believe in a heavenly Father who loves his children with unconditional fervor and whose forgiveness knows no bounds.

I love you, Daddy.

Hatred stirreth up strifes:
but love covereth all sins.

Proverbs 10:12

Chapter One

Spencer, Texas
February 1887

After two years, they'd finally cut him loose. Gave him a new suit of clothes and everything. Funny, though. The shame of the convict stripes still clung to him, as if tattooed horizontally across his skin. Levi Grant rolled his shoulders under the slightly-too-tight coat he'd been issued and wondered how long it would take to get reaccustomed to ordinary clothes.

Or to get the smell of turnips out of them.

A farmer had let him ride in his wagon bed for the last ten miles or so of his journey from Huntsville. Levi's feet had welcomed the respite, but now, standing outside the parson's small box-shaped house, second thoughts needled him.

His future hinged on making a good impression. The Bible and recommendation letter in his knapsack fueled his hope, but his past dragged behind him like the lead ball that used to be shackled to his leg. The Father might have forgiven his prodigal ways, but the world was full of parabolic older brothers who would either resent the second chance he'd been given or condemn him outright. Not that he would blame them. Christian charity could only be expected to stretch so far.

A gust of cool February wind jarred him from his thoughts and pushed him forward. The Lord had led him to the preacher's threshold—the least Levi could do was knock on the door.

He climbed the steps onto the porch, ducking under a barren rose trellis. Winter had temporarily robbed the latticework of its color, but the promise of spring lingered in the twining stems.

Levi rapped a knuckle against the door and waited.

Seconds ticked by. He shifted from one foot to the other. An urge to run burgeoned inside his chest until his lungs found it difficult to expand. He blew out what little air was left in them and paced to the rail. Had he been wrong to come? Forcing himself to breathe evenly, he began to count the number of pickets in the fence across the yard. He'd barely made it to seven when the door clicked open behind him. Levi spun around. Seeing a woman, he yanked his hat from his head.

"Can I help you?" The tiny lady finished wiping her hands on her apron and looked up at him, her eyes widening only slightly as she took in his size.

"Levi Grant, ma'am. I'm here to"—*See? No*—"talk to David Cranford." The pause hadn't been long, but she'd blinked, a sure indication that she'd noticed. Years of avoiding *S* sounds in his speech had made him adept at finding substitutes, but it still took his brain time to recognize and reject the

S words that came to mind automatically.

"Mr. Grant, of course. We've been expecting you. Please, come in." A warm smile blossomed across her face as she pulled the door wide.

Levi swiveled sideways to edge through the opening without grazing his hostess. His size came in handy when pounding iron, but it was a hindrance around delicate ladies in delicate houses.

She led him to a parlor full of treacherous knickknacks and spindly chairs and left him there with the impossible task of making himself comfortable while she fetched her husband.

Choosing the most substantial piece of furniture in the room, Levi cautiously lowered himself onto the green tapestry sofa, wincing with each creak of the thin oak legs. He slung his knapsack off his shoulder and into his lap, then reached inside for the letter from his chaplain and mentor, Jonathan Willis.

Soft footfalls sounded in the hall. Levi shoved the sack aside and lurched to his feet, still clutching the letter.

"Mr. Grant. Welcome to Spencer." A thin man with dark hair graying at the temples strode across the parlor carpet, his hand outstretched. "Jonathan wired that you were coming."

Levi handed over the letter and gripped the man's hand, careful not to squeeze too hard. The preacher was a good head shorter and probably a decade older than Levi's thirty years, but his eyes exuded kindness and a blunt honesty that communicated his knowledge of Levi's past without casting judgment.

"Please, sit."

Levi bent slowly to retake his seat on the sofa while David Cranford settled into an armchair. He opened the letter Levi had given him but barely scanned the contents before folding it back up and slipping it into his coat pocket.

"You'll be glad to know that everything is in place," Cranford said. "Mr. Spencer accepted my recommendation and forwarded the lease papers to our bank. You should be in business by the end of the week."

Levi swallowed what moisture he could summon from his arid mouth. “No interview?”

“Not a formal one, no. We’ve been without a blacksmith for nigh onto four months now. And with spring planting around the corner . . . Well . . . let’s just say the townsfolk have not been shy in vocalizing their dissatisfaction. Mr. Spencer was anxious to find a blacksmith, and I was happy to recommend you to him. As long as his representative finds no glaring faults in you, things should go smoothly.”

No glaring faults? Levi nearly laughed aloud. His faults glared brighter than streaks exposed by sunlight on a freshly cleaned window. His only hope was to hide them from this representative until he’d had a chance to prove himself.

“Did you tell him about . . . ?” Levi cleared his throat but couldn’t quite spit out the rest of the question.

The preacher shook his head. “No. And I see no reason to enlighten anyone at this point. It has no direct bearing on your ability to perform your duties.”

Levi relaxed into the cushioned sofa just a bit. He had a chance, then.

"The truth will come out eventually, though," the man cautioned, "and it would be better for it to come from you than somewhere else, but I believe a man has the right to demonstrate his character by his actions instead of being weighed solely by his past mistakes.

"I've known Jonathan Willis since our days at seminary," Cranford continued. "He speaks highly of you, Mr. Grant. And that's good enough for me. I'll gladly introduce you to Mr. Spencer's agent and reiterate my recommendation."

"Thank you." Levi had not expected such generosity. Didn't deserve it. Yet he'd not be so foolish as to reject it. He'd spent enough time in foolish pursuits.

" 'There is therefore now no condemnation to them which are in Christ Jesus.' " The preacher patted the leather cover of the Bible sitting on the round parlor stand between the arm of his chair and the sofa, his gaze intent. Almost as if he were trying to bore a hole through Levi's hide to embed the truth of the words into his soul.

Levi turned his head away from the man's scrutiny to stare instead at a porcelain shepherdess guarding a shelf on the front wall. He knew the passage from Romans 8. He even believed it. Yet no matter how hard his brain tried to convince his heart, self-reproach still clung to him like a parasite.

"You're a new man making a new start."

Levi jerked his head around.

"Leave the guilt behind, son."

"Leave the other book on my desk. I'll shelve it for you later."

Eden Spencer tried to hurry her last patron out, an elderly woman who moved slower than a bug on flypaper. Normally she didn't mind chatting with Pearl after closing time, but today she did. Norman Draper had strolled past her window five minutes ago, portfolio in hand—no doubt on his way to get the new blacksmith's signature on the building lease. Before she'd even had a chance to talk to the man. Eden pressed her lips together to keep her irritation at bay as she helped Pearl with her scarf.

Why was it that no one on the town council took her role as her father's representative seriously? What if she found the new smith unsuitable? If the banker jumped the gun with the papers, it would make sending the man on his way vastly more difficult. Thank goodness Emma had stopped by earlier to let her know the smith had arrived. Now, if she could just hurry Pearl along a bit, maybe she could dash across the street to the parsonage in time to prevent any rash action on Mr. Draper's part.

"Here's your book, Pearl." Eden placed the small volume of poetry into the older woman's hands.

"Thank you, dear. My afternoons would be dreadfully dull without something new to read every now and again."

"I'm glad I could help." Eden swung her door open, ignoring the chilly breeze that ruffled her skirts. She took Pearl's elbow and guided her down to the street, taking extra care on the steps. Then she bid the woman a quick farewell and darted back into the house, where she snatched her black cashmere shawl from the hall tree and flung it around her shoulders. Plunking a bonnet on her head, she let the ribbons flap freely as she loped down the front walk. Loped, not ran. Running would be unseemly.

"Whoa there, little lady. What's the hurry?"

Eden groaned. Sheriff Pratt's office was around the corner on Main Street, and he had taken up the habit of watching for her from his rear window. The town matrons found it sweet the way he escorted her around town. Eden found it a nuisance.

"I'm afraid I can't talk, Sheriff. I'm late for a meeting." She offered an apologetic wave as she bustled past without slowing her pace. She had just about reached the churchyard when he lunged in front of her, forcing her to choose between halting and colliding with his person. She opted for the halt.

"Is that any way to talk to your betrothed?" His syrupy voice set her skin to itching.

Eden gathered her shawl a bit more tightly about her. "I'm not your betrothed, Sheriff. I refused your proposal three weeks ago."

"And nearly busted my heart in the process, but I forgive you."

She didn't want to be forgiven. She wanted to be left alone.

Sheriff Pratt clasped the crown of his felt hat and dragged it from his head down to the general vicinity of his heart, or more precisely, the area above his belly paunch.

"I'm just letting you know the offer's still on the table. In case you decide to reconsider." He smiled at her and winked, but the gesture seemed void of true affection. The man might want to marry her, but Eden doubted his reasons had anything to do with tender feelings. He probably figured tying himself to a Spencer would be good for his career. He was up for reelection, after all.

"Thank you, Sheriff, but—"

"Conrad, darlin'. Call me Conrad."

Eden stiffened. "Sheriff Pratt . . ." She emphasized the formal address. "I appreciate your kind consideration, but my answer remains unchanged. Now, if you'll excuse me?"

His smile tightened, but apparently the gentleman in him won out. He extended his hat in a sweeping motion as he stepped aside. "I'll wish you a good evening, then, Miss Spencer."

"Thank you. And a good evening to you." Eden nodded and moved past. Her conscience pricked a little over having been short with him, but after the indignity she'd suffered five years ago, she was in no hurry to commit herself to another man. Especially not to one who wore a gun. Violence only begot more violence, and she couldn't imagine aligning herself with a man who had blood on his hands—even if he stood on the right side of the law.

Having reached the parsonage, Eden thrust aside all thoughts of the sheriff and raised her hand to knock. Emma Cranford answered swiftly.

"They haven't signed anything yet, have they?" Eden asked as she breezed past the preacher's wife, focused solely on making her way to the front room, where the men were congregating.

Soft laughter echoed behind her. "Are you planning to storm the castle, Eden?" There was more teasing than chiding in the question. Nevertheless, it succeeded in slowing Eden's step and getting her to turn around and face her neglected hostess.

"I'm sorry, Emma. I didn't even greet you, did I?"

"Never mind," she said as she shooed Eden toward the parlor. "We've been friends too long for me to be offended by such silly details. I know not to get in your way when you're on a mission." She smiled in the forgiving way of hers that relieved Eden's conscience even while it made her silently promise never to repeat the infraction.

"Go on. Get in there before Mr. Draper bullies them into signing without you."

Eden nodded her thanks and spun back toward the parlor.

Male voices grew louder as she approached, Mr. Draper's being the most adamant. ". . . no telling when Miss Spencer will get around to making an appearance. You know how women are. If Calvin Spencer gave his approval, that's all I require."

"I'm sure she'll be along short—"

"Well, *I'm* here now. But I won't be for long. I have a town council meeting to attend. And if Mr. Grant wants to lease the smithy, he'll sign the papers now."

Storm the castle, indeed. Bristling, Eden set her shoulders for battle and swept into the room. "If Mr. Grant wants to lease the smithy, he'll have to gain my approval or the papers will be meaningless."

The banker turned hostile eyes on her and opened his mouth, most likely to inform her that his papers were legal with or without her approval, but David Cranford managed to forestall the argument by jumping to his feet and rushing to her side.

"Miss Spencer! So good to see you." He wisely positioned himself between her and the banker. "May I introduce you to the man who recently applied to be our new blacksmith?"

As David stretched his arm out toward the sofa, a man rose to his feet. Slowly. Well, it wasn't so much that his movement was slow, but that there was a great deal of him to unfold from where he sat.

At some level, her mind registered the preacher's voice as he made the formal introduction, but the rest of her attention remained riveted on the giant in Emma's parlor. If the mythical Hercules had been inspired by an actual person, this man would surely be a descendant. She'd never seen such broad shoulders.

Her gaze moved from his shoulders to his face. Square jaw. Firm lips. Straight nose, barring the bump on the bridge, where it looked like it'd been broken. Everything about him was hard—except his eyes. Vulnerability shone in their gray depths. Or at least she thought it did. He shifted his regard to the floor so fast, she couldn't be sure.

David cleared his throat, and Eden blinked, realizing she was expected to speak. "Pleasure to meet you, Mr. . . . ah . . . Mr. Grant."

"Ma'am." He nodded to her, his gaze barely brushing her chin before falling again to the floor.

Good heavens. How was she supposed to conduct an interview with a man whose size was so startling she could scarcely manage a coherent greeting?

Chapter Two

Levi forced his gaze away from the auburn-haired beauty standing beside David Cranford. *This* was Mr. Spencer's representative? He'd been prepared to face a man like Mr. Draper—professional, practical, and more than a bit pompous, but a woman who looked like she belonged in some rich man's drawing room? He'd be lucky to string a handful of words together under her scrutiny.

It wouldn't be so bad if she were older, or pinched-faced or something. Even having her look down her nose at him would help. But, no. She had to be young, and prettier than a spring meadow in her green dress with the flowery ruffles. Yeah, he'd noticed. Noticed the way her eyes widened when she got a look at him, too. Wished he could tell if it was fear or appreciation that prompted that reaction.

"Come. Have a seat, Eden." David Cranford ushered her to a chair near his own and waved Levi and Draper back into theirs. "We might as well get this business done while everyone is here."

The banker grumbled something about interfering women, but Levi ignored the muttering as he retook his seat on the sofa. Draper might not think too highly of the female, but Calvin Spencer obviously did, and Levi had no intention of alienating the man's representative, no matter her gender.

"Miss Spencer runs the library down the street," Cranford explained to Levi as the lady removed her shawl and bonnet, draping them across the arm of her chair. "And since Mr. Spencer resides in Austin, she also serves as her father's representative on town matters."

Draper heaved an audible sigh. "Let's forgo the explanations, shall we? All Mr. Grant needs to know is that Calvin Spencer owns the blacksmith shop he wishes to lease, and that, for some unfathomable reason, our founding father wishes his daughter to give her approval before the papers are signed."

The banker dipped his chin toward the young woman, his voice brittle. "If you'd be so kind as to get this interview underway, Miss Spencer? Some of us have places to be."

Levi dug his fingers into his knees, disgusted by the man's attitude. He wanted to glare him into repentance, but instead, he turned toward Miss Spencer and tried to apologize with his eyes. "I'd be glad to"—*Answer your questions?*—"tell you whatever you need to know, ma'am."

"Thank you, Mr. Grant." She offered him a small smile, and he returned the gesture, relief uncoiling the knots in his belly. "And please, call me Miss Spencer. *Ma'am* makes me feel decrepit."

Her smile widened, and Levi tried to match it while the knots reasserted themselves in his stomach and climbed into his throat.

"You're far from decrepit," he assured her.

Her eyelashes fluttered as her gaze dipped to her lap, and Levi exhaled, grateful to have extricated himself for the time being, even though he knew he was doomed to offend her in the future. Her name had so many S's in it, he'd hiss worse than a steaming kettle if he attempted to pronounce it. And if *ma'am* got her dander up, too? Well, he was sunk.

"So tell me about your work experience, Mr. Grant." Miss Spencer's lashes lifted, and her eyes glowed with purpose. "I'm sure Mr. Cranford has expressed our town's need for a blacksmith, but let me assure you that I'd rather prolong our search than employ a smith who offers shoddy craftsmanship."

Regardless of the opinions of the men in the room, the lady took her responsibilities seriously. Levi checked his posture, rolling his shoulders back slightly to make sure he was straight, then met her gaze head on. Time to get down to business.

Deliberating over each phrase, he pieced together a halting answer. "My father . . . taught my brother and me the trade. I've manned a forge . . . from the time . . . well, from the time I could hold a hammer."

"And where are you from?"

He couldn't say Huntsville. One, because he really couldn't *say* it. And two, because everyone knew of the state prison there. Such a response would provoke too many questions. However, he'd not dishonor his new commitment to Christ by lying, either.

"I . . . grew up in Caldwell."

"That's south of here, isn't it?"

Levi nodded. "Yep. Near Hearne." He turned away from her for a moment, hoping to cut off the line of questioning that was growing increasingly uncomfortable. The unspoken code of the West was to let a man's past alone. He didn't know if that held true in employment interviews, but he'd do his dead-level best to invoke it if possible.

Miss Spencer shifted in her chair, as if sensing his unease, but instead of pressing the issue as he would expect from a woman determined to prove her mettle, she hesitated. For a time-stretching moment, she peered into his face as if searching for proof of his character, then blinked and steered the conversation in a different direction.

"You mentioned working with your father. Have you ever operated your own shop?"

"No, ma'am." As soon as the *ma'am* left his tongue, Levi slammed his lips closed, but it was too late. Miss Spencer's eyebrow twitched, and Levi dropped his gaze like a schoolboy trying to avoid a teacher's scolding.

"Mr. Grant comes highly recommended," the preacher interjected in an effort to smooth things over. "Your father found his references quite satisfactory."

"I'm aware of that." Miss Spencer's brow arched even farther, but at least this time she was looking at someone else. "Yet it is still up to me to ascertain the smith's suitability. So, Mr. Grant . . ." Her attention fixed on Levi once again. "Do you have any written documentation vouching for the quality of your workmanship?"

Levi forced himself to meet her stare without apology. "No."

He hadn't actually plied his trade in close to six years. But his time as a bare-knuckle fighter combined with the eighteen months spent breaking rock at the Granite Mountain labor camp had kept him fit. He didn't doubt for a moment that he could swing a sledge as well as he ever had. Maybe better. Seeing as how this time around he actually *wanted* the job.

"Give me a month," Levi urged, glancing at the banker and the preacher but focusing on the woman across from him. "If you find my work . . . inadequate . . . you can take back your offer."

Eden held the man's gaze. His offer was fair. More than fair, really—seeing as how he could have leveraged his skill against their obvious need in order to take advantage of the situation. But he hadn't. No, he'd answered her questions forthrightly, and treated her with respect. There was an earnestness about him, too, that made her want to trust him. Not that she was foolish enough to trust a man she'd just met, but he'd wisely given her exactly what she needed to say yes—a way out if things turned bad.

"Can we write that into the lease, Mr. Draper?"

The banker scowled at her. "Would doing so get me out of here in the next fifteen minutes?" He deliberately pulled his watch from his vest pocket, checked the time, and clicked it shut before raising his eyes back to hers.

Eden bit back the retort that sat heavily on her tongue. Instead she favored him with a tight smile. "Having such a stipulation in place would assuage my concerns concerning Mr. Grant's lack of references. Surely, it would only take a minute to add such an amendment to the lease papers."

She turned to David Cranford. “Do you have pen and ink, Mr. Cranford?”

“Of course.” The preacher pushed to his feet and crossed to the desk that stood in the corner. With a dramatic sigh, the banker followed.

Eden fiddled with the bonnet strings that draped over the arm of her chair and into her lap. Even though she and Mr. Grant were not alone in the room, it suddenly felt as though they were. She glanced in his direction, and her gaze collided with his. They both smiled, then quickly looked elsewhere. Well, Mr. Grant looked elsewhere. Eden couldn’t seem to find another object in the room on which to focus. But it wasn’t as if she *wanted* to look at him. The man was as big as a mountain. Where else was she supposed to look?

He certainly possessed an abundance of brawn. Eden’s attention flittered over his arms as he leaned forward and balanced his forearms on his knees. The fabric of his sleeves seemed too meager to contain the muscles within as it stretched over his biceps. The heavy aspects of ironwork would be no hardship for this man. It was unfortunate that his intellect hadn't developed to the same extent as his physique. Then again, he wasn't interviewing for a position as schoolmaster, so what did it matter? Except that it did matter—to her—a bit more than it should.

A vague feeling of disappointment had circulated through her when she first heard him speak. Why his halting verbiage should bother her, she had no idea. It wasn't as if she had any personal attachment to the man.

Eden sat up straighter in her chair, uncrossing her ankles and then crossing them again in the opposite direction. She forced her eyes away from the blacksmith, glancing behind him to where Mr. Draper stood hunched over the desk, penning an addendum into the lease contract. Unfortunately, Mr. Grant chose that moment to straighten his own posture, the top of his head moving to block a good portion of the banker's back and half of the preacher's arm from her view. Eden bit the inside of her lip.

For heaven's sake. She was tempted to think he had somehow discerned her intention to ignore him and taken action to prevent it. But, no. The man was just restless. He lifted a hand and scratched a spot behind his ear as he turned toward the window. When he finished, a small tuft of hair stuck out, somehow making the gargantuan man seem almost boyish. Eden's lips curved slightly before she pressed them back down into an indifferent line. His thick, dark brown hair was cropped into short waves. She wouldn't call them curls; that descriptor sounded much too feminine for a man as rugged as Mr. Grant. However, the strands looked as though they would easily wind around a person's finger . . . should a . . . uh . . . person's finger have cause to be in his hair.

The smith glanced back at that moment, and Eden dropped her gaze to her lap—where her right index finger had apparently wound itself up in her bonnet ribbon while she'd been contemplating the man's hair. She immediately extricated the iniquitous digit and gave it a firm glare.

She wasn't in the market for a man, and even if she were, she'd never be attracted to one who lacked wit and intelligence. It was not that she didn't respect a man who worked with his hands. Skilled tradesmen were crucial to a town's economy. Nonetheless, she couldn't imagine spending her life with someone who was unable to converse with her about Dickens or argue the merits of Twain. Love of literature encapsulated too large a part of her not to share.

"It's ready, Mr. Grant." The banker cleared his throat, effectively cutting off Eden's wayward thoughts. "Come, read over the lease agreement. Mr. Cranford can serve as witness."

The smith rose and strode across the rug toward the desk. Eden jumped up and followed, an insistent inner voice demanding that she be allowed to read the addendum before the men signed it. She clamped her teeth closed against it, though. Mr. Draper already thought her enough of a harpy without her questioning his honor. Besides, David Cranford had observed the banker's edits, and she trusted the minister's integrity.

Mr. Grant nodded to the men as he accepted the contract. He swiftly reviewed the page, as if the legal jargon presented no difficulty for him, which caused Eden to raise a brow. That didn't fit her image of him. Then again, the man was eager to obtain employment. He was probably just putting on a show—pretending to read in order to make a good impression before signing the papers.

Once Mr. Grant and the minister signed their names, Norman Draper stuffed the lease into his portfolio and held out his hand to the blacksmith. "Welcome to Spencer."

Mr. Grant smiled and gripped the man's hand. "Thank you. . . ."

There he went again. He opened his mouth to say more, then didn't.

"One of our council members, Luther Colby, owns the local hotel and has offered to put you up tonight free of charge." Mr. Draper collected his hat and tucked it into the crook of his arm. "Should you require additional time to search for more permanent accommodations, all subsequent charges will be your responsibility."

The blacksmith nodded.

"Claude Barnes down at the livery has been filling in as temporary farrier, so he can show you around the shop."

"I'll . . . come by tomorrow morning."

As the men shook hands and thumped each other on the back, Eden retreated and fetched her shawl and bonnet. She needed to be going, too. Verna would have a conniption if she showed up late for dinner—what with the Ladies Aid meeting tonight.

She slid the shawl around her upper arms and wandered back toward the kitchen to say her farewells to Emma. But before she left the parlor, she cast a final glance over her shoulder—and found the blacksmith watching her.

"Have a good evening, ma'am." The deep voice vibrated through her like the low timbre of a concert cello. The only discordant thing about it was that he still called her *ma'am*. Perhaps he had forgotten her request. He'd been focused on securing employment, after all, not social connections. A little reminder might be in order.

"Congratulations on your appointment, Mr. Grant," she said. "And please, do call me Miss Spencer."

A strange look passed over his face, almost as if he were battling a rising frustration. Why on earth would he be frustrated with *her*? Hadn't she just wished him well?

She tied her bonnet ribbons into a bow beneath her chin as she waited for him to answer, her hackles rising as each silent second ticked by.

Finally, he managed to spit out a "Thank you" accompanied by one of those generic nods he seemed so fond of. Either Mr. Grant had some sort of mental blockage when it came to names, or he didn't deem hers worth remembering.

Eden turned and made her escape, telling herself in no uncertain terms that the tiny ache in her chest was a touch of indigestion, nothing more.

Chapter Three

Eden made every effort to banish Mr. Grant from her mind as she welcomed the members of Spencer's Ladies Aid Society into her home for their weekly meeting later that evening. However, the new blacksmith seemed to be all anyone could talk about.

"My Chester told me everything over supper," Hattie Fowler informed the ladies who clustered around her the minute she arrived. The woman hadn't even removed her cloak. Yet she didn't seem to mind. She just flapped her wings and gathered her chicks closer.

Hattie loved nothing so much as being the purveyor of social information.

"Norman Draper reported all the pertinent details to the council, and Chester reported them to me. The man's name is Levi Grant, and he used to work in his father's smithy down in Caldwell."

Immediately, an image of Mr. Grant rose in her memory, and not the imposing one that was easier to dismiss, either. No, hearing his first name summoned the picture of him with his boyishly mussed hair made all the more charming when contrasted against his very mannish musculature.

The moment Eden felt her mouth begin to tip upward at the corners, she shook off the recollection and stepped forward to touch Hattie's arm. "Let me take your wrap, Mrs. Fowler."

"Thank you, dear." Hattie managed to hand over her brocade cloak and matching lace cap without forfeiting any momentum. As she prattled on, answering questions and expounding opinions, Eden slipped into the smaller private parlor across the hall and gently deposited the items on the settee with the other coats and hats.

When she returned, she attempted to skirt the group of ladies standing in the center of the reading room so that she could check on Verna in the kitchen, but Melody Cooper called out and stopped her.

"There you are, Eden. Come here. Come here." Her hand rotated in small, frantic circles as she waved Eden closer. "You must tell us."

"Tell you what?" Eden asked as she approached, propping up her hostess smile with an extra rod of patience.

"What the new smith looks like. Hattie told us you were there."

"Yes, Eden. Tell us." Hattie stared at her—not unkindly, but in a fashion that left Eden with the impression that the woman wished her to hurry and be done with it so she could continue holding court.

"Well, there's not much to tell, really. He's tall and looks to be fairly strong. I imagine he'll do a fine job." She began to edge away.

"But is he handsome?"

"Does he wear a beard?"

"How old would you say he is?"

"What color is his hair?"

The barrage of questions peppered her like tiny bullets. The firing squad closed in on her, their eager faces swimming in Eden's vision as panic rose in her chest.

She should have stayed in the parlor with the cloaks.

God proved merciful, though, and sent rescue in the form of Emma Cranford. The minister's wife had just secured a cup of warm cider from the sideboard and started making her way back to the center of the room when Eden spotted her.

"Oh look. There's Emma." Eden redirected their attention with only a twinge of guilt for subjecting her friend to the next round of pecking. "Mr. Grant was in her home all afternoon. I'm sure she could describe him better than I."

The instant heads swiveled in Emma's direction, Eden hied off to the kitchen.

"I got the fritters nearly done," Verna informed her without looking up. Her housekeeper cranked a sifter over a pan of fried apple dough, snowing sugar on the cooling treats.

"Take your time. Everyone is still milling around and talking."

"Hmmph. They'll be talkin' about how there ain't no food set out if we don't get these trays finished."

Eden wouldn't mind such a conversational shift, but Verna took pride in her service, and Eden couldn't sacrifice that for the sake of her mental comfort. So she took up a clean silver tray and began arranging the sugared morsels upon it.

Verna gave the sifter a final shake and set it aside to configure her own tray. "If I hadn't had to wait dinner on you, these things woulda been ready by now."

"I know." Eden squeezed one more fritter into the center of her tray and wiped her sugary fingers on the towel draped over Verna's shoulder. "No one will mind. Once they get a taste of these goodies, they won't care when they were set out. All they'll be able to talk about is how wonderful they taste."

"Ach. Get on with ya."

Eden took up the tray as Verna shooed her out of the kitchen.

Verna and Harvey Sims had moved with her from Austin to Spencer five years ago. Those first few months away from her mother and father had nearly done her in, but the Simses kept her from burying herself in pity over the event that drove her from her home. They treated her like a daughter—dispensing unwanted advice, interfering in her affairs, taking her to task when they thought she needed it—and she adored them for it.

In fact, it was Verna who had inspired the idea of opening a lending library. She'd been dusting the shelves and grumbling about how Eden had more books than any one person ought to have. Yet behind that complaint, Eden recognized an unspoken challenge. Conviction seized her in that moment, and with it sprang a new sense of purpose—to share her love of literature and learning with others in the community, especially the children.

As she mingled with her guests in

the reading room, offering fritters from the tray she carried, Eden eyed the bookshelves that lined three of the four walls, the chairs and lamps strategically placed throughout the center of the room and near the windows, the corner where she read to the children on Friday afternoons. Peace settled into her heart, chasing away her earlier upset. Yes, this was what the Lord had called her to do. The path that led her here might not have been of her choosing, but as he promised, God had worked it out for good.

"Ladies, if you would take your seats, please. It's time to begin the meeting." Emma Cranford stood behind Eden's library desk at the front of the room and called the meeting to order.

"As head of the Charitable Aid Committee, I would like you to know that we have prayerfully considered all the members' suggestions for organizations we might support this year with monies collected during our annual fund drive."

Eden quietly placed her tray on the sideboard, a tickle of anticipation fluttering in her belly. Last year they had raised over two hundred dollars and stitched nearly thirty quilts for the Seeds of Hope Foundling Home and Orphanage in Austin, where she used to volunteer.

The ladies generally selected different projects each year, but the church that ran the home had been so appreciative that the committee allowed her to resubmit its name for consideration this year. After all, who could possibly be more deserving of aid than orphaned children?

"We've decided to fund a mission that is rich in spiritual promise and moral fortitude."

Yes . . . Eden leaned forward, bracing her palm on the corner of the sideboard.

"This year we will be facilitating a Bible drive for the residents of the Huntsville state prison."

Eden's arm went limp, and the sudden loss of support threw her off balance. Her knee bumped the table, rattling the cups and saucers by the cider urn. A few ladies seated in the back of the room turned censorious looks her way. Eden smiled and held up a hand of apology as she straightened her posture.

"Now, I realize this choice might seem odd to some of you . . ."

Odd? Make that completely nonsensical. Eden bit the inside of her cheek. How could the committee possibly favor helping criminals over children?

". . . but open your minds to the possibilities. I have personally been in contact with the chaplain who serves in the Huntsville prison, and he has supplied me with several moving stories of conversions that have taken place during his tenure there. However, he is concerned that without a physical representation of the gospel to cling to and immerse themselves in after they are released, these new believers will fall back into their old ways. We, ladies, are in a position to meet that need."

Emma spoke with passion and zeal, as if the years of listening to her husband's sermons had imbued her with his oration skills. And she was succeeding in winning over the crowd. Religious fervor fairly crackled in the air.

"Now, I'm sure some of you have questions, so I'll open it up for discussion."

A timid hand inched up to half-mast in the middle of the room.

"Yes, Bertha?"

The young woman stood. "Will we have to visit the prison or come into contact with any of these . . . convicted persons?"

Emma smiled and shook her head. "No. After the Bibles are ordered and shipped, my husband will deliver them to the chaplain. Our only duty is to collect money from neighbors and friends here in Spencer, just as we have done in the past."

Bertha nodded and took her seat.

As others raised questions, Eden's indignation built. Evangelism was all well and good, but it seemed rather pointless to sow all of one's seed in rocky soil and expect anything to take root. These were convicts, men who willingly chose a life of sin. Violent men—Eden swallowed the growing lump in her throat—men like the instigators of the riot that had nearly killed her father when she was twelve. Just thinking about that awful day made Eden's toes curl down like tiny claws within her shoes.

Wouldn't it be wiser to sow seed in tender, undeveloped ground? Soil too young to have been corrupted by deceitful thorns and stony hearts? Unlike those who had already turned their back on godliness once and would likely do so again.

Eden's hand shot up in the air. Emma recognized her with a nod of her head.

"I think the idea of raising money for prison Bibles is a lovely idea, but I fear it might be a little impractical."

"How do you mean?"

Eden weighed her words. Emma was a godly, kindhearted woman. And her friend. She had no wish to insult her in any way, but she had to give voice to her concerns. "I appreciate the compassionate spirit that led the committee to make this selection, but I wonder if it is the best stewardship of the money we collect. Most of these men are uneducated and illiterate. What good will a Bible do them if they can't read the truth it contains? And let's not forget that these men already turned their backs on morality and righteousness once, if not repeatedly, when they chose to commit unlawful acts."

Ladies bent their heads together, and low murmurs broke out across the room.

"Miss Spencer makes a valid point," Emma conceded. "In fact, those are some of the very issues we struggled with in making this choice. Jonathan Willis, the chaplain at the Huntsville prison, has assured me that he will only distribute copies of Scripture to men who have attended his Bible studies and worship services. But even if nine of every ten men who receive a Bible never open it, isn't it worth our participation for the one soul who does? Jesus himself said that there is more joy in heaven over one sinner who comes to repentance than for the ninety-and-nine just persons who need no repentance."

The fire that had burned inside Eden began to sputter.

"We are called to be sowers, ladies. It is not our business to decide which soils are most likely to give success, for the Lord rarely confines himself to areas dictated by human wisdom. We are to scatter seed. God will give the increase. And I believe he will give great increase, indeed, if we join him in this endeavor."

Her voice rose on a crescendo, and applause erupted. Without much enthusiasm, Eden joined the ovation, clapping her fingertips limply against her palm. Her heart still sided with the children at Seeds of Hope, but she could no longer argue in good faith that the Huntsville cause had no merit. Her spirit had perceived too much truth in Emma's defense.

So she would do her duty. She would solicit funds for prison Bibles and even contribute her usual personal sum to the effort. She'd not particularly enjoy it, but she'd do it.

Then another thought hit her, this one causing a whole different type of disturbance to Eden's system. Her assigned merchants to approach for donations would be the same as in years past, those with businesses on the west end of Main Street. The saddler/boot maker, the livery owner, and . . . the blacksmith.

Chapter Four

"Well, here she is." Claude Barnes twisted the key in the padlock that kept the wide double doors chained together.

Levi's gaze traced the outline of the stone structure. It looked nothing like the wooden building his father had used, yet an odd sense of coming home settled over him as the livery owner pulled the first door wide. The hitch in the older man's gait made the going slow, so Levi stepped forward to take over the task.

"The place ain't 'zactly been kept

up." Barnes relinquished his hold on the door. "The council only gave me the key so's I could take care of shoein' when the need arose. Not to be a caretaker."

Levi shrugged. "I can clean."

The man's rigid posture relaxed, and a smile cracked his white-whiskered face. "Glad to hear it. You ever get bored, feel free to come over to my place and muck stalls." He slapped Levi's arm and chortled as he led the way into the smithy. Levi grinned and followed.

A large brick hearth sat on a stone foundation in the center of the workshop, its chimney funneling up through the roof. Levi was pleased to see a lever rod hanging down from a chain at about shoulder height. If he was to be working alone, having a way to pump the bellows without leaving the forge would be essential. He'd have to inspect everything, of course, but not having to rig his own pull rod would save time. Levi gave it a yank, and when a stream of air stirred the dirt and ash in the cold hearth, he nodded in satisfaction.

He moved to the anvil and tested its height, swinging an imaginary sledge. It might be set a bit low for him, but it stood mounted close enough to the hearth that he would be able to maneuver between the two with only a quarter turn. Whoever designed the shop knew what he was doing.

A wooden rack a few feet away boasted a selection of tongs, chisels, scroll forks, punches, and hammers. Sledges and vises littered the floor, along with leftover rod iron and discarded horseshoes. The Lord had truly blessed him. With the twenty dollars paid to him by the state after his release, plus the sixty-five cents a day he'd earned breaking granite at the labor camp for eighteen months, he'd come to town with a little over three hundred dollars to his name. And he'd spent a good chunk of that paying for the first two months' rent in advance that morning at the bank. All he owned were the clothes on his back, a spare shirt, and the Bible the chaplain had given him. He would have never been able to afford to stock the smithy on his own.

A mouse skittered across Levi's path, darting away from the sunlight. More scratching sounds echoed in the back corners. The place smelled of dust and disuse, but there was a familiarity, too. Charcoal, leather, and iron. The smells of his father.

Levi ran his hand over the cold anvil, moving from the squared heel, down across the chipping block, and out to the pointed end of the horn. He could hear the pounding of the sledge, see sparks shower from red-hot iron, hear his father call for him to pump the bellows or hand him a twisting bar while his brother acted as the striker. The smithy had been a place of tradition and pride for the Grant men. Until Levi's rebellion. Maybe today would be the first step in reclaiming the family honor he'd lost.

Barnes stepped into Levi's line of sight and pointed to a large dark circle in the middle of the plank floor. "The smith afore you took to drinking," he said. "Dropped a hot coal into his kindlin' bucket one day and tried to put out the flames with the contents of his whiskey bottle." Barnes looked up and gave Levi a grave look. "Didn't work too good."

Levi shuddered. "He dead?"

"Naw. Got a few new scars to impress the ladies with is all. Gave 'im a good scare, though. Decided to skip out the next day. I hear tell he's got a pig farm over in Williamson County now."

"Huh." What else could he say to a story like that?

"Ain't a drinkin' man, are ya?" Barnes scratched at his whiskers, shooting him a glance from the corner of his eye.

"No."

Not for the last two years, anyway. Levi had practically lived in saloons and barrooms prior to that. Not so much for the liquor—mostly for the fights. But that was his old way of life. He'd not return to that path. The Lord had given him a second chance. He didn't aim to squander it.

"Good. Then I'll leave the key with you." Barnes tossed it to him, and Levi snagged it out of the air. "You got a place to bed down?"

"I . . . ah . . ." *Stayed? Slept?* Levi cleared his throat. "Colby . . . put me up at the hotel. But I'll need to find . . . a room . . . of my own before long."

"Well, it ain't nothin' fancy, but the wife and I got a shed out back o' our place with a bunk and a stove. You could come and go as you please, no one to bother ya. Oh, and you'd be welcome to take your meals with us. Georgia would insist on it. That woman don't believe in lettin' a man fend for himself in the kitchen." Barnes winked at him and patted the slightly rounded midsection on his otherwise wiry frame. "Not that I'm complain', mind you."

Levi grinned, warming to the old man. He couldn't recall the last time someone had approached him with genuine hospitality. The preacher and his wife had been kind, but there was something about Claude Barnes that put Levi at ease. Made him feel accepted. Normal.

'Course, that was probably because the man thought him a blacksmith, not a convicted felon. Guilt jabbed him in the belly.

"Therefore if any man be in Christ, he is a new creature: old things are passed away; behold, all things are become new."

The verse from 2 Corinthians he had spent days meditating on before his release rose from his memory to beat back the shame and unworthiness that twined like fast-growing jungle vines around his soul.

He *was* a blacksmith. Like his father before him. And like his father before him, he would become a man of integrity.

"How much?"

Barnes kicked at the spokes of an old wagon wheel that had been left propped against the wall by the previous owner. "Three dollars a week. Less, if you're willing to help out with the chores."

"Deal." Levi stuck out his hand. Barnes shook his agreement, his grip firm and assured, his eyes taking Levi's measure. Levi held his gaze, giving silent promise that the man would not have cause to regret his offer.

"Well, then. I'll leave you alone to get your bearings." Barnes thumbed his suspenders away from his plaid flannel shirt and released them with a painful-sounding snap. "Give you a holler 'round six and we can head out. Georgia'll have supper on the table."

"All right. Thank y—"

A low growl cut Levi off. He spun toward the doorway, where a brownish-gray dog crouched in the opening, baring his teeth. A chunk was missing from his left ear and his ribs were visible through the matted fur on his side, giving him a desperate, almost savage appearance.

Barnes stood nearest the animal. He held out a conciliatory hand. "Look who's paying a call. What're you up to, Ornery?" The rumble in the dog's throat deepened.

Levi edged closer to the forge hearth, where a sledge stood on end, its handle about level with his knee. He didn't want to hurt the critter, but if the animal attacked, he'd be ready.

"Don't worry," Barnes said in a hushed voice. "Ornery hardly ever bites. He's just the cussedest dog you ever wanna meet. Showed up 'bout a year ago. I'm not sure from where. Don't like people. Other dogs, neither. Give 'im a wide berth and he'll leave you alone. Won't ya, boy?"

The livery owner took a step back and the growling stopped.

"See? I—"

With a yip, the dog's ears perked up and a small whine resonated in his throat. He lifted his head and seemed to stare directly at Levi, tilting his jaw to the side.

Soon Barnes was looking at him, too, with a nearly identical tilt to his chin.

Levi let go of the sledge handle and extended his hands in front of him, palms out. "I'm not going to hurt you, Ornery."

At the sound of Levi's voice, Ornery let out a sharp bark and bounded forward. Thinking he was about to have a mouthful of canine teeth tearing at his throat, Levi raised his arms to fend off the beast, but the dog only pushed his front paws into Levi's abdomen and tried to overcome him with pants of pungent dog breath.

"Well, I'll be."

Levi met the livery owner's gaze over the dog's head, the awe on the other man's face heightening Levi's confusion.

"Son, I think you've just been adopted." Barnes shook his head in disbelief, a wide smile breaking out across his face. "I'll leave you two to get acquainted."

"But . . ."

Barnes waved him off, still shaking his head as he left.

Arms hovering at his sides, Levi looked back down at Ornery. New cuts overlapped old scars above his eyes and around his ears. A patch of fur was missing on his snout, as if the skin had been scraped so raw the hair couldn't grow back. Levi slowly brought his arms in and began rubbing the mongrel's head. Ornery's pants increased as his eyes slid closed. When they opened again and stared up at him, Levi felt it. The kinship.

Ornery was a fighter, too.

"You looking to retire, boy? That why you came to me?" Levi hunkered down beside Ornery to pet him proper. "Maybe we can help each other. I'll keep you out of trouble and you keep me out of trouble. What do you think?"

"I think staying out of trouble is always a good policy for newcomers in my town."

At the sound of the masculine voice, Ornery immediately stiffened and growled a warning. Levi craned his neck to scrutinize the man in his doorway. With the sun behind him, the brim of his black felt hat cast shadows across his face, but one detail glared at Levi from its position on the right side of the man's unbuttoned coat.

A tin star.

Chapter Five

Levi deliberately stayed down an extra moment before rising, trying to gain control of his panicked pulse. The sheriff was just making his rounds. That was all. Yet Levi couldn't quite banish the notion that his criminal past would somehow be evident to the lawman once he faced him eye to eye.

Ornery continued to growl, so Levi used the dog as an excuse to tarry. "Quiet, boy." He rubbed Ornery behind the ears, then slowly pushed to his feet. His height worked to his advantage, bolstering his confidence as he straightened to stand a good three or four inches taller than the sheriff.

"You the new smith?" The question came out like an accusation.

"Yep. Levi Grant." Levi offered a small nod. The stiffness of the man's jaw didn't foster the impression that a handshake would be welcome.

"Conrad Pratt. Sheriff." He jerked his chin in Ornery's direction. "Better watch yourself around that mutt. I seen 'im tear a dog's throat out once. Lost me twenty dollars on that fight."

A sick ache churned through Levi's stomach, but he kept his face a disinterested mask. He'd always hated the dog and cock fights that were used to warm up the crowds before one of his bouts. Men could choose to make a living with their fists. Animals were forced into it, usually through cruelty and abuse until their God-given temperaments were twisted into something barbarous.

"I think his owner up and left him one day after a loss. I thought about shootin' him to put him out of his misery, but the thing slunk off before I got around to it. So far he ain't done more than growl at folks, but I'm tellin' you now, if he ever turns aggressive, I'll put a bullet through his skull faster than you can spit."

Levi stepped to the side, blocking Sheriff Pratt's view of Ornery. "I'll keep an eye on him."

"You do that." The sheriff finally turned his attention from the dog and focused on Levi again. The man took his time sizing him up, lingering overlong on his face. "Have I seen you around these parts afore? There's something about you that strikes me as familiar."

"Hmm." Levi chose his words carefully. "I don't know why. I've . . . never been here . . . before."

The sheriff narrowed his gaze. Levi bit down on his tongue and tried to swallow, but his saliva seemed to solidify into a ball and lodge in his throat. If Sheriff Pratt bet on dog fights, there was a good chance he'd attended his share of bare-knuckle brawls, as well. Had he seen the Anvil fight?

"Well, it'll come to me eventually. Always does." He shrugged his shoulders under his coat, as if brushing off the thought for the time being, and straightened his Stetson. "Welcome to Spencer, Grant. Treat the people here fairly. Keep yourself on the right side of the law, and you and me will get along fine. Mess with my town, and I'll bury you. Got it?"

Levi dipped his chin in acknowledgment. Nothing like a friendly how-de-do to make a fella feel at home.

"Good." The sheriff tapped the brim of his hat in salute. "See ya around."

Levi tapped his own brim in response, deciding it'd probably be in his best interest to see the sheriff as little as possible. The man obviously enjoyed throwing his weight around, and Levi had no desire to be the one to catch it.

And his first order of business was setting his new workshop to rights and taking inventory of his tools and supplies.

After the sheriff left, Ornery settled down and curled up in a corner to supervise. Levi appreciated the company.

The dog didn't require conversation, and if Levi happened to say something that hissed a bit, Ornery didn't notice or care.

By late afternoon, Levi had a pretty good idea of what he would need to purchase. The previous smith had kept a healthy heap of scrap iron piled up behind the building. Old tools, broken hinges, axles, plows, horseshoes, anything that could possibly be welded or reshaped. He'd need to order several pounds of iron bars and rods for new projects as well as a couple dozen bushels of charcoal. There were enough supplies and fuel to keep him in business for a few weeks, but if any large projects came in, he'd come up short.

With no hot coals to ignite the forge in the morning, he'd need to come in early to build an appropriate fire. The kindling box was full, though, probably thanks to Mr. Barnes, so there was nothing left to do until tomorrow. Levi figured he had a couple hours before it would be time to meet Claude at the livery, and since Ornery had wandered off a while ago to wherever stray dogs went in the afternoon, he decided to explore the town.

He'd already seen most of the east side, having stayed in the hotel and eaten at the café last night. He'd visited the bank after treating himself to a cinnamon bun at the bakery next door.

A wagon and team rumbled out from the livery, heading toward him. Levi waved to the fellow on the driver's seat and waited for him to pass before crossing to the opposite side of the road. He introduced himself to the man who ran the saddle shop and let it be known that he'd be open for business on the morrow.

The saloon came next, with its entrance discreetly, or not so discreetly, tucked around the corner. Only two horses stood hitched outside at this early hour, but someone was pounding out a vigorous tune on a piano, as if the house were packed. Bawdy lyrics popped into Levi's head, lyrics he used to sing with his cronies after a drink or two. Lyrics that now heated his neck with shame as he fought to oust them from his mind. He lengthened his stride, trying to outrun the words and the images they induced.

He evoked a hymn from memory to replace the tavern song and started humming, *"O for a faith that will not shrink, Though pressed by ev'ry foe . . ."*

The rest of the verse eluded him, but he kept humming the music, louder and louder until the saloon was out of earshot. So intent was he upon clearing his mind that he marched past the boardinghouse, general store, drug store, and butcher before sight of the sheriff's office drew him up short.

" 'Scuse me, mister. I'm late." A young boy pushed past him and dashed down the side street that veered to the right.

Eager to avoid the sheriff and curious about where the kid was rushing off to, Levi followed. He recognized this road. The steepled church and parsonage beckoned to him from the end of the lane. But the boy didn't clamber up to either of those doors. Instead, without knocking, he plunged into a large two-story frame house. Levi assumed it was the boy's home until he moved closer and caught sight of a small wooden sign hanging from the eaves of the covered porch. *Library*.

A yearning began to grow within him. He'd started reading books to aid his efforts in circumventing his speech problem and discovered along the way that he truly enjoyed getting lost in a book.

In grade school, Levi dealt with his lisp by trouncing any kid who teased him. His size and quickness gave him an advantage over other boys, even those two or three years his senior. But he'd had to deal with his dad's belt and extra chores every time the teacher sent him home for fighting, so he began searching for another way around his problem.

In his sixth grade year, the school board hired a new teacher, a short, thin fellow with spectacles and pointy chin whiskers. The first day he caught Levi in a fight, he pulled him aside.

"Levi," he'd said, "fighting doesn't make these kids think more highly of you. It simply makes you a bully."

Levi hadn't been too sure of that at the time. He'd seen the respect in the eyes of the other kids after he pummeled an eighth grader who thought it funny to call him a baby. Yet this diminutive teacher was the first person to address his problem directly, so he listened.

"If you want to change their opinion of you, you must change your behavior. If they poke fun at the way you speak, expand your vocabulary so that you can substitute other words that are easier to say correctly."

"How?"

"Read. Everything you can get your hands on. Read until words become your friends. Then when you need to find one, they will jump into your mind, waving their hands for you to pick them. And you can select whichever you like, just like a captain choosing a stickball team."

So Levi read—stories, almanacs, history books, even the Bible. After school. In between chores. In his bed by candlelight. It took months before he noticed a difference, but he did notice one.

By the time he quit school at fifteen to work with his father and brother in the smithy, he'd learned to disguise his lisp by eliminating trouble words from his speech. The only unfortunate consequence of this strategy was that it led him to pause and stumble while searching for replacement words. But he preferred to run the risk of people thinking him simple rather than degrade his manhood with infantile diction. Reading had provided a way for him to maintain his self-respect, and in the process, gave him a source of pleasure he'd not expected.

In fact, a portion of his first prizefighting purse had gone toward buying a copy of Verne's *Around the World in Eighty Days.* He must have read that book more than a dozen times before the saloon owner who managed his fights seized it along with the rest of his belongings the day he was arrested.

Levi stared at the little wooden sign. It creaked slightly as it swung in the breeze. Would he find a copy inside?

He stood in the street for a moment, debating whether or not he should go in. Hadn't the preacher said something yesterday about Miss Spencer running the library? Levi frowned. He hadn't made the best of impressions on her. Miss Spencer had no way of knowing how difficult it was for him to say her name, so it was understandable that she'd been miffed when he ignored her invitation to use it. Perhaps he'd be better off exploring the inventory at the general store.

On the other hand, if he was going to make a home for himself in this town, he couldn't avoid the woman forever.

Besides, he really wanted to see her book collection.

Stepping onto the path that led to her doorstep, Levi found himself surrounded by dormant rosebushes. They lined the walkway and bordered the length of the porch as well. The place would be a riot of color in a few months, when spring brought the hibernating flowers back to life.

He paused before climbing the three stairs to the porch and brushed the worst of the dust from his trousers. Then, spotting the *Open* sign in the window, he followed the boy's example and entered the house as if it were any other business establishment.

Only it wasn't. It was a home. A woman's home. And the minute Levi crossed the threshold, he felt about as out of place as a railroad spike in a keg of two-penny nails. There were flowers everywhere. Gilt ones in the wallpaper, woven ones in the rug, wooden ones carved into the hall tree a few paces away. He swore he could even smell them.

Levi took off his hat and hung it on the tallest hook on the hall tree, its masculine brown design contrasting sharply with the two frilly bonnets below.

A voice carried to him from the doorway on the left. Letting it lead him, he entered a large, open room lined with bookshelves on three walls. In an instant, he forgot the flowers, forgot his discomfort, and simply drank in the sight.

The prison library in Huntsville had

been larger, but for a personal collection, this was tremendous. A woman perusing the shelves to his right turned to him and smiled as she slid a book free. Levi nodded in return and looked beyond her to the gathering in the back corner.

A group of about fifteen children of various ages sat on the floor, engrossed in the telling of a story. Eden Spencer perched on the edge of a spindly tapestry chair before them, reading aloud. He could only see her profile, but even from a distance he easily discerned the animation in her features and heard the intensity in her voice.

Not wanting to disturb the recitation, he moved as quietly as possible to the opposite side of the room.

Books on cattle, farming, and animal husbandry filled the first bookcase, along with an extensive assortment of horticultural guides. Levi ran his finger along a spine decorated with a bouquet of roses and chuckled quietly to himself. The woman did love her flowers.

But that wasn't all. There were also

history texts, sermon collections, handbooks on steam engines, and medical advisors. Etiquette guides and cookbooks, carpentry manuals and a series of bound lectures. A reference section contained encyclopedias, atlases, and two dictionaries. He even found a book entitled *Practical Horseshoeing* by Mr. G. Fleming. Levi made a note of what shelf it was on, just in case he discovered he had forgotten more than he thought he had about being a farrier.

He reached the back wall and found an extensive collection of children's literature, poetry, and essays. And when he turned from the bookcase, he found himself nearly on top of Miss Spencer.

She had just begun to close her book when the children began clamoring for another chapter. A featherlight laugh floated out from her as she opened the cover once again, her finger still holding their place as if she'd known all along she would read more.

Levi backed away, afraid that if she saw him it would interrupt the magic. There was something so different about her here—something joyous and unguarded, elements that had been missing from their previous encounter. Yesterday at the parsonage she'd been all business, but here she was carefree and alive. The children obviously adored her, and she them.

"'One night,'" she read, her voice subdued, "'a few days after James had left, I had eaten my hay and was lying down in my straw—'" she paused to yawn and stretch with theatrical flair—"'fast asleep, when I was suddenly roused by the stable bell ringing very loud.'" Her speech accelerated and she leaned forward. "Bong! Bong!" A couple of the children giggled at the face she made as she imitated the bells.

She went on to tell of a lad named John and his urgency in waking the horse, Black Beauty, and their desperate ride to fetch the doctor for his ill mistress. The poor horse gave his all, and in turn, fell ill himself, thanks to the faulty care of a young stable boy. A lung inflammation, they said. Yet Beauty's ride had saved the mistress's life, and despite his sickness, he did not regret his efforts.

"All right, children. That's all for today."

A collective moan rose from the group.

"But what happens to Beauty?" one young girl near the front asked, her eyes wide and a bit moist.

Miss Spencer reached out a hand to stroke the child's cheek. "You'll have to come back next Friday to find out, Anna."

"But, Miss Spencer . . ."

A boy yanked on one of Anna's pigtails, cutting her off. "He dies."

Anna's bottom lip started trembling. The boy snickered.

"Joseph. Stop teasing your sister." Miss Spencer set the book aside and gathered Anna into her lap, wrapping her arms around her.

Before she could offer any comforting words, though, a stoic young lady spoke up from the back. "Beauty won't die," she stated with matter-of-fact assurance. "We're not even halfway through the book yet. It wouldn't be called *Black Beauty* if the horse died at the beginning."

"Very astute reasoning, Gussie." Miss Spencer turned back to the child in her lap. "That makes sense—don't you think, Anna?"

"Uh-huh."

"Good." She gave Anna a hug and stood the child up on her feet. Apparently that signaled the end of the session, for the rest of the kids scrambled up, as well. "Don't forget your school books and lunch buckets," Miss Spencer called out to them. "And be careful walking home. I'll see you next week."

She leaned to the side to retrieve her book from the floor, then stood. The children filed past in a mass, but she reached out to touch the arm or shoulder or back of each youngster that moved within reach. It was almost as if she didn't want to let them go.

They shouted their good-byes and she waved, standing still until the last child disappeared through the doorway.

Levi enjoyed the warm scene so

much, he wasn't prepared when she suddenly spun around.

Her gaze flew to his face and she jumped back, a gasp vibrating the air between them.

Like an idiot, he just stood there staring at her, the only thought running through his brain being that her pale green eyes reminded him of the lacy lichens that grew on the old oak tree behind his father's house.

She clutched the book to her chest like a shield. "What are *you* doing here?"

Chapter Six

"I'm sorry. That came out wrong." Eden stared at her shoes for a minute before gathering enough courage to look the blacksmith in the eye again. He didn't say anything, but the shock on his face softened into a hint of a smile. She hoped that signified forgiveness.

She hadn't meant to be rude. It was just that Levi Grant was the last person she'd expected to see in her library. Male visitors were rare anyway, but seeing this particular one standing so large and so . . . well . . . close, must have disabled the part of her brain that usually kept her from blurting uncensored thoughts.

Stretching her lips into a polite curve, Eden attempted another greeting. "Is there something I can assist you with, Mr. Grant?"

"Wanted to . . . look at what you had here." He nodded toward the shelves on the far side of the room. "You've got a good collection."

A little thrill of pride shot through her, even though the fellow paying the compliment probably couldn't distinguish Shakespeare from Sophocles. "Thank you. My father started gathering tomes for his personal use before I was born, and when I mentioned that I wanted to open a lending library here in Spencer, he generously donated many of the books you see on the north side of the room. My tastes run more toward literature and novels, so that is what you will find on this side." She released one hand from *Black Beauty*'s cover long enough to gesture at the shelves along the wall on her left.

He nodded.

She fought to keep her eyes from

rolling in the direction of the ceiling. Dipping his chin seemed to be his answer for everything.

When he remained silent, she held out her book and indicated with a raised brow that she needed him to step aside so that she might replace it on the shelf. "Excuse me, please."

He moved out of the way, and she slipped Anna Sewell's autobiographical horse story between Laura Howe Richards's *The Joyous Story of Toto* and Robert Louis Stevenson's *Treasure Island.* She straightened and caught him watching her.

Her breath got tangled up in her throat. What was it about this man that put her so on edge? Was it his size? She was sure his arms boasted a larger circumference than her head, yet she felt no threat of violence from him. No, it had something to do with his eyes. There was a hint of apology in them, as if he knew he wasn't measuring up to her expectations. And the vulnerability she'd glimpsed on their first meeting was there, too—at least it had been until he shuttered it. The combination left her with the odd urge to reassure him. And that scared her.

Her judgment regarding the masculine gender had proven faulty in the past. How foolish would she prove to be if she developed soft feelings for a man who couldn't even remember her name? Better to offer what assistance she could and hurry him along.

Eden stepped toward the shelves on the north wall. "Is there something in particular I can help you find?"

Most males of her acquaintance only visited the library when they needed a specific piece of information, usually a manual or reference book of some sort. However, when she glanced back at Mr. Grant, his attention was fixed on the south wall, not the north.

"Do you have Verne?" He crossed through the open corner where she conducted her readings and began perusing the fiction spines.

"Verne?" She could think of no book with that title.

He twisted his neck to peer at her over his shoulder. "Verne," he repeated. "The author?"

"Oh. Jules Verne. Of course." What a ninny he must think her. "Yes. I have several of his titles." She bustled past the blacksmith to the last bookshelf and crouched down to reach the bottom row. "*Journey to the Centre of the Earth*. *From the Earth to the Moon. Twenty Thousand Leagues Under the Sea*." She withdrew each book as she called out the title, shifting it into the crook of her left arm. "*Around the World in Eighty Days. The—*"

"That one."

"*Around the World in Eighty Days*?" Eden looked up at him.

He nodded.

Of course he nodded. The man hoarded words as if he were being charged a dollar for each one he uttered.

She handed the book up to him and returned the others to the shelf. As she reached for the edge of the bookcase to aid her balance in standing, a hand cupped her elbow. A large, warm hand that lifted her to her feet so easily she felt more like a puppet than a person with muscle and sinew of her own.

Her gaze melded with his, and an unexpected stirring meandered through her abdomen. She lowered her lashes at once and hid her discomfiture behind a mumbled thank-you.

As soon as she regained her full height, Mr. Grant removed his hand, and one completely irrational corner of her heart actually regretted the loss. Just because a man was strong didn't mean his commitments were, she reminded herself. Eden had felt secure with Stephen, too, right up until the day he accepted her father's money and left her behind with a wedding dress that would never be worn.

She shook out her skirts, ignoring the fact that they were perfectly tidy, and cleared her throat. "Well, feel free to have a seat as you look over your book." She motioned to a nearby armchair that cozied up to a library table and lamp.

He gave it a glance, then looked down at himself. "I think I'll . . . go over there." He tipped his head in the direction of the reading corner.

"All right." Too late, Eden realized

he'd have a difficult time squeezing himself into the chair she had offered. It obviously hadn't been crafted for a man of his proportions. However, any chair that had been would surely swallow her usual female patrons, so he would have to make do. It wasn't like he would be a regular visitor or anything. The giant hardly strung more than two words together at any one time. What could he possibly want with her books?

He was probably trying to impress her so she'd send a favorable report back to her father. Probably trying to give himself a veneer of sophistication. Although, why a blacksmith would think anyone cared if he could read or not escaped her.

As she watched him lower himself to the floor and brace his back against the wall, another, much more disturbing, thought found purchase in her brain. What if he was trying to impress her for more personal reasons?

Mr. Grant looked her way and smiled before stretching out his long legs. He crossed his ankles and opened the book across his lap.

Eden spun around, her breath hitching. *Oh dear.* That wouldn't do at all. She couldn't have him coming in all the time, pretending to be interested in literature simply because she'd expressed a preference for it. People might get ideas—matchmaking ideas. Wouldn't the busybodies in town love to pair up the bookish spinster with the brawny blacksmith, making a to-do about opposites attracting and all that nonsense? It would be humiliating.

Especially because the whispers would start again. Whispers about how any man interested in a bluestocking like Eden Spencer must be after a piece of the Spencer fortune. Rumors would circulate about her last fiancé and the scandal that tainted her with his leaving. Questions would arise about whether or not her father would buy off another of her suitors, and how much it would cost him.

She'd spent the last five years of her life silencing those whispers. She couldn't bear to have them return.

Then she heard one . . . right in her ear. “Is that the new smith?”

“Oh . . . Mrs. Draper.” Eden reined in her runaway thoughts. “Yes. I believe it is. Mr. Levi Grant.”

“Ah. I thought so. Norman told me the man was abnormally large.”

Eden followed the woman’s gaze and peeked at Mr. Grant. Sure, his legs were longer than most and well-muscled, and his torso put one in mind of a sturdy tree trunk, but she wouldn’t say his size was *abnormal.* She’d seen ranchers and quarry workers who exhibited similar statures. Well, perhaps not quite as tall. Or as strapping. But close.

“I imagine size would be beneficial in a job like his,” Eden said.

The banker’s wife sighed. “I suppose. Still, it will take some getting used to. I smiled when he came in, but to tell you the truth, I was praying the whole time that he wouldn’t come too close. One never knows what kind of behavior to expect from a man like that. If he were ever to lose his temper, he could probably snap a person in two."

Eden bristled. Why, Mr. Grant had demonstrated more gentlemanly behavior toward her yesterday than Lydia's husband had. And today, despite her ruffled feathers, he'd been polite and even assisted her to her feet.

"I've been in the man's presence on two separate occasions, and he has always conducted himself in a courteous and civilized manner. I'm sure you have nothing to fear from him."

"Perhaps you're right." Lydia Draper gave her a probing look. Only then did Eden realize her defense of the blacksmith might have been a tad too spirited. She rushed to change the subject.

"So, would you like to borrow that book?" Eden glanced pointedly at the volume in the woman's hand.

"I don't know." Lydia opened the cover and thumbed through a couple of pages. "Do you think I'll like it?"

Eden made out the embossed title. *Lady Audley's Secret*. "Well, there are some elements to the story that you might consider somewhat shocking, but it has an intriguing plot with mysterious identities and a man bent on uncovering the truth. You can always try it and if it doesn't fit your tastes, you may return it."

"Shocking, you say?"

"There is a touch of scandal and certainly a great deal of deception, but the ending is quite satisfying. Right triumphs, as it should." Eden chose to keep quiet about the fact that Lady Audley turned out to be a madwoman, a bigamist, and nearly a murderess. She wouldn't want to spoil the mystery should Lydia decide to read it.

"All right," the banker's wife said as she handed the book over to Eden. "I'll give it a try."

There was a bit of a sparkle to the woman's eyes, giving Eden the distinct impression that the shocking nature of the story might have actually increased its attractiveness. She hid a smile as she moved to her desk and opened the wooden box that held the cards for each book in her collection. Flipping through the alphabetical stack, she spotted the author's name, Mary Elizabeth Braddon, and pulled free the small card for *Lady Audley's Secret*. She noted the date, Lydia's name, and the book's title in her ledger and handed the book into Mrs. Draper's keeping.

"I hope you enjoy it."

Lydia tucked the book under her arm. "Thank you."

As the woman departed, Eden added the extracted card to her Borrowed Books box and took a moment to peruse the other cards inside to see if anyone needed a gentle reminder about returning their selections.

All at once she sensed someone's presence. Eden stilled, her head bowed over her box. Mr. Grant. It had to be. He was the only patron currently in the library. Yet she hadn't heard his approach. Strange that a man his size could move so quietly.

Her heart thumping an uneven rhythm, Eden looked up. "Yes?"

"May I borrow it?" He set the Jules Verne novel on her desk with the same care one would use for a crystal vase or other delicate item.

Eden fought back a rising panic. She

needed to discourage this man from becoming a regular visitor. After her slip with Lydia Draper, she was already in danger of having her name linked with his. If Mr. Grant started frequenting the library on a regular basis, it would only add grist to the rumor mill. But what could she do? She couldn't bar the man from her reading room when he'd done nothing deserving of such drastic treatment. She needed something subtle, something . . .

An idea budded.

She leaned forward, lacing her fingers together as she pressed her palms onto the cover of the book, scooting it slightly toward her chest. "I would be happy to lend you this book, Mr. Grant, if you can come back in two weeks."

"Two wee—" His brow furrowed as he cut himself off. "Why?"

"I'm sorry to disappoint you, but I have a policy about lending books to people who do not have strong ties to our community." A policy that had been in place for all of ten seconds, but he needn't know that. "I have to protect my inventory, you see. If someone were to borrow a book and then leave town for one reason or another, I'd have no way to recover the lost item. You only arrived in Spencer yesterday, sir, and while I've no doubt that you will soon establish yourself, until that day comes, I must restrict your borrowing privileges."

She hoped that in two weeks he'd be so busy at the smithy, he'd have no time for books. Or her.

Which would be for the best.

Really.

His gaze strayed to the placard propped on a wire photograph easel at the corner of her desk, and the frown lines between his eyes relaxed.

"You open at noon every day?"

"Except Sundays." Eden spoke slowly while her brain rushed ahead. Surely he wasn't considering—?

"I'll come by tomorrow, then."

With supreme effort, Eden held her head erect and even managed a weak smile in parting as he bid her good day. But the minute she heard the front door close behind him, she slumped forward, her hands barely unlacing in time to catch her plummeting head.

Only *she* could so successfully achieve the very thing she so wanted to avoid.

Chapter Seven

Spending his lunch break at the library was quickly becoming a habit. And a rather pleasant one at that. Not only did Levi get the chance to renew his acquaintance with old friends like Phileas Fogg and Passepartout in their wild adventures around the world, but he also enjoyed the opportunity to observe the enigmatic Miss Spencer.

Levi dragged his mind from the pretty librarian in order to examine the weld on the wagon rim he'd just pounded into place. After dunking it in the slack tub for fast cooling, he gave the circle a few quick taps with his hammer at various intervals, listening for the clear, bell-like sound that indicated a well-rounded rim. A hollow thud would mean he'd have to start over. He struck the iron rim a final time, and the resultant ping filled him with satisfaction. Ornery let out a guttural moan—half howl, half whine—at the sound.

"You like that, too, do you?" Using his tongs, Levi set the rim on the flat stone work surface at the end of the forge. "We'll have to file it and fit it to the wheel later. After the library." He crouched down to rub the dog's neck. "A man ought to have a break in the day, don't you think?"

His father had always claimed that his afternoons were more productive when he went home to eat lunch with Mama. Of course, the vitality he found probably had more to do with being in the company of the woman he loved than with the break itself. But surely the short time spent away from work played a role, as well. After all, Levi had no wife, yet his daily trips to the library invigorated him. A quiet retreat away from his tools and the constant heat of the fire. A chance to get lost in a fictional adventure for thirty or forty-five minutes. He looked forward to the midday escape.

Eden Spencer's image sprang to mind. All right. So maybe he looked forward to seeing her, too. What man wouldn't? He'd been separated from female company too long not to appreciate the view of shapely curves and a comely face. Eden Spencer possessed both. As did several of Spencer's other young ladies. Yet there was something particular about the prickly librarian that drew his attention time and again. What that was, he couldn't say, but it drew him all the same.

Levi ruffled the dog's fur a final time, then gave Ornery two firm pats on the side before stretching to his feet. He strode to the back corner of his shop, where a second tub of water sat atop a three-legged workbench he'd propped up with the broken handle of a garden hoe. The table leaned backward and to the left, but as long as he didn't overfill his washtub, it suited his purposes.

Unwilling to show up at the library smelling like a mule, Levi hung up his leather apron, pushed his suspenders off his shoulders, and stripped out of his work shirt. He scrubbed his face, neck, arms, and chest and then dried off with a flour-sack towel Mrs. Barnes had lent him. Leaving the sweat-stained shirt to air out on a peg, he took down his only other shirt, the one he wore with his suit coat, and pulled it over his head. After doing up the buttons, tucking in the tails, and snapping his suspenders into place, he turned around for inspection.

"What do you think, boy? Will I do?"

Ornery looked up at him, stared for half a minute, and then turned and padded out the back door.

"Fine lot of help you are," Levi called after him.

The dog seemed to crave privacy as strongly as he craved companionship, a strange combination. He waited by the shop doors every morning for Levi to arrive and enjoyed a bowl of dinner scraps and an occasional scratch behind the ears. But every afternoon he left. Levi had yet to decide if the increased traffic the shop generated later in the day scared him off, or if he simply experienced a canine urge to explore the countryside and chase rabbits. It was a puzzle he might never solve.

Much like Miss Spencer.

A wealthy, beautiful woman like her should have married years ago. Yet she hadn't. Why? And why did she pretend to be cool and aloof when he knew very well a warm heart beat within her? He'd seen it in the way she interacted with the children during the reading on Friday. And he'd seen it again on Saturday. As he'd turned up her walk, he'd witnessed her hand off a cloth-wrapped bundle to a lad of about eight. As the boy dashed past him, Levi smelled freshly baked bread and something savory that might have been ham. A truly uppity woman would have scolded the child for bothering her, not given him hot food.

However, when it came to adults, she presented a more reserved disposition. After services on Sunday, she'd flitted from one female cluster to another, a polite smile gracing her lips, yet she never once penetrated past the fringe. Did the townsfolk consider her an outsider, or was she the one putting up barriers?

Levi pushed the questions to the back of his mind and stepped out onto the street. He waved to Claude, who was checking the harness on one of his rigs while a woman with a big hat and even bigger bustle waited in the shadow of the livery. He couldn't see her face, but he dipped his chin and fingered the brim of his hat anyway, not surprised when she made no visible response.

A line had formed in front of the café, and his stomach rumbled as the aroma of beef stew wafted toward him. He ignored the pangs, though. Mrs. Barnes had packed him a couple pieces of cold chicken and one of her soft yeast rolls. He'd eat when he got back to the shop. Levi turned away from the café and walked down the side street that led to Miss Spencer's library.

Over the last couple of days, he'd

fallen into a routine. Walk in, hang up his hat, nod to the lovely lady behind the desk, collect his book, and settle into the corner, where he could sit unobtrusively on the floor instead of crushing one of her dollhouse-like chairs with his decidedly un-doll-like physique. The two of them usually had the place to themselves while others lunched at home or at the café, but they rarely conversed. She, because she apparently had no such desire. He, because silence was the safer path.

Today, however, the sound of her voice greeted him as he trod up the walkway toward a door that stood ajar.

"Please go outside. I really don't want to hurt you."

Levi pulled up short.

"No. Not toward me. To the door. The door!" She squealed, and Levi bounded forward, taking the stairs in a single leap. He threw the door wide and brought up his fists, ready to take on the unseen threat.

"Get it off! Get it off!" She held her skirts away from her body and twisted her head to the side as if trying to put as much distance as possible between her and the invader clinging to the dark green fabric of her dress.

A cockroach. A big ugly one—three, maybe four inches long, its wings still slightly askew.

"Please." Miss Spencer whimpered, and the sound galvanized him to action.

Levi opened his hand and swiped the oversized beetle from her skirt. Then, before the thing could scamper into a dark corner, he crushed it with a stomp of his boot, wincing at the audible crunch that echoed in the now-quiet hall. He scraped his sole over the carcass like a horse pawing the ground, and sent the bug sailing out the door.

"Did you have to squish him?"

Levi jerked his eyes to Eden Spencer's face. What had she expected him to do? Tie a leash around its neck and take it for a walk?

"Don't get me wrong," she said, as she raised a shaky hand to fidget with the button at her collar. "I appreciate your removing that beastly insect from my person." She shuddered slightly, and her gaze dropped to the darkened spot on the hardwood floor that evidenced the roach's demise. "However, I can't abide violence against any of God's creatures. Even horrid, wing-sprouting behemoths."

"I don't like it, either," Levi said, recalling the vow he made in the Huntsville chapel the day he chose to hand his life back over into the Lord's keeping. "But if . . . I need to take violent action to . . . protect another, I will."

Not for himself. Only for another. Never again would he fight for sport, pride, or self-defense—only if the well-being of someone else hung in the balance. Although, the speed at which he'd clenched his fists and charged when he thought Miss Spencer was in trouble concerned him. Old habits died hard. The fighting impulse had taken control of his body before his mind had a chance to piece together what was happening.

Sending the Lord a silent plea for more self-discipline, Levi ducked around Miss Spencer, not wanting to see any more condemnation in her eyes. Crushing a bug was no sin, but her accusations prodded his guilt. If the woman was upset at him for killing a cockroach, he hated to think what her reaction would be if she ever discovered what he used to do for a living. Or what happened during that last prizefight . . .

Never again, Lord. I swear, never again.

After he hung his hat on its customary top hook, he strode into the reading room and collected his book from the shelf. The quiet rustle of a woman's skirts echoed behind him. He didn't turn. In fact, he lengthened his stride until he realized there was something different about the corner he usually sat in. The vacant space had been filled with a large leather wing chair. A sturdy chair. A masculine chair. A chair he'd never seen before.

He did turn then.

"I thought you might prefer it to the floor." She met his eye briefly, then looked away. "Harvey brought it in from my father's study. Since Father rarely visits, I doubt he'll mind if we borrow it for a while. I can use it for my story time, as well."

Levi stared at the woman before him, her thoughtfulness pouring light into a place inside him that had long been darkened. A place that reminded him of family and acceptance, of belonging. His mind scoffed at the tender reaction stirring in him. It was just a chair—leather, wood, some stuffing. It wasn't new or even really his. But the gesture left him shaken nonetheless. He'd not received such a gift since he left home so many years ago.

Miss Spencer waved her hands in the air as if his response was unimportant to her, but Levi caught the sidelong glances she shot his way as he kept silent.

"If you don't like it, I'll ask Harvey to move it back."

He tried to shape his gratitude into words, but before his sluggish tongue could spit them out, she exhaled a heavy breath, and her arm flopped to her side.

"You know what? I'll just go fetch

him right now. He's probably in the kitchen with Verna." Her face flushed as she spun away from him.

She didn't understand.

Levi tossed his book onto the seat of the chair and lunged forward. He snagged her hand and tugged her to a halt. Still, she didn't look at him. He wanted to call to her, to urge her to face him. Using her given name would be too presumptuous, though, and calling her Miss Spencer would embarrass them both. So, letting go of her hand, he cupped her shoulders and gently forced her around.

He waited, his hands holding her in place.

Finally she looked up, her bottom lip trembling slightly. Perhaps he should have smiled to ease her nerves, but he couldn't. That sort of surface smile would only cheapen the sentiment he wanted to express.

"I like it. Very much. Thank you." He gazed into her eyes while he spoke, hoping that somehow she would comprehend the depth of his gratitude despite his inadequate words. Those mossy green eyes peered back at him, and for a moment the chair, the library, the house—all of it—disappeared. All he saw was her. Then she blinked, and the world returned.

Levi released her shoulders and stepped back, dredging up the very smile he'd rejected earlier to cover his own sudden bout of nerves.

"Well," she said, "enjoy your book."

He nodded, and a strange look passed over her face, almost as if she were trying to contain a giggle. What in the world did that mean?

As he settled into the leather seat, he opened to the page where he had left Phileas yesterday, but his gaze kept drifting over the edge of the book to follow Miss Spencer as she wandered about the room, straightening shelves that were already tidy.

A man could get used to such a view. Levi looked his fill until Miss Spencer swiveled to inspect a bookcase near his corner. He ducked his head so fast, vibrations ricocheted down his spine. After that, Levi maintained continuous visual contact with Mr. Verne's pages, but when he took his leave thirty minutes later, he couldn't recall a single word he'd read.

Chapter Eight

Later that afternoon, Eden asked Verna to watch the library for her so she could run the errand she'd been putting off all week. Tomorrow, the Ladies Aid Society would expect a report on the progress of the fund drive. Eden had yet to solicit a single penny beyond the twenty dollars she'd withdrawn from her own account.

As she moved to the hall, she glanced through the window to judge the weather. The sun had been shining most of the day, so she doubted she'd need a cloak. Her pleated shoulder cape should offer sufficient protection. Besides, it was more flattering to her figure. Not that she was trying to impress anyone. It was simply a matter of properly representing the Society.

Eden collected the short black cape from the closet beneath the stairs, swung it over her shoulders, and fastened it under her chin. She checked her appearance in the hall-tree mirror, pleased with the way the cape complemented the dark green of her dress and the jet buttons at her cuffs. Taking down her black straw bonnet, her gaze strayed to the empty top hook, the one belonging to Mr. Grant. Or rather, the one he tended to use. Eden cleared her throat and jabbed a hatpin through the knot of her chignon. Just because the man was habitual about where he hung his hat was no reason for her to consider the spot his. On impulse, she yanked an umbrella from the cylindrical stand beside the hall tree and slapped its curved wooden handle onto the hook in question.

There. That was better.

She gave the umbrella a sharp nod,

then spun and marched toward the front door, snatching her handbag and black kid gloves from the hall table as she went.

As Eden made her way down Main Street, the smithy loomed large in her peripheral vision. Nevertheless, she kept her focus straight ahead. She would visit the saddle shop and livery first, hone her pitch on men she'd known for years—men who didn't look at her with penetrating gray eyes or rescue her from mammoth-sized beetles.

Turning her back on Mr. Grant's place of business, Eden took a deep breath and pushed open the door to the saddlery. The smell of new leather and harness oil filled her senses. It wasn't an unpleasant aroma, just stronger than she preferred. Trying not to inhale too deeply, she made her way to the counter.

Alex Carson set down the shoe leather he'd been stitching at his worktable and rose to greet her. "Good afternoon, Miss Spencer. Ready for that new pair of walking boots? I got some pebbled goatskin in that would make a handsome pair of gaiters." He stepped around the counter and started moving to the adjoining room, where his boots and shoes were displayed. An expert in all things leather, the man served as the town cobbler as well as saddler.

"No, thank you." Eden stopped him before he could get too far. "I'm afraid I'm not shopping today. I'm here on behalf of the Spencer Ladies Aid Society."

"Ah, I see." The man smiled and strode back to the counter. "Time for the annual fund drive, is it?"

"Yes, sir."

Mr. Carson reached behind the counter and brought out his till. "What deserving cause have the good ladies of Spencer chosen this year? Orphans again?"

"No. Although the reconstructed shoes you sent along with your cash donation last year were a true blessing. My contact at the Seeds of Hope Orphanage was delighted at the gift. Children outgrow their shoes so fast, and the ones that are handed down are worn to shreds. Having several new pairs makes a big difference."

The man's face reddened a bit, but his smile widened as he opened the till and fingered a ten-dollar greenback. "I was glad to help, miss. Will you be needing shoes again this year?"

"No. We are raising money for prison Bibles this year."

Mr. Carson looked up from the till, the corner of the bill he'd been holding sliding back into its slot. "Prison Bibles?"

Eden silently sympathized with his reluctance. But her opinion was not what mattered. She was there for the Society, not herself, and she would do her best to honor the ministry the Lord had led them to, even if it was not one that spoke directly to her heart.

"I know it seems an odd choice," she said, setting her handbag on the counter next to the till. "However, our preacher and his wife fully endorse the idea. The Cranfords are personally acquainted with the chaplain in Huntsville who will be receiving the Bibles, and they assure us that Mr. Willis is a godly man of sound judgment who knows what he is about. The Bibles will be distributed only to convicts who attend weekly Bible classes and worship services. Those who demonstrate a spiritual commitment will receive a copy as a gift upon their release."

Mr. Carson scratched at his beard. "I can't rightly say that buying Bibles is a bad idea, but I'm not sure I want them going to criminals. My brother, the one up in Jewett, was robbed last year. The thief shot him in the arm and made off with a week's worth of earnings. His arm ain't worked right since. If he didn't have that boy o' his, he would've had to close up shop." The saddler dropped his hand from his chin to massage his shoulder as his gaze swept over his merchandise. "It might seem un-Christian to you, but I can't see my way to helping men who would steal from decent folk and not think twice about shooting them for their trouble."

Eden couldn't blame the man. She hadn't been in favor of the idea either. Yet, instead of thanking him for his time, she felt an inner urging to make a final plea.

"What if your donation led to the conversion of one of those criminals? What if he repented of his past sins, and after his release, did his best to 'go and sin no more'? Then, because of you, there would be one less man who thought stealing acceptable, one less man who would turn a gun on another. One less soul in Satan's grasp."

Mr. Carson shook his head and released a small huff of disbelief. "Do you really believe that's possible, Miss Spencer?"

" 'With God all things are possible,' " she quoted softly.

"Possible," he allowed, "but knowing human nature the way I do, I'd say it weren't very probable."

Eden shrugged. "You may be right. I've found myself thinking much the same thing. But giving these men Bibles certainly won't cause any harm, and if there's a chance that one or two of them might actually commit their life to Christ as a result of our fund drive, well then, I consider it money well spent."

Her words hung in the air between them, and Eden was surprised by how much she meant them. It was no longer salesmanship on her part; somewhere in the midst of her defense, her heart had changed. Maybe Mr. Carson needed time to adjust, as well.

"If you'd like to think about it, I could come back tomorrow."

"That's all right." He smiled at her and reached back into the till. "I know you ladies do good work, and you're right—giving Bibles to prisoners will do no harm. I'd be happy to contribute."

Eden held out her hand in anticipation, but instead of the ten-dollar bill he'd been fingering earlier, Mr. Carson dropped two silver dollars into her palm. Masking her disappointment, Eden conveyed her thanks and left the establishment. Two dollars might not be as much as she had originally hoped for, but it would cover the cost of three or four of the Bibles Emma planned to order. It was still a blessing.

She made out a little better at the livery. Mr. Barnes donated five dollars and graciously offered free use of his wagon if Mr. Cranford needed it to deliver the cases of Bibles to Huntsville at the conclusion of the drive.

The blacksmith shop was the only business left on her list.

Steeling herself, Eden strode through the gaping double doors and into the warmth of the smithy. The glow of the forge in the center of the shop beckoned to her, but the interior was dim. Her toe struck something hard on the floor. A clanking racket echoed off the walls as she stumbled forward.

"Look out!" someone yelled.

As she caught her balance, she turned her face toward the man's voice and found herself on the wrong end of a fretting horse. Its rear leg kicked out. Eden spun away, tensing for the blow. But before the hoof could connect with her head, a pair of massive arms scooped her up and smothered her against a wide chest.

"Oomph." Her rescuer moaned, and

Eden knew the horse had taken its pound of flesh after all.

"You all right, Levi?" a man called. "Sorry 'bout that. Red don't like unexpected noises."

"Yeah. I'm fine." He carried her several feet away before lowering her to her feet. Then he gently peeled the protective cocoon of his body from around her and peered into her face. "Are you hurt?"

"No." Eden's legs trembled, though, and she grabbed his forearm to steady herself. He stilled and stared at her gloved hand as if it were a ladybug that had alit upon him, delicate and dainty against his corded masculinity. Embarrassed, Eden released him and dropped her hand to her side.

"Thank you, Mr. Grant," she said softly as she tugged her sleeve cuffs back down over her wrists. "That's twice in one day you've come to my rescue."

"Glad to help, ma'am."

Again with the *ma'am*? The warmth his gallantry had evoked cooled several degrees. Why could the man not remember her name? It was the same as the town, for heaven's sake! How difficult could it be?

"Really, Mr. Grant. One would think that after living in this town for nearly a week and making numerous visits to my library, you would extend me the courtesy of learning my name."

"I know your name, Eden."

Her eyes shot to his.

"I know your name." The intensity in his gaze left no doubt of his sincerity.

"Hey, Levi." The owner of the recalcitrant horse spoke up, and Mr. Grant looked away. "I think I got 'er settled down. If the lady don't mind waitin', you can finish shoein' her now."

Mr. Grant . . . Levi . . . raised a brow at her in question.

"Go ahead. I'll just stay out of Red's range over here in the corner." And try to restore her pulse to a normal rhythm.

He stared at her for a moment in a way that had her despairing of ever regaining control of her runaway pulse. Then, with a nod, he returned to work.

Taking slow, even breaths, Eden

wandered to the back wall. A makeshift wash station had been rigged from pieces of broken furniture to support a basin the size of a horse trough. She smiled and ran a finger across the rim, until an unwelcome thought intruded.

If he'd known her name this whole time, why did he not use it when she specifically requested he do so? Was he playing some kind of game at her expense? She peeked over her shoulder to where he stood bent at the waist, Red's back hoof cradled in his lap upon a leather apron. Every once in a while Levi would stroke the animal's flank and murmur words she couldn't make out. But they must have been soothing, for the horse remained calm and cooperative. Somehow she couldn't quite picture this patient, gallant giant amusing himself in a spiteful way at another's expense.

Eden turned back to the table. A discarded scrap of towel sat lonely and forgotten in a wadded heap. She picked it up, shook out its creases, and folded it into a tidy rectangle. She laid it beside the washtub and straightened the white shirt that hung askew from a peg to her left. It was the one he'd worn to church and for his visits to the library. Was it the only good shirt he owned? She tilted her head to examine his work clothes. The trousers were the same dark brown ones she'd become accustomed to seeing stretched out across her reading-room floor. Now that she thought about it, she'd never seen him wear a different pair. He must have fallen on hard times. Perhaps she should forgo asking him for a donation. She'd not want to embarrass him or take funds he could ill afford to give.

The door at the back of the shop stood open. Maybe it would be best for all concerned if she left before he could ask why she had come.

Eden stole another glimpse at Levi. He looked to be finished. The horse was standing on all fours as the two men discussed something—payment most likely. Careful to mind her steps so as not to repeat her earlier mistake, Eden picked her way toward the back entrance. However, the moment she exited into the waiting sunshine, a shaggy gray creature with death in his eyes leapt from behind a pile of scrap metal to bar her path.

Chapter Nine

Levi heard Ornery's familiar growl behind him as he pocketed the fifty cents he'd just earned from replacing two shoes. He dropped his hammer and rasp into the toolbox at his feet and turned to address the mutt.

"Quiet, boy. You don't want to frighten . . ." The sentence disintegrated as he took in the scene.

"I'm afraid it's too late for that," Eden offered in a plucky voice that quaked only a little. She made no move to face him, though. Ornery consumed her full attention.

"He won't hurt you," Levi said as he stretched out his stride to cover the distance between them in as quick and nonthreatening a manner as possible.

"That remains to be seen."

Levi moved up behind her, so close they were nearly touching. Eden leaned backward ever so slightly until her shoulders brushed his chest. The soft sound of her exhale stirred the air as she pressed against him. In that moment, he felt more like offering the dog a treat than taking him to task for his inhospitable manner. But he'd be a cad to take advantage of her fear, so he cupped her shoulders for a brief second to fortify her, then stepped away.

"Quiet, Ornery." Levi hunkered down and rubbed the dog's ears. The growl gave way to a whine before Ornery surrendered to the pampering. With a small leap, he raised both front paws onto Levi's raised knee, silently demanding that Levi scratch his belly, as well. "You big fraud." As he reached down to bury his fingers in the fur on Ornery's underside, Levi cast a reassuring glance in Eden's direction.

"Come pet him. He might look mean, but only . . . on account of him being . . . hurt by . . . virulent men." He stopped rubbing Ornery's stomach long enough to wave her closer. "Come on. I won't let him hurt you. Prove you're a friend."

Eden raised a skeptical eyebrow, but she inched forward. Levi grinned. The woman had gumption.

"Here. I'll hold him."

She bit her lip as she moved closer. Finally, she crouched beside him. "Should I pat his back or rub his belly?" Her hand hovered uncertainly.

"Belly," Levi said. "He'll be a faithful devotee if you do that."

Eden tilted her head and gave him a curious look. It was the first time she had taken her gaze off the dog. Levi winked at her. Her cheeks flushed pink, making him feel like a young swain courting his first girl.

She turned back to the dog and tentatively stretched out her gloved hand.

"It might be better if you took off the glove. Let him . . . get to know your . . ." *Scent, fragrance, odor?* He was *not* going to use the word *odor*. But everything else had the dreaded *S* sound. ". . . your identifying aroma."

Again with the quizzical glance. "My scent, you mean?"

Levi nodded.

"All right." She unbuttoned the fastener at her wrist and pulled each finger free.

Levi blinked and refocused on the dog. When her slender hand crept back into his line of sight, he took hold of it and brought it close to Ornery's nose. The dog sniffed and then ducked his head under their joined hands as if letting them know it was time to commence with the petting.

Eden giggled. "I guess he approves of me."

"Yep." The dog had good taste.

They stayed hunkered beside each other for another two or three minutes as they rubbed and scratched Ornery until his manner more closely resembled that of an overgrown pup than a trained killer. Levi's fingers occasionally brushed against Eden's in the forest of scraggly gray fur, but she didn't seem to mind. So it was only natural for Levi to take her hand and help her stand when Ornery finally grew weary of the excessive attention and bounded away.

Her hand fit into the crease of his palm like a rivet in a customized hinge. It seemed a crime for her to slip it free. Nevertheless, he released his hold the moment she tugged. He stepped back to give her some space and leaned his back against the doorframe. As he watched her slide her glove back into place, he searched his mind for something intelligent to say.

"You need ironwork done?" Levi clamped his jaw shut over the inane question. Apparently, intelligent was too lofty a goal in his present distracted state. Fine ladies like Miss Eden Spencer didn't frequent smithies during their shopping expeditions. They perused dry goods stores and milliners' shops. If she'd needed blacksmithing done, she would have sent her man, Harvey, not trudged down here herself.

Yet here she stood, so she must require something of him.

"Actually, I came here in regard to another matter, but I . . . well . . . I'm not sure I should follow it through." Her gaze flitted past him to his washstand, then fell to the dusty ground at her feet.

What did his washstand have to do with anything? And why was Eden back to acting so uncomfortable? A sudden dread knifed his gut.

"Did . . . an individual complain about my work?" Levi gripped the edge of the wall for support. He was supposed to have a month. It hadn't even been a full week.

"No." Eden's head shot up and her green-eyed gaze melded with his. "Nothing like that. I assure you."

"Good." Levi let go of the wall and straightened, taking his hat from his head long enough to wipe the sweat from his brow with his sleeve. Then he settled the hat back into place and contemplated the woman before him. "If not that, then what?"

"Well . . ." Eden blew out a breath. "All right. I'll tell you, but don't feel obligated to participate. You haven't had time yet to solidify your business. I understand that. And so will the other ladies."

Levi held up his hand to stop her, his head spinning. "Whoa, there. What are you talking about? What other lady—er—women?"

"I'm here as a representative of the Spencer Ladies Aid Society." She drew back her shoulders and lifted her chin. "Each year, we conduct a fund drive to collect monies for worthy causes. Last year, the donations we accumulated procured quilts, shoes, clothing, and school supplies for the children at the Seeds of Hope Orphanage in Austin. I had the honor of overseeing the delivery, and I'll never forget the joy on those young faces when the children opened our crates."

He could well imagine. Her face lit up even now as she talked about it, her love for the children as obvious as a footprint in newly turned soil. If ever a woman was meant to be a mother, it was Eden Spencer. A pity she'd never married.

"This year, the committee chose a

different ministry to sponsor. We are garnering funds for prison Bibles."

Levi sucked in a shocked breath. He felt as if he had just fallen into a vat of molasses. No matter how hard he tried to get his mind or body to move, everything seemed to be stuck on those two words. Prison Bibles. When she mentioned Jonathan Willis and Huntsville, however, he snapped out of his stupor.

Did someone suspect? It couldn't be coincidence. The connection between this fund drive and his past was too uncanny to be explained away by chance. But what did it mean?

"Who . . . ah . . . came up with the idea?"

"Our preacher's wife, Mrs. Cranford. She and her husband are acquainted with Mr. Willis, the chaplain who requested the Bibles."

The vise around his heart loosened a notch. The Cranfords. Of course. Maybe it was innocent after all. Then again, he'd probably be wise to test the waters a bit.

Levi studied Eden's face closely. "I know Jonathan. Good man."

Eden's brows bunched together. "You do?" Her surprise seemed genuine, not the expression of one gathering evidence to confirm a scandalous hypothesis.

"He put me in touch with the . . . with Dave and Emma. Recommended me for the job here."

The creases in her forehead receded. "Oh, I see. I'm glad to hear you speak well of Mr. Willis. I trust the Cranfords, of course, but I'll admit I was a little hesitant about this venture. It seemed wrong somehow to collect funds to help criminals."

An ache throbbed in Levi's gut, and he doubted it had anything to do with the bruise from Red's hoof. This was why he kept his past a secret. Felons were a low class of society—despised, feared. And for good reason. Yet even they deserved the chance to hear the good news, the chance to turn their lives around. And when they did, shouldn't the blood of Christ wash away their stigma as well as their sin?

It should, but it didn't. Not in the eyes of most, anyway. Even Jesus warned of the lingering consequences. The father welcomed the Prodigal Son into his home with unwavering love and forgiveness. However, when the older brother looked at his sibling, all he saw was the greedy fool who had squandered half the estate. Irresponsible. Worthy of condemnation. Never to be trusted. Levi fully expected to be treated with similar attitudes should his past become known, but hearing a hint of what was to come from the lips of a woman whose good opinion he coveted sprinkled poison over the sprig of hope he'd cultivated over the last week.

He clenched his teeth as Eden rambled on about how he needn't feel pressured to give. He was still establishing his business, after all. No one would expect him to make a donation. He could contribute to next year's cause.

But next year's cause wouldn't stir his soul like this one. Next year's wouldn't be personal. Next year's wouldn't give him the chance to pay back the man who showed him the way home.

"Pardon me for a minute." Levi interrupted Eden's string of well-intentioned excuses. "I'll be right back."

It wasn't a coincidence that God had laid this particular mission on the hearts of the Spencer ladies at the same time he brought Levi to their town. The Lord was offering Levi a choice—distance himself from his past by declining to help or fight for the souls of men he'd roamed the yard with. He hesitated only a second before reaching for the key in his trouser pocket.

Levi stretched his arm up to the high shelf he'd installed above the washstand. Taking down the metal box he sought, he slid the key into the lock and gave it a quarter turn. The lid released. He moved aside the small ledger where he tallied his daily profits and expenditures, and gathered up every bank note and coin in the box. He counted it out and made a note in the ledger. Fourteen dollars and sixty-two cents. The money he'd earned combined with the money he'd staked himself at the beginning of the week.

"What are you doing?"

He turned to find Eden less than a yard away. "Here." He held the fistful out to her. "For the drive."

She shook her head, her eyes wide. "I . . . I can't. That's all you have." She tried to push his arm back, but Levi locked his elbow and refused to budge.

"Levi, please. It's too much." The plea in her voice touched his heart, but it was the sound of his name on her lips that spread warmth through him like hot coffee on a winter morning.

He smiled at her beautifully befuddled face. "Take it, Eden. For Jonathan and . . . the men." Gently, he took her hands and placed the money in her palms. Then he pressed her fingers closed by wrapping his own hands around her smaller ones. "A Bible can change a life. I know."

Eden gazed up at him, understanding finally dawning in her eyes. One corner of her mouth curved slowly upward. "All right. Thank—"

"Hey, shmith!"

Levi snatched his hands away from Eden, a guilty heat creeping up his neck. He spun toward the slurred voice bellowing at him from the front of his shop.

"Come out and fashe me, you murderin' dog."

"What in the world?" Eden stepped up beside him, craning her neck to see who was there.

Levi pushed her behind him, his heart as heavy as a stone. "Wait here. I'll deal with it."

The jig was up. As he navigated his way around the forge, he stole a glance back at Eden. At least he'd done one good deed before his past caught up with him. He just wished she wasn't the one witnessing his fall.

"It's your fault he's dead!"

The minute Levi stepped into the doorway, the stranger lunged at him. Unprepared for the fist that flew at his face, Levi took a hard blow to the jaw and staggered back into a plow that had been brought in for repair. It clattered against the floor as he tripped over it.

"Levi!"

He heard Eden call his name, but it was little more than a dim buzz as his senses honed in on the man rushing toward him. For a moment, he was back on the fight circuit, his opponent charging. In a single fluid motion, he thrust his body up over his feet and closed his hands into fists. He narrowed his focus, zeroing in on the man's chin. All else faded from his awareness. One sharp jab ought to send him sprawling.

As the man lumbered into range, Levi drew his arm back, his muscles tight and ready to lash out. But then the man's face changed. No longer was he a stranger. His face became the one that had haunted his dreams for the last two years. The man he'd killed.

Chapter Ten

Eden rushed forward, intent on helping Levi. Although how, she wasn't quite certain. She doubted a stern lecture on the ills of violent behavior would deter the man bearing down on him.

Before she reached his side, however, Levi sprang to his feet like some kind of wild jungle cat, his fists clenched. Eden stuttered to a halt. His eyes had gone so hard she almost didn't recognize him. A chill passed through her, and suddenly she feared not for Levi but for the loud-mouthed drunk charging him. Nausea roiled in her stomach.

He was just like all the rest. Why had she expected anything different? He was a man. A strong, burly man. Of course he would answer violence with violence. It was the barbarian way.

Levi cocked his arm, and Eden raised her palm to block the view of what was to come. Yet in the instant before her hand fully shielded her face, Levi's countenance changed. Peeking between her fingers, she watched his arm slacken. He wasn't going to retaliate? Her heart leapt.

Then it plunged as she realized his change of heart left him unprotected. The other man fell on Levi, muttering vile curses and swinging sloppy punches.

"Stop it!" she screamed, but the man paid her no heed.

She had to help. Moving behind the aggressor, she reached for his suspenders, intending to yank him backward, but Levi caught sight of her.

"No, Eden! Back off. He'll hurt you."

And he nearly did. Sensing a threat from behind, the man whirled and clipped Eden's shoulder. Not hard, but enough to toss her sideways and prove how ineffectual she was against him.

As she bumped against the shop wall, Levi growled and surged forward. The man shrank back, but when Levi still didn't throw a punch, he stepped in and threw one of his own. Levi dodged to the left and at the same time slammed his palm into the man's fist, absorbing the blow. Then he curled his fingers over the man's hand, immobilizing him. His opponent struggled to pull free, but Levi held fast.

"Wilson! What in tarnation are you doing?"

Eden spun around to find Claude Barnes hustling across the yard separating his livery from the smithy. Never had she been more grateful for a nosy neighbor.

"He attacked Mr. Grant with absolutely no provocation," she called out as Claude jogged past, but the man ignored her. Instead he hurried to aid the foul man he'd called Wilson. The name struck a chord of familiarity with her, but Eden failed to place it. All she knew was that this Wilson had shown Levi no mercy, even after the much larger blacksmith had exhibited the virtue first by restraining his own aggression. The fellow deserved to be brought up on charges.

When Mr. Barnes reached his side, Wilson stopped trying to wrench his arm free. His anger crumpled into child-like sobs. “He killed my boy, Claude. He killed him.”

Mr. Barnes wrapped his arms around the man and nodded to Levi to let go. He did, and Wilson slumped to the ground, causing Mr. Barnes to have to crouch down beside him to keep his hold.

“You been drinkin’ again, ain’tcha?” Mr. Barnes sniffed at Wilson’s clothes and scrunched his face in distaste. “You gotta lay off that whiskey, brother. It ain’t gonna bring John Junior back. It’s just gonna make you worthless to the rest of your kin. How’re you gonna plant your fields next month if you’re locked up for assaultin’ this here fella? How’re Betsy and the girls supposed to live if you’re too busy drownin’ your sorrows to take care of them, huh?

Grief is a hard land to dwell in, but pouring liquor down your throat only makes it harder to find the path out."

Eden edged closer, compassion for this man reluctantly stirring her heart. She drew abreast of Levi and glanced up at him. A small cut on the corner of his mouth oozed blood, but what struck her the most was his stillness. He didn't turn at her approach. Didn't smile or ask if she was all right after her tussle. All he did was stiffen slightly as he stared straight ahead, into nothing. She moved in front of him, but his gaze never wavered. It hovered above her as if tied like a clothesline to a high spot on the far wall. An air of doom surrounded him, sending a shiver through Eden's shoulders.

"I miss him, Claude," Wilson said, grabbing Mr. Barnes's arm as he visibly fought to contain his sobs. "He shoulda been fourteen today. Woulda been if *he* had just fixed the axle rod right."

Wilson pointed an accusing finger at Levi, and for one horrible moment, Eden wondered if Levi really was responsible for the boy's death. But then a memory clicked in her mind. A broken axle. Young John Wilson being thrown from the buckboard seat and run over before the horses could stop. The churchyard funeral. She hadn't known the family well, but she recalled how the mother had wept and how forlorn the two little girls had been.

"It was a year ago." Eden softly voiced the thought aloud. "Mr. Grant was not even here then."

"W-What?"

"The gal's right, Wilson. Even if shoddy work led to the axle breaking, which we can't know fer sure, Levi here ain't the one responsible. You been punishing an innocent man." Mr. Barnes pulled Wilson onto his feet and dusted the fellow off. "Just be glad he didn't strike back. The way he's built, he'd probably a-knocked all your teeth out with one tap. Come on. I'll see you home."

Mr. Barnes led the grieving father away. Wilson mumbled something that could have been an apology, but it was too quiet and slurred to be coherent.

Behind her, Levi's boots scratched

against the hard-packed earth. Eden turned to see him reach out for the wall as if in need of support. "Fourteen?" The whispered word fell from his lips, tinged with disbelief. "Not a man, grown?"

Eden stepped closer. "No. He was a boy. Thrown from a wagon."

Levi's eyes widened, and he blinked repeatedly. "Not a fighter?"

"A fighter?" Eden's brows drew together in confusion. "What are you talking about?"

He shook his head fiercely, like a dog expelling water from its fur. It left his hair quite mussed, but his eyes cleared, and Eden felt as if he once again was truly aware of her presence.

"Are you all right?" she asked, cautiously touching his arm.

Levi's gaze found her fingers, and his lips lifted at one corner in a tiny smile. "I'm fine. A bad memory caught up to me for a minute, but . . . it left."

His eyes met hers, and she longed to ask him about that memory. Yet she swallowed her questions. She knew firsthand how painful it could be to have someone dredge up the past. It wouldn't do their fledgling friendship any good to press Levi for answers he clearly didn't want to give.

"I heard you had a scuffle," a male voice announced in overloud tones.

Eden flinched and yanked her hand away from Levi's arm. "Sheriff Pratt," she said, willing her cheeks not to blush. "I'm afraid you missed all the excitement."

The lawman's gaze traveled meaningfully from Eden to Levi and back again. "Don't know about that, darlin'. Seems to me I got here just in time."

There was no stopping the warm flood that washed over her face at his insinuation. The sheriff glared at her in disapproval before turning narrowed eyes on Levi.

"I warned you about stirring up trouble, Grant. A customer from the Hang Dog told me a fellow at the bar claimed your poor workmanship cost a boy his life. And that the man aimed to take a piece of your hide in payment. Where is he?" The sheriff stepped into the shop, his neck stretching from side to side as he searched. "I figure a drunk ain't no match for you. His friends carry him off already?"

Eden bristled. "Don't be ridiculous, Sheriff. Mr. Wilson is unharmed. Claude Barnes is seeing him home."

Sheriff Pratt eyed Levi more closely. He rubbed the pad of his thumb over the edge of his mouth, mirroring the location of Levi's split lip. "Got in a lucky punch, did he?" The lawman smirked. "Guess you're not as tough as I thought. Size ain't everything, is it?"

Levi simply stood there, mute.

"Still, I want you out of my town. Can't have kids dying because of your sloppy work."

Eden gasped at the man's audacity.

"Not my work," Levi finally offered in his defense.

However, those three little words were far from sufficient to Eden's way of thinking. She marched up to Conrad Pratt, indignation tearing at the seams of her control. "This is outrageous. You can't oust a man from town on the word of some . . . some drunkard without even verifying the veracity of his story. What kind of lawman are you? The boy who died was young John Wilson, and the accident was over a year ago. Mr. Grant is innocent of any wrongdoing. It was all a misunderstanding."

"That's a mighty spirited defense, *Miss Spencer*." The way he looked her up and down as he drawled her name made Eden cringe. "Seems odd, you takin' up for a man you hardly know. Unless, of course, you *know* him far better than you've let on."

"Watch it, Pratt." Levi's voice echoed behind her, steel lacing his tone.

The sheriff took a menacing step forward, anger mottling his cheeks as he shifted his gaze to Levi. "You're the one who should watch it, Grant. The Spencer family is well respected in this town. I won't stand for anyone besmirching Miss Eden's reputation. She has no business being here alone with you, and I aim to see her home straightaway." He grabbed Eden's elbow and began yanking her toward the road.

"Of all the high-handed, rude behavior . . ." Eden muttered as she tripped along behind him. She longed to whack Sheriff Pratt across the side of his head with her handbag and snatch her arm free of his biting hold, yet she knew antagonizing the man would only make matters worse. So instead, she called out a parting word to Levi over her shoulder.

"Good day, Mr. Grant. Thank you again for your generous donation to the Ladies Aid Society fund drive. Your gift will be a blessing to many, I'm sure."

"Glad to help, ma'am. Let me know if you encounter any other project I can help with." The way he glowered at the sheriff's back left little doubt as to what other project he was referring to.

"I will, sir. Thank you." She tried to wave, to reassure him she was fine, but all of the twisting she'd been doing to glance behind finally tripped up her feet. Eden stumbled into the sheriff, who released her elbow in order to wrap his full arm about her.

"I got ya, darlin'."

"I'm not your darling." Eden planted her feet and turned accusing eyes on the man at her side. "How could you insult me like that? Insinuating that I had done something improper?"

"What was I supposed to think?" he hissed at her. "I stride in expecting to break up a brawl, and instead I find you cozying up to the smith, talkin' all quiet-like, touchin' his arm. Looked mighty intimate to me."

He loosened his hold and Eden stepped free, ducking her head as she brushed a spot of dust from her skirt. "The man had just been attacked. I was simply ensuring that he was all right before I took my leave."

Well, there might have been a bit more to it than that, but Conrad Pratt need not be privy to every detail. The man was far too intrusive as it was.

"Now, if you'll excuse me?" She brought her gaze back up to meet his. "I believe I'll see myself home." Eden forged down the road, praying the sheriff wouldn't cause a scene in front of the ladies who had gathered on the boardwalk by the general store. The three women made a good show of being absorbed in their chatter, but

Eden caught the curious glances cast in her direction as she approached. The kind of glances that reminded her of whispers and scandal and pity—three things she'd spent the last five years trying to escape.

Thankfully, the sheriff let her go without another word. However, the thud of his footsteps followed her the short distance home, the sound filling her with an odd sense of foreboding.

Chapter Eleven

On Friday afternoon, Levi walked into the Spencer bank with his first deposit jangling in his pocket. His profits from a week at the forge were meager at best, especially after having donated everything in his till to Eden's fund drive on Wednesday, but like a kid who'd earned his first dime carting supplies or mucking stalls, the sense of accomplishment he carried rendered the dollar amount unimportant.

Taking his place in line, Levi glanced up to the clerk's barred window and spied a familiar black bonnet perched atop a lovely coil of auburn hair. He'd seen Eden at the library just a few hours ago, but his stomach danced as if he hadn't seen her in ages. Who would've guessed viewing the back of a woman's head could have such an effect on a man?

Levi grinned, then sobered. He needed to keep a tighter rein on his reactions. The scuffle with the drunk a couple days back proved that his past could catch up to him at any time. He had no business pursuing more than a friendship with Eden Spencer, no matter what the back of her head did to his insides.

"Thank you, Adam." Eden's soft voice carried in the quiet lobby, as did the click of her purse clasp after she tucked the bills she'd received within its folds. She had just begun to turn when the outside door swung inward and crashed into the wall.

Levi spun around. Three men charged into the bank.

"Draper!" the first one yelled as he shoved past Levi, "Get your sorry hide out here!"

One fellow blocked off the entrance with a crossed-arm stance as if to make sure their quarry didn't escape while the other prowled about the room kicking at chairs with enough force to overturn a few while he heated the air with curses.

The first man reached the clerk's window and pounded his fist against the bars. "Get Draper. Now!"

The clerk scurried away, as did Eden. She backed toward the side wall, her hands out before her in a placating manner. Levi moved to go to her, but before he took more than two steps, the second man snatched up one of the chairs he'd been kicking and hurled it at Levi's head.

"Stay where you are, cowboy."

Levi lurched back and twisted his face away, leaving his shoulder to deflect most of the blow.

His assailant grabbed a second chair and drew it back. "Mind yer own business and nobody'll get hurt. All we want is that no-good, swindlin' banker."

Levi said nothing, just rubbed his shoulder and stared the man down. It was a little late to promise that no one would get hurt. The fellow finally lowered the chair, then straddled it as he placed himself between Levi and the man at the front, the one yelling for Draper.

The trio wasn't armed as far as Levi could tell, unless one counted the chair, so it was doubtful they intended to rob the place.

"You too afraid to face me, Draper?" The first man pounded on the bars again, and the sound of coins quivering in an open drawer rattled from the other side. "You think you can just steal my brother's land and not be held accountable? Come out here and face me like a man."

Levi was plotting the best way to circumvent the man with the chair to get to Eden, when the crazy woman actually stepped closer to the ringleader.

"Gentlemen, please. Whatever injustice has transpired, this angry display will only make matters worse. Please, calm yoursel—"

"Shut up, lady," the first man snapped. "This don't concern you."

"It most certainly—"

"Eden," Levi said through his clenched jaw. "Be quiet."

Her gaze locked with his, and the panic in her eyes made his heart throb worse than his shoulder.

"Get out of my bank, Monroe. You and those mangy brothers of yours."

Draper had finally made an appearance, but it was the shotgun he carried that drew everyone's attention. He jabbed the barrel through the bars, making Monroe step back.

"You gonna shoot me, Draper? I shoulda expected as much from a dirty dealer like you."

Levi inched toward Eden while Draper distracted the men.

"Will hadn't made a payment in four months. I warned him I'd foreclose if he couldn't find the money a fifth time."

"A decent man would wait until the next crop comes in."

"I run a business not a charity, Monroe. Now, get out!" Draper cocked his weapon and aimed it at the man's chest.

The brother at the door suddenly

cried out in pain and fell to his knees as Sheriff Pratt forced his way in, gun drawn. "Everybody down!"

Levi lunged for Eden. He shielded her with his bulk, not trusting Pratt or Draper to keep their bullets to themselves. Eden trembled and her breath came out in shallow little puffs.

"Out," she begged as she tugged on his arm. "Levi, I need to get out."

He tipped his face slightly toward her while keeping an eye on the sheriff. "All right."

The two Monroe brothers near the counter had their hands raised, but their mouths continued to call curses down on the banker as they slowly sank to their knees. Emboldened by Pratt's presence, Draper unlocked the inner door and stepped out from behind the counter.

"I want these men arrested, Sheriff."

"What for?" one of the brothers demanded. "We're not robbin' the place. You're the one who should be locked up for threatening me with that shotgun."

"Close your trap." The sheriff glanced

around the room, his eyes widening when he caught sight of Eden. He then scowled at Levi, a muscle in his jaw ticking where he ground his back teeth together.

Levi met his gaze. “Let me take her home, Pratt.”

The lawman checked on the Monroe brothers before looking back at Levi. He huffed out a disgusted breath, then strode to the door and yanked the last Monroe to his feet, dragging him away from the entrance. “Go on. Get her out of here.”

Levi made his way to the door with Eden sticking to him like a shadow.

“But you better hightail it back here and give me your statement, pronto.” Pratt glared at Levi as he passed, making his objection clear.

Levi would have promised almost anything to get Eden out of that powder keg. He nodded. “You have my word.”

Eden needed no urging to hurry. The minute she stepped clear of the bank, her arms and legs pumped with such haste, Levi struggled to keep up. When they reached her yard, Levi reached a hand out to slow her before she could disappear into the house.

"You going to be all right?"

She pivoted so fast, her handbag whacked him in the arm. "What is it with men, that they think yelling and pounding on things will get them what they want? Or throwing punches or waving a gun. It's all so . . . so . . . stupid!"

Her eyes still had a bit of the wild, panicked look to them that he'd seen earlier in the bank, but a glow of righteous indignation dominated. Her cheeks flushed from the brisk pace she'd set, her chest heaving slightly from the exertion, wisps of her hair waving in the breeze—she was like a virago rising up to take mankind to task for their deficiencies.

"First that grieving man attacks you for no good reason other than he feels sorry for himself and wants to spread the misery around," she started, gesticulating wildly, "and then a pack of wolves descends upon the bank, snarling and pouncing in the hopes of frightening their prey enough to get him to concede to their demands. Did they care who else might be inside when they charged through the door? No! They were too caught up in their own rage. Not five minutes before they arrived, the Cooper girls were skipping around the lobby while their mother made a deposit. Just imagine the disaster if those Monroe men had arrived a few minutes earlier. It's unconscionable!" Eden's arms flung wide, sending the handbag dangling from her wrist flying through the air until it snagged on a rosebush.

"Then Norman Draper with his shotgun and the sheriff with his strong-arm tactics—why, it's a miracle we got out of there unscathed!"

Levi kept his mouth shut, letting her say what she needed to say. He didn't try to explain a man's need to assert himself among his peers or point out that the sheriff's strong-arm tactics had proved effective in defusing the situation at the bank. Who was he to defend the actions of the men who had earned her scorn? He'd done far worse.

Silently, Levi reached around Eden to retrieve her handbag from a thorny branch. He picked off the tiny sticks that clung to the lacy fabric and handed it back to her. She accepted his offering and let out a long sigh.

"I'm sorry, Levi. I had no call to vent my spleen on you like that. I just . . ." She turned away from him and started walking toward the porch. "I felt so trapped and helpless. It was as if someone had turned the clock back and I was twelve again, and . . ." Her voice trailed off as she reached the railing.

He thought she was going to disappear into the house, but she sank down onto the stairs instead. There wasn't enough room to squeeze in beside her, but Levi wasn't about to strand her with her memories, not when her eyes begged him to stay. So he followed her to the porch steps and leaned against the newel post at the base.

"What happened when you were twelve?"

She dropped her purse in her lap and grabbed hold of one of the curved railing spindles. "My father took me to a political rally where one of his friends was speaking. Mother was supposed to go, but she didn't feel well, so Daddy asked me to accompany him."

A wistful smile touched Eden's face as she gazed out across the yard. "I felt so grown up and special on his arm that day. The hall was terribly crowded, though, and when the speaker droned on and on I grew impatient. Daddy went to fetch me some lemonade, and while he was gone the riot started."

Levi stiffened. "Riot?"

"Apparently my father's friend had bought several mills in the area only to close them down in order to sell the land to the railroad. The townsfolk heralded him a hero because his deal brought the railroad, and with it increased prosperity for all their businesses. But the unemployed mill workers took a different view, and after building up their courage at the local saloon, they stormed the meeting hall.

"They fired shots in the air while casting aspersions on anyone siding with a man who would steal bread from their children's mouths. People panicked and pushed and shoved to try to get away. I screamed for my father, but he was too far away to get to me, and everyone was pressing against him to try to exit the building. Some of the men tried to subdue the troublemakers and confiscate their weapons, but the mill workers fought back, and soon it was nothing more than an all-out brawl.

"The noise was deafening as everyone scrambled to escape. I was too scared to move, afraid Daddy wouldn't be able to find me if I wasn't where he left me. But as the brawl grew, it moved closer to the stage. Closer to me. Then one large fellow took a blow to the face and fell backward. Right on top of me. I lay beneath him as he rolled back and forth, trying to get up. I couldn't breathe. The fall had knocked the wind out of me, and I thought I was dying."

The girl must have been frightened out of her wits. No wonder the standoff in the bank had spooked her so badly. Levi hunkered down beside Eden and tried to meet her gaze, but she was too lost in her memories to notice.

"The man finally rolled off and I sat

up, gasping and sputtering. I could hear Daddy calling my name. He pushed his way through the mob and was nearly to me when another gun went off. I couldn't even scream. All I could do was watch Daddy grab his head and fall to his knees.

"I crawled over to him. Blood covered the side of his face and stained the shirt Mother had given him for Christmas."

Levi reached for her hand. When he touched her, she startled and returned to the present. Offering him a small smile, she tugged her hand free and got to her feet. Levi rose, too, standing quietly as she brushed the dust off her skirts.

"He was fine, of course," Eden continued, with a tone that tried to convey that everything else was fine, too, but Levi wasn't fooled. "The bullet had just grazed him."

"I'm glad."

The faraway look came over her again, but after a second or two she blinked it away. "My goodness. Here I am rambling about something that happened ages ago when the sheriff is waiting for you." She scurried up to the door and laid her palm on the handle, clicking the latch open. "Thank you for seeing me home, but you better hurry back to the bank. The sheriff's not known for his patience."

"Pratt will keep." He wasn't going anywhere until he was sure she was going to be all right.

Eden dipped her chin, but when her eyes lifted to meet his, they held an intensity that made his chest ache. "You're one of the few men I've met who has found a way to keep his life free of aggression, even when provoked. This world needs more men like you, Levi."

Then she turned and went into the house, leaving him staring at the closed door while his stomach churned over the lie he was letting her believe. Maybe he'd been believing a lie, as well. Thinking he could walk away from his past. Eden might respect Levi the blacksmith, but she'd never forgive Levi the prizefighter.

Chapter Twelve

After all the unpleasant excitement involving the attack at the smithy and the standoff at the bank, Eden found the routine of the following week a blessed relief. She doubted her pulse had accelerated past a steady plod during the last ten days. Well . . . except for when Levi stopped in for his daily read.

As he was doing now.

Eden forced her gaze to remain on the letter she was writing to her father instead of allowing it to wander in the direction of the man sitting in the corner of her reading room. Her self-discipline proved ineffectual, though. Just knowing he was there prompted that annoying little flutter in her abdomen that had been getting worse of late.

The two-week waiting period she had imposed on Levi's library privileges had expired last Friday, and each day since, she'd held her breath as he pushed up out of her father's chair and then exhaled when he slid his book back onto the shelf instead of bringing it to her desk with the request to borrow it. She had become rather accustomed to his visits, and though they still said no more than a handful of words to each other during the daily encounters, there was something comfortable about sharing the room with him.

Afraid she'd actually miss the hulking fellow should he decide to read at home, Eden had yet to remind him of their agreement. However, her rising curiosity about another matter prodded her to broach the subject. She wished to conduct an experiment.

Eden finally glanced up from the letter and snuck a peek at the blacksmith. She nibbled on the end of her penholder as she contemplated him.

Ever since the day she went to the smithy to solicit a donation, she'd been cataloguing the unexpected words that emerged from Levi Grant's mouth. With his halting speech and preference for minimizing conversations, she had initially assumed he was a bit, well . . . uneducated. Not that she had ever thought him lacking in wit or practical knowledge, per se, but he hadn't exactly struck her as an intellectual sort—the type who could analyze Melville's symbolism or comprehend the depths of Thoreau's reflections. Yet as the list secreted in her desk drawer grew ever longer, she began questioning her first impression.

Levi turned a page in his book, the movement sending Eden's gaze scurrying back to her desktop. Perhaps the best choice would be to leave things as they were. He'd probably not take kindly to her snooping, no matter how cleverly she disguised it. They'd developed an agreeable acquaintanceship over the past weeks. In fact, she considered herself more at ease in his company than any other man outside of Harvey or her father. So why risk losing that ease just to assuage her curiosity?

Eden set the pen aside and smothered a sigh. Because she was no longer content with easy and comfortable when it came to Levi Grant. It was like skimming through a novel without fully engaging with the story until a well-turned phrase or powerful bit of imagery snagged her attention, hinting at depths previously unnoticed. How could she continue skimming when a richer experience awaited?

Casting a quick glance at Levi to ensure he was still absorbed in his reading, Eden inched her desk drawer open and lifted her library ledger away to retrieve her list. The paper rattled slightly as she pulled it free, the sound echoing loudly in her ears. She darted a nervous look across the room, but Levi's attention never wavered from his copy of Verne's *A Journey to the Centre of the Earth*. He had moved on from

Around the World in Eighty Days the middle of last week.

Eden's heart rate slowed, and she turned back to her list. She'd been careful not to label the page in case someone should stumble upon it. To anyone else it probably seemed an odd collection of words that had no bearing on one another, but to her it represented a mystery—one she was eager to pursue. She had added many words to the list since the day of the fund drive. Words like *virulent*, *devotee*, and *identifying aroma*.

At church last Sunday, she overheard him compliment Mr. Cranford's sermon as being a "compelling pontification." He could have just as easily called it a speech or message, but he'd chosen *pontification*, and the word rolled off his tongue without the slightest bobble. Then today when he arrived, she'd made some comment about the weather, how the sun had cleared away the clouds, and he'd answered by saying that the firmament exhibited fine form indeed. Firmament? Most people would refer to it as the sky or possibly the heavens if they were in a poetical mood. But firmament? The only time she ever used that term was when singing Joseph Addison's hymn in church.

Levi Grant was a blacksmith by trade, not a schoolmaster or lawyer or gentleman of privilege. Yet every once in a while, he spat out a chunk of vocabulary so above his station, it signaled to her like a flare. The man might be an ironworker, but his mind seemed to be filled with more than a simple farrier's knowledge. Eden ran a finger down the length of her list. Dare she test the depths?

She bit her lip for a moment in indecision, then snatched up a fresh piece of writing paper, determined to take action before she lost her nerve.

Levi reached the end of chapter ten, where the impatient professor and his level-headed nephew had just secured a guide for their subterranean adventure. Tempted to turn the page to see how they got on, Levi forced himself to close the cover instead. He could check in with them tomorrow. Today he had chain links to repair, a garden cultivator to weld, and a pair of axes to reface. Not as exciting as descending into a volcano shaft, but with the heat of the forge, the smithy might be almost as hot.

He smiled to himself and rose to his feet. Several years ago, he would have chafed at having to put aside a pleasurable activity for the drudgery of work. But that boy no longer existed. He'd been replaced by a man who'd grown to appreciate honest labor. It gave him purpose and even a bit of pride when a customer nodded approval to a job well done—not the fierce bolt of gratification that used to shoot into him when he knocked an opponent to his knees, but a quieter satisfaction that meandered through him like a clear stream, nourishing and sustaining him from within.

Surprisingly, Levi found he preferred the steady stream to the scorching bolt. Except when that bolt originated from a more feminine source.

Levi's gaze sought out Miss Spencer. *Eden*. All she had to do was smile to release those little frissons of lightning in him.

As that thought crossed his mind, she glanced up, and Levi realized he was wrong. She didn't have to smile. All she had to do was look at him.

Heaven help him. He was in a bad way.

And over a woman he couldn't be more wrong for. Eden deserved a man who could provide for her in the same manner her father did, a man who wouldn't tarnish her with his past, one who could carry on long, genteel conversations with her as they sat by the fire on a cold winter night. Levi was none of those things. So he hid his growing feelings and tried to talk himself out of them. But it did no good.

Yep. He was in a bad way.

Levi drew a corner of his mouth upward, thinking the smile more than actually shaping it. However, Eden must have noticed, for she answered with a tiny curve of her lips that suggested a similar mindset. Levi's chest tightened. Twenty feet or more separated them, yet in that moment, it seemed he could feel her breathe. Then Eden dropped her gaze back to the desk. As if nothing out of the ordinary had just occurred, she dipped her pen into the inkwell beside her arm and returned to the letter she'd been writing.

Digging his fingers into the binding of his book, Levi made his way to the shelves. He stared at the slot where the title belonged, yet his hand refused to move. Maybe he should stop visiting the library so often. He'd waited his allotted two weeks. He could take the book with him and read it by lamplight in his room. By himself. With no distractions.

But he craved those distractions.

"Mr. Grant?"

Levi spun to face his hostess, a disconcerted knot in his belly. Had she guessed his thoughts? Praying his features portrayed nothing deeper than friendly interest, he raised a brow, inviting her to continue.

"It occurred to me today while you were reading that I have been remiss in my duty." Eden straightened from her seat in a graceful motion, her deep blue skirts cascading into place to brush against the floor. As she came around the corner of the desk, her fingers trailed along the edge of the wood, the white lace at her wrist drawing his gaze to the delicate appendages. "You have proved yourself a stable member of this community; however, I have yet to loan you a book outside these walls."

The formality of her tone and the way she didn't quite look him in the eye wrenched his stomach further. Maybe she *had* guessed his thoughts and was politely trying to discourage his interest. It was probably for the best. Hurt like a punch to the gut, though.

Glad he still had the book in his hand, Levi summoned a smile and closed the distance between them. He couldn't blame her for having discriminating taste. What he could do was make things easy on her. No point prolonging the awkwardness for either of them.

He held out the book to her. "I'd . . . enjoy . . . reading in the evening. And I won't have to bother you every day, either."

"You've not been a bother, Levi." She dipped her chin, her voice soft, and Levi found himself wanting to believe that more than simple courtesy lay behind her words. Eden stroked the cover of the book and then raised her face to look at him. A shyness lingered in her eyes, but there was warmth, too—a warmth that quickly penetrated his chest and enlivened his hope.

"Your chair will remain in its place so that you may visit as often as you like. Some patrons prefer the atmosphere here." She turned from him to survey the room. "I myself find the shelves of books soothing. I often come here after hours with a quilt and a cup of tea to relax with a story or a bit of poetry before retiring for the night."

The picture forming in his mind was so vivid Levi couldn't dispel it. Eden, her hair down, a quilt wrapped around her shoulders, stockinged feet peeking out from beneath her hem. Would she recline on the settee or curl up in a chair? Levi shot a glance at the stuffed leather chair across the room. Did she use *his* chair?

Another image flashed through his mind. He in the leather chair, a book in hand. Eden coming to join him. He'd stretch his arms wide, and she'd sit on his lap, leaning her head on his shoulder as she opened a volume of Browning or Keats. His arms would close around her as he turned his attention back to his own book, so accustomed to her presence that words wouldn't even be necessary. . . .

"Forgive me. I'm rambling." Eden blushed and moved past him to reclaim her seat behind the desk.

Levi blinked and quickly refocused, afraid his inattention had embarrassed her. But what could he say? That he hadn't been listening because he was too busy imagining what it would be like to hold her? The ache of it still filled his chest.

"Anyway," she was saying, "you can keep the book for up to two weeks." Eden jotted a note in her ledger, listing the date, the name of the book, and his name. "After that, I'll send the hounds after you." She favored him with a grin as she handed the book into his keeping.

Levi chuckled, thankful for her easy forgiveness of his rudeness. "I'll guard it with my life, dear lady."

"See that you do."

On his way back to the shop, Levi met up with Ornery. The dog trailed his heels from the library to the smithy. Apparently Eden had won over his hound so convincingly that the fellow was doing her bidding even before she asked.

"I'll take care of the book, boy. Don't worry." Levi grinned and bent to rub the dog's head. When they entered the shop, Levi made his way to the back and was about to slide Mr. Verne's story onto his tall shelf next to his money box when he noticed something jutting out from among the pages. Something that hadn't been there when he'd been reading it earlier. He was sure of it.

Levi lowered the volume and fanned the pages. A folded piece of stationery stood up from the center of the book, the edges slightly apart. He tipped the book toward him for a better look and found his name staring up at him from the top of the page.

Chapter Thirteen

Levi reached for the paper, his pulse suddenly throbbing in his veins. Just as his fingers brushed the nearest corner, however, Ornery set in to growling. The dog jerked his head toward the shop entrance and barked a warning. Sure enough, a wagon rumbled past the wide double doors and pulled to a stop.

The note would have to wait.

Levi spared a second to caress the side of the paper with one knuckle, then snapped the book shut. Taking care not to scratch the cover, he set it up on the shelf, wishing he could shelve his thoughts of Eden as easily. Moving quickly, he stripped out of his good shirt and hung it on the peg by his washstand. He slid his work shirt over his head and did up the buttons. The cotton, still slightly damp from his morning labors, chilled his skin as he stuffed the tails into his waistband and stretched his suspenders over his shoulders.

A solid-looking fellow hopped down from the driver's bench and ambled in Levi's direction. Ornery's growl thickened in his throat.

"Enough, boy." Levi rubbed the animal behind the ears with one hand while retrieving his leather apron with the other. He strode forward to meet his customer, tying the apron around his waist as he went.

"Afternoon." Levi nodded to the man and held out his hand.

The fellow pulled off his tweed flatcap, revealing a shock of orange-red hair and youthful features. His palm met Levi's. The kid wasn't more than nineteen or twenty in Levi's estimation, but his tanned face and strong grip testified to his workman status.

"Good day to ye." He spoke with a touch of brogue, his sentence lilting up at the end. "I be Duncan McPherson."

"Levi Grant. What can I do for you, Duncan?"

The lad grinned as if the expression was a habitual part of his countenance. "I bring work if ye've the time for it." He slapped his cap back on his head and tucked his thumbs into the shallow pockets of his black flannel vest. "I'm a driller out at Fieldman's Quarry, and our smith has all he can handle keepin' our chisels and bits sharpened. The boss wants two dozen new jumpers made to his specifications by next week, and Wally ain't got time to fill the order. Some of the gents heard of ye openin' shop and thought ye might be up for the job. I got a couple o' jumpers in the wagon in case ye're nae familiar with the tool."

"I'm familiar." Too familiar. Acid climbed up from Levi's stomach to burn the back of his throat. He swallowed it down and cleared the passage with a rumbled cough. "I'd like to . . . ah . . . take a gander at them, though. Judge the length, diameter, preferred weight."

"Aye. So ye do ken the tools. The boss man'll be pleased." Duncan's grin widened even farther. "I'll go fetch the jumpers." He spun around and loped off. Levi stared after him, but his mind refused to follow.

A quarry? He'd no idea there was a quarry so close to Spencer. Not that the knowledge would have changed his decision. He had no place else to go. But a quarry? The ridges on his back that told the tale of his time in the labor camp at Granite Mountain seemed to suddenly grow nerve endings. His shirt rubbed against them, and vivid memories of the whippings the sergeants doled out crashed through his brain.

Due to his strength and skill with a hammer, Levi consistently met his rock-breaking quota, and since he kept his head down and his mouth shut, he usually escaped the guards' notice. Until they decided to enlist his aid.

When the guards chose to mete out

punishment, they ordered prisoners to hold their fellow convicts down as a way to further demoralize the group. Levi became a favored choice for this duty. At first he refused, thinking to take the licks himself rather than aid the sergeants. He had enough blood on his hands from his fighting days, and his conscience was not eager for more. As expected, the guards awarded him with twenty lashes for his disobedience. The whipping tore up his back, but what the sergeants did next tore up his soul. The man he'd originally been asked to restrain received a second beating on top of his already bloodied flesh in order to teach Levi a lesson. He never refused again.

Duncan strolled through the doors, two long metal rods balanced atop his shoulder. The boring tools clanged against each other softly as he moved. Levi shook off his memories and stepped forward to meet the younger man. Duncan stood the rods on end between them. The shorter of the two reached Levi's chin, while the other towered well past the top of his head.

"You drill granite?" Levi asked as he picked up the smaller rod. It was flat on the driving end to accommodate hammer strikes and appeared to be made of iron except for the chisel-shaped tip, which would have to be steel to stand up to the force of boring into stone.

"Granite? Nae. Fieldman quarries limestone." He handed Levi the second jumper to inspect. "Me da cut granite back in Scotland afore the fever took him, but 'round here, limestone's more common." He shrugged. "Don't matter much to me. I'll drill anything they want so long as they pay me wages. I'd like to dress stones one day like me da instead o' drilling 'em, but I got to do me time in the pit first."

Levi ran his hand along the taller jumper, trying not to think of his own father. Had Levi been more like young Duncan and been willing to do his time, the last few years would have turned out much differently. He couldn't change the past, though. All he could do was move forward. Yet he was reluctant to move forward in a direction that led to a quarry.

"Let me check my bar iron." Levi carried the jumpers to the back of his shop. The shorter tool was thicker, about an inch and a half in diameter, whereas the longer one was only about seven-eighths of an inch wide. The first also had an iron ball welded to the middle to give it greater weight for when the drillers pounded it into the hole.

Levi took stock of his supply and determined he would have ample iron to complete the project. The income he'd receive from the job would go a long way toward covering his expenses. He might even be able to set a little aside to start saving up for his own place. Filling an order this large in a timely manner would boost his reputation among the townsmen, as well.

So why were his intestines cramping at the idea of taking it on?

It wasn't as if he were supporting abusive overseers. Duncan looked hale and hearty, with a ready grin that spoke more eloquently than any sworn vow of the favorable working conditions at the local quarry. The labor was no doubt grueling but honest—motivation provided by a fair wage instead of a whip.

Surely a small-scale operation like Fieldman's Quarry, one he hadn't even heard of until today, did not use convict labor. While within the prison walls, inmates learned quickly of the different places where they could be leased out. Cotton plantations, railroads, sawmills—all owned by companies looking to save on labor costs without care for the working conditions of the men in their employ. The only reason convicts were sent to Marble Falls to work the quarry at Granite Mountain was because of the push to get stone cut and shipped to Austin for the rebuilding of the capitol. Therefore, it was highly unlikely that anything similar to what he'd experienced was taking place at Fieldman's.

Maybe if he could keep from visiting the quarry in person, he could supply the tools without reliving his nightmare.

Setting his jaw, Levi circumvented

the garden cultivator and pile of chain waiting for him near the forge and rejoined the quarryman. "A dollar fifty for each weighted jumper. One eighty-five for the longer one."

"Done." Duncan pushed away from the support beam he'd been leaning against. "Can ye have 'em ready by the end o' next week?"

Levi mentally tabulated the other jobs he'd already committed to, then estimated the hours needed to complete one of the custom drills. "I think I can manage that. I don't have a wagon, though. You'll have to come pick them up."

"Can do." Duncan's grin flared to life again as he reached out to shake Levi's hand. "Ye're makin' me a hero, Mr. Grant. It's pleased the boss will be, and that's a fact."

Levi couldn't help but smile at the kid's enthusiasm. "Call me Levi."

Duncan nodded. "Levi, then. 'Tis a fine name to be carrying."

Levi shook his head and chuckled softly. "Keep your flattery for the women, Duncan."

"Why do ye think I'm practicin'?" Duncan winked at him. "I got me a bonny lass to impress. She's a shy one, but I'm determined to coax her out of hiding." He wiggled his eyebrows and lifted his knees in a high-stepping jig as he danced his way through the doors, leaving Levi with a hearty dose of laughter rumbling in his chest.

That kid could charm the horns off a bull. Levi doubted the bonny lass would resist for long.

Images of another bonny lass floated through his mind. A lass with mossy green eyes and hair that caught fire when the sun glinted upon her auburn tresses. One with a willowy figure exuding grace and refinement and a smile that set his heart to racing every time she aimed it his way. One who was so far above him, he'd be a fool to pursue her.

Levi's grip on the jumper rods tightened. His gaze slid past the forge to the shelf along the back wall and the book lying upon its ledge. The note inside called to him, and his foolish heart longed to answer.

But he had work to do—work the Lord had provided. He'd not forsake his responsibilities. The note would keep.

Levi propped the jumpers against the north wall and hefted the thick pile of chain onto the slab at the end of the forge. As his fingers sought out the faulty links, he strove to put Eden from his mind. Not an easy task.

At the end of the day, he finally gave himself permission to collect the book, but as an added exercise in self-discipline, he refrained from opening it until he was alone in his shed at the Barnes' homestead. Somehow he managed to talk horses with Claude, compliment Georgia's skillet ham and dried-apple pie, and even launder his work shirt with a borrowed tub and washboard without thinking of the note more than a couple dozen times.

So when he finally sat on his cot, book open in his lap, lantern glowing from its hook in the shed's ceiling, he wasn't prepared for the hesitation that suddenly immobilized him.

Anticipation had grown within him as

the day progressed until he felt ready to burst. Yet now that the time had come to read Eden's note, he froze, fearing disappointment. Most likely it merely contained a few friendly words of apology over not urging him to borrow a book sooner. He had no reason to expect more, regardless of the titillating possibilities his imagination had been spoon-feeding his heart all evening.

Castigating himself for making more of things than was warranted, Levi snatched the folded slip of paper and pried it open.

Levi,

Over the course of our brief acquaintance, I've deduced that you are a man who prefers to keep his own counsel. While I, on the other hand, enjoy a spirited sharing of ideas, even when those ideas represent opposing perspectives.

He jerked his face toward the ceiling as he blew out a hard breath. It always came down to that, didn't it? His speech or lack thereof. He didn't have Duncan McPherson's glib tongue and never would. As he'd feared, Eden suspected his growing feelings and was kindly pointing out the reasons why they wouldn't suit.

Of course, he knew why they didn't suit better than she. Although that knowledge had done precious little to temper his affection.

Was she spoken for? Sherriff Pratt had certainly acted possessive with her on the day he'd found her at the smithy, calling her *darlin'* and shooting Levi warning looks that carried enough heat to scorch a man's hide. But the thought of Eden with that man made Levi ill. Something about Pratt rubbed him the wrong way. Maybe it was his heavy-handed manner or his threat to shoot Ornery. Then again, maybe it was just because the man had more right to court Eden than Levi ever would.

Levi closed his eyes and steeled himself as he faced her letter once again. Might as well take his punches like a man. Opening his eyes, he read the rest of the note.

Please feel no pressure to respond, but should you be interested, I would very much like to hear your impressions of the book you are reading. Do you consider Professor Von Hardwigg to be a passionate explorer whose absolute faith and zealous determination lead him to scientific triumph? Or is he a man with an obsession who carelessly endangers his nephew's life by rushing into an ill-advised expedition without adequate concern for the consequences?

I know you have not yet finished reading this novel, so if you prefer to respond after completing it, I will be happy to wait upon your convenience.

Eden

By the time he reached her signature, Levi's heart rate had tripled its pace. Far from pushing him away, Eden was actually giving him the chance to deepen their acquaintanceship.

Levi stood so fast, he knocked his head against the lantern. He winced and raised a hand to steady the lamp as he slid out from under it. Two steps took him to the door, but when he pulled it wide, wintry air assaulted his bare chest, reminding him of his inappropriate attire. Grabbing his freshly laundered shirt from where it hung across the back of the room's single chair, he pulled it over his head, not caring that the wet cotton suctioned to his skin like an icy leech.

He hunched his shoulders against the wind and trudged past the barn to the Barnes's back door. After pounding twice, he folded his arms across his chest and fidgeted from foot to foot. Finally, Claude appeared.

"Need something, Levi?"

"Yep." He looked at his disheveled host, feeling only a twinge of guilt for disturbing his evening. "Got any writing paper?"

Chapter Fourteen

Eden sat at her library desk, staring down at the packets of dried flowers scattered across the tabletop without really seeing them. Her sketchbook lay open before her, blank. A pencil poised between her thumb and forefinger angled toward the page; however, no inspiration stirred it to motion.

"I brung you some tea." Her housekeeper placed a steaming cup on the edge of the desk, rattling it against the saucer with more volume than was strictly necessary.

Eden sighed and dropped her pencil, along with her pretense of working. "Thank you, Verna." She offered the woman a small smile and reached for the china cup. The bitter aroma succeeded in sharpening her dulled senses a bit as she lifted the tea to her mouth. "Maybe your special brew will enhance my concentration. My mind seems trapped in a fog this afternoon."

She sipped the warm beverage and savored the sweetness of the honey that gentled the pungent blend of black teas. Verna always managed to find the right balance between the sweet and the strong.

"You're pining over that man, aren't ya?"

Eden sputtered. The tea sloshed and dribbled onto the white paper of her sketchbook. She hastily returned the cup to its saucer and tore out the stained page, hoping to prevent the liquid from bleeding through.

"Really, Verna." Eden crumpled the ruined paper in her palm. "You come up with the oddest notions."

Her housekeeper gave her one of those looks—the kind that made her squirm like a little girl caught in a fib. "So I guess it's just coincidence that your concentration troubles started up about the same time that big feller stopped comin' by? What's it been—a day or two?"

Three, actually, but admitting she'd been counting would only validate Verna's argument. So she chose a bland reply, hoping to throw the too-perceptive housekeeper off the scent. "I had grown accustomed to Mr. Grant's visits during the lunch hour, that's true. Perhaps the change in routine has affected me more than I realized." Eden tried to make it sound as if the possibility had not occurred to her until that moment.

Verna's gaze narrowed. Eden glanced away. Subterfuge was apparently not one of her strengths.

Eden didn't know what to expect from her brash housekeeper next, but it certainly wasn't for the woman to lay a tender hand on her arm.

"Ain't nothing wrong with having feelings for the fella, Eden. He seems a decent sort. In fact, I should prob'ly be encouraging it after all the nights I sat awake prayin' for you—askin' the good Lord to bring you a man that'd treat you right."

Eden inhaled a sharp breath. Praying for God to bring her a man? After Stephen left, she'd vowed never again to word such a request. It took her aback to learn that someone else had been wording it for her.

No, she'd spent the last five years begging the Lord to help her find contentment in her spinster status. And he'd been faithful. She had her library, her Ladies Aid work, the children's reading hour. She could come and go as she pleased, spend her money as she deemed fit, all without the hassle of first gaining a man's permission. And if the loneliness sometimes ate away at her like water poured on a sugarloaf . . . ? Well, God had seen her through the last five years. She figured he could be depended upon to see her through the next fifty.

Eden cleared her tightening throat. "Verna, you shouldn't ask for such things. I—"

"You deserve a good man," the

housekeeper declared, her voice surprisingly stern. "Not like that fella who couldn't see past his pocketbook. A man like my Harvey." Her voice softened as her attention drifted out the window to rest on the man who was hoeing the weeds from the flower beds. "One who will offer you his coat when you're cold or cut you a bloom from his favorite rosebush just because he was thinkin' about ya while he worked. One who'll take your sass in good humor and sass you back when ya need it."

She'd never heard Verna talk so. Harvey and Verna Sims had been a fixture in her life for so long it was hard to imagine them as people with lives of their own—people in love. Yet as she listened to her housekeeper describe their relationship, a profound longing for a similar connection stabbed Eden's heart.

Stephen had bought her gifts, escorted her to parties, and showered her with compliments and pretty declarations. But looking back, she realized none of those actions measured up to the standard Verna had just set. They'd been mere flattery, lacking depth and substance. Why hadn't she recognized them as such? She'd always considered herself intelligent, educated. How could she have been so deceived?

Her thoughts flew to Levi. Was it happening again? He was as different from Stephen as a mountain was from the prairie, but that was no guarantee that her budding feelings could be trusted.

Give me a discerning spirit, Lord. Please don't let me fall prey to romantic delusions again. Help me see the truth.

"Drink your tea, gal, and forget I said anything. I oughtn't have stuck my nose where it didn't belong." Verna wiped the trail of spilled liquid from the side of the cup with a corner of her apron and gave Eden's shoulder an awkward pat. "I reckon you're wise enough to take a gander at what lies beneath the surface before makin' a judgment on a fella's character. You never were one to make the same mistake twice."

Eden snatched her cup and drew it to her lips to avoid having to manufacture a suitable reply. Her already-bruised heart winced at the reminder of her past folly, but as Verna bustled off to see about a batch of cookies for the children who would start arriving in an hour, the encouragement hidden in her statement seeped into Eden's consciousness.

Verna was right. She wasn't the same gullible girl she'd been when Stephen came calling. She was older. Wiser. Better able to guard her heart against insincerity and deception.

Yet, if her heart was so wise and protected, why did the fact that Levi hadn't visited the library since she'd written him that note leave her feeling vulnerable and achy inside?

Levi's fingers fumbled over the buttons on his good shirt as he tried to make himself presentable. He gritted his teeth and rubbed his damp palms down his trouser legs for the fifth time in as many minutes. Then he tilted his chin out of the way and tried again. It was like threading a needle without looking. Useless fingers. A growl echoed in his throat that set Ornery to whining. He glared the dog into silence and finally managed to shove the last minuscule button through its hole.

"Ha!"

Ornery met his shout with a bark that sounded more exasperated than congratulatory.

"Yeah? Well, you oughta try it." Then again, the dog's paws would probably prove more dexterous than Levi's clumsy mitts.

He should have gone at lunch. There would've been fewer people around. Less chance of making a fool of himself. But he'd had a set of those quarry drills in the fire and couldn't leave them unfinished. He quit work early to compensate, but if he didn't put boot leather to road—and soon—he'd end up at the library after all the kids tromped in for their weekly story time. He'd never get the chance to talk to her then.

Levi's gaze shifted to the shelf, where the corner of his borrowed book peered at him from over the ledge. The pages gapped a bit in the middle, but the slit wasn't wide enough to reveal the sheets of paper stuffed inside. Had he written too much? Not enough? Did she even remember she'd asked the question?

He rubbed a hand over his face and blew out a quivering breath. Then, before he could lose his nerve, he snatched his coat from its peg, grabbed the book, and marched out of the shop.

As he strode up the library's walk, he caught sight of a man stooped over a bush. "Hey, Harvey. They budding yet?" He and Mr. Sims had struck up an acquaintanceship over the last couple of weeks, bonding over the simple fact that they both wore trousers—an uncommon occurrence in an establishment dominated by women. Not counting the boys who attended the reading hour, most of the library patrons were of the feminine persuasion. And according to Harvey, when the Aid ladies descended on Thursday nights, there were so many hens in the coop, even the bravest rooster knew to make himself scarce until they left.

Harvey straightened and waved, a small pair of pruning shears in his hand. "Good to see you, Levi. Got me some new leaves comin' in. Spring must be on its way."

"Yep. I imagine Eden'll be out here . . . helping you before long." With all the gardening books on her shelves and floral fripperies in her house, the woman must take great pride in cultivating her roses.

"Eden?" The man's face scrunched up in disbelief. "Heavens, no. I'd not let that girl touch one of my plants if she begged for a week. No way, no how."

"Aren't they . . . Don't they belong to her?"

"Sure enough. She picks 'em out of the catalog and tells me where to plant 'em and how to tend the soil. Why, she had me make compost with fish heads and fruit peelings after reading about it in a magazine. Fish heads. I never heard o' that. But I did what she said, and last year we had the biggest blooms yet. Yessir, she knows a lot about 'em from all her reading. But don't let her near an actual plant." He scratched a spot on his forehead, leaving a smear of dirt above his graying brows.

"Why not?" If she knew what she was doing, what was the harm? And why did she let her employee bully her out of her own garden?

"The gal is pure poison to plants. Don't know how she does it, but every plant she tends turns up dead or near to it. Poor thing. It grieves her something awful."

Harvey shook his head and tipped it back to meet Levi's eye. "She and I made a pact a few years back. I tend the flowers at the house, and she can play with the ones that grow wild outside of town. Even got her daddy to buy her a piece of land on the other side of Lone Oak Hill, where the bluebonnets and Indian paintbrush grow thick as a carpet every spring. She'll take a book and go sit out there for hours at a time. Even after the bluebonnets fade, she'll keep makin' trips off and on through the summer and fall to collect flowers for her press. She dries 'em and makes pictures. Real purty ones. She's got a tender touch when the things are already dead, but a live plant? It'd wither at the sight of her comin'."

Levi gazed at the curtains that fluttered in the window that opened to the library. It must be hard on Eden to love something so much and have to keep her distance. At least she could still enjoy the beauty of the flowers and the glory of their fragrance.

His thoughts turned to the book he carried and the private correspondence hidden in its folds. Was he kidding himself? Would his sullied past poison a woman like Eden? Perhaps, like the roses, he was only meant to admire her from afar.

"Don't let me keep you out here, son. Go on in." Harvey smiled and made shooing motions at him. Levi stared at him as he bent back to his work.

But . . . what if he wasn't toxic? What if God could take the garbage of his past and turn it into something that could help Eden flourish, like the kitchen scraps that nourished the roses? Levi's fingers tightened on the spine of his book. He couldn't just walk away if there was a chance of making a life with her. The possibility was too sweet to forfeit without at least trying to cultivate it. He only prayed that God would make things clear to him before he did anything to hurt her.

It's in your hands, Lord.

Taking a deep breath, Levi climbed the steps and opened the door.

Chapter Fifteen

Women's voices floated to him through the hall as he hung up his hat.

"I was so glad to hear you agreed to put together another pressed-flower piece for the spring auction. The one you donated last year brought in top dollar. At yesterday's meeting, those of us on the fund-raising committee agreed that we needed to convince you to contribute another. I hope we didn't pressure you too much."

"Not at all." Eden's gentle laugh drew Levi into the main room. She was sitting at her desk, tiny yellow and blue flowers forming a rainbow arch across her work space with various shades of green leaves in between. "I love making art out of the flowers I collect. And truth be told, my personal parlor is quite cluttered with my previous efforts. I'd be happy to have one of my designs grace someone else's wall."

"And the money it provides will help buy a new blackboard for the schoolhouse. The one they have now is so cracked, Miss Albright's tidy penmanship is barely legible." Emma Cranford stepped to the side of Eden's desk and peered down at a sketchpad on the tabletop. "Have you come up with a design yet?"

"No." Eden sighed. "Usually inspiration strikes when I experiment with the dried flowers, placing them one way and then another until a pattern forms in my mind. But even after taking samples from each of the packets and pairing them in countless combinations, ideas are still eluding me today."

Levi tried to steal a glance at the paper from over Mrs. Cranford's head, but he was too far away to see anything. Not wanting to elicit the ladies' attention, he made no move to close the gap. Instead, he hovered in the background, hoping the preacher's wife would conclude her business in time for him to speak to Eden before the children descended.

"The wreath you made last year was lovely."

"Thank you, but don't you think a fresh design would bring a better price? Something different from last year." Eden tapped her fingers on the table's edge, her nails clicking lightly against the wood. "I've made wreaths, hearts, garden scenes. I even tried a butterfly once." As she rattled off her list, she turned her head, her exasperation evident. Until she noticed him. Her features softened, and Levi's pulse accelerated. She didn't smile exactly, but there was something about her eyes that told him she wanted to.

Then Mrs. Cranford spoke again and reclaimed Eden's attention. "You'll find your inspiration somewhere, dear. Don't fret. The auction is a month away. You have plenty of time." The woman eased away from the desk and began buttoning up her cloak.

"You're right." Eden stood and escorted her to the hall entrance, her gaze finding his for a moment before skittering away. "It was kind of you to come by, Emma. Please give my regards to your husband."

"I will. By the way, did I tell you that David expects our shipment of prison Bibles to arrive soon? Maybe by next—Oh! Mr. Grant. I didn't realize you were standing there." The woman blushed, and Eden gave her a questioning look.

"Ma'am." Levi dipped his chin and averted his gaze. Eden wouldn't know of his connection to the prison Bibles, but Mrs. Cranford did. Discovering his presence at the same time she'd spoken of them had obviously flustered her, and he worried that Eden would somehow piece things together.

"Well, I must be off. Have to see to David's supper, you know." Mrs. Cranford bustled down the hall.

Eden said nothing, just watched her go.

When she turned to face him, Levi

tried to think of something to say to break the silence that was growing more awkward with every second that passed. But his brain was mush.

Eden's focus bounced between his face and a spot somewhere on the wall behind him. Then she moved back to her desk and braced her arms upon it, as if the solidity helped restore her equilibrium.

Maybe he should try something similar. He felt as unbalanced as a horse with mismatched shoes.

"Welcome back, Mr. Grant." The smile that had been in her eyes earlier finally found its way to her lips.

Warmth radiated through him and loosened some of the tightness in his chest. He smiled in return and stepped up to the desk. Glancing down at the flowers scattered there, he blurted out the first coherent thought he could grasp. "Make a bouquet."

"A bouquet?" Confusion laced her tone. She looked down as he peered up, their gazes crossing and holding for a brief moment before hers dropped the rest of the way. "With dried flowers?" Her hand fluttered over the blooms like a butterfly afraid to land. "They're much too delicate to—"

Levi captured her hand in his. "No. In a picture." He drew her hand down to the open sketchpad. "For the auction."

Her slender fingers trembled against his palm as he gently pressed her hand against the paper. He trailed his fingertips over her knuckles, all the way to the ends of her rounded nails as he slowly withdrew. Her breath caught, and when she tipped her chin up, her mossy eyes had darkened to a deep sage.

All he had to do was lean forward, cup her cheek, and press his lips to hers. She would taste like heaven. He was sure of it. Longing burgeoned inside him, until it nearly overran his good sense. He wanted that kiss more than he wanted his next breath.

But he didn't have the right. Not yet.

Levi straightened.

Eden blinked a few times, then stared down at the blank sketchpad. "A bouquet . . ." She murmured the words, testing them out. Then all at once, she dropped into her chair, snatched up a pencil, and took the paper in hand. Hesitant at first, she drew a few exploratory lines but then picked up speed until the pencil fairly flew over the paper. "A framed bouquet. Yes. A *bridal* bouquet. Fit for a trousseau, an anniversary gift, a wedding."

She spared a couple of seconds to look up at him, and her beaming smile made Levi feel as if he'd just knocked out John L. Sullivan for the heavyweight championship. "It's a perfect idea, Levi. Perfect."

Eden turned back to her sketch, mumbling something about an oval frame and touches of lace and ribbon. He didn't follow most of it, but then, he was concentrating more on the way her eyes sparkled with creativity and how the tip of her tongue peeked between her lips while she concentrated on her drawing.

"There." She tilted her head and examined her handiwork, then stood and turned the sketchpad around for his inspection. "What do you think?"

I think you're beautiful. His eyes shifted from her face to the paper. "I think . . . you've got talent."

The sketch was rough since it'd been drawn hurriedly, but even so, the flowers exhibited dimension and life as they bunched together above slender stems arching gently from the confines of a bowed ribbon.

"It will look better with colorful blossoms and lacy accents." She seemed ready to say more but clutched the drawing back to her chest and gave him an apologetic look. "Listen to me rambling on about flowers and ribbon when I'm sure you don't care a whit about such things."

She might be surprised what could interest a man when spoken of by the right woman.

"Sorry." She tossed the sketchpad into her chair.

"Don't be," he said. "I like . . . viewing your joy."

Eden cocked her head and gave him one of those quizzical glances that made him feel like she was searching out his secrets. Not ready for her to discover them yet, he opted for a diversion.

"I'm done reading the book." He held out Verne's *Journey to the Centre of the Earth* to her.

She took it from his hand and stroked the cover, not quite meeting his gaze. "Did you enjoy the story?"

"Yep. I—" Before he could tell her about the sheets of paper tucked into the pages, a herd of footsteps pounded up the front stairs.

"Howdy, Miss Spencer," a young voice called out from the hall. "We're here."

Eden pivoted toward the sound, then turned back to him. "The children. I'll have to log this in later." She pulled open a desk drawer and laid the book inside. After she closed the drawer, she reached a hand out to him as if to touch his arm but stopped herself short of making contact. Levi repressed his disappointment.

"Please stay as long as you wish, Mr. Grant," she said, stepping aside to put more distance between them as the school kids filed into the reading room. "If you find a book you would like to borrow before I finish with the children's story, just leave it on my desk and I will deliver it to you tomorrow."

Then she left.

All the fretting he'd done over what to say to her about the book, and their time together expired before he could even broach the subject properly. The kids swarmed her, and Levi tried not to resent their appearance. Not too tough a task when Eden's delight was as plain to see as the sun on a cloudless day.

He wandered over to the bookshelf containing the fiction titles and glanced at the spines. Hunkering down, he pressed his finger into the crevice where Verne's *Journey* belonged. Would Eden look for his written response or just shove the book back onto the shelf? He shuddered to think of someone else running across his letter. He'd have to stop by tomorrow when she first opened to check the book. If the papers were still inside, he'd simply slip them into his coat pocket and dispose of them later without anyone being the wiser.

Then again, hadn't she said that she would deliver his selection to him tomorrow should he find a book he liked? If she came by his shop in the morning, that would afford him the opportunity to ask her about the note as well as spend time in her company. A pleasant prospect. Levi grinned. *I'd better find a book.*

Touching a finger to the top edge of each spine, he perused the books. He supposed he could just snatch the first one he came to, yet that felt too much like a pretense. He wanted an excuse to visit with Eden, but not at the price of deception. Guilt already hounded him for not being entirely forthright about his past. He hadn't lied—just hadn't expounded on things. Nevertheless, if their friendship evolved into something deeper, it'd be only natural for Eden to start asking questions about his family, his work, his experiences. He'd have to confess. Everything.

If there was any hope of keeping her, it would be found in proving he could be trusted in other matters—demonstrating a pattern of integrity that spoke to the man he had become, not the man he'd once been.

On a shelf above the Verne tales, Levi lingered over a title that struck him as familiar. *Ivanhoe*. He'd never read it, but if he remembered correctly it was one his old schoolmaster had tried to interest him in before he left home. A story of knights and hidden identities. Appropriate reading for a man who struggled to hold on to his nobility as well as his secrets. Levi slid the book from between its neighbors and pushed against his knees to stand.

The steady sound of Eden's voice called to him as she read to the children. And when his eyes found her, everything inside him went still. She was sitting in his chair. *His* chair. Just as he'd imagined. Well, not exactly as he'd imagined. Eden perched on the edge like a dainty bird on a branch, but that didn't mean she wouldn't tuck her legs beneath her and curl into the cushions when no one was around to see. Her auburn hair down, lying in waves about her shoulders; a knitted throw over her lap to hold back the evening's chill; her restrictive clothing traded in for something softer . . .

Eden looked up from her story, and Levi blinked away the vision. Her sentence rambled to a halt, and he feared his thoughts were evident on his face. She stared at him for half a second, then cleared her throat and resumed her recitation of Black Beauty's adventures.

Time to go.

Suddenly feeling large and conspicuous, Levi strode to Eden's desk and quietly placed *Ivanhoe* on top of her sketchpad, taking care not to disturb the flowers scattered across the table's surface. Then, with a parting glance, one he told himself not to make but was helpless to resist, he stored up a final picture of Eden in the stuffed leather chair and took his leave.

Chapter Sixteen

For the first time since she began hosting the reading hour over a year ago, Eden had to fight the urge to cut the session short. She'd been keenly aware of Levi's presence as she settled the children and found her place in the story, but when she glanced up and found him looking at her with such . . . well . . . pining, she nearly dropped the book from her lap.

Never could she recall a man looking at her in such a manner. Warmth spread through her as if she'd just climbed into a steaming tub, yet her mouth was bone dry. Rattled by her reaction, she'd done the only thing she could think to do—return to her reading. Unfortunately, vocalizing the words on the page did little to regulate her quivering pulse. Even after Levi left, her attention wavered from *Black Beauty* to the book she had stashed in her desk. Levi's book.

Had he responded to her questions? Eden found her eyes wandering to the desk whenever she looked up to smile at the children. With each minute that passed, the urgency to examine that book swelled until she began stumbling over her words. A few of the children looked at her oddly, but she managed to muddle through. The minute the last child scampered down the front steps, however, she locked her door and flew to her desk.

To prove to herself that she did still harbor at least a modicum of self-control, she first tidied her work area by returning all her dried flowers to their appropriate paper packets and storing them in the hatbox she had stashed beneath her desk. Then she folded the sketchpad closed and recorded Levi's latest selection in her lending log before finally granting herself permission to open *the drawer*.

There it sat—a mahogany-red cover, the title embossed in gold. She traced the lettering with a finger, suddenly nervous. Would she find what she'd hoped for within the pages?

Eden bit the edge of her tongue as she lifted the book from the drawer and placed it on her lap. Propping the spine in the dip between her knees, she fanned the pages until they fell open of their own accord, revealing folded sheets of writing paper. Her heart pounded and her hand shook as she reached for them. She'd grown so accustomed to disappointment, she'd almost forgotten how to react when it didn't occur.

She had just laid hold of Levi's letter when the door to the kitchen swung open. "Supper's on, Eden. Quit your dallying."

Slamming the book closed, Eden felt a ridiculous heat climb up her neck and into her cheeks. "Be right there. I . . . um . . . need to take something up to my room first." Grabbing her hatbox by the strap and hoping her housekeeper would pay more heed to it than the book she covertly tucked under her arm, Eden dashed toward the stairs. Levi's letter would have to wait a while longer.

Once dinner had been consumed and the dishes washed, Eden bid Verna and Harvey a good-night, ignoring the raised eyebrows her early departure garnered. She climbed the stairs with purposeful restraint, not wanting the echo of hastening footsteps to feed their curiosity. After her earlier conversation with Verna, Eden preferred keeping the subject of Levi Grant closed to further discussion. At least for now. She needed time and privacy to sort out her feelings on the matter before venturing into those waters with anyone else.

Eden quietly clicked her door shut and leaned her back against it as she drew in a deep breath. Her gaze fell unerringly upon the dark red book on her writing desk. Anticipation sizzled along her nerves, leaving her a bit lightheaded.

"Pull yourself together, girl," she murmured as she pushed away from the door. "It's just a note, for heaven's sake."

A note that could contain anything. It could be filled with insightful literary discourse or unintelligent ramblings. For all she knew, the pages might be nothing more than her own note returned with a single page from Levi stating his desire not to participate in her little experiment. He was busy establishing his business, after all. Just because he took time out of his day to read didn't mean he'd sacrifice more time to indulge her bookish whim.

Angry at herself for getting all worked up over a few scraps of paper, Eden marched to her burled walnut French writing desk, threw open the book cover, and yanked out the folded pages. Eden separated the sheets and counted. Four—and none of them looked familiar. Levi had written her *four* pages. Her legs began to quiver, suddenly too insubstantial to hold her upright. She grabbed the back of her chair for support and lowered herself upon the needlepoint seat.

She smoothed out the paper crease with her finger and pushed Verne's book out of the way to make room for more important reading.

His handwriting didn't have the elegant quality of a refined gentleman, but his strokes were strong and definitive, making his penmanship easy to decipher. If only the man himself were so easily read.

Eden,

I cannot tell you how happy I was to discover your note. I look forward to deepening our acquaintance through this correspondence.

A little thrill shot through Eden. Her instincts had been correct. The man was educated. His writing bore witness to the fact. The scripted words spreading across his page were penned with simple eloquence, nothing at all like his broken speech. She swiveled her knees to fit more directly under the top of the desk and leaned forward over the letter.

> **I know that I appear to be tight-lipped at times. However, this is more by necessity than choice. It shames me to admit this to you, but I want you to understand that my lack of words in no way indicates a lack of desire to communicate. There are certain types of words that I physically cannot say correctly. Therefore I avoid them, even when silence is the only way to do so.**

Her eyes reached the end of the first page. Eden lifted her head and stared thoughtfully at the framed pressed-flower garden that hung on the wall above her desk. It made perfect sense. Was it a stutter? Slurred speech? A lisp?

It was hard to imagine a man of such physical strength being unable to control something as small as his tongue.

Yet his strength of mind must be equal to that of his body. Constantly editing his speech to mask a deficiency? Eden couldn't imagine such a feat. Levi might feel shame, but she felt nothing but admiration for his adaptability and self-control. And a bit of self-condemnation for her earlier misjudgment of his intelligence.

Eden shifted the top page to the bottom of the stack and continued reading. Levi spent the next three pages answering her question about Verne's fictional professor and citing examples from the book. His arguments were well formed, but it was the personal insight he gave at the close of the letter that most spoke to her heart.

> **I understand that Professor Von Hardwigg's irrational obsession is necessary to propel the action of the story. After all, the tale would be dreadfully dull if the fellow took sufficient precautions to eliminate all danger. However, I cannot condone his choices, even if things did end**

well. Selfishly putting one's own desires above the welfare of a family member is unconscionable. It is an act of betrayal that destroys relationships. I know. I made a similar mistake once and have seen the heartache spawned by such a choice. Perhaps in time the Lord will mend the rift in my family that my actions created. I pray so. Until that day, I live to become the man I should have been.
Levi

Eden let the pages fall to the desk and fell back in her chair. What could he have possibly done to cause such regret? She could feel his sorrow, his contrition, and she ached for him. Yet the cynic within her rang warning bells that were impossible to ignore. He betrayed those he cared about once. Who was to say he wouldn't do so again?

On the other hand, the fact that he accepted the blame for his past choices and strove to rectify them spoke to his integrity. Stephen never demonstrated such honor. He took her father's money and disappeared without a word of apology or even explanation.

But if she let herself care for Levi and he broke her heart . . . Perhaps this peek into the blacksmith's past was the Lord's way of directing her onto a different path.

Or maybe it was a challenge to trust her future to her Lord's keeping despite her fear. How was she to know?

Releasing a sigh, Eden refolded the letter and crossed to her bureau. She opened the carved jewelry box that sat in the center by the mirror and pulled out a hair ribbon—a silver one to match Levi's eyes. She wrapped it loosely around the pages and tied the ends into a bow. Then she opened the top bureau drawer and secreted the letter beneath her unmentionables.

What would you have me do, Lord?

Eden removed the pins from her hair and dragged her brush through the strands.

My head tells me one thing. My heart another. Which voice is yours?

As she switched the brush to her

other hand a snippet of a verse drifted into her awareness. Something about love casting out fear.

She paused midstroke and set the brush down, not caring that her hair was only half groomed. She needed to find that verse. Eden retrieved her Bible from the bedside table and sat on the edge of the mattress, flipping pages. She scanned 1 Corinthians 13, but it wasn't there. She found several verses in Romans that dealt with love, yet not the one she sought. Growing frustrated, she fingered a thick section of pages and flopped them over. To 1 John. A sense of rightness resonated inside her. She began skimming the chapters, and finally, in chapter 4, she found what she'd been looking for.

"There is no fear in love"—she mouthed the words as she read them—*"but perfect love casteth out fear: because fear hath torment. He that feareth is not made perfect in love."*

All this time she'd thought it God's will that she be a spinster. She had grown content with that expectation, taking satisfaction in the wisdom she'd gained through her experience with Stephen. No man would dupe her again. But what if living alone was never part of God's plan for her? What if she chose that life because it was safe—because she was afraid?

Dear God, I don't want my fear to be a barrier to the blessings you are trying to bestow. Cast out my fear, and help me to trust in your perfect love. But also grant me a full measure of wisdom. Do not let me be led astray by my own desires. If it is not your will that I pursue a relationship with Levi, I pray that you will stop me. Make your message so clear that I cannot argue it away. Protect me, Lord, and show me the way that I should go.

Eden closed the Bible and clutched it to her breast, as if spiritual discernment could somehow spill through the wall of her chest directly into her heart. However, her uncertainty did not abate.

Levi made a mistake, one he obviously regretted and hoped to rectify. Hadn't she done the same thing? It was easy to blame Stephen for everything, but she'd played a role in it too.

There'd been hints of his weak character that she'd turned a blind eye to and questions she'd purposely left unasked.

This time things would be different. Eden replaced her Bible on the table and strode back to her desk. Opening her stationery box, she removed several sheets, then unscrewed the lid on her inkstand and dipped her pen into its depths. As she inscribed Levi's name across the top of the first page, she vowed to keep her eyes open and her ears pricked. Maybe—just maybe—this time she would discover a love she could trust.

Chapter Seventeen

After she delivered a note to Levi tucked between the pages of *Ivanhoe* on Saturday, she hadn't really expected to receive another note until he finished reading the book, but he surprised her.

Following the service on Sunday, he managed to slip one under the cover of her hymnal while she chatted with Georgia and Claude Barnes. He stood quietly behind the livery owner and his wife near the edge of Eden's pew, never saying a word. She tried not to look his way, afraid her growing interest would be apparent to anyone who happened to observe her. Nevertheless, she was aware of every movement he made. She noticed him glance over his shoulder and wave to Alex Carson, the saddler. She noticed him shifting his weight and stretching his neck from side to side as if his clothes had suddenly grown uncomfortable. She noticed the crumpled brim of his hat as he clutched it unnecessarily tight in front of him.

Until he dropped it.

It slid down the back of the dark polished wood of the church pew and landed directly over her hymnal, which was stacked atop her Bible on the bench seat.

She wouldn't have thought much of it except that when he bent to retrieve the hat, he fumbled several times before finally taking possession of it again. Then, when their eyes met, he pointedly looked at the book and then back to her. Something inside her stomach quivered at the wealth of meaning behind that glance, even though she had no earthly idea what that meaning entailed.

Eden immediately picked up the

books and clasped them to her chest. Levi's eyes crinkled at the corners while his mouth maintained its straight line, and Eden couldn't stop her foolish heart from imagining that he'd done so in order that she might be the only one privy to his smile.

It was hard to believe nearly a week had passed since then. And Eden and Levi had exchanged letters nearly every day.

Knowing he wouldn't be able to finish *Ivanhoe* before she would be ready to send along another letter, on Monday Eden had taken it upon herself to loan him a second book and deliver it in person. He'd caught on and had exchanged it the following day. They were on the third of a six-volume set of Washington Irving's essays. Yet this particular volume had sat on her desk unclaimed all day yesterday and again today.

Eden laid her hand atop the volume of essays that was to serve as their next receptacle and gazed out the window. She'd been doing that for hours.

Waiting for Levi to appear on her walk. But he hadn't come.

Had Levi lost interest already?

Eden gritted her teeth and pressed the pad of her finger into the corner of the book cover with increasing strength until the resulting discomfort brought her back to her senses.

Where did this spinelessness come from? This wasn't who she was—who she wanted to be. So Levi hadn't come by yesterday. Or today. There could be a hundred reasons to explain his absence that had nothing to do with her.

Levi was not Stephen, and she refused to let her ex-fiancé's abandonment turn her into a pusillanimous female who sat around wringing her hands while her own insecurities corroded her heart. If Levi couldn't come to her, then she'd go to him.

Eden surged to her feet, snatched up the book, and marched over to the hall tree. Staring herself down in the small square of mirror between the hat hooks, she jabbed a pin through her favorite straw bonnet and settled her fringed black shawl over her shoulders like a warrior's chain mail.

"I'm going out, Verna," she called, pausing by the entrance to the reading room to pull on her gauntlets . . . er . . . gloves.

The kitchen door pushed in, and Verna propped it open with a hip as she dried her hands on her apron. "You want me to wait supper on ya?" She raised her eyebrow in a manner that clearly suggested an affirmative answer would not be welcome.

Tempted to assert her authority just to prove to herself that she did indeed have a spine, Eden shoved her fingers into the holes of her right glove and bit back the rejoinder that jumped to her lips. When she finally composed herself and looked up, Verna stood in the same spot, eyebrow still raised.

The longevity of the expression struck Eden as funny.

She smiled, and as she did, the desperate drive to reestablish a sense of control over her world dissipated. Oh, she had no intention of wilting back into a boneless heap of insecurities again, but seeing Verna in all her crotchety glory reminded her that she wasn't alone. And that made all the difference.

"I don't plan to be gone long," Eden said. The thaw working its way through her spirit lent her voice a warmth she had not felt seconds ago. "But if I've not returned by the time you and Harvey are ready to eat, don't wait on me. I can fend for myself."

"Yeah, well . . ." Verna straightened and fidgeted with the ruffle on her apron bib. "I'll put a plate in the warmin' oven for ya."

"Thank you. I'll be back soon." Eden waved to her housekeeper and slipped out the front door.

No longer feeling militant, she sauntered down the street, enjoying the cool breeze against her cheek and the hum of activity along Main Street as patrons shuffled to and fro in an effort to complete their errands before shopkeepers closed for the day. As she neared the Drug Emporium, the door opened and Bertha Springer and her daughter emerged.

"Hi, Mith 'Penther." Gussie curled

the greeting around the peppermint stick in her mouth, leaving her S's by the wayside.

Eden frowned a bit. Is that what Levi would sound like if he didn't guard his words?

"Augusta Jane! You know better than that." Bertha bent over and yanked the candy out of the girl's hand. Gussie narrowed her eyes and slowly wiped the stickiness from her mouth with her sleeve, as if intentionally breaking another etiquette rule in retaliation.

Hoping to avoid a scene, Eden tried diverting the girl's attention. "What story do you think we should read after we finish *Black Beauty*, Gussie? We'll probably reach the end next Friday."

"I don't know." She shrugged. "Maybe *Swiss Family Robinson* or *Treasure Island*. I've heard those have pirates. I like pirates."

Eden could well imagine. Gussie Springer was a bloodthirsty little thing. She loved adventure stories, always asking questions like how deep of a hole an Indian arrowhead would leave in a man's back or what exactly a person's face would look like after falling victim to a stampede. Eden had hoped that Black Beauty's tale would make her and the other children more sensitive to the harm such violence provoked, but apparently Gussie had been immune to her efforts.

"Those are good suggestions." And they were. Eden had read both and found them entertaining, even with the pirates. "Perhaps we'll put it to a vote."

Gussie shrugged again. "All right."

Bertha smiled an apology for her daughter's poor manners and bid Eden a good day.

Eden watched them make their way across the street, trying not to listen to the hissed lecture being issued. She shook her head and restrained a grin. Despite the stomach-turning questions the girl was prone to ask, Eden treasured her time with Gussie and the other children. Who knew? Maybe Gussie's fascination with wounds and death would lead her to a study of medicine. Curiosity needed to be fed, and Eden found purpose in nourishing young minds.

She continued on her way, her bootheels clicking against the planked boardwalk in a rhythm that soon had her humming. The tune persisted even after she moved down to the dirt of the street and waited for an opportunity to cross. A wagon rumbled by, the driver lifting a hand to the brim of his hat. Eden nodded in acknowledgment, then gathered a handful of skirt as she prepared to step forward.

"Miss Spencer!"

Eden turned and stifled a groan, the fabric of her skirt sliding through her gloved fingers in resignation. "Sheriff."

He approached from the direction of the saloon, and a faint odor of spirits followed him. "You're looking lovely today. As always." He winked and made an annoying little clicking sound with his mouth. He probably meant it to be charming, but Eden failed to see the allure in being clucked at in the same manner one would a horse.

"Where're you headed?"

Eden opened her right arm slightly to allow Sheriff Pratt a glimpse of the book she carried. “I have a delivery to make.”

He raised a brow. “When’d you start making house calls?”

Uncomfortable with his scrutiny, Eden waved her hand in the air as if to dismiss the significance of her outing. “I’m simply helping out a friend who couldn’t make it to the library today.”

Sheriff Pratt glared at her, then seemed to catch himself. A smile suddenly sprouted beneath his well-trimmed mustache. “Well, shoot, Eden. Had I known you’d deliver, I woulda ordered books from you weeks ago.”

Why did that statement make her feel like a worm had just crawled across the back of her hand?

Eden lifted her chin. “It’s not a customary service, as you well know. This was a special circumstance. Now, if you’ll excu—”

“Who’s it for?” His tone remained light, but he shot a glance across the street, targeting the blacksmith shop as if he were sighting down the barrel of a rifle.

“That’s really none of your concern.”

Eden picked up her skirts once again and inched toward the street, eager to escape the growing unease the sheriff's company generated.

"Whoa there, darlin'." He took her arm and tugged her away from the road. "I'm just asking a question. No need to get all uppity."

Before she could decide whether or not to apologize, he reached around her back and snatched the volume of essays from her hand. "What do we got here? Some kind of storybook?"

She lunged for the book. He laughed and twisted away, blocking her efforts. Panic coursed through her. What if he discovered the letter?

"Really, Sheriff. Must you act so juvenile?" Eden tried to hide the fear quivering through her with a dose of disdain. "Give me my book, please." She held out her hand in silent demand, but her tormentor ignored it.

"If it's for that blacksmith, it probably has lots of pictures." He snickered and held the volume at a level even with his eyes.

Eden's chest tightened. "My book?"

she said again, a note of pleading working its way into her tone. But it was no use. He'd already started fanning the pages.

"What's this?" He growled and pulled the folded sheets free. "You're writing him letters?" Accusation dripped like acid from his tongue as he speared her with a glower and thrust the papers into her face.

She seized the note and tried to yank it free, but he held fast. "Mr. Grant asked my opinion on a literary matter. These are just some of my thoughts. Nothing to concern you." She pulled again, and this time he let go. Eden quickly hid the letter in the folds of her shawl.

"Everything you do concerns me, Eden." He spat the words at her out of the side of his mouth as he smiled and tipped his hat to a middle-aged woman several paces away who had turned to gawk. After a final curious look, the woman smiled and moved on.

Eden frowned up at Conrad Pratt. His high-handedness was really getting out of hand. Perhaps it was time to get her father involved. A few well-placed words, maybe a threat or two from the town's founder, and she'd be safe from any further unwanted advances. But then again, she wasn't a little girl anymore, running to Daddy instead of solving her own problems. She could handle the sheriff. She just needed to hold her ground until he finally tired of the battle and turned his attentions elsewhere.

"My book, please?"

"I'll not have you ruining your reputation before we say our vows," he ground out. "Respectability is everything in my business." He shoved the book at her chest.

Eden teetered back a step as she secured an arm around the volume. "I thought protecting the citizens of Spencer was your business."

He glared daggers at her, clenching his jaw so tight she thought she heard a tooth chip. But having the letter and book safely in her possession again freed her to vent some spleen.

"Despite your stubborn insistence, Sheriff, I'll not be saying vows with you.

So do me the honor of staying out of my affairs." With that, she turned her back and swept out into the street, feeling good about the setdown she'd delivered.

Until she reached the opposite side and glanced back.

Sheriff Pratt leaned menacingly against the wall of the Hang Dog Saloon, his black coat tucked back behind the holster at his hip. As he stroked the handle of his Colt, he stared across the street. But not at Eden. No, the heat burning from his eyes was directed at the man who had just emerged from the smithy.

Chapter Eighteen

Levi shouldered the last of the jumpers and carried them out to where Duncan was waiting with the wagon.

"This be fine craftsmanship, Levi." Duncan crouched in the wagon bed inspecting the weld on the weighted drill and the sharpness of its tip. "Aye. Ye ken what you're about, for certain."

Bending forward, Levi let the rods slide down his shoulder and through the crook in his arm until the ends met the ground. The jumpers rattled together as he took them between his hands and angled them toward Duncan.

"I've . . . hammered a drill or two . . . in my day."

"Have ye, now?" Duncan grinned at him as he levered the shafts to the rear of the wagon. He gave a nod and both men released their grips, letting the tools clatter against their counterparts. "Well, if ye're ever in need o' a job, I'll put a word in for ye with the boss."

Levi raised an arm to wipe the sweat from his brow as well as to hide the wince he couldn't quite contain. Work at a quarry? God forbid. It'd been hard enough to stomach making the drills. Walking through the pit again would be a living nightmare—shadows of the men he'd restrained lurking behind each slab, their agonizing cries echoing off the rocks. No. He wouldn't take Duncan up on his offer. Not for all the gold in Texas.

"I think I'll keep on here for now," he said, his tone dry.

"As ye should." Duncan brushed the dust from his hands and hopped over the side with a nimble ease that Levi envied. "Ye cannae waste the talent the Lord's given ye, now, can ye?"

The question pierced Levi's soul, resurrecting his guilt for doing just that for so many years. "No. Not anymore."

Duncan's jovial manner receded for a moment, replaced by a consideration that surprised Levi with its depth. But just as quickly as it appeared, it vanished again behind the lad's ready grin.

"Well," he said, "I suppose we should be settlin' Fieldman's account, then." He reached beneath his vest, most likely to retrieve their agreed-upon sum, but Levi never saw the money. Something beyond the younger man's shoulder captured Levi's attention.

Duncan turned his head and let out a low whistle. "Ach. Now, there be a lass with a bonny look to 'er. And I'm thinking it's nae me she's coming to see."

Levi dragged his gaze away from Eden to glare at the smiling Scotsman. It had little effect, though. Duncan lifted his eyebrows in a knowing manner and winked before schooling his features into a serious mien so false it elicited a reluctant smile from Levi.

"Here's your payment, Mr. Grant," Duncan said in an absurdly formal tone. "Fieldman sends his thanks."

Levi stuffed the bank notes in his trouser pocket, his eyes again drifting to Eden. She lifted a hand in greeting from the other side of the wagon, hanging back to avoid interrupting his transaction.

"I'll be on me way, then," Duncan said in an overloud voice, shooting Levi a final wink before gamboling up to the driver's seat. "Ma'am." He touched the brim of his cap and nodded to Eden, then took up the reins and maneuvered the wagon down to the street.

Levi crossed behind him and ran a hand through his unruly hair. He hadn't visited the barber since coming to Spencer, and now his hair curled more than a man's should. He always made a point to comb it down before paying a call on Eden, but there wasn't much he could do about it this time.

"We've missed you at the library, Mr.

Grant." Her beautiful eyes were full of questions.

He stepped closer, wanting to touch her arm, stroke her cheek, anything to convey his regret. But he was covered in perspiration from working the forge, so he shoved his hands into his pockets and did the best he could with words. "I've . . . uh . . ." Levi cleared his throat, his gaze dropping to the dirt. "I've had to work late to . . . complete a job for the quarry." He lifted his head. "I meant . . . to come by. . . ."

"So it was just your work that kept you away?" She peered up at him, a shimmer of vulnerability in her eyes.

"Of cour—" Levi bit down on his tongue at the last second. "I mean . . . You didn't think I . . . ?"

"It doesn't matter."

But it did. He could tell by the way the lines around her mouth softened at his reassurance. She seemed to understand his intent even with his blundering speech.

"I brought you a book." She opened her arm a bit to reveal a cover that matched two others he'd perused recently. "If you're still interested . . . in Mr. Irving's writings."

Levi grinned, and the tension between them evaporated. "Lately I've become right fond of the fellow."

Her lips stretched wide in a smile that lit up her face. She ducked her head as she held out the book to him, but he caught her peeking up at him, and his heart swelled within his chest. He took the book from her hand, intentionally grasping it in such a way that his fingers brushed against hers. Even though she was wearing gloves, he knew she felt the contact by her tiny indrawn breath and the fact that she hesitated several seconds before pulling free.

Could it really be possible that Eden Spencer felt something more than friendship toward him? He didn't deserve such a gift. But he wasn't about to shy away from it, either.

"Will I see you in church tomorrow, Mr. Grant?"

"Yep. I'll be there." He wanted to hear his given name on her lips again, but understood her need for formality.

Though no one was around, they were still in public, and he suspected she used it to create a bit of distance between them, as well. He would respect that and let her set the pace.

"Good. I'll look for you then." She reached down to grasp her skirt, lifting the hem out of the dust. Her shawl slipped from her shoulder to her elbow. Levi stepped close and gathered the soft wool in his palm. Slowly, he dragged it up her arm and back over her shoulder. He smoothed it into place, enjoying the feel of her fine bones beneath his touch. A tremor passed through her as his thumb grazed the edge of her neck, and satisfaction surged inside him.

She might be setting the pace, but he wasn't above giving a little nudge every now and then.

Levi turned his attention to her face. Her wide eyes stared back at him like a doe, wary and unsure. Yet there was a touch of longing in evidence, too. Finally, she blinked and broke free of her stillness.

"I'll be on my way, then. Have a pleasant evening."

"You too."

He watched her go, the dark green fabric of her dress acting like a magnet for his gaze. Seeing this shy side of her was new. Since the day they'd met, Eden always seemed to be charging forward—confident, independent, opinionated. And admittedly, those opinions had not always been too favorable where he was concerned. Yet the more she revealed of herself in her letters, and the more he learned to look past her oh-so-proper shell, the more he realized that a tender soul resided within her, one easily bruised, if he didn't miss his guess. Hence her reluctance to expose it.

His view of her faded until only an occasional flash of green caught his eye as she wove through the townspeople. Knowing he still had a pile of projects to organize after setting them aside for the quarry job, Levi sought out a final glimpse of green, then turned to head back into the shop. He didn't take more than a step before his path was blocked. By a scowling lawman with loathing in his eyes.

"Enjoying the scenery, Grant?"

Levi ignored the bait. "You got . . . a bar in the jail needing work, Pratt? Or are you here to gab?"

Moving sideways, Levi tried to step around him, but the sheriff cut him off and thrust his finger in Levi's face. "Stay away from Eden. She's mine."

Something hardened inside Levi at the claim, and it was all he could do not to grab the man's finger and snap the bone in two. He balled his free hand into a fist as he struggled to control his fury. "I don't recall her mentioning a beau."

Sheriff Pratt dropped his arm and shrugged. His mouth curved into a cocky grin that set Levi's teeth on edge. "Doesn't matter. I've made my position clear to her. It's just a matter of time before she reconciles herself to the idea."

Reconcile herself to sharing a life with Pratt? The thought made Levi ill.

"Spencer is my town, Grant. And I aim to keep it that way. Taking Eden to wife will solidify my standing in the community."

"Noble of you." No doubt he expected such an alliance to put Eden's father in his pocket as well as give him sway over the town council. Levi's right bicep twitched as he slowly lowered his focus to the sheriff's jaw.

"What?" Pratt sneered. "You think you can offer her something better? As my wife, she'll have acceptance and respect from everyone in town, something she's lacked as a spinster. Something she'd certainly never have with a beggar like you."

Levi jerked his gaze back to the man's eyes.

"Oh yes." The sheriff nodded, smugness coating his words. "I know about your measly account at the bank. You're practically living off this town's charity. Eden is accustomed to a life of means. She'd never consider marriage to a man like you. Any friendship she's extended has been strictly out of pity. The woman always did have a soft spot for lost causes. That's all you are—a cause, like those orphans down in Austin she's always collecting things for. Add to that your secrets . . . and, well, I think we both know who Eden would be better off with."

Secrets? Levi's chest ached. He didn't say a word. He couldn't. What did Pratt know?

As if he could smell Levi's fear, the sheriff stepped closer, his face mere inches from Levi's own. "I plan to do some serious looking into your past, Grant. Seems there's a handful of years unaccounted for between the time you left your father's shop in Caldwell and the day you started work here in Spencer."

Levi held his ground without so much as a blink. Yet all the while, his insides quivered.

"I'm real good at ferreting out the truth. That's my job, after all."

A snarl echoed, and for a moment, Levi thought Pratt had issued it. Then the snarl became a bark as Ornery stalked out of the smithy, teeth bared, eyes locked on the sheriff.

Pratt lunged back and drew his Colt, the barrel aimed straight at the dog's skull. "Call him off, Grant, or I swear I'll do the town a favor and put a bullet between his eyes."

"Ornery. Down." With effort, Levi uncurled his right fist and motioned with his palm for the dog to sit. Ornery complied but continued to growl and snap at the interloper.

Pratt backed away, his eye on the dog, his finger on the trigger of his gun until he decided Ornery was no longer a threat. A couple yards away, he holstered his weapon and turned his attention to Levi once more.

"Remember what I said, Grant. You're no good for her, so keep your distance. I'd hate for her to get hurt. People caught in the middle often do."

When the man disappeared into the saloon across the street, Levi strode to the large smithy doors and jerked them closed. Rage and despair battled within him until he thought he might explode from trying to contain them.

He set Eden's book on the edge of a nearby sawhorse and braced his arms against the crosspiece. Clenching his jaw, he dug his fingers into the wood until the contraption started shaking against the ground from the force of his grip. With a growl, he released the sawhorse and turned toward the wall, hands fisted. A discarded branding iron lay on the floor a few feet away. Levi snatched it up, and with a yell deep enough to rival thunder, bashed it into the stone wall. Again. And again. And again. All his fury, all his fear that what Pratt had said was true were bludgeoned into that wall until the circular tip of the iron broke free and flew across the room to clatter somewhere behind him.

The sound ricocheted through Levi and halted him midswing. Muscles trembling, he lowered his arm. The iron was bent and mangled. The stones in the wall were chipped and bore traces of the metal used to abuse them.

A whine brought Levi's head around. Ornery sat cowering behind his tool rack.

Disgusted with himself, Levi dropped what was left of the branding iron and hunkered down with his hand out. "Forgive me, boy. I let him get the better of me for a minute there. I won't hurt you. Come here."

Ornery's watery eyes spoke of betrayal and distress, piercing Levi's conscience. But the dog obeyed. Hesitantly at first, he padded up to Levi and licked his hand. Levi rubbed his ears and patted his side, then hugged the beast to him as his anger melted away to leave a heaviness that pressed in on his heart with unrelenting force.

Conrad Pratt was right. His secret did have the power to wound Eden. But that didn't mean he'd meekly step aside and let the sheriff manipulate the situation. No. He'd find a way to protect Eden from Pratt and—if the Lord was merciful—from himself, as well.

Chapter Nineteen

After supper with Claude and Georgia Barnes, Levi hiked back to town, needing to occupy his hands. Claude had given him permission to bed down at the livery on nights he chose to work late, and even though the repairs that had piled up while he completed the quarry job would probably keep until next week, Levi craved a distraction from the thoughts that had been spinning in his head since his encounter with the sheriff.

As he worked the bellows to breathe life back into the forge's coals, Levi grew steadily more despondent. Maybe Pratt's words were the warning he'd asked the Lord to send. The sheriff seemed too full of himself to be a vessel for a divine message, but then again, God had been known to talk through donkeys before.

Levi grinned at the comparison.

Then frowned at the ramifications.

He raked new coals into the hot pocket at the center of the forge and stared at the mound as it slowly turned bright red. Eventually, the center grew white, ready for work, but Levi made no move to reach for the plowshare that waited to be reshaped.

Had Pratt been right about Eden only extending friendship to him out of pity or some sense of community obligation? He'd discounted the idea at first, certain he'd detected interest in her demeanor as they'd exchanged letters. But what if his own desire was coloring his perception?

And then there was the money issue. His father had always provided a dependable living for his family as a blacksmith, but even in his best years, he could never have supplied Levi's mother with the type of finery Eden enjoyed every day. Would she be willing to give it all up? Would it be fair to ask her to?

What about the library? It was her passion. Her life. He couldn't imagine her being happy without it. Could he find a way to rent the space from her father or build her a separate building somewhere?

He didn't own a second pair of trousers, let alone property. And he likely wouldn't own property for quite some time. What exactly did he hope to offer a woman like Eden?

He couldn't even provide an unsullied name. Prison records tended to leave blemishes.

An urging from deep within prompted Levi to seek confirmation for his suspicions that the Lord was indeed telling him to steer clear of Eden. Yet too afraid the confirmation would come, he couldn't bring himself to pray. He wasn't ready to give her up.

So he pounded out his frustrations on the anvil instead. For the next two hours, he hammered a preliminary weld on the plowshare, punched screw holes into a dozen butterfly hinges, and started repairs on a set of bench springs for a farm wagon.

But the labor didn't help. By the time he shut things down, his mood had only darkened.

Levi locked up the smithy and trudged toward the livery. Halfway there, music from the saloon called to him. He looked over toward the building. Light glowed from within. Voices carried across the street. The Hang Dog offered companionship, distraction. The chance to forget for a while.

Levi adjusted his course.

No one showed up to stop him. Not even Ornery. The mutt was probably off cavorting with a pretty little female somewhere. No sympathy at all for his master's troubles.

He lengthened his stride.

Thirst struck him—a thirst so deep he started salivating. How well he remembered the taste and the way it made him feel. The rounds of beer and whiskey shots in celebration of his latest prizefighting victory. The hurrahs from his cohorts. The respect in men's eyes. The way the sporting girls would flash him hungry looks and find a way to stroke his chest or arm as they passed by, serving drinks. He didn't even have to watch his speech. Everyone slurred and stumbled over their words.

It was freedom.

The door stood open, promising camaraderie. Promising acceptance.

The bank notes from the quarry job burned so hot in his pocket that heat seeped into his leg. He reached down and curled his fingers around the cash, then climbed the steps to the entrance.

Something in his gut told him to stop, but the lively piano music drowned out the quiet voice whispering to his heart. Levi hesitated for a moment, but a burst of laughter from inside the Hang Dog urged him forward.

Then a man staggered through the opening and caught Levi's arm to steady himself. The sour smell of alcohol wafted up from his mouth as he spat out an apology.

"Betsy begged me not to come. Said

she'd leave if I didn't quit. I tried. I really did. But the memories keep coming back." The man turned up rheumy eyes, and the light from inside the saloon fell across his face. A jolt of recognition flashed through Levi. It was the man who'd attacked him at his shop, the man who'd lost his boy.

"Don't go in there, feller. It won't help." He pushed off of Levi and wobbled down the walk. He reached for the wall to steady himself and looked back over his shoulder. "It never helps."

Like a two-edged sword, truth sliced through Levi and nearly stole his breath. The relief he'd hoped to find in this place had nothing to do with freedom. It was slavery.

What am I doing?

A rush of nausea hit him, and Levi dashed around the corner into the alley. He stood hunched over, hands braced against his knees, panting. Like a dog. A dog who'd run away from his master in order to rummage in the garbage of his own will.

Lord, I'm sorry.

Levi straightened and pressed his

back to the wall, the muted piano music fading out of his consciousness. He pulled his hat off and tipped his chin up toward heaven. Black filled his vision. No stars, no moon, just darkness.

I'm weak, God. So weak. I don't deserve your forgiveness, but I ask for it anyway. Change my heart. Make me new.

His eyes slid closed as the familiar weight of guilt bore down on him. Hadn't he made vows to avoid the trappings of his old life? He'd been in Spencer a month and never been tempted in this way before. Why now?

Eden's face swam before him.

He'd been walking in faith. Until tonight. He'd let his desire for Eden outweigh his desire to follow the Lord's path. He'd refused to seek God's will because he feared it wouldn't coincide with his own. And in the process he'd left himself open to attack—attack from an opponent who never pulled his punches.

The words of the Prodigal Son came back to haunt him. *"I am no more worthy to be called thy son."* Levi bent his head, unable to look in heaven's direction. Why did he even try to change? He'd never be good enough.

As the thought formed in his head, a barrage of Scripture hit him as if some unseen angel had reached into his seed bag, grabbed a handful, and flung it at him.

"For all have sinned, and come short of the glory of God; being justified freely by his grace . . ."

"A man is not justified by the works of the law, but by the faith of Jesus Christ . . ."

"For I will be merciful . . . and their iniquities will I remember no more."

"If we confess our sins, he is faithful . . . to cleanse us from all unrighteousness."

"There is therefore now no condemnation . . ."

Levi trembled as those seeds took root in his soul. Grace. Cleansing. Forgiveness. No condemnation.

No condemnation—with all he had done? The prison chaplain had made him memorize these verses, but never before had they penetrated his heart to such an extent. They were meant for other Christians, those who didn't have blood on their hands, those who hadn't betrayed their families and their God with such flagrant selfishness. No, he was the unworthy prodigal, hanging his head in shame, trying to make up for all his past mistakes to earn back his Father's love.

"But you don't want me to earn it, do you?" Levi whispered as his gaze climbed back up to the night sky, truth resonating in his soul. "I *can't* earn it. I can only accept it. Your gift."

Levi raised a shaking hand to his face and scrubbed away the moisture that pooled in his eyes.

I understand now. Thank you.

Pushing away from the wall, Levi straightened, ran his hand through his curls, and repositioned his hat on his head. He felt taller. A grin tugged at his mouth. Taller. Imagine that.

Guilt no longer weighed on him. Regret? Yes. Repentance? Assuredly. But guilt? It had finally slid from his shoulders, and the relief he'd been seeking poured through Levi like a cleansing stream. Gone was the desperate drive to redeem himself. Christ had already done that job.

Laughter gurgled in his throat at the irony of his misplaced efforts. No, he couldn't redeem himself, but he could demonstrate his thankfulness and love by extending God's grace to others and living in a way that brought glory to his Lord. And that he vowed to do.

Starting now.

As if the angel who'd earlier showered him with Scripture had heard him, something new hurled from the heavens to slap against his head. But this time there was a definite physicality to the projectile. Levi grasped it with his hand. It was slender, a bit scratchy, and definitely still attached to something above him. He pivoted to face the wall, and scanned up to the second story.

Who would drop a rope into a saloon alley?

Chapter Twenty

Levi craned his neck. A window above him had been propped open, and sounds filtered down to him. Shuffling. Scraping. What could have been drawers slammed shut. Then, after one particularly loud bang, a woman's voice pierced the quiet of the alley.

"Get out! I ain't servicin' you."

Deep masculine tones vibrated in answer, but the man spoke too low for Levi to make out his words.

"I don't care what he promised you or how much you paid. I ain't no whore!"

Something crashed.

"Stop! I work in the kitchen. Leave me alone!"

Levi shoved his hat onto his head and leapt for the rope to scale the wall. But before he could fully plant his feet, a metallic clank echoed like a strike from one of his hammers, followed by a dull thud. *Did he hit her?*

Levi scrambled, straining against the rope as he hoisted his large frame toward the window. A third of the way there, he glanced up in time to see a petite pair of arms shove something through the opening. He barely had time to turn his face before a gunny-sack plowed into him, knocking his hat from his head and his feet from the wall as he instinctively twisted to protect himself from the blow.

Then, as he dangled midair, curling his biceps to keep himself from slipping, a stocking-clad leg thrust out of the window, followed by more feminine parts encased in white petticoats.

Apparently the woman was alive and well.

Not wanting to frighten her, Levi dropped to the ground on quiet feet, collected his hat, and waited. If what he overheard was accurate, the gal had gotten herself into quite a pickle. If she'd let him, maybe he could find a way to help her. If not, well . . . at least he'd make sure she didn't fall on her backside as she navigated her way down.

She grunted and groaned but made good progress. Levi picked up her bag and positioned himself in the middle of the alley so as not to jump out at her from the shadows. When her feet finally hit the ground, she swiveled from side to side, looking for her belongings.

Levi held his arms out wide and tried to make himself appear as nonthreatening as possible. Not an easy task for a mountain-sized ex-prizefighter.

"I've got it, ma'am."

She gasped and braced her back against the saloon wall. Her attention darted to the bag, to him, to the end of the alley, and back to the bag.

Afraid she'd try to make a run for it before he could assure her that he meant no harm, he set the bag down in front of him and stepped back. "I'm not going to hurt you," he said. "I'd like to help if you'd let me."

The woman was a mere girl. A tiny little thing with big eyes suspended in a face as pale as the moon. Well, pale except for the reddened portion along her jaw.

Slowly, her shock gave way to determination as she eyed her bag. She lifted her gaze to him once again and straightened away from the wall just a bit. "You drunk?"

Levi shook his head. "Nope."

She leaned forward and sniffed. He fought the urge to smile.

The girl slid a step closer. "Whatcha doin' in the alley?"

"Praying."

Her face scrunched in disbelief, and she eyed him as if worried about his mental stability.

He couldn't hold back his chuckle. "Odd, I know." Keeping his arms out wide, he shrugged. "I thought I wanted what the Hang Dog offered, but at the la . . . final minute, I remembered all the trouble that kind of help can lead to. Thought I'd be better off trying God."

"Mister, I lived in saloons my whole life, and you're the first feller I met who ever figgered that out. Don't know much about the God part, but I seen enough trouble over liquor, cards, and women to—"

A masculine moan echoed from above, cutting her off. The girl must have hit her assailant pretty hard to have knocked him out for so long.

She darted a glance up at the window. "Crikey! I gotta git."

She grabbed the gunnysack and dashed away from Levi. Not wanting to leave her unprotected, he followed. After rounding the corner of the saloon, she halted at the edge of the side street and twisted her head from left to right as if trying to determine which route would prove safest.

"You got a location in mind?"

The girl shot a glare at him over her shoulder. "Away," she snapped before turning back toward the street. "Now leave me alone, mister. I ain't your problem."

Yet Levi couldn't shake the feeling that she was.

"I know people who would take you in. The wife of the town preacher would—"

"I ain't going to no church lady's house! All that holier-than-thou snubbin'? No thanks! I'd be better off hidin' out in a barn somewhere."

Levi wanted to argue, to explain that Emma Cranford was not that way at all. If she could host a man like him in her parlor, she could handle a runaway saloon dweller with grace, too. But he knew it'd do no good. The gal was scared and fixin' to dart into the night if he didn't come up with another idea, and quick.

"What about a library lady?" The words slipped out before the idea had fully formed.

The girl's head swiveled so fast, he thought it might detach from her neck. "You know Miss Spencer?" Her face was a mask as she spoke, but even in the darkness, Levi could make out the longing in her gaze.

"Yep." He prayed he wasn't making

trouble for Eden by bringing her into the situation, but knowing how she felt about children, he figured she'd be willing to help.

"I done heard about them stories she tells the school kids. You think she would let me—"

The sound of a man yelling shot panic into the girl's eyes. She flattened herself against the side wall and slowly peeked around the corner. Jerking her head back, she panted like a trapped animal. Thinking to put himself between her and what threatened her, as well as hoping to catch a glimpse of the man responsible for her fear, Levi strode forward. Before he could angle himself around the corner, though, the girl threw her puny strength against him.

"Don't!" she hissed. "He'll see ya."

Levi resisted at first, but then her voice lost its toughness and took on a childlike pleading. "Please, mister."

He complied, shifting his stance to merge again with the shadows.

She stole another glance around the side of the building, and this time her shoulders sagged with relief when she returned to her place. "He's leaving."

"You made up your mind yet on where to go?"

She met his gaze. "I reckon I'll give the library a try."

A tapping from outside roused Eden from her doze. She startled awake. The book she'd been reading dropped to the floor. Blinking, she took stock of her surroundings and tried to recall what had awakened her.

Another tap, louder this time, carried to her from the front door. She slid her feet into a pair of house shoes, checked to make sure her wrapper was properly done up, shuffled to the front room, and parted the curtains to peer out.

Levi?

She couldn't make out his features, but no one else in town stood so tall and broad. It had to be him. What was he doing at her door so late in the evening?

Eden moved from the window and

made her way down the hall to unlatch the door. "Levi, why are you—"

Her throat suddenly closed in on itself as she discovered he was not alone. What was he doing with a girl? Especially one so young and pretty?

"Can we come in?" Levi asked in a low voice.

"I'm not exactly dressed for company, Mr. Grant."

She watched his gaze travel over her, lingering on her hair. Only then did she remember that it hung free, nearly to her waist. He swallowed, his Adam's apple bobbing up and down as he stared. The warmth in his eyes soothed her in a way words could not.

Eden pulled the door wide and showed them to her personal parlor.

"Why don't you have a seat, Miss . . . ?"

"It's Chloe, ma'am. Just Chloe. Ain't got no last name." She spoke the shocking statement with bland acceptance as if such a thing were of no consequence, then lowered herself onto the sofa. Chloe settled the sack she carried on her lap, hugging it to her chest as if it were a toddler in danger of crawling away.

"A pleasure to meet you, Chloe. I'm Eden." Somehow it didn't seem right to introduce herself with her surname when the poor child didn't have one of her own to offer. "If you'll excuse me for just a moment, I need to have a word with Mr. Grant."

The girl nodded and squeezed the bag more tightly as her wide-eyed gaze darted around the room.

Eden led Levi out into the hall. "What is going on?" she whispered.

"I'm hoping you can help her." Levi rubbed a spot on his chest and dipped his chin to avoid looking at her face. "The kid . . . had nowhere to go."

"Where did she come from?"

"The Hang Dog. Found her climbing out a window."

"The Hang Dog? You brought a girl from the saloon into my house? How could you? She has to leave." Eden took a step toward the parlor, but Levi's large hand closed around her wrist. Gently, but with enough power to bring her to a halt.

"Hold up there." He looked her full in the face now, and the plea she read in his eyes softened her heart. She ceased pulling against his hold.

He stroked the tender skin on the underside of her arm. "Hear me out, will you?"

She hesitated a second, then nodded.

Levi released his grip on her arm and let out a heavy breath. "From what I can gather, the girl worked in the kitchen, not in . . . uh . . . entertaining. Until tonight, when a man paid to . . . break her in."

Eden covered her mouth with her hand and shook her head in denial. Chloe couldn't be more than fifteen. What kind of animal would put a price on her innocence?

"Chloe fought him off, though," Levi continued. "Knocked him out and climbed through the window. I tried to . . . get her to go with me to . . . talk to Dave and Emma Cranford, but the girl wanted nothing to do with them. I worried about her bolting. I told her I knew you, and . . . now we're here."

She could hear the unasked question. Would she take Chloe in?

Her heart ached for the girl, it truly did, but opening her home to a young woman who made her living in a saloon? Unthinkable. "I can put together some food and rent her a room in the hotel for the night. I'll give you the funds to buy her a ticket on the morning train to wherever she wants to go. She can make a fresh start in a new town." Pleased with her solution, Eden relaxed.

However, Levi didn't seem too enthusiastic about the suggestion. The way his mouth turned down made Eden's stomach clench.

"A new town won't fix the problem," he rasped. "Without a job or family, you know where the girl will end up."

"But what will people think, Levi?" Eden crossed her arms over her churning stomach. "I have my reputation to consider."

As soon as the words passed her lips, her mind flew back to her conversation with the sheriff. He'd claimed reputation was everything, and she'd belittled him for such a superficial attitude. And here she was doing the same thing.

Levi peered into her eyes for several seconds, his disappointment in her palpable. "You can't control what people think, Eden. You can only control how you live. Do you live to protect your reputation—or to care for a child in need?"

Eden bit her lip and turned her face toward the wall to hide the tears welling in her eyes. He was right. So right. Jesus asked his followers to deny themselves, take up their cross, and follow him; to present themselves as living sacrifices. Putting Chloe on a train might have soothed her conscience at first, but not now. Not when her soul was convicting her that it was time to deny herself and act sacrificially.

"She can stay," Eden whispered to the wall.

"What?"

She sniffed and looked to the ceiling for a moment to push the moisture away from her eyes, then turned to face Levi. Clearing her throat, she met his gaze and spoke with conviction. “She can stay.”

Chapter Twenty-One

The knot in Levi's gut uncoiled at Eden's concession. He touched her shoulder. "Thank you."

She gave a jerky little nod, then turned and pulled away. The tears in her eyes had not escaped his notice, and he questioned the rightness of pushing her to take Chloe in. A woman's reputation was nothing to trifle with, and Eden had reason to be concerned. But surely her standing in the community would overshadow the girl's unfortunate upbringing. In fact, having Eden as her champion could open a new world to Chloe, a world of respectability and perhaps even faith.

However, as Levi followed Eden back into the parlor, a troubling thought took hold. Had he been pushing strictly for Chloe's sake, or had he been paving his own road to acceptance? His brow furrowed. When Eden suggested sending Chloe away, the first thought that flashed through his mind had not pertained to the girl's welfare. No, he had speculated on the likelihood of Eden sending *him* away when she learned of his own shameful past. Convincing her to open her heart to Chloe could make it that much easier for her to open her heart to him.

Yet at the same time, he knew Chloe's arrival on the heels of his vow to the Lord had not been coincidence. God had used his presence in that alley for Chloe's good. He was sure of it. Bringing her to Eden was the right thing to do. He just had to be careful not to stir his personal motives into the mix.

When they crossed the threshold into the parlor, Chloe jumped to her feet. "I'm sorry, Miss Spencer. I never shoulda let him talk me into coming here. A girl like me ain't fit company for a fine lady."

Levi stopped in the doorway, blocking the exit with his bulk. The kid had that bolting look about her again.

Eden took a more direct approach. She hurried to Chloe's side and wrapped an arm around her shoulders. "Well, I'm not sorry at all that you came. In fact, I believe Mr. Grant did us both a favor by bringing you here." Eden glanced back at him. Her lashes dipped shyly as if in apology for her earlier reluctance, but the sincerity shining in her eyes made him proud of her in a way that went beyond simple admiration.

"You'd . . . you'd let me stay?" Chloe asked, incredulity written on her face.

Eden smiled at her. "Yes."

Chloe tossed her bag onto the sofa and swiveled out of Eden's hold in order to face her squarely. "I ain't no loafer. If I stay with you, I'll earn my keep."

"I'm glad to hear it." Eden succeeded in keeping her face straight, but Levi could hear the smile in her voice. "Mr.

Grant tells me that you have experience in kitchen work. Is that correct?"

"Yes'm. I mostly scrubbed pots and pans at the Hang Dog, but I can throw a meal together when it's called for. I'm real good with eggs. Old Nell couldn't stomach cookin' when she was hung over, so I handled breakfast for anyone who managed to get outta bed afore noon. It was usually just me and Roy, the barkeep, but he never complained 'bout my eggs and coffee. 'Course he's sweet on Mama, so he might not a said nothin' on her account."

"Your mother works at the saloon?"

Levi had started walking toward a chair but stopped at the tightness in Eden's voice. Chloe picked up on it, too, for she crossed her arms over her chest and set her jaw.

"That make a difference?" the girl challenged. "It ain't too late for you to change your mind. She's done her best by me, and I ain't ashamed to claim her. If you got a problem with that, say so now."

"Calm down, kid," Levi said, trying

to ease the growing tension in the room. "Give her a minute to take it in."

Eden bit her lip but held firm to her determination. "I'd never ask you to disown your mother, Chloe. I apologize if I gave you that impression. I guess I just assumed you were on your own. Hearing about your mother caught me off guard. Nevertheless, if you are interested in staying, you'd be welcome here."

Chloe uncrossed her arms, though her eyes remained wary. "All right, so long as we're clear." Her chin dropped as she scuffed the toe of her shoe against the rug. "Sorry I snapped at you."

Levi looked from one female to the other. "You two going to be all right?"

Eden kept her focus on Chloe while she answered him. "We'll be fine. We just need some time to get to know one another—that's all."

Chloe offered no disagreement.

"Good. I'll be on my way, then."

Eden finally looked his direction and he gave her a teasing wink. "Wouldn't want to . . . mar the reputation of . . .

the two of you by lingering too long after dark."

A smile tugged the corners of Eden's mouth upward, and Levi's pulse responded. Now that Chloe was safely transferred into her care, he was having a hard time keeping his mind off the fact that Eden looked even better with her hair down than he'd imagined. And when he passed the reading room on his way out and caught sight of a book lying half open against the leg of his chair as if it had just toppled to the floor, he picked up his pace to the door.

A man could handle only so much evidence of his fantasy being reality without wanting to bring the rest of it to life, as well.

After Levi left, Eden ushered Chloe upstairs to one of the spare bedrooms. She had to admit, the girl didn't look like what she would've expected from one who lived in a saloon. Her dress was plain and prim, an ordinary gray muslin buttoned clear to her neck. No unseemly flesh on display, no flashy colors to attract a man's attention. The girl's face was clean of all cosmetics, and Eden couldn't smell any evidence of perfume as she leaned close to help her unpack her bag.

"So, how old are you, Chloe?" Eden shook out a petticoat and folded it against her chest.

"Sixteen."

Eden paused for a moment, then opened a drawer in the bureau and laid the petticoat inside. "I would have guessed younger."

"That's because of Mama's disguise." Chloe undid a few buttons on her dress to reveal a tight binding around her breasts, then fastened the dress closed again. "This and my drab clothes usually kept men from noticin'. Although Mama warned me never to let myself be caught alone with a man, 'cause some liked 'em young and wouldn't care about my lack of experience."

Chloe spoke with such nonchalance, as if protecting herself from vile advances were an everyday occurrence. Of course, in her world, it probably was. Eden bit back a moan and turned away from the girl, ostensibly to lay out a nightdress upon the bed, but in reality she hoped to hide her pity. How could the Lord allow an innocent child to grow up in such a place? She thanked God that Levi had convinced her to take Chloe in. The child deserved a place to sleep where she could be safe, where she could learn the ways of womanhood without worrying that some inebriated cowboy would manhandle her.

"We planned to leave Spencer soon," Chloe said, drawing Eden's attention. "Mama knew I was gettin' too old to hide in the kitchen much longer. We was gonna take the train and act like we didn't know each other so that I would be free to look for work in a café or restaurant somewheres. I guess we waited a little too long."

Eden sat on the edge of the bed and peered up at the girl. "What happened?"

"Bad timing." Chloe shrugged. "I know better than to go into the main room after dark, but Old Nell's bottle run out, and she sent me to fetch another from Roy. Mr. Salazar, the owner, was hobnobbin' with some gent at his special table in the corner. I saw the man in the Hang Dog afore, but never upstairs, so I didn't think much of it when I caught 'im looking at me."

Chloe dumped the last of her belongings onto the bed beside Eden. A brush tumbled out along with a deck of playing cards. She took up the cards, slid them out of their box, and began manipulating them as if they were an extension of her hands. Chloe's gaze fixed itself somewhere on the wall above the bureau as she lowered herself to the corner of the bed. But even without her attention, the cards danced in and out of her fingers like drilling soldiers responding to her silent command. Not a single one stepped out of formation.

Eden didn't hold with gambling and card playing, especially for a young lady, but the shuffling action seemed to soothe Chloe, and heaven knew the child deserved some soothing after all she had been through.

"Mr. Salazar found me in the kitchen a few minutes later," Chloe continued, her voice small and sounding far away. "He told me to go up to my room but not to lock the door. His friend wanted to visit me. Just to talk, he said. But I knew different. A man's got more on his mind than talkin' when he comes to a gal's room."

Eden's heart cringed. Letting instinct guide her, she picked up the brush that lay on the bed between them and scooted closer to Chloe.

"I told 'im I wouldn't let his friend in my room. Mr. Salazar said I would or he'd make things hard on my ma."

Eden untied the ribbon at Chloe's neck and pulled the brush through a few strands. The girl stiffened at her touch at first, then seemed to relax. She even turned her back to allow Eden greater access as she resumed her tale.

"I knew what to do then. Mama and I'd worked it all out. I was never to give in to threats, Mama said. No matter what. That's how they control you, and she made me promise to never let no man control me. So I went up to my room and locked the door. Then I got the rope I kept under my bed, tied it to the bedpost, and let it down out the window. I threw my stuff in a sack and was ready to go when the man showed up. Salazar'd given him a key."

This Salazar person should be horsewhipped, Eden decided. He and his friend. Maybe it was time for the Ladies Aid Society to take a more active role in ridding Spencer of its more unsavory element. She'd have to bring up the suggestion at the next meeting.

"How did you escape?" Eden had already worked through all the tangles in the girl's hair, but she kept stroking, hoping it would help Chloe feel safe.

"I yelled at him to get out, but he forced his way in. Said he'd paid for my time. He hit me." She hunched her shoulder up toward her jaw, and Eden saw the beginnings of a bruise near her chin. "But I was ready for him. I clobbered him over the head and knocked him out cold."

The brush stilled in Eden's hand. "You knocked him out?" The girl was smaller than she was, no match for a full-grown man. "What on earth did you hit him with?"

Chloe glanced over her shoulder, a smirk quirking her lips. "A chamber pot."

"A chamber . . ." A giggle rose up in Eden. She tried to hold it in, but it erupted out her nose. Chloe chuckled at the indelicate snort, and soon both of them were laughing so hard their eyes watered. The release was heavenly.

"Oh, Chloe," Eden said as she wiped at her eyes and struggled to catch her breath. "I think I'm going to like having you here."

Chapter Twenty-Two

The following evening—on the Lord's Day, no less—Levi found himself once again outside the Hang Dog. It was still early, the sun had yet to disappear behind the hills west of town, but that fact did little to ease Levi's nerves. A noble mission had brought him here this time instead of his own willfulness, but that didn't mean he wouldn't weaken once inside.

With a quick prayer for added strength, Levi took a deep breath and stepped into the saloon. The place was nearly empty. A lone cowboy stood at the far end of the bar, staring into his beer while three old-timers played poker at one of the tables. A spirited tune echoed from the piano beneath the stairs, but the detached expression on the player's face neutralized the happiness of the notes. A pair of women in exposed corsets, leaning against either side of the instrument, straightened from their positions and gave Levi a thorough examination.

He turned away, his mind dangerously flooded with images of plentiful bosoms and limbs encased in black stockings. He swallowed hard and concentrated on his task.

The note Eden had given him seemed to press against his chest from within his pocket. She had presented it to him after church that morning on Chloe's behalf. The girl had chosen to stay behind and keep an eye on Verna's pot roast, although Eden shared his suspicion that her true motive for missing services had more to do with her fear of running into the man who'd accosted her than her desire to baste a hunk of beef.

Wisely, Eden had not pressured her to attend. But perhaps unwisely, she'd promised to get word to the girl's mother that Chloe was safe. Levi wasn't about to allow Eden to traipse into the Hang Dog to deliver the message herself, so he'd volunteered for the duty.

The barkeep glanced over at him and set aside the glass he'd been wiping clean. Slinging the dishtowel over his shoulder, he moseyed down to Levi's position. "What'll it be, friend?"

Levi eyed the bottles on the shelf behind the man's head. He'd probably draw less attention to himself if he ordered a drink. But the minute that rationalization entered his brain, he evicted it. Better not give the devil a foothold. He forced his gaze back to the barman. "You Roy?"

The thin fellow raised an eyebrow. "Yep. Who's askin'?"

Levi lowered his voice. "A friend of Chloe. I have a note for her mother."

Stillness came over the man for a moment, then he blinked and jerked back into action. "Beer it is." He grabbed a glass and unstopped the spigot on the keg behind him. Rich amber liquid flowed into the glass, forming a foam on top. He plunked it down in front of Levi.

"No, I didn't—"

"Ah, you're in the mood for some company, are you? I can fix that." He motioned to someone at the back of the room. "Violet? Come here, honey. This gent's in need of some . . . conversation."

Heat rose up from Levi's collar. "You don't under . . ." The word strangled him. But it didn't matter, for Roy leaned in close and hissed in his ear.

"No, mister. *You* don't understand. Salazar worked Vi over good when Chloe turned up missin' last night. If he catches her swapping messages with you, he's bound to hand out more of the same. I ain't about to let that happen. You got something to say to her, you do it my way. And make it convincing."

Levi dipped his chin an inch to let the man know he'd cooperate, then turned to face the woman sashaying in his direction. For Chloe's sake he'd do all he could to minimize the amount of trouble his being there might cause her mother. Unfortunately, minimizing her trouble meant maximizing his own. Not an encouraging prospect.

A man at a back table lit a cheroot, the flare of his match briefly illuminating his swarthy face. Levi hadn't noticed him when he'd first entered the tavern, but that was probably due to the fact that the man wore all black and lingered among the shadows. The possessive way he watched Violet move across the room, though, hinted at his identity. Salazar.

Committed to playing an uncomfortable role, Levi leaned an elbow on the bar and pivoted to face Violet. He let his gaze rake over her as would be expected, but he schooled his mind to see her as Chloe's mother, not as a vehicle of pleasure. And amazingly, that simple change in perspective truly altered his perception.

The woman was small-boned, like her daughter, but stood several inches taller. When she reached his side, she curled her hand around his bicep, a practiced pout on her lips. She drew little lines on his arm with her fingernail and peeked coyly up at him from the corner of her kohl-darkened lashes. "Such marvelous muscles," she purred. "So strong. You and I are going to have us a mighty fine time."

Her face looked young—younger than he'd expected—but her eyes had a flatness to them that reminded him of men who'd been trapped behind prison walls so long they'd given up on ever being released. She rubbed her leg against his and leaned seductively into his side, yet the only thing that stirred in him was sorrow. What had happened in her youth to lead her to this place?

Levi smiled down at her, cupping his palm over her fingers. It might not be within his power to save her, but he could offer reassurance that her daughter would not suffer the same fate. "Got a room where we can . . . talk?"

"Sure thing, handsome. Follow me."

Salazar's stare burned into Levi's

back as he climbed the stairs, but the man made no move to rise. Thankful for each step that increased their distance from his table, Levi stayed on Violet's heels until they closed themselves behind her door.

The moment the latch clicked into place, however, Violet turned on him. "Where is Chloe?"

Startled at her quiet vehemence Levi staggered backward. "How . . . how did you know?"

The woman's eyes were far from flat now. They sparked with fire and a mother's passion that lent her deep blue eyes a violet hue. More than a flower had inspired her name.

"Roy signaled me before we left the bar." She waved the explanation away impatiently. "Now, tell me where she is."

"At the library," Levi finally spat out. "Unharmed."

Violet lifted a shaky hand to her throat. "Thank God. Maybe he does hear a whore's prayers after all."

Levi winced, recognizing the pain of self-loathing. He reached into his shirt pocket and pulled out the note Eden had written, hoping it would ease the woman's mind. "Here. The lady who took her in wanted me to give . . . a note to you."

She stared at it, making no move to reach for it. Instead she twirled back toward the door and unhooked a filmy lavender dressing robe from a nail that protruded from the wood. Keeping her back to him, she slid her arms into the sleeves and tightened the sash. Then with one hand holding the material closed at her neck, she turned and accepted the folded paper.

After she scanned the few words on the page, Violet pinned Levi with a look. "Can I trust this Eden Spencer to treat my girl good? I've heard of the Spencers. Know her daddy practically owns the town, even though he spends most of his time in Austin with his political cronies. People like that usually avoid people like Chloe and me. At least here, I could keep an eye on her."

"But not all the time," Levi said quietly.

Some of the starch went out of her

at that. "No. Not all the time." She turned her face away from Levi and gazed about the room. "I want better for her than this. I always have. We knew she'd have to leave one day, I just never figured how much losin' her was gonna hurt."

Something clenched in Levi's gut. This was the kind of pain he'd caused his own mother. His father, too. And unlike Chloe, it wasn't necessity that had driven him away but selfishness.

Did his parents ever think of him? Did they miss him? Or had they been so hurt and disappointed by his poor choices that it was easier for them to forget they had a younger son? Levi hadn't heard anything from them in years. Of course, he'd made no effort to contact them, so they wouldn't know where to find him if they wanted to. They would have heard the news of his incarceration, though. Everyone in the surrounding counties would've been privy to that juicy tidbit. Yet not once had he received a letter or visit or any indication that they wanted to see him.

Maybe once his shop was turning a

decent profit and he'd accrued enough funds to build a house . . . Maybe then he'd try to contact them. If they didn't want to see him, he'd find a way to live with that, but at the very least, he'd like to learn how they were faring. If his folks were in good health. If Pop still ran the smithy, or if he'd handed the reins over to Aaron. Did he have any nieces or nephews? Aaron had been courting a girl from Hearne when Levi left. It was easy to imagine him married and settled. Aaron had always been one to follow the conventional path, the one Levi had scorned. Now he longed for the simplicity and contentment such a life represented.

Of course, contentment would require the right partner with whom to share this life. A particular auburn-haired librarian with mossy green eyes came to mind.

Violet let out a sigh and turned back to him. "How did you meet up with Chloe?"

Levi did his best to fill her in on what had transpired in the alley and later at the library. She asked a few pointed questions about Eden, then decided they had hidden behind closed doors long enough to make the ruse believable.

Levi pulled a couple coins from his pocket and dropped them onto the dresser by the door, hoping it would be enough to satisfy Salazar. He nodded to Violet in parting and reached for the doorknob.

"Muss your clothes a bit before you go."

Levi raised a brow at her. Coming upstairs with her had been bad enough. He didn't want to reinforce his supposed lack of morality to anyone who cared to notice his exit.

She grabbed at his shirt when he hesitated too long and managed to tug most of one shirttail free before he batted her hand away. "Don't be such a prig," she said with a huff. "You can straighten yourself up as soon as ya leave. It'll be easier for both of us if everyone assumes we were havin' a good time. Fewer consequences."

Violet wrapped an arm around her ribs, and Roy's heated words came back to Levi. He hadn't thought much about the punishment the barkeep had mentioned because he hadn't noticed any bruises. But there were more places to hit a woman than the face—especially if one didn't want to mar his merchandise.

So, with a frown, Levi allowed her to undo his top button and put a kink in his left suspender. Praying no one from church would be anywhere nearby, he made his way downstairs and out the front door in record time.

Suddenly, he had a lot more sympathy for Eden's desire to protect her reputation.

On Monday morning, an hour before the library was due to open, a knock sounded on Eden's door.

"Verna, can you answer that?" Eden called out from the reading room, where she sat at her desk using a pair of toothpicks to glue down a dark pink phlox bloom on the stiff art paper that served as the canvas for her pressed flowers. She'd adhered the stems of her bouquet last week, had the background leaves in place for texture and dimension, and was finally ready to add the flowers—her favorite part, and the most delicate. She hated to leave before being certain the glue had set.

"Chloe and me are up to our armpits in bread dough," Verna answered from the kitchen. "You'll have to get it yourself."

Eden sighed as she pushed to her feet, holding on to her toothpicks until the last possible second. Relieved when the flower maintained its position, she gingerly eased her hands away from the bouquet and hurried to the door.

A woman in a tan-and-blue-striped walking suit stood on the porch, her back turned. At the sound of the door clicking open, however, she spun around. She blinked several times, and she peered past Eden's head as if trying to see into the house.

"This the library?"

"Yes, ma'am. But I'm afraid we don't open until noon. Perhaps you could return in an hour?" Eden tried to keep her voice polite, but the woman had yet to look her directly in the eye, and the rudeness was starting to rankle.

"I didn't come for a book." The woman finally brought her attention to Eden's face. "I come to see my girl. I'm Chloe's mother."

Chapter Twenty-Three

In all of Eden's etiquette lessons, no one had ever taught her the proper manner in which to welcome a prostitute into her home. Which probably explained why she just stood in the doorway, blinking stupidly at the woman on her porch.

"Chloe *is* here, ain't she?"

Violet's question snapped Eden out of her fog. "Yes. Of course." She stepped back and swung the door wide. "Please, come in."

The woman swept past her, and Eden had to admit that she hid her identity well. Just like Chloe, her face was scrubbed clean of paint, her dress was modest and well tailored, even her hair was done up in a fashionable chignon. If her eyes hadn't been so cold and her grammar so atrocious, she could have been mistaken for one of the women of the Ladies Aid Society.

Determined not to be caught gawking again, Eden closed the door and bustled forward to lead Violet into the reading room. "Chloe is in the kitchen. If you will follow me through here?"

The carpet muffled their footfalls, and a pervading awkwardness muzzled their tongues. Eden pushed open the swinging door to the kitchen. "Chloe? You have a caller."

The girl glanced up sharply, her flour-covered hands stalling in the midst of their kneading. "But, Miss Eden, you know I don't wanna see any—" Her eyes widened as Violet stepped into the room. "Mama?"

A smile began taking shape on her face until her gaze veered over to Eden. All at once, she turned her attention back to the bread dough, folding and punching it with great vigor. "You shouldn't a come here, Mama. It ain't proper. I sent you a message that I was safe. You shoulda left it at that."

Violet fiddled with the strings on her reticule. "I needed to see for myself."

Did Chloe not want to see her mother, or was she afraid Eden might banish her from her home because Violet showed up on her doorstep? It was true that the woman's presence discomfited her, but she'd told Chloe on the night she arrived that she didn't expect her to disown her mother, and Eden aimed to keep her word.

"Chloe, you and your mother can visit in my parlor, if you'd like. Or up in your room. Verna can finish the bread dough."

" 'Course I can." The housekeeper crowded in, scooting Chloe's breadboard over to her side of the table. "Go on and wash up. I'll put a kettle on. When you and your ma finish catchin' up, you can come have a cup of tea."

Chloe hesitated, clearly unconvinced. Eden nodded at her and smiled. "There will still be plenty to do after your visit. We can spare you for a while."

That must have finally convinced the girl that they weren't going to toss her out on her ear if she took a break, for she did an abrupt about-face to the pump and rinsed the flour from her hands and arms. She reached for the apron strings behind her back, then stopped. Flattening her palms along the front of the white cotton as she turned, she pressed the fabric against her stomach as if to say she had no intention of giving up her place. Then she set her jaw and strode toward the doorway.

"Come on, Mama. I'll show you my room."

Eden and Verna watched them go, saying not a word until the sound of retreating footsteps echoed on the staircase.

"I think that girl might be a little tired of livin' in saloons." Verna's dry understatement brought a smile to Eden's lips.

"She did seem a mite reluctant to leave her post." Eden met Verna's eyes, and the two shared a silent laugh. "It's a good sign, though," Eden said, sobering. "If she's going to be successful in creating a new life for herself, she's going to have to work hard and not be swayed by the familiarity of old habits. I don't want to stand between a mother and her child, but if Violet cannot leave the Hang Dog, there will have to be some level of separation between her and Chloe. I fear it will be hard on both of them."

Eden crossed to the cookstove and took down the kettle from above the warming oven and carried it to the water pump. After filling it and setting it directly over the firebox on the left side of the range, she turned to find Verna staring at her, a thoughtful look on her face.

"What?" Eden reached a hand to her hair. Had a pin come loose?

"Nothin'." Verna shook her head as she plopped the bread dough into a buttered bowl and covered it with a towel. "I'm just proud of you is all."

"Proud of me?" Eden's heart twitched as she sucked in a quivery breath.

Verna wasn't one to hand out compliments with any great frequency. "Why?"

The housekeeper wiped her hands on her apron and leaned back against the table as she met Eden's gaze. "You're learnin' to put your hurt aside and invest yourself in helping someone else."

Eden's brow crinkled as she puzzled over Verna's words. "But haven't I done that all along? Volunteering at Seeds of Hope and organizing clothing drives for the children? Not to mention the projects I've undertaken with Ladies Aid here in Spencer. Everything we do is to help the unfortunate or improve our community."

"I'm not talkin' 'bout charity work." Verna moved the bowl of bread dough to the cabinet near the window so the sun's warmth would aid in the rising. "I'm not saying them things aren't worthy activities. They are. But they're not the same as getting involved in the life of one particular person. 'Specially when that person has nothing to offer you in return.

"Your mama, bless her soul, taught

you all the niceties of playin' hostess and makin' others feel important, but she also taught you to always put your right foot forward in order to impress those above ya. She's so set on helpin' your daddy's career, sometimes she forgets to look past what's best for her to what's best for someone else." Verna fiddled with the lid on the flour bin for a moment, then looked up with a piercing stare. "Even her own daughter."

The strength ran right out of Eden's legs, and she grabbed the back of a chair for support. "You knew?"

She shrugged, but her eyes held compassion. "One of the maids overheard yer parents arguin' that night, and . . . well . . . You know how folks talk."

Eden sank into the chair. She'd spent so much energy over the years convincing herself that her mother's betrayal had been unintentional, that she'd only been looking out for the best interests of the family as a whole. Yet hearing Verna confirm her darker suspicions brought the pain back in stunning force.

It was the night Stephen broke their engagement. After learning what had occurred, Mother stormed into the bedroom to confront Father and slammed the door. Mother *never* slammed doors. Eden's room was across and down the hall, but sound carried—especially when one made a point to listen.

"What were you thinking, Calvin? Offering money. Of course he took it. Stephen Hartshorn is an ambitious man. It's one of the reasons we approved the match. Eden needs a husband who has a mind for the future."

"But he doesn't love her. I can't consign my only daughter to marriage with a man who cares more for his fortune than his wife's happiness. I tested him, and he failed. He's not worthy of her."

"Worthy of her? It was a solid match. They got on well enough together, and his family has advantageous connections that would have benefited us. How could you throw that all away? Now not only does Eden not have a husband, but we are left to deal with the humiliation

of her practically being left at the altar. It will take months if not years to recover from this fiasco. . . . Perhaps she should spend some time with my sister in Galveston. The change of scenery would do her good, and it would give us a chance to rally from this setback."

Eden had stopped listening after that. And the following day she began making arrangements to move to Spencer. She'd not burden her family with her humiliation.

The touch of Verna's hand on her shoulder brought her back to the present.

"Your mother loves you, Eden. Never doubt that. She just gets a bit blinded now an' again."

"I know." Eden forced a smile. "And you're right. Worrying constantly about what others think can be debilitating." She reached up to clasp Verna's hand, drawing strength from the older woman. "When Levi first showed up with Chloe, I tried to send them away." Shame washed over her as she confessed. "My first instinct was to protect myself from possible scandal. But now, even though I only met the girl last night, I can't imagine abandoning her to an uncertain fate. She's changed me."

Verna gently tugged her hand free, patting Eden's shoulder as she went. "Chloe didn't change you, child. The Lord done that piece of work. And I'm proud of you for lettin' him have his way."

Warmth permeated Eden's soul at her housekeeper's words, undoing the last of her anxiety knots. The Lord was at work. First through Levi and now through her. What was there to worry about?

But an hour later, after tea and a private conversation where Eden promised Violet that Chloe could stay for as long as she wanted, her confidence in the Lord's provision started to waver. For as she and Chloe walked Violet to the door, Hattie Fowler, president of the Ladies Aid Society and Spencer's self-appointed morality matron, charged through the library entrance and stuttered to a halt, her mouth gaping like a landed fish.

Eden's heart hammered against her ribs. Should she introduce the women? Hattie might consider such an introduction offensive, yet failing to say anything would surely be an insult to Violet and Chloe. Before she could decide on the proper response, Violet pulled on her gloves and edged forward.

"Thank you for your assistance, Miss Spencer," she said, surprising Eden with her genteel tone. The woman had a bit of the actress in her, it would appear. "I don't expect to have need of your services again, but it was kind of you to accommodate me this morning before your usual business hours. Good day." Violet nodded to Hattie as she moved past. Hattie swept her skirts out of Violet's path and pressed her back to the wall to increase the distance between them.

"I'll head back to the kitchen now, ma'am." Chloe bobbed a lopsided curtsy and scurried away, leaving Eden alone with the sputtering Hattie. The woman fanned herself with her hand as if trying to stave off a swoon.

"I am shocked to the core, Eden Spencer. Shocked, I tell you."

"Here. Let me show you to a chair." Eden took her arm and led her into the reading room, steering her to the chair closest to the hall, the one at her desk. "Can I bring you some tea?"

Shaking her head, Hattie dropped her handbag into the vacant chair instead of herself and paced along the short length of the desk. "Do you know who that woman was?"

The venom flavoring her enunciation killed the hope Eden had harbored that Hattie wouldn't recognize Violet. After all, Eden hadn't known her identity until she'd mentioned Chloe. But Hattie had lived in Spencer longer and made it her business to know everyone. She probably even knew the local prairie dogs by name.

Eden scratched a spot behind her right ear and raised her gaze to the ceiling. "You mean the, ah, woman in the striped dress who just left?"

"Of course that's who I mean!" Hattie pivoted with such speed, Eden was forced to take a step back. The woman's brow was plowed with deep furrows, but she fought to regain her composure by taking a deep breath. The tight lines on her face gradually smoothed into a more reserved countenance. "Well, perhaps you didn't know." She grabbed the fingers of her left hand and massaged them. "I admit that I didn't recognize her myself, at first. It was the girl that tipped me off."

"Chloe?"

Hattie nodded. "She's the one they send to our store for supplies."

Eden frowned. "Who?"

Hattie leaned forward and whispered in a hoarse voice, "The saloon managers." She glanced about the room as if fearful the books would overhear, then clutched Eden's elbow and dragged her toward a pair of chairs beside a small lamp table.

Once they were both seated, she tugged on Eden's arm until their heads were in close proximity. "Several years ago the ladies of Spencer campaigned for temperance. We spent many hours outside the Hang Dog singing hymns and carrying signs. During that time, I saw the women who worked there, and that *person* who just left your library was one of them. She's a . . . a . . . Well, she's a harlot—that's what."

Her face flushed, Hattie finally released Eden's arm and sat back in her chair to fan herself again.

"I'm sorry you're so upset, Hattie. But you heard what she said. She'll not be coming back anytime soon." Although, if she did, Eden would welcome her. Hattie didn't need to know that, though.

"What about the girl?" Hattie stopped waving her hand through the air and accosted Eden with a steely look. "She seems to be making herself at home in your kitchen."

Eden sat straighter, determined to hold firm to her commitment even while her stomach churned with dread. "Chloe is a new addition to my staff. She was looking for a more respectable way to make a living than cooking for the residents of the saloon, so when she came to me, I offered her a position. She is a great help to Verna."

"You *hired* her?"

"Well, why not? Aren't you always encouraging us to better our community by helping those less fortunate? That's all I'm trying to do."

Hattie puckered, as if the taste of her own words soured her tongue. "But bringing her into your home? Your place of business, where decent folk will be forced to mingle with her? She's not one of your orphans, Eden. She's a girl of exceedingly low moral character who will only cause you grief. If you want my advice, I say send her packing before word gets out. She's old enough to be on her own. Give her money if you need to assuage your conscience, but get her out of your house. Having her here will only cast aspersions upon your character."

Eden swallowed the retort that sprang to her lips. Offending Hattie would only stir up more trouble. She could handle a few aspersions. It was better than sacrificing her character in truth by sending Chloe away.

"I appreciate your concern, Hattie, and will consider your advice. But enough of that." She clapped her hands to her knees and stood, forcing her lips into a smile. "Surely something else brought you here today. Would you like to see the progress I'm making on the art piece for the auction?"

The older woman looked none too pleased by the change of subject but allowed Eden to steer the conversation onto a less rocky path. She murmured approval over the pressed-flower bouquet when Eden laid out sample blossoms and showed her the design sketch. They spent several minutes discussing Ladies Aid business and even chatted briefly about what books Mr. Fowler might consider carrying in the dry goods store, both ignoring the currents of tension flowing beneath the polite surface.

When Hattie took her leave, she made no further comments regarding either Chloe or Violet, but Eden couldn't escape the feeling that the issue was far from resolved.

Chapter Twenty-Four

Levi closed up shop late on Friday afternoon, and whistled as he crossed the road. He couldn't remember having a better week. Not even when he took out three opponents in three rounds back in '84. For the first time in ages, he felt comfortable in his own skin. He'd finally turned loose of his guilt and discovered a new lightness in his heart. He no longer wasted time bemoaning his mistakes and worrying about his future. Instead, he focused on his work and on helping the people around him.

When Claude asked him to reinforce the chicken coop two days ago, he'd hummed while he hammered; whereas last week he'd somberly chopped firewood as if it were some kind of penance rather than a simple farm chore done in exchange for room and board. He found more joy in his forge work, too, and his customers responded. The smithy was turning a modest profit, enough that he'd splurged yesterday and bought himself a pair of heavy denim trousers for work so he could save his wool ones for Sundays.

Tipping his hat to the lady who ran the bakery as she pulled her door closed, Levi smiled as much to himself as to her. Things had been improving with Eden, too. After the excitement over the weekend, they had picked up their letter writing again. And with each letter, their literature discussions became more and more overshadowed by personal matters. Eden wrote him about Violet's visit and the untimely arrival of Mrs. Fowler, as well as sharing everyday concerns—such as how she struggled to find just the right centerpiece flower for her pressed bouquet. Knowing she trusted him with such private matters gave him hope that she might be coming to care for him in the same manner he did for her.

If he timed it right, he would arrive at the library just as the school kids were leaving from their story hour. Being with the children always seemed to put Eden in a good mood, and if a man wanted to, say, ask a lady to supper at the café, her being in a good mood would greatly increase his chances of success.

Levi turned down Oak Street, repositioning the book containing his latest note under his arm. He'd begun sharing things about his family with her, revealing innocent bits and pieces with the goal of making his background more palatable. He figured it'd be easier to swallow if he doled it out in small bites. This time he'd mentioned the teasing he'd been subjected to as a boy due to his impaired speech and how that led to his first schoolyard fight. He was nervous about how she might react to the violence, but if they were to share a future together, he'd have to eradicate the secrets between them sometime. Might as well test the water.

He strode up the walk and clasped the door handle. Taking care to keep the hinges quiet in case the story was still in progress, he slipped inside. He didn't hear Eden's clear voice dramatizing Black Beauty's tale, nor the buzz of childish enthusiasm. They must have finished early.

Levi hung his hat on the hall tree and wandered into the reading room. He searched for Eden.

Odd. She wasn't at her desk. He didn't see her near the shelves either. "Eden," he called. "Are you here?"

A tiny creak echoed at the far side of the room. Levi turned to find the kitchen door slightly ajar. "Eden?"

The door inched open a bit farther, then all at once it flung wide. "Mr. Grant! Oh, Mr. Grant, you have to help me. I don't know what to do."

"Chloe?"

The girl burst into the room and sprinted toward him, stopping just short of a collision. “Verna and Harvey took the afternoon off to visit some friends outside of town, and Miss Eden begged me not to leave. But I’m worried about her. She was so upset.”

The girl wasn’t making any sense. “What happened?”

Chloe’s lip trembled and her eyes shimmered with unshed tears. “It’s ’cause of me. That’s why they didn’t come. I told her I’d leave, that I never meant to cause her no problems. But she begged me to stay. Said she couldn’t bear it if I left her, too. Said she needed me. What am I s’posed to do, Mr. Grant? Is it better for me to stay or to go?”

Levi took the book from beneath his arm and set it on Eden’s desk. He gently clasped her upper arms. “Abide, Chloe.”

“A-what?” She scrunched up her nose as if the word smelled funny.

“Abide. Remain. Linger.” Levi rolled his eyes toward the ceiling. This would be so much easier if he could just say *stay*. His lisp was a blasted nuisance.

Finally simplicity found its way onto his tongue. "Don't go."

"You sure?" she asked, but her body sagged with relief in his hold. "The kids might come back if I left."

The children? That's who hadn't come? He closed his eyes as a deep ache radiated through him. *Eden*.

Levi opened his eyes and focused a firm stare on Chloe. "You need to be here."

He couldn't have her running off to who knew where—or worse, back to the saloon. Eden wouldn't want that, either. Levi waited until Chloe nodded her assent before he released her.

"What about Miss Eden?"

"I'll find her." As he spoke, he strode out to the hall and grabbed his hat. Chloe's footsteps followed him. "Do you have any idea where . . . Eden went?" he asked as he headed for the door.

"No. All she said was that she needed some time by herself and not to wait supper on her."

Levi set his jaw. "I'll find her."

"Good." She held the door for him as he exited to the porch.

He scanned the area, not finding anyone resembling Eden. He itched to begin the search, but before he could get his feet to walk down the path, he cast a final stern look at Chloe.

She seemed to understand his meaning, for she stood a bit taller, lifting her chin. "Don't worry," she said. "I'll be here when you get back."

Levi nodded to Chloe, then marched down the walk. He heard her latch the door and prayed that she would indeed stay put.

He paused at the edge of the street, turning his head in both directions. Where would Eden have gone? His first instinct was to look for her at Emma Cranford's place. But if she truly wanted to be alone, she wouldn't have sought out her friend. So where else?

Eden would be on foot since Harvey and Verna took the buggy. She couldn't have gone far, but he had no idea where to start. He rubbed a hand over his face and closed his eyes once again.

She shouldn't have to carry this bur-

den by herself, Lord. Let me help her. Show me where to look.

Instead of opening his eyes, Levi searched his memory for clues. He thought back over the letters she had written, the talks they'd had. Nothing resonated.

Unable to stand still any longer, he sent one last plea heavenward for guidance, then started walking away from town. It would be hard for her to be alone when surrounded by neighbors, after all.

He passed the church and continued along the rutted road, heading northeast. The schoolhouse rose in the distance, and Levi slowed his step. Would she have come this way? Surely seeing the school would only remind her of the children who had failed to appear at the library. Why cause herself more pain?

Levi kicked at a stone along the edge of the road in frustration. It skipped and rolled over the dirt and yellowed prairie grass until it thumped into the trunk of a sweet gum tree.

Why won't you help me? Levi's heart

railed at God. Hadn't God led him to Chloe when she needed assistance? Why not Eden? God was supposed to work all things together for good for those who loved him. But what was good about this? Eden opened her home to Chloe and lost what she held most dear. Where was the justice in that?

He growled and kicked another stone, harder this time. It sailed off the toe of his boot and ricocheted off the same tree.

Eden had agreed to take Chloe into her home because he asked her to. He'd pushed her. This was his fault. He had to fix it. Had to make it right somehow.

Tearing his gaze away from the tree, Levi trudged forward a few more steps. As he moved, however, a flash of color tugged at his peripheral vision. He glanced back at the sweet gum. There beneath its branches grew a clump of dandelions, their cheerful hue a testimony to the onset of spring.

Spring . . . Wildflowers . . .

Thank you, Lord.

He knew where to go. Levi swung toward the south and spotted a rise with a solitary oak standing guard at the top. Lone Oak Hill. The other day in Eden's yard, Harvey had mentioned her fondness for wildflowers and the piece of property her father had purchased for her. It was a retreat of sorts, a place to escape.

Levi left the road and set off across the open fields, stretching his stride. His boots crunched against the twigs and low-lying brush that covered the area, but except for dodging the occasional mesquite, he kept his path aimed straight for the tree on the hill—and the woman waiting on the other side.

Eden's breath hitched as she inhaled, the pain in her chest marking the death of her dream. Swiping her crushed, damp hankie beneath her nose, she gazed out over the pastureland and tried to imagine the riot of color that would emerge in a few weeks. All she saw, however, were clumps of dead grass and naked branches. Where was the hope of new buds, the promise that beauty would triumph over desolation? She'd come here seeking comfort, but the barrenness only intensified her grief.

She needed to go. She'd cried enough tears. Chloe would be worried. If the girl was still there.

Eden wrapped her arms around her middle and rocked back and forth, a moan vibrating in her throat. Her bones ground against the rock beneath her with each backward tilt, as if to emphasize her inability to escape the pain. Why had Verna chosen today to go visiting? She needed someone to lean on, someone to hold her and tell her everything was going to be all right. Someone to care.

"Eden?"

She jerked her head around, her throbbing heart leaping at the familiar voice. Her blacksmith. She didn't know how he'd found her, and frankly, she didn't care. All that mattered was that he'd come when she needed him most.

With a tiny cry, Eden jumped from

her rocky perch and threw herself against Levi's chest. The tears she'd thought had been exhausted returned with a vengeance. Starving for comfort, for a sympathetic touch, she sobbed in gratitude as much as in grief when his arms folded around her back.

"I'm here, darlin'," he crooned, caressing her hair and laying a kiss atop her head. "I'm here."

He was so warm and strong. Eden longed to melt into him and forget all her worries. His hands rubbed long strokes along her back, soothing her like he would a restless mare that needed a shoe. The technique worked. His deep voice rolled through her, unclenching the tightness in her stomach, and soon her sobs dwindled into hiccups.

She dabbed at her face with her handkerchief but couldn't bring herself to step away. As if he sensed her need, Levi scooped her into his arms and carried her back to the rock she used for sitting. But instead of depositing her there, he tucked her closer and sat down with her in his lap. He didn't say anything, just held her. And it was perfect.

Once her breathing resumed a deep and even rhythm, Levi broke the silence. “Want to talk about it?”

She tipped her chin up to look at him, and he smiled in encouragement. Then he ran his finger around the edge of her face, collecting loose hairs the wind had pulled free from her pins and placing them gently behind her ear. A tremor ran through Eden at his touch, the concern in his storm-gray eyes only heightening the sensation. This was a man she could trust—a man who could keep her safe, even from heartache.

“I should have expected something was amiss when Hattie Fowler suddenly volunteered to host the Ladies Aid meeting at her home last night.” Eden sniffed and lifted her balled-up hankie to her nose.

Levi shifted his position for a moment, then tugged the soiled linen from her hand and replaced it with a clean cotton square.

“Thank you,” she said.

He nodded, and Eden found herself

suddenly wanting to smile. How often had she silently castigated him for that nod, thinking him dim-witted, when first they met? Now the gesture was so dear to her, she preferred it to a worded reply.

"For the last few years, the ladies have met at my house because of the larger rooms. Then yesterday, Emma stopped by to tell me that Hattie felt they had been imposing on my hospitality too long and decided to hold the meetings in her parlor for the next several months. I assumed her change of heart had something to do with the run-in she had with Violet, but I thought she was just uncomfortable. I didn't imagine she'd spread the story to everyone in town, warning mothers to keep their children away from the library for fear of the bad influence Chloe might have on impressionable minds."

Levi stiffened, the tension in his muscles palpable.

"I know," she said. "It makes me angry, too."

"Maybe with time . . ."

Eden sighed. "Maybe, but I'll not pin my hopes on it."

She fell quiet. The soothing motion of Levi's chest expanding and contracting eased her sorrow. His right arm supported her shoulders, and his fingers drew lazy circles on her sleeve above her elbow. A new emotion rose in her, something fluttery and light, with a warmth that permeated all the corners of her heart. Then his left hand cupped her chin and lifted her face to meet his gaze. For one delicious, completely irrational moment, Eden thought he would kiss her. And she wanted that kiss. More than anything.

But sanity returned as he began speaking to her instead.

"I'm . . . I regret . . . the trouble you're having." He frowned and Eden could almost see his mind scrambling for the right words. "I really didn't think anything bad would happen. I thought you would be a good . . . model for Chloe and that the girl would feel . . . inviolable in your home." He glanced away for a second, then drew in a deep breath and directed his gaze back toward hers. "I never meant for you to get hurt. Forgive me?"

"Oh, Levi. There's nothing to forgive." Eden pulled back to look him more fully in the face and propped her hand on his shoulder. His very wide, muscular shoulder. Determined not to get distracted by her growing awareness of his masculinity, she banished the ill-timed observation and focused again on their conversation.

"When you brought Chloe to me that night, I resisted at first because of fear and selfishness. But then you challenged me, and it was as if scales fell from my eyes, revealing my true nature. I am the only daughter of a wealthy man. I've never been in need. In fact, I've been indulged most of my life. I thought I was righteous because of the causes I supported and the moral life I lived, but with Chloe sitting in my parlor, the Lord laid a new conviction on my heart.

"Jesus' love led him to a cross. What had I sacrificed for him in return? I had given money, but I had plenty, so that was no hardship. I had given time when

I volunteered at the orphanage and opened my home to the Ladies Aid group. But that cost very little. My love for God must be shallow indeed if I was loath to help a child just because I feared for my reputation. How could I claim to be a living sacrifice if I was unwilling to lay anything of value on the altar?"

Levi dropped his chin. "You humble me."

"You humbled me first." The irony made her smile. "The Lord knows I needed it." His head shot up and shook in vigorous protest, but she cut him off before he could say anything. "God spoke to me through you, Levi. You were his instrument. And I thank you."

Silence fell over them again, but it carried more peace with it this time. Eden gazed out across the fields, and suddenly the landscape didn't seem so barren. She could envision the places the bluebonnets would bloom and see the sunrise colors of the Indian paintbrush in her mind. Though she hated to leave the shelter of Levi's arms, the time had come. She'd absorbed enough of his strength to stand on her own.

When she pulled away from him, he moved with her and helped her to her feet. He stayed close, as if he shared her reluctance to separate.

"I'm going to miss reading to the children," Eden said, a touch of wistfulness lingering in her tone, "seeing their faces light up with interest and intelligence as the story unfolds, being a part of their lives. I probably needed them more than they needed me over the last few years. Yet even though my heart grieves the loss, I can see new purpose lying ahead. God directed me to Chloe, and I won't let pain over the past inhibit me from meeting the future."

Eden gazed out over her field one more time, then turned to look up into her blacksmith's face. "There's just one thing I must do first, before I can completely let it go." She tentatively touched Levi's sleeve. "Come with me?"

Chapter Twenty-Five

Awareness passed through Levi at the touch of Eden's fingers upon his arm. Go with her? The earth would have to open beneath his feet to stop him.

He nodded his answer, and a smile blossomed across her face with all the glory of a rainbow emerging after a storm. Such a remarkable woman. And one he wanted so badly to claim as his own.

Stepping away from him, she bent to retrieve a small drawstring bag from the far edge of the rock where they'd been sitting. She clutched it lightly to her chest, then pointed to a trail that curved between two large oak trees.

"We can go this way. It winds around to the north, up past the schoolhouse, where we'll meet the road that leads back to town."

He held out his arm to her as she neared. She glanced at his face in silent question, then lowered her lashes against pinkening cheeks and slid her left hand into the crook of his arm. An unexpected surge of possessiveness stabbed through him as he matched his stride to hers. It felt so right, having her at his side—like she belonged there.

As they passed between the two oaks that stood like natural posts to an invisible gate, an idea began to take shape in Levi's mind. The trees were smaller than the one atop the hill, but the two little ladies were elegant in their own right. They grew too far apart for their branches to form a canopy. However, he could easily aid their efforts. Some scrolled ironwork, a decorative arch, botanic details fitting for a woman who loved flowers . . .

"You should see this place once spring is fully upon us," Eden said, breaking Levi's train of thought. "Wildflowers cover this field like a rainbow touching the earth."

"Harvey told me you like to come here."

She smiled at him again, and Levi doubted any wildflower could match Eden in beauty.

"So that's how you knew where to find me." Her eyes shone, still a little red around the edges from her tears, but happiness glowed in their depths now. Happiness he had a part in putting there. Happiness he hoped to keep there always. If she'd let him.

"My father bought this property for me two years ago for my twenty-fifth birthday. See that clearing over there?" She pointed to a spot about a hundred yards to the south. "I'd like to build a house there someday. One with a big plate-glass window in the front so I can sip my tea and watch the flowers grow."

Eden leaned into his side as she stepped around a hole dug by a ground squirrel or some other burrowing creature, and Levi couldn't help but picture himself behind that same window, moving up behind Eden to touch his lips to the sensitive skin along her neck.

She'd smile and ask about his day. He'd wrap his arms around her and say that the best part of it was coming home. Then perhaps a little girl with reddish curls and moss-green eyes would run into the room, call him *Daddy*, and latch on to his leg. He'd swing her high into the air and laugh at her delighted squeals.

"It wouldn't be anything as grand as my father's house in town," Eden said. "Just a cozy little cabin where I could escape every now and again. I don't think I could reside here all year. Not by myself, anyway. I'd be too nervous so far from town."

She cast a slow glance at him, and his heart hit his ribs like a sledge against the anvil. Was she hinting at something? Or just making conversation? Either way, he'd gladly volunteer to keep her company.

Levi cleared his throat. "A cabin out

here would be ni . . . um . . . inviting. A pretty location."

"I've always thought so." Her focus shifted from his face back to the ground, but the shy smile that lingered on her lips did odd things to his insides.

The path led them around Eden's field and over the east side of Lone Oak Hill. Occasionally she would point out a place where a particular wildflower grew and tell him about it—what time of year it was most likely to bloom, its color and shape, whether or not it had a strong fragrance. She chattered about how she would carry her small flower press out to the fields several times during the year to search for the perfect blooms to cut and press for her collection.

She continued to ramble on about her flowers as they walked, not minding that the conversation was markedly one-sided. He appreciated that about her. Since they'd started exchanging letters, she seemed less flustered by his limited speech. She didn't look at him with disdain or patronize him by trying to finish his sentences for him as others were apt to do. She simply waited patiently for him to spit out his words, and that acceptance made communication much less burdensome.

It was easy to imagine a life spent with this woman.

They met up with the main road and before long came upon the schoolhouse. Eden veered toward it, releasing his arm to take the lead. Curious about her intent, Levi followed her into the yard, where the wind pushed a pair of vacant rope swings and an abandoned seesaw plank tilted over a log. The place looked somewhat eerie without the children playing there. It must have been devastating for her to wait, book on lap, for those same kids to pour into her library, only to have them never show up.

Perhaps she felt the need to try to reason with the teacher, to explain about Chloe. Or maybe she felt compelled to express her displeasure over the matter. It would certainly be within her right to do so, though he had a hard time picturing her haranguing the schoolmarm. Especially since Eden seemed to have made peace with the situation.

Instead of walking up the front steps, Eden skirted around the outside until she reached a small room protruding from the main building. Levi hung back as she climbed the three steps to the stoop and knocked on the door.

A young woman answered. "Miss Spencer." The name came out on a squeak, and a guilty flush stained the teacher's cheeks. "I'm so sorry about what happened. I truly am. I tried to talk them out of their decision, but Mrs. Fowler is on the school board and she threatened my position if I didn't abide by their wishes."

The flustered woman reached for Eden's hand but then seemed to realize a pencil was still woven through her fingers. She fluttered about for a bit like a bird that couldn't choose where to land, then stabbed the writing utensil through the thick knot of hair atop her head, leaving the end to protrude like a stiff Indian feather. Having freed her hands, she captured one of Eden's between her palms.

"I was told to inform the children that there would be no more trips to the library for stories, that we would spend the time in our McGuffey readers instead. None of the children were happy about it, I can tell you, but they knew better than to cross their parents."

"Please don't fret, Miss Albright." Eden gently extricated her hand only to place it comfortingly upon the teacher's arm. "I don't blame you for any of this. That's not why I came."

"Then why are you here?" The woman darted a glance over to Levi, only now realizing Eden wasn't alone. Her eyes widened. He smiled and put a finger to the brim of his hat, but she continued staring, as if she expected him to huff and puff and blow the schoolhouse down around her ears. He was tempted to pucker up just to see what she would do but restrained the impulse.

Eden released Miss Albright's arm to

stretch open the top of her drawstring bag, and the movement successfully regained the teacher's attention. "I came to bring you this."

A book. With a very familiar cover.

"We were so close to the end," Eden said, handing her copy of *Black Beauty* to Miss Albright. "I hate for the children to be left hanging. Would you read the remainder of the story to them sometime next week? I've marked our place with a scrap of ribbon."

Miss Albright moved slowly to accept the book, her eyes searching Eden's face.

But Eden's smile remained fixed, giving no hint to the upheaval he knew must be going on inside her.

"That is very kind of you, Miss Spencer. The children will be delighted, I'm sure." Miss Albright lowered her gaze as she ran her hand over the illustrated cover.

"We had also been discussing our next selection." Eden bit her lip as if to stem her emotion. Levi took a step closer but stopped when she pasted her smile back into place as the teacher raised her head. "If you would like to continue to read to the children, I would be happy to loan you whichever books you would like."

"I . . . um . . ." Miss Albright dropped her chin.

"If you don't feel comfortable coming by the library, you can mention a title to me at church, and I'll see you get it." Eden hesitated. Miss Albright fiddled with the pencil stuck in her hair, her eyes still downcast. "Or you could send a message through Mrs. Cranford if that would be easier for you."

Finally the teacher looked Eden in the face. "Forgive me for being so timid, Miss Spencer. It's just that I can't afford to lose my position. With my father ailing, my family depends on the income I can send them."

"I understand. But the school board doesn't disapprove of the books themselves, only the people whom one might come in contact with while at the library. So if we take the library out of the equation and work through Mrs.

Cranford, they shouldn't be inclined to raise any objections."

Miss Albright appeared to find her backbone, for she straightened her posture and gave Eden a sharp nod. "You're right. The children shouldn't be kept from being exposed to literature simply because their parents don't approve of the person who dusts the shelves where it is kept. I'll be looking for you in church, Miss Spencer."

Levi wanted to pump his fist toward the sky over the small but pivotal victory. Instead, he waited for Eden to bid Miss Albright a good day, then handed her down from the stoop, squeezing her fingers and sharing a smile with her as they headed back to town.

There would be people who disparaged not only Eden's decision to keep Chloe under her roof but her character, as well. Levi had no illusions in that regard. Yet as he tucked her hand into the crook of his arm, he vowed to do all he could to soften the sting of the coming barbs. A man protected his woman, after all. And Lord willing, one day Eden *would* be his.

Later that evening, Eden sat at the desk in her bedroom, penning a letter to her father. As usual, she updated him on the local happenings—the latest Ladies Aid projects, town council issues, social news, and church activities. Taking pains to ensure her report didn't read like a gossip column, she reiterated only the facts, allowing her father to draw his own conclusions.

When she scraped the nib across the stationery to confess her part in the library scandal, her habit of keeping things factual helped her contain her emotions. In as rational a manner as possible, she outlined her reasons for encouraging Chloe to stay and the ramifications that followed. Her pulse fluttered as she concluded the telling.

She'd always hated disappointing her father. When she'd been seven, she ruined his razor by using it to trim the rosebushes in her mother's garden. The look he gave her when he found out nearly crushed her soul. No whipping was needed. Her torture was already complete. She never wanted to see that look on his face again. That's probably why she stayed with Stephen so long, even when, deep down, she knew he didn't love her. She'd rather have gone through with the wedding than disappoint her father. Thankfully, he'd saved her from herself—although, in the end, she'd still been a disappointment, at least according to her mother.

Would Daddy approve of her choice to keep Chloe? Or would he be upset at the scandal it was causing? After all, it was his house, not hers, that was sheltering a young woman from the saloon.

Eden took a deep breath and twisted in her chair to focus on the photograph of her parents in the frame beside her bed. Her father's eyes sparkled as he gazed out over the room. Mother would be in a dither over this mess, for certain, but something told Eden her daddy would understand.

Turning forward again, her mind drifted to another man who understood, whose stalwart support had comforted her in a way not even her father could match.

Eden reached for another piece of paper and dipped her pen into the ink. She paused, letting the penholder lean against the side of the inkstand. Her feelings were new and a bit frightening as she considered leaving herself vulnerable to another possible heartbreak, but they'd grown too deep for her to ignore.

Should she keep the news to herself and wait to see how things played out with Levi, or should she solicit her father's blessing and advice?

Levi appeared to be everything she wanted in a man. He was a man of faith, he loved literature, and rarest of all, he shared her views on violence and aggression. What man could be more perfect? A year ago, she would never have believed it possible, but she trusted him. Completely. And so far he'd lived up to all her expectations. When he'd held her today out at the field, her heart had recognized the truth—she was in love with Levi Grant.

Swallowing the last of her uncertainty, Eden took hold of the pen and set it to paper.

Daddy, I've met a man. . . .

Chapter Twenty-Six

The following Tuesday evening, Levi sat sideways on his bed surrounded by balls of crumpled paper. He read over his latest attempt and moaned. No matter how he tried, he couldn't seem to find the wording that would allow him to reveal another part of his past without completely alienating the woman he loved. Closing his eyes, he banged the back of his head against the wall.

In his last two letters, he managed to make his violent beginnings palatable by sugarcoating them in the innocence of childhood. And Eden had swallowed them. She'd written about her experience with the boys in her reading group and how she'd caught them reenacting a battle scene outside her home after story hour one afternoon. They'd been sword fighting as pirates until one boy's stick missed. Instead of crossing with his opponent's sword, it lashed the bigger boy across the face. Retaliation ensued until she'd been forced to send Harvey out to break up the scuffle.

She'd gone on to reassure him that she thought no less of him for his childhood antics. What mattered to her was that he'd had the maturity and insight to grow out of those aggressive tendencies. Unlike other men.

If only she knew.

And therein lay the problem. If she knew the truth, chances were good she'd never again look at him the same way. She'd not run into his arms for comfort as she had in the field. She'd probably run in the opposite direction. Instead of seeing his strength as protection, she'd see it as a weapon. What if she came to fear him? He couldn't bear that.

Would it really be dishonest to withhold his past? Surely there were things about her that he didn't know. Why reveal something that would only kill the feelings that were growing between them? What good would that accomplish? He could tell her later. After their love was secure and deep. After marriage bound her to him. Maybe after they'd had a child and fortified their ties.

Coward.

Levi winced. He was afraid to lose her. Afraid that choosing God's way would mean forfeiting a life with the only woman he'd ever loved.

Was this how Abraham felt when God asked him to sacrifice his son? Did his feet drag as he trudged up the mountain? Did his resolve weaken as he tightened the ropes on Isaac's wrists? Did his hand shake as he raised the knife? Or was his trust in God so complete that fear had no hold on him?

I want to trust you, like Abraham did. Give me the courage to step out in faith. A sense of certainty filled him, cutting through his fear to convict his heart. *You are the God of truth, and if I am to be your follower, I, too, must walk in truth.*

Levi opened the oak lap desk he'd borrowed from Georgia Barnes and pulled out another sheet of stationery. Knowing what he had to do, he dipped his pen into the ink and set the nib to paper.

Sweat beaded on his forehead as he wrote. A drop rolled into his eye, the salt stinging the inner corner. He rubbed at it with the tail of his shirt and immediately returned to writing. As if his soul were purging, he poured himself onto the page. Telling her everything. About rejecting his family in favor of quick money and counterfeit respect. About the thrill he found in being the best, the strongest, the victor. About the man he unintentionally sent to meet his Maker with a mighty right jab. About being sentenced to two years in prison for involuntary manslaughter.

That wasn't all that flowed from his soul, however. He also wrote of how the horrors of the Huntsville labor camps humbled him. How he rediscovered his faith through the influence and teachings of a prison chaplain. How he rededicated his life to following God and made a vow never to raise a fist against another human being again.

He made no excuses. But he did plead for understanding.

Levi closed the letter by sharing with Eden the regret he felt over betraying his family. The lesson had nearly destroyed him, but he'd learned it well. He would never turn his back on a loved one again. Never.

By the time he finished, night had dipped into the wee hours of morning. He set the six written pages aside and collapsed onto the length of the bed. He'd purged himself of the past. Only time would tell if he'd forfeited his future.

Wednesday morning found Eden and Chloe sitting around the reading room desk, part of their new routine. During library hours, Verna tutored Chloe in the culinary arts and had the girl help her with the cleaning and household errands in order to avoid any unpleasant encounters with patrons. Although Eden had started wondering why they bothered. They hadn't had a single visitor outside of Levi all week. But maybe with time things would return to normal. Meanwhile, Eden used the morning hours to instruct the girl in reading, writing, and sums.

Chloe absorbed the lessons like the sand soaked up the tide—little by little. She loved to listen to stories but struggled to read them herself. Her spelling and penmanship . . . Well, they offered much opportunity for improvement. And the only way Eden could get her to do sums was to use a ledger and fill it with pretend wages from her imagined employment at the café. Having had little to no schooling in the past, learning did not come easily to Chloe, but she wanted so badly to improve herself that once she realized the practicality of a skill, she threw herself into the task with dogged determination.

"I don't see how readin' the Bible is gonna help me read recipes or a menu. Shouldn't I be practicin' on a cookbook or something?" Chloe looked up from the pages in front of her and frowned.

"There is more to be gained from reading than simply an improved proficiency in recognizing words. Reading has the power to shape one's mind. And there is no better book than that one for mind shaping."

Chloe grumbled under her breath but dutifully returned her attention to the gospel of John. Borrowing a primer from Miss Albright would have been easier for the girl, but Eden hoped the exposure to God's Word would plant some seeds in Chloe's heart. With all the uncertainty surrounding the young lady's present circumstances and future prospects, she needed something firm to hold on to—something like faith.

After a few minutes, Chloe raised her head. "That Jesus feller was pretty smart, getting them to drop those stones like that."

"I thought you might like that story." Eden jotted a final number in Chloe's ledger. "Did you notice how he forgave the adulteress instead of condemning her? God is more interested in showing mercy and giving people a second chance than in pointing fingers and reminding them of all they've done wrong."

"Except for them rock-toters."

Eden smiled. "You're right. Those *rock-toters* were the religious leaders and should have known better. They were so busy trying to prove themselves righteous, they forgot to show love. Jesus had to remind them that they weren't as perfect as they thought they were."

"You think he'll ever get around to remindin' the folks around here?"

"I imagine he will, in his own way." Eden wrapped an arm around Chloe's hunched shoulders. "It might be hard for a while, Chloe, but not everyone in Spencer shares Mrs. Fowler's opinion. You've got me and Verna and women like Emma Cranford on your side, and if you'll ever see your way to coming to church with us, I bet you'd find there are more, as well. Georgia Barnes, for one. She and Claude are the couple Mr. Grant is staying with, and I doubt you could find two more kindhearted people. I have faith the others will come around in time. Even Hattie Fowler."

"I ain't so sure about that, but I'm tired of hidin' away when I ain't done nothin' to be ashamed of." She shrugged away from Eden's hold and straightened her spine. "Maybe I *will* go to services with you. It'd do all those old biddies right to have to drop their rocks for a while. People in God's house ain't supposed to throw stones, you know."

Eden bit her tongue to keep her amusement contained. The saying had more to do with glass houses than the Lord's house, but the same principle applied, she supposed. And while there would certainly be an abundance of horrified looks and ruffled feathers at first, Eden could think of no better way to help the townsfolk grow accustomed to Chloe's new position in their society. Plus it had the added benefit of exposing the girl to more spiritual teachings. David Cranford's sermons had a way of pricking hearts and encouraging weary souls. Perhaps between the two of them, they could scatter enough seed for something to take root.

"You know what we should do?" Eden closed the ledger she'd been preparing sums in and smiled at Chloe. "Go shopping."

Chloe's brows rose so high they nearly disappeared into her hair. "Shopping? Instead of sums?"

"Every lady needs a Sunday bonnet to wear to church. I think I recall seeing one or two in the mercantile that would look lovely on you."

Chloe's face fell a little. "You think Miz Fowler will sell one to me?"

"She sold groceries and supplies to you on behalf of the saloon when you ran errands, didn't she?"

"Yeah . . ."

"Well then. We don't have anything to worry about, do we? Besides, I'll be the one making the purchase for my new employee, so we'll have leverage. The Spencer name carries some weight around here. Might as well use it to our advantage."

Chloe nibbled on her lower lip. "You sure?"

"Absolutely." Eden pushed to her feet, tapping the ledger with the end of her pencil. "We still have forty minutes before I need to open the library, so it's either shopping or arithmetic. What's your choice?"

"Shopping." Chloe jumped up from the desk, a sparkle in her eye. "Facing Miz Fowler hurts less than doing all them sums!"

Eden burst into laughter.

The two were still smiling when they entered the dry goods store. Hattie Fowler, however, was not. Eden pretended not to notice the shopkeeper's sour face, choosing to wave and greet her with a cheerful hello before shepherding Chloe to the corner where dress goods and sewing notions were stored.

They tried on several hat styles and settled on a simple straw bonnet with an upturned brim and a wide blue ribbon decorated with a small spray of white flowers.

"This will match your blue calico

quite nicely, don't you think?" Eden asked as Chloe took it from her head and handed it into her keeping.

"You sure this one wouldn't be better?" Chloe plopped a pink behemoth covered in ostrich plumes onto her head and struck a pose that set Eden to giggling. The hat stood a good foot above the girl's head, threatening to swallow her whole. "Or maybe this one." Chloe replaced the feathered headpiece with one sporting a bright yellow bird of indistinct heritage perched amid an array of silk leaves and chenille pompons protruding from either side. When Chloe starting whistling and flapping her hands like bird wings, tears pooled in Eden's eyes from the hilarity of it all.

"Stop it," Eden whispered hoarsely as mirth continued to tickle her throat. "You're going to get us into trouble." She peeked around a display of lace trim to find Hattie scowling in their direction. But for once in her life, she didn't care. She couldn't remember the last time she'd felt so young and carefree. Being with Chloe was like having a little sister, and Eden treasured the joy of the moment.

They managed to restrain themselves under Mrs. Fowler's disapproving looks while she completed their transaction and placed Chloe's new hat in a bandbox. But when they exited to the boardwalk and spotted a yellow-bodied warbler sitting on the hitching post, the two looked at each other and dissolved into another round of laughter.

"Bless me soul, if it ain't a couple o' heather pixies come all the way from Scotland to brighten me mornin'," a strapping young man addressed them from the street, dragging his wool cap off his head to reveal a shock of bright red hair. The man glanced briefly at Eden, but his attention quickly veered to Chloe and remained there, a light of fond familiarity warming his expression. "Me name's Duncan, miss. Duncan McPherson. I'd be honored to carry that package for you."

Chloe blushed prettily and lowered her lashes with a shyness at odds with her usual bold, plainspoken manner. Eden looked from one to the other. She could have sworn the two knew each other by the way he'd looked at Chloe and the way she edged closer to him, a hint of a smile playing on her lips. Yet Mr. McPherson had introduced himself as if they were strangers.

"Thank you, sir. That's very kind of you."

Eden's brows shot up as Chloe handed the bandbox to the young man, who vaulted up to the boardwalk to accept it. Usually the girl went out of her way to avoid men, but something about this McPherson fellow was different. He treated her as a gentleman did a lady, even though it seemed this was not his first encounter with her. Chloe needed the normalcy of being accepted, of being appreciated. And what could be more normal than a sixteen-year-old girl flirting and stepping out with a handsome young man on a well-traveled street?

"Chloe? If you feel comfortable with Mr. McPherson's escort, I'll allow him to see you back to the library while I pay a call at the smithy."

Eden carefully gauged the girl's reaction. Any hint of reluctance and she would immediately rescind the offer. But the girl fairly glowed with delight.

"Perhaps I can save Mr. Grant a trip by collecting the book myself that he had planned to bring in today."

"Chloe." McPherson whispered the word in a near-reverent tone. "All these months, I had wondered." He gazed into her face. "'Tis a bonny name. For a bonny lass." He offered his arm, and with a happy flush, Chloe accepted.

Eden watched the two walk several steps, wondering if she should follow. Then Chloe glanced over her shoulder, her wide smile giving Eden all the assurance she needed. They would be fine. More than fine, if she didn't miss her guess.

Grinning, Eden strolled down the street in the opposite direction. As she neared the smithy, her stomach fluttered, much as she imagined Chloe's had done a few moments earlier.

Levi. She never dreamed she'd find a man so perfect. He wasn't wealthy, he didn't come from a politically connected family, but none of that mattered. She'd be proud to walk on his arm anywhere, even at one of her mother's events.

Lost in her thoughts, she neglected to call out to him as she picked her way around the forge. A splashing sound drew her to the rear of the shop.

Ornery came out to meet her, and she stopped to pat his head and rub his ears. "Hey, boy. Where's Levi?" she asked in a low voice. The dog turned and bounded toward the back corner. Eden followed until she cleared the far side of the forge. The sight that greeted her stole her breath.

Levi stood at the washstand, stripped to the waist. The damp hair at his neck glistened and curled, tempting Eden to see for herself if the strands really would wind themselves about her fingers. But even that thick sable hair couldn't distract her from the impressive display of male musculature before her. Levi rubbed a towel over his chest, the tiny scrap seeming woefully inadequate for the task. Eden's mouth went dry. He lifted the rag to his head briefly, then moved it to his back, his movements growing awkward as he tried to reach behind him.

An absurd urge to assist him shot through her. Then the rag moved lower, exposing more of his skin, and a new sensation washed over her. Sorrow.

Puckered skin glared at her, the remains of deep welts, where the flesh had been ripped and torn. Thick white lines crisscrossed over his back. Up and down. Side to side. One upon the other. Her own back ached as if trying to share in the pain of the lashes he had suffered. Tears welled in Eden's eyes.

"Levi," she moaned. "What happened to you?"

Chapter Twenty-Seven

Levi spun around.

"Eden?" he croaked. For a moment he just stared at her, shock dulling his brain. Then he noticed her chin dip and her lashes lower over her eyes, and all at once reason returned. He snatched his clean shirt from the peg on the wall and thrust his arms into the sleeves as he twisted away from her.

The stubborn buttons refused to go through their holes. Levi's thick fingers fumbled over the simple task. Blasted things. Why couldn't he button the stupid shirt?

Because she had seen. Levi's fingers halted, and he inhaled a shaky breath. Eden had seen the truth of his past written across his back. All the ugliness he had tried to forget shouted out his mistakes in gruesome detail. He'd thought he'd made his peace with sharing his history with her, but somehow words on a page seemed easier for a person to accept than the blatant testimony of mutilated skin.

Levi's thoughts scattered, though, the instant she touched him. The muscle in his back twitched, but everything inside him stilled as the coolness of her hand penetrated the cotton of his shirt. Levi squeezed his eyes shut, her touch both magic and torture. He held his breath as she traced the ridges between his shoulder blades.

"Who did this to you?" Her voice came out in a broken whisper, and when he finally turned to face her, he saw tears leaking from the corners of her eyes. Tears for him, for his pain.

Tears he didn't deserve. For behind them, he could read the assumptions in her face. She believed he'd been treated unfairly, abused for no reason. And while it was true that the heavy-handed sergeants took pleasure in subjugating the inmates with a harshness that was unjustified, he was far from innocent.

Eden had not withdrawn her hand when he turned, and now it hovered lightly upon the side of his arm. He reached up and covered it with his palm, then brought those precious fingers to his mouth. He laid a kiss on their tips.

"There issth—" He slammed his lips closed. How could he slip like that? Now of all times. As if he wasn't about to give her enough reasons to despise him. Levi bit down on his tongue and breathed through his nose. Back in control, he started again. ". . . much you don't know about me, Eden. My former life."

Deep furrows wrinkled her brow, but she brought her free hand up to his mouth and brushed her fingers over his lips, as if to comfort him for his stumble, as if to prove it didn't repulse her. Tenderness welled up inside him.

He loved this woman—her spunk, her intellect, her tender heart. It was that tender heart he wanted to protect. But he couldn't spare her the hurt he was about to cause, not if there was to be any hope for the two of them sharing a life together. He could only pray for the Lord to speed her healing. And her acceptance.

"I know all I need to know, Levi." The creases on her face smoothed, and she smiled. "You are a gentle, kind man of faith. You work hard and are more generous with your earnings than anyone I know. You—"

"Quit, Eden."

Little frown lines crept back between her eyebrows, and he hated himself for putting them there. But he couldn't stand to listen to her glowing description. It was too tempting to let her keep her delusions. "You *don't* know me, Eden. Not the whole truth, anyway."

"What are you saying?" She bit her lip.

"I've kept particular information hidden from you. Information I didn't want you to learn becau—"

"You . . . you lied to me?"

She tugged her hand free from his grasp, and it felt as though she were pulling his heart from his chest. On instinct, he reached out to her and clasped her upper arm. But she just blinked up at him, like an animal caught in a trap.

"I didn't lie to you, Eden." He chafed her arm, alarmed at the way the color was draining from her face. "But I've done . . . more than one thing in my life that I'm not proud of. And they could have an impact on you if . . . well, if you and I . . ."

Feeling as if he were about to be dragged off to prison all over again, Levi clutched Eden to him and pressed his cheek to her hair. Inhaling deeply, he breathed in the light, flowery scent that always seemed to cling to her. She did not resist his embrace, but neither did she encourage it, and it scared him down to his marrow.

"I care about you, Eden. More than you can fathom," he whispered hoarsely into her hair. "I want to be open with you. I want you to tru . . . er, to believe that you can rely on me, that you can . . . build a future with me."

She said nothing, just stood limp in his arms. A stone sank in Levi's belly. Gently taking her arms in his hands, he laid a kiss on her forehead, then set her away from him. Curling his fingers into fists to keep from reaching for her, he cleared his throat.

"I planned to give you a letter today." He pivoted back toward the washstand and pulled down the book with the bulging cover that sat waiting on the high shelf. When he turned back, he held the book in front of him, not yet extending it to her. "I think the Lord knew I needed to have it ready." Levi glanced up and met Eden's shuttered gaze. He bit back a sigh. "I wrote everything down," he said. "All you need to know."

He willed his hands to move and pushed the book through the tension-filled air between them. She stretched out to receive it, her movements stilted. For a moment the book connected them, but then she drew it toward her, and Levi had to let it go.

Eden stared at the ground, her eyelids shielding her from the man she'd thought she'd known. Whatever tale his letter told, she wasn't going to like it. Of that she was certain.

A shiver crawled over her. She should have brought a shawl. To fight off the chill. But the cold seemed to originate within. Making her numb. She hugged her arms around her middle, not caring that the book bumped against her hip. Not caring about much of anything.

"Eden, I—"

She shook her head. She couldn't bear any more words. Not now. It was as if someone had snuffed the light and left her alone in the dark. Everything once familiar and comforting now had a sinister edge. She could feel disaster lurking, ready to pierce her with its secrets. She had to get away—to find the light again, before the darkness suffocated her.

She retreated a step. Then another. Ornery nudged the back of her leg with his nose and whined. Eden ignored him. Without meeting Levi's gaze, she turned and staggered toward the entrance.

The bright sunlight did nothing to dispel the blackness that had wrapped itself about her heart. Eden rushed past people and shops along the street, seeing nothing more than a dark blur.

Home. She needed to be home.

Her house stood only a block and a half away, yet it seemed an eternity before her feet found the beloved walkway that led to her front porch. As she ascended the steps, the door opened.

"I was just changin' the sign," Verna greeted.

"Put it back." Eden pushed past her housekeeper. "The library's closed today."

"What?"

Eden could feel Verna's eyes on her as she headed for the stairs, but she offered no further explanation. All she could focus on was getting to her room before she completely fell apart.

Chloe waved from the open doorway of her bedroom. She wore her new bonnet and a sunny smile that dimmed as Eden strode by without acknowledging her with more than a glance.

"Miss Eden? What's wrong?"

The girl's voice followed her down the hall, but Eden couldn't have explained even if she wanted to. How could she? Her reaction didn't have an explanation yet. Just emotion. All she knew for certain was that she was about to shatter, and she didn't want anyone around to witness it.

Finally reaching her sanctuary, Eden stepped inside, closed the door, and leaned her back against it. She closed her eyes, squeezing a tear from between her lashes. The droplet rolled down her cheek, tingling against her skin. It came to the edge of her face and dipped under the ledge of her jaw to cling to her throat. Why wouldn't it fall? Why couldn't it just release her and let her be?

Eden scrubbed at it, desperate to remove the feel of it from her skin. But as she scrubbed, more tears fell. She couldn't erase them fast enough. Tremors attacked her legs next, stealing her strength. She wobbled to the bedpost, grabbed it for support, and sank to the mattress. She dropped the book Levi had given her atop the quilt. The cover flopped at the gentle jarring and a packet of folded papers several pages thick bounced into view.

Seeing the familiar ivory stationery brought the chill back to her bones. Her eyes glued to the visible edge of the letter, Eden lowered herself to lie on her side near the book and curled her knees up toward her chest. She clasped the hem of the sateen coverlet and pulled it up over her shoulders, burrowing into its folds. It took several minutes for her shivers to subside, but once the warmth from the bed quilt seeped past her clothes to relax her muscles, she found the courage to reach for Levi's letter.

It took longer to find the courage to open it. She set it on the bed in front of her and traced the line of the fold with her finger.

This was Stephen all over again. She knew it, in the core of her being. Levi might not be abandoning her in order to pursue his fortune, but whatever was in this letter was going to prove that he was not the man she thought him to be. Just as Stephen hadn't been. Only this time the hurt cut far deeper. For unlike Stephen, who had not inspired more than a warm admiration in her, Levi owned her heart. Like a fool, she'd surrendered it to him bit by bit until nothing was left.

A burst of anger erupted inside her. She hated secrets. Hated lies. Hated that the man she thought she loved had hidden things from her. It wasn't fair. Why was she always the one paying the price for the faults of others? Why couldn't a man just be who he appeared to be? Was that so much to ask?

Eden lurched up onto her elbow and grabbed the letter. Enough secrets. Time for the truth.

She waded into Levi's confession, but in a matter of seconds her horrified spirit was drowning. Her lungs burned and her stomach cramped as she struggled to keep her head above the darkness that threatened to sweep her away. Not even in her wildest imaginings could she have predicted such violent atrocities.

Rebellion against his family.

Prizefighting.

Prison.

God help me.

She'd welcomed the attentions of a killer.

Chapter Twenty-Eight

Later that afternoon, Levi closed up shop a few minutes earlier than usual. His concentration hadn't been worth a hill of beans anyhow. If Claude hadn't stopped him with a well-timed question, he would have given the man's new mare five shoes instead of four. Thankfully, his friend just gave him a hard time, accusing him of thinking too much about a certain pretty librarian. While his mind *had* been consumed with thoughts of Eden, it hadn't been memories of her shapely curves or winsome smile that had interfered with his shoeing. No, it'd been the way the compassion in her eyes had dulled to a blank sheen of shock when he'd hinted at his past and the way she ran from him without a word about what she was thinking.

Levi ran a hand down his face as he exhaled a long breath. Surely she'd read his letter by now. How had she reacted? She'd been so upset when she left the smithy, so hurt. The lost look in her eyes would haunt him for days. And she'd hadn't even known the full story at that point. What had the truth done to her?

He wanted to go to her, see how she was faring. Maybe offer to answer her questions. Anything to end this agony of not knowing.

With a grunt, Levi hauled the oversized double doors into place and threaded a chain through their handles and padlocked them together. He trudged down to the library, his heavy heart weighing down his feet. Each step sapped his strength. By the time he reached Eden's porch, he felt as spent as if he'd gone ten rounds with a bruiser.

Glancing heavenward, he sent up a silent plea for God to provide him with the right words and clasped the doorknob. The latch didn't budge. Frowning, he tried again, only to notice the *Closed* sign in the front window. Odd. Eden rarely locked up early.

Levi fought to subdue the trepidation that clawed at his chest. Pulse thrumming, he made a loose fist and knocked on the door. And waited.

Finally the portal opened, and in a rush of last-minute protocol, Levi yanked the hat from his head. Verna Sims peered out at him through the half-opened door.

"Sorry, Mr. Grant. The library's closed today."

It had been closed all day?

Levi crushed the brim of his hat between his fingers as that disheartening piece of information sank in. "I've no need of a book, ma'am," he hurried to get out before she could shut the door. "I've come to pay a call on Eden, if I may."

"Miss Spencer ain't taking callers. You'll have to try back tomorrow." She moved again to close the door, but Levi shoved his boot into the shrinking crack. The housekeeper narrowed her eyes at him. Usually Verna Sims greeted him with friendly banter and an offer of cookies. Yet today, if he'd had a pick, he could have chipped enough ice from her frosty demeanor to chill a vat of lemonade.

He had no idea if the woman knew about the contents of his letter, but one thing was clear—she knew he was somehow responsible for Eden's upset and wasn't about to let him do any further damage.

"Plea—" He shook his head, frustration mounting. "Would you tell her I'm here? I'd like to talk to her, to explain. Make it better, if I can."

Some of the fight seemed to go out of her, and the painful pressure against his foot relaxed as she stopped trying to shove the door against it. "If you can make it better, you'll have my undyin' gratitude."

She opened the door wide and led

him to the parlor, the one where he'd delivered Chloe that night nearly two weeks ago, the one with the framed pressed flowers that he'd never be able to look at without thinking of Eden.

"I ain't never seen her this bad," Verna murmured in a tone that Levi couldn't tell if he was meant to hear or not. "She's been closed in her room all afternoon, ignorin' me *and* Chloe. Harvey tried to coax her out by finding some tiny new buds on the bushes out front to show her, but she wouldn't stir herself to look at 'em." Verna wagged her head and clucked her tongue. "The girl didn't even hole up this bad after that Austin feller up and—" The housekeeper clamped her lips shut and scowled at him as if he'd somehow tricked her into revealing more than she'd intended.

"Wait here while I go ask her."

Verna left and Levi paced.

There'd been a man in Austin? A man as in a paying-court kind of man or more of a business-associate kind of man? And what had he done to upset her? Levi's hands balled into fists as the urge to retaliate on Eden's behalf swelled within him.

Until he realized that whatever that fool in Austin had done hadn't hurt her as much as he had this morning. Levi pulled up short of the north wall and tossed his hat onto the sofa. Releasing a sigh, he unclenched his hands and stared at the miniature garden in the frame in front of him.

Eden and her flowers. He reached up with a finger and lightly stroked the glass over the tiny blooms she had fashioned into a springtime vista complete with painted wood slivers arranged like a picket fence and matching trellis to add a touch of domestication to her wild blossoms. He could sense her joy in the picture as well as her desire to have their beauty close at hand and recalled her dream of building a house in her wildflower field. Her own personal garden of Eden.

Eden's Garden.

That's it! The vague idea he'd been carrying around in his brain of constructing an arched entryway for the space between the two oaks at the edge of Eden's field suddenly crystallized into a concrete design. It had been years since he'd done any ornamental work, but the rest of his skills had returned with little practice. Maybe those would, as well.

It would be the perfect gift. Something large to express the depth of his feelings. Something personal and intimate. Something permanent to symbolize his unchanging love and dedication to her. Perhaps when she saw it, she'd realize the true nature of his heart and start to trust him again.

A throat cleared behind him. Levi spun around.

"She don't want to see you." The housekeeper shrugged. "Sorry."

His spirits deflated a bit, but his new project idea filled him with purpose. He'd fight for their future, even if Eden was too fragile to join him. He'd fight enough for both of them.

"I'll try again tomorrow."

Verna nodded, a glow of respect in her eyes. Levi collected his hat and allowed the housekeeper to show him out.

He might not have made any headway with Eden, but as he strode down the street toward the livery to meet up with Claude, renewed hope brought a lightness to his step. Levi smiled at the sky, thanking God for sparking the idea for that entry arch. Having a project would occupy his thoughts and his hands for the next several days, maybe even weeks, depending on how many embellishments he decided to add. He'd never been good with words, so perhaps it was time to start talking with his hands.

Wednesday rolled into Thursday, which rolled into Friday, which rolled into Saturday. And every evening Levi was met at Eden's door with the same response. She didn't wish to see him. The library remained closed, too, ensuring he couldn't sneak past her defenses.

Yet he was determined to persevere. She needed time, and he'd give it to her, but he would also do everything in his power to prove himself. If that meant being turned away from her door every day for a month, then he and his knock-roughened knuckles would keep coming back until she finally agreed to see him. Jacob worked for seven years to earn Rachel. Eden was worthy of a similar effort.

Levi poured his soul into crafting his gift, spending hours after supper hammering out delicate leaf shapes and welding them to the scrollwork that would comprise the top of the arch. By the time he covered his work with a tarp on Saturday night, the main arch piece had been completed, and Levi was pleased with his progress. Next week he would start on the lettering.

The wagon ride to church on Sunday took a toll on Levi's nerves. As Claude and Georgia chatted amiably on the bench seat above him, Levi sat in the bed with his spine braced against the front board.

Eden had closed the library to avoid seeing him. Would she forgo worship services to accomplish the same task? He doubted it. Her faith would take precedence. The thought of finally seeing her filled him with an anticipation that had his insides as twisted and snarled as a discarded fishing line.

When he entered the building, his gaze gravitated to the pew where Eden usually sat with the Simses. He recognized the back of her Sunday bonnet and the knot of auburn hair beneath it. He willed her to turn, to look his way. Her head never moved. People shuffled around her, visiting with neighbors, but Eden's stiff posture welcomed no conversation.

Not wanting to cause her further distress, Levi hung back, deciding to try approaching her after services. He took his place on the bench beside Claude as the quiet hum of voices died down. The preacher got up to make announcements about those of the community who were ill, the need for donated clothing and household items to replenish the church's poor box, and a reminder about the upcoming Ladies Aid auction to benefit the Spencer school fund.

As the minister invited the congregation to bow their heads in prayer, Eden turned to the tiny woman seated at her right and smiled. It wasn't directed at him, and it was just a small curve of the lips, but it was enough to lift Levi's spirits. When the lady turned to meet Eden's eye, his spirits lifted even higher. Chloe was here. Levi bowed and followed the preacher's prayer while adding his own praise for bringing the young girl out of hiding and asked that she might be welcomed with an air of grace from the people in the pews.

He also couldn't help giving private thanks for the provision of a safe conversation topic to broach with Eden. They both wanted what was best for Chloe. If he focused on that common ground, perhaps Eden would be more willing to open up.

When worship concluded, Levi quietly suggested to Georgia that she might like to meet Chloe, and as he knew she would, the big-hearted woman set off to intercept the child at once. Levi trailed in her wake, his eyes fixed on Eden.

She had on the green dress with the flowery ruffles that she'd worn the first day he'd met her at the preacher's house. She'd seemed so stoic and guarded that day, nothing like the warm, emotional creature he'd come to know over the last weeks. Yet even then he'd felt drawn to her.

The closer they came to the Spencer pew, the more erratic his pulse throbbed. Georgia clasped Chloe's hand and introduced herself. The girl's eyes shot to his, and Levi smiled and nodded encouragement to her. Soon the two were knee-deep in feminine chatter. Well, Georgia did most of the chattering, but Chloe got a few words in every now and then. Eden hovered like a mother hen with a new chick yet said little. And although he stood beside Georgia as part of the group, Eden never once looked at him, a fact he found most frustrating.

Stepping behind Georgia, Levi edged toward Eden. She immediately retreated between the benches and turned her head away from him to fiddle with the ribbon marker protruding from the top of her Bible. Feeling predatory, Levi pursued. How were they to get past this awkwardness if they never spoke to each other? Eden had hidden from him for four days. When iron cooled too long it became hard and unresponsive. If she was ever going to soften, he was going to have to apply some heat.

"Great to find Chloe here." He spoke in a low rumble so the others wouldn't hear and leaned his hip casually against the back of the pew in front of him. "I knew you would be good for her."

She flinched a little at the sound of his voice and kept her face averted.

"Eden," he whispered after glancing around to be sure no one was paying them any heed. "Eden. Look at me." Levi lightly grasped her elbow and tried to tug her around to face him.

"Don't . . ." She resisted the pressure of his hand. "Don't touch me."

Scalded by her words, Levi dropped her arm.

Slowly her chin lifted and rotated toward him. Her lashes swept up, and she finally met his gaze. And as the darts plunged into his chest, he wished she hadn't.

Those beautiful, mossy green eyes of hers overflowed with anguish and disillusionment. But what froze his heart was the hint of disdain she couldn't quite conceal.

She'd made up her mind. It was over.

Chapter Twenty-Nine

Eden bit her lip and fought to keep her tears from falling as she watched Levi exit the church building. He'd not said another word to her after releasing her arm, just looked at her with eyes that mirrored her own agony and backed away.

She'd known it was going to hurt to see him again. That's why she'd avoided the happenstance for as long as possible. She would have pled a headache and stayed in bed this morning, too, if it hadn't been for Chloe. No matter how tempting the prospect of hiding, she couldn't abandon her new friend when she'd finally shown interest in attending services.

Why had Levi betrayed her by pretending to be something he wasn't? Had it all been an act to secure her affections so he could later secure her bank account? Why would God let this happen to her a second time?

And why couldn't she get the pain in his eyes out of her head?

Her heart still yearned for him. Even knowing the truth, a traitorous part of her still longed to feel his arms around her, to feel his lips brushing her hair. But she must remain strong. Levi had purposely misled her. Beneath that gentle exterior lived a brute who had gloried in the violent destruction of other human beings. He couldn't be trusted. And where there was no trust, there could be no love.

The sooner she managed to convince her heart of that fact, the sooner she could put the whole wretched mess behind her.

"My dear Miss Spencer. You're looking lovely today." The sheriff had sneaked up beside her while she'd been woolgathering. As if she didn't have enough man trouble without Conrad Pratt adding to the mix.

"Thank you, Sheriff." Eden tried to discourage further conversation by looking past him to the small cluster of women standing where she'd left Chloe. She meant simply to act as if she were seeking feminine company, but her concern grew genuine when she failed to spot Chloe in their midst.

"Now that the weather's turned warmer," the sheriff was saying, "I thought you might like to go driving this afternoon. I reserved one of the buggies at the livery for us."

Distracted, Eden frowned back at him. "What?"

"How 'bout I pick you up around three?" From his smooth maneuvering of blocking her escape from between the pews, to his pretentious grin, to his slicked-down hair, everything about Conrad Pratt just seemed . . . oily. Eden fought off a shiver.

"Today is not a good day for me, Sheriff. Now, if you'll excuse me, I need to find Chloe." She tried to sidle by, but the bounder refused to remove himself from her path.

"You ran a great risk, taking that little strumpet into your home." His lips were so close to her ear, she could feel the hotness of his breath against the side of her face. She tilted her cheek away from him. "Luckily, most of the townsfolk seem to have decided that your efforts to reform the gal are a sort of pet project and don't hold the association against you. But if I hear word that Vi has paid you another call, I'll have to insist that you get rid of the girl."

She turned to face him, her molars clenched tightly to hold her polite mask in place for the benefit of any who might glance their way. "Insist all you like, Sheriff," she whispered, steel lining her quiet tone, "but I make the decisions for me and my household. Not you. Now get out of my way before I cause a scene guaranteed to wag tongues."

For a second or two, his eyes bored into hers with sharp displeasure. Then all at once, the intensity melted away, and his oily smile slipped back into place. "You're a spirited filly, Eden. I like that. One of these days you'll get used to my hand at the reins and quit your buckin'. For now, though, I'll let you have your head. Just don't go forgettin' who you belong to. Hear me?"

Before she could lash him with a scathing retort about no man owning her, he spun away and clapped Dave Cranford on the shoulder, complimenting the fellow's sermon in a voice that seemed to boom after being so hushed moments earlier.

Navigating her way out from between the pews, Eden sidestepped the sheriff and moved into friendlier territory. Emma Cranford and Georgia Barnes welcomed her into their circle with a smile.

"Did you happen to see where Chloe went?" she asked as soon as the conversation lulled.

Georgia nodded her head toward the door. "I think I saw her follow Levi outside."

Levi.

Eden had no desire to face him again,

stirring up desires and longings that she still hadn't fully suppressed. And after her confrontation with the brash Conrad Pratt, the blacksmith's quiet manner would tempt her even more. Yet her concern for Chloe wouldn't allow her to play the coward. Levi had probably left by now, and she needed to make sure Chloe hadn't been cornered by Hattie Fowler or some other dragon who might be unkind.

Excusing herself from the group, Eden made her way to the door and descended the steps to the churchyard. She squinted against the bright sunlight and held a hand to her stomach to try to master the fluttering within. As she inhaled a steadying breath, she glimpsed the undeniable form of Levi already a dozen or more yards away, trudging past her home on his way to Main Street. Relief mixed with regret inside her. She told herself to quit staring and look for Chloe instead, but she couldn't seem to pry her gaze away from Levi. Then she saw him stop at the pecan tree that marked the corner of her property, and all else slid from her mind.

He didn't look at the house, nor did he look back toward the church. He simply reached out his hand to touch the tree and hung his head. The breadth of his spread fingers nearly spanned the width of the trunk, and for a reason she couldn't explain, Eden felt the gentle pressure against the small of her back as if he were touching her, not the tree.

Agonizing seconds ticked by as he prolonged the moment. Then his hand lifted and balled into a fist. Eden sucked in a breath, an ache stabbing her heart. Here it was—the truth. Levi might seem tender, but his aggressive nature was about to assert itself.

Yet he didn't strike out at the tree in anger or frustration as she expected. No. He simply tapped the pad of his fisted hand against the bark of the tree. Once. Twice. Then he opened his fist as if releasing the last scraps of something precious to float away on the wind.

Eden's legs buckled beneath her,

and she clutched the newel at the bottom of the church steps to keep from crumpling into a heap. Her heart throbbed with such force within her breast, her whole being felt bruised. As Levi rounded the corner, her vision blurred beneath a misty haze of tears waiting to fall.

Why did letting him go hurt so much? She should feel relieved at his departure, comforted by the rightness of her decision. So why did she feel as though she'd just been cleaved in two? He'd hidden things from her, purposely misled her. Separating herself from him and the certainty of further hurt was the right thing to do—the *only* thing to do.

Wasn't it?

"Something's wrong with Mr. Grant." Chloe's voice jarred Eden from her thoughts. The girl had come up beside her. "What did you say to him in there?"

Eden blinked the moisture from her eyes and released the railing post to brush at her skirt. "N—" Emotion clogged her throat. She coughed a bit to clear it and tried again. "Nothing.

We barely exchanged more than a sentence or two."

"Ah." The girl nodded as if that explained everything. "You're still sore over that letter he wrote you, huh?"

People began filing out of the church and the urge to flee became too great for Eden to ignore. "I don't want to talk about it, Chloe." She lurched away from the steps and crossed the yard in long strides, intent on getting to her front door as quickly as possible.

Chloe wouldn't leave her alone, though. She dogged Eden's heels from the churchyard to the house. Her presence set Eden's teeth on edge. It took all her self-control to keep from snapping at the girl. Which made no sense. Chloe had done nothing wrong.

Eden tugged off her bonnet and tossed it haphazardly onto the hall tree. Chloe did the same, only she took much more care, ensuring that her new hat was properly secured on a lower hook. Hoping the girl would head directly to the kitchen, Eden made a beeline for the stairs. But again, Chloe followed.

Halfway up, Eden spun around. "I'm going to lie down for a while. Why don't you check on Verna's roast?"

Chloe just stared up at her as if she hadn't heard a single word. A scream built at the back of Eden's throat.

"You should forgive him, you know," Chloe said. "Whatever he did, don't let it tear the two of you apart."

Eden exploded. "You have no idea what you're talking about, Chloe! None at all!" She stormed up the stairs and into her room, slammed the door, and slapped her Bible onto her writing desk with enough force to set her inkstand wobbling.

But not even the closed door kept Chloe out. She marched into the room, closed the door behind her, then crossed her arms and braced her legs apart as if preparing for battle.

"I ain't gonna let you sit up here and fester anymore, Miss Eden. You done enough of that already. You ain't just hurtin' yourself now. You're hurting Mr. Grant, and I can't let you do that."

How dare the girl invade her bedroom and throw accusations around!

As if *Levi* were the wronged party. “Oh, and Mr. Grant is perfect, isn’t he?”

“No, ma’am. He ain’t.” Chloe’s quiet rebuttal brought Eden up short. “I don’t know what he said in that letter that’s got you so riled, but if you can’t see the good man he is, you need to unscrew them eyeballs of yours and try on a different pair.”

Eden just stood there blinking, her mind too sluggish to accomplish any higher-functioning task.

“I lived my whole life in a saloon. If it’s one thing I know, it’s men. I seen weak men, brutal men, men with twisted minds, and men who think they own you just because you fall into their line of sight.” She turned her head away at the last description, her gaze sliding to the wall somewhere behind Eden.

“But once in a while, I run into the honorable type. They’re so rare, they stand out like a stallion in a barn overrun with vermin.” Chloe’s eyes found Eden’s again. “Levi Grant is that kind of man.”

“I thought so, too.” A sudden weariness overtook Eden. She reached for the edge of the bed and sat down. "He rescued you, Chloe. It's only natural for you to feel the need to defend him, but he told me things—dreadful things that he has done, worse than you could ever imagine, worse than—"

"Murder?" Chloe interrupted, stepping away from the door.

Eden froze. "What?" she rasped.

"Worse than murder?" Chloe hammered her again, relentless. "Ain't that what the preacher man talked about this mornin'? That Paul fellow . . . No, Saul . . . No . . . Oh, fiddlesticks. It don't matter what his name was. The guy was a bad egg, remember? He made his livin' hunting all them Christians, putting them in prison and stuff. He even helped kill one of 'em."

Had *that* been the subject of Dave Cranford's sermon? To be honest, Eden couldn't recall a single word. She'd been concentrating too hard on not thinking about Levi.

"That fellow had an ugly past," Chloe said, "but God set him right. The guy ended up writing half the Bible or something."

Eden shook her head. "This is different."

"Why?"

Chloe stalked her until the toes of their shoes were practically touching. Eden had to look up from her place on the bed to meet the girl's gaze, and when she did, the force of it nearly pushed her backward.

"Why is it different?" Chloe demanded. "Because *you're* the one hurt by it?"

"No!"

"You told me God was more interested in offering second chances than pointing fingers at past mistakes. What about you, Miss Eden?"

The question ripped a painful hole in her defenses. Her mind scrambled to fill it in with justifications. Levi had purposely misrepresented himself to her, hidden things . . .

"He didn't have to tell you, you know." Chloe's words blasted another section of carefully constructed rationale to smithereens. "Most people wouldn't have. They woulda just kept their mouths shut and hoped you never found out. But not Mr. Grant. He trusted you with his secrets. And what'd you do? You held 'em all against him—that's what."

Chloe narrowed her eyes in accusation, then dropped her arms to her sides and spun toward the door in a huff. She grabbed the handle and hesitated.

"He ain't perfect, Miss Eden," she said, twisting to face the room a final time, "but neither are you. All this time you had me fooled. I never took you for a rock-toter."

Chapter Thirty

A rock-toter. The image seized Eden by the throat and shook her until the scales finally fell from her eyes. All at once she could feel the weight of the stone in her hand as if it were physically present. Large. Heavy. Her fingers barely long enough to curl around its edges.

Then, in her mind's eye, she saw Levi standing on her porch, asking to see her after she'd read the letter. She'd refused, hurling her first stone against his shoulder. He'd rubbed the spot but returned to knock again the next day.

And she'd thrown another rock, this time connecting with his ribs. He kept coming back, and she kept pitching stones, her aim getting deadlier with each toss. Until today when she finally pulverized his heart.

The shock in his eyes when she told him not to touch her crashed through her mind—much like the look of a man who'd just received a bullet to the chest and could only register a flash of disbelief before life drained out of him.

"Levi," she moaned. "Oh, Levi. I'm so sorry."

Eden covered her face with her hands and wept. How could she have been so callous? So self-absorbed? Never once had she thought about how he might be feeling. Never once had she considered that he had given her a precious gift in trusting her with his secrets. No, she'd been too busy trampling that gift with her self-preservation efforts.

Never once had she let herself contemplate that God had forgiven Levi's past and helped him create a new identity in Christ, just as he had done for

Paul. For admitting such a thing would strip away her justifications and leave her vulnerable. And that prospect was too terrifying to bear.

And therein lay the crux of her problem. She didn't trust God to direct her steps. When trouble loomed, she altered her course, convincing herself she was displaying wisdom and the courage of her convictions. Yet in actuality, she was surrendering to fear, letting it control her in place of the Lord's hand.

Forgive me, Father.

Eden dried her face with her sleeve, sniffed a few times, and then slid off the edge of the bed to kneel upon the rug like she had as a child saying bedtime prayers.

I failed to seek your will, didn't I? I let fear cast out love instead of trusting your perfect love to cast out my fear.

Eyes closed, Eden let her forehead drift down to rest on the mattress. She wanted to explain her sin, to offer excuses for her behavior, but for once, she shoved her justifications aside and simply prostrated herself before her

Lord. She'd spent enough time in the self-righteous robes of the Pharisee. Time to find the humility of the tax collector.

"God have mercy," she whispered.

How could her heart have hardened so quickly? She loved Levi, admired him for his spiritual strength and his physical restraint. A man who had not fully surrendered his brutish ways would have fought back when attacked. Yet despite his size and the certain knowledge that he could flatten his weaker opponent with one well-aimed fist, Levi had not swung a single punch at Mr. Wilson the day the man had accosted him at the smithy. And in the bank that same week, he'd gone out of his way not to provoke the angry men that stormed the building, even after one of them threw a chair at him. All he did was see to her protection.

Levi was a man who took in abused dogs, rescued girls from saloon alleys, and donated most of a week's income toward the purchase of prison Bibles.

Prison Bibles. The ache in Eden's breast intensified. No wonder he was so eager to contribute. It was in prison that he rediscovered his faith and recommitted himself to the Lord. Snippets of his letter came back to her, parts that had faded into the shadows the first time, invisible behind the glaring accounts of his prizefighting.

Opening her eyes, she twisted toward her bureau and rummaged through the top drawer until she found the letter. Eden rearranged her skirts and sat on the floor, leaning her back against the bed. She reread every word he had written, this time ignoring the shock of the violence in order to focus on the quieter message. Her heart grieved for the boy he had been, teased for his speech until he started fighting for respect with his fists. She heard his regret over the way he left his family, turning his back on his father's training to pursue a self-serving way of life. And this time when she read the account of how his blow unintentionally killed a man, she felt *his* horror instead of her own.

Had she been guilty of the same offense? Had she killed the love that had been growing gently between them with the callous blow she'd delivered as they'd stood in a *church*? She saw again his bowed head as he pressed his palm into the pecan tree and the way he stepped away as if saying a final good-bye.

Please, God. Let it not be too late.

She had to go to him. Now. Too much time had already been wasted.

Eden shot to her feet. She vaguely remembered Verna's voice calling her to lunch but had no idea how long ago that had been. The afternoon could be half over.

Without further thought, she dropped the letter onto her bed and threw open the door. As she dashed down the stairs, she nearly collided with Chloe, who was ascending with a plate of roast beef, vegetables, and bread. Eden yanked her skirt back just in time to avoid getting gravy on her bronze silk.

"Miss Eden," Chloe gasped. "I was bringing you something to eat."

"Don't have time." Eden squeezed past her on the narrow stairway. "I'll eat later." She was nearly to the bottom when Chloe's worried voice stopped her.

"Are you all right?"

Eden turned back to look at her.

The girl ducked her head, her thumbs fidgeting along the edge of the plate. "I . . . uh . . . I shouldn't a said those things. It weren't my place. I'm sorry."

Eden bounced back up the three stairs she'd just come down and clasped Chloe's shoulders. "Don't be sorry. Not for any of it."

The girl glanced up, and Eden smiled. "I needed someone to wake me up, and God chose you for the job."

"God chose *me*?" The wonder and confusion on Chloe's face broadened Eden's grin.

"Yes, he did. And you executed his plan perfectly. Now I've got to do my part." Eden released Chloe's arms and charged toward the front door, sparing no time to collect her bonnet.

Stretching her legs into the longest stride she could manage, she hurried down Main Street toward the smithy. The wide double doors were chained shut, so she circled around to the back, determined not to let anything keep her from making her overdue apology. The back door stood partially open, but everything was dark inside.

"Levi?" She pushed the door wider, its creak echoing in the silent shop. As she listened, a rhythmic tapping sounded from within. It came closer, and Eden's heart raced.

"Levi? Is that you?"

The tapping sped up. Eden backed away. As she grabbed her skirts to flee, a gray head emerged, its viscious jaws spread wide in a deadly . . . yawn?

"Ornery! You scared me out of my wits." Eden's chastisement dissolved in a giggle as the dog finished his tongue-lagging yawn with a guttural whine and padded up to her, his nails no longer tapping as he left the wooden floorboards of the shop behind.

"Crazy mutt." She smiled and bent down to rub his ears. "So, I guess Levi's not here?"

Ornery stretched a foreleg out in front of him. Eden wanted to think he was pointing a direction but knew he was simply getting the kinks out from his nap. She patted his side a couple times, then straightened. Levi had never mentioned anyplace in particular that he liked to spend his time. Well, except the library.

Eden frowned, ashamed of the way she'd barred him and everyone else from the reading room in order to hide away from her problems. What a coward she'd been. But no more. Eden grabbed hold of her skirts and marched back around to the street. She would find Levi and apologize. She'd not shy away from him or anyone else, no matter how awkward the conversation. Levi deserved the best she could offer, and if her best wasn't good enough to win back his favor, maybe it could at least repair their friendship.

There was only one other location she could think of to look for him, and it would be a bit of a hike in Sunday silks and her dress boots with the high French heels, but the urgency inside her compelled her forward.

After the mile and a half hike to the Barnes' homestead, that urgency remained firm, even though everything else on her had wilted. Her chignon flopped loose and off center against her neck, perspiration clung to places it had no right to cling, and her feet screamed for a soak in a tub of cool water, but she pressed on.

The only trepidation came when she stood on the front stoop of the Barnes home and raised her hand to knock. A hummingbird took flight in her stomach, and the arm that had swung so purposely at her side a moment before now quivered with uncertainty.

Would he refuse to see her, as she had done him? What if he sent her away?

"Don't back out now, Eden," she whispered under her breath. Then, before any other questions could pop up to plague her, she rapped her knuckles against the door.

Mercifully, Georgia answered quickly. Eden had barely exhaled two steadying breaths before the door opened.

"Eden?" Georgia's gaze moved up and down taking in her bedraggled state, the woman's brows knitting together more tightly the longer she stared. "Has something happened?" She glanced past Eden's shoulder at the buggy-less yard. "Goodness, girl. Did you walk all the way out here from town?"

"Yes." Eden swallowed. "I need to speak to Levi. Is he here? It's a rather pressing matter."

Georgia pulled the door wide and gestured for Eden to enter. "He's here. Fool man's been out back choppin' wood as if winter hadn't already bowed out to spring." She shook her head. "He's nearly worked through that pile of mesquite Claude cleared off the north acreage last fall. I'm worried he'll take after my peach trees next. I may have to ask Claude to hide the ax."

Eden managed to smile at the jest, but Georgia must have seen the anxiety in her eyes, for she steered her toward a small parlor to the right. "Have a seat, honey. I'll go fetch him for you. Might take him a few minutes to wash up, but I'll let him know it's important."

"No. Please don't trouble yourself. I'll go find him." She couldn't stand the thought of sitting still and waiting for him to come. It would be too easy for him to have her sent away. If she caught him unaware, he might be more inclined to listen. Besides, she doubted he had told Claude and Georgia all the details of his past. And if he hadn't, she didn't want to risk one of them accidentally overhearing their conversation. Perhaps they would handle the truth better than she had, but she'd made things difficult enough for Levi without running the chance of his landlord evicting him due to his felonious past.

Georgia gave her another odd look, but she didn't argue. "All right, then. Come through the kitchen. I'll fix up a glass of water for you to take out to him." She gave Eden another raised-brow inspection. "Looks like you could use one, too."

This time, Eden's smile curved with more enthusiasm. "Thank you, Georgia," she said as she reached up to tidy her hair. "That sounds wonderful." She didn't have time to do much more than reposition a few pins, but at least the twist she had fashioned that morning no longer flopped around like one of Ornery's ears.

Accepting the filled water glasses, Eden headed out to the porch, stealing a sip from hers as she proceeded across the yard. The cool liquid refreshed her parched throat and gave her dry mouth some much-needed moisture. She followed the loud cracks of wood splitting, navigating the hard-packed path that led to the barn. After circling the side, she caught sight of Levi standing over the chopping stump. He'd shed his shirt, draping it atop the corral post near the lean-to that sheltered a stack of firewood that already reached the low roof. She couldn't imagine where he planned to fit all the pieces that were strewn on the ground at his feet.

As she watched, he grasped a large log and dropped it onto the stump. He raised the ax, and Eden's mouth dried again at the play of muscles across his back and shoulders. So strong, yet so controlled. He was no brute. He was beautiful.

Not even the scars detracted. They made her heart throb in sympathy over the pain he had endured, but they no longer darkened her opinion of him. God used those stripes to humble him, Levi had said in his letter, so that he would be receptive to the prison chaplain's message. How could she not love them as a part of this faithful man who had won her heart?

And how could she put off for another minute what her heart urged her to say?

After he swung a second time to split the log, Eden stepped closer. Taking a breath, and praying for guidance, she parted her lips. "Levi?"

He straightened from his bent position, his movements so slow Eden felt each second tick by. A chunk of split wood dangled from his left hand, the ax hung suspended in his right, but he did not turn to face her.

"I brought you some water." She extended the glass to him even though he couldn't see it. Recognizing the foolishness of the gesture, she pulled her arm back.

"Please, Levi?" she begged. "Please look at me."

With a flick of his wrist, he flung the wood aside. Then, with measured deliberateness, he set the ax head on the ground and leaned the handle against the chopping stump. Only then did he turn.

Chapter Thirty-One

Levi steeled himself as he bent to set the ax down. That voice. The voice from his dreams. It cut through him with bittersweet agony. Why had she come? She'd communicated her distaste quite clearly that morning. Yet here she was, pleading with him to look at her. Determined to hide his turmoil, he schooled his features into the stoic mask he'd perfected while in prison and slowly turned to face her.

"Would you care for a drink?" She held out a glass of water to him.

Levi stared at her. What was her

game? And why did she have to look so pretty with her cheeks flushed and stray curls falling loose about her face?

He raised an eyebrow at her in question but made no move to take the glass from her. She bit her lip, straightened her shoulders, and took a step toward him.

"You've been working hard," she said. Her gaze traveled from his face to his chest. The pink in her cheeks deepened, yet her eyes didn't skitter away. "Take the water."

A perverse part of him wanted to ignore her offering, to make things as uncomfortable for her as she'd made them for him, but his heart wouldn't allow it. He took hold of the glass, careful not to let his fingers touch hers, and lifted it to his lips. He gulped down the contents in a single guzzle, not noticing whether the water was warm or cool, sweet or bitter. He just drank to get it done, then set it aside on the chopping stump.

Eden timidly sipped at her glass, then set it on the stump next to his. She had trouble meeting his eyes—her gaze kept straying to his torso. It was good to know he wasn't the only one affected by the attraction that continued to hum between them despite the emotional distance that now pushed them apart.

But then, what good was attraction without love to lend it depth and meaning? Levi paced to the corral fence and grabbed his shirt. He poked his arms into the sleeves but only fastened a couple of buttons before crossing his arms over his chest.

"You didn't come all the way out here to bring me water. What do you want?"

She flinched at his brusque tone. "I want to talk."

Levi blew out an impatient breath. "I think you made your opinion clear already. Go home, Eden. And don't worry. I won't bother you anymore." He unlaced his arms and turned away to pick up a new log.

"But I want you to bother me!"

What?

Eden lunged forward and seized his wrist. Too stunned to protest, he offered no resistance as she yanked him around to face her and pressed his back against the slatted fence. “You don’t have to say anything. Just listen, all right? When I’m finished, if you still want nothing to do with me, I’ll honor your wishes.”

His wishes? Wasn’t she the one who wanted nothing to do with him?

“Will you hear me out?”

How could he not with those green eyes pleading with him? Levi nodded, feeling as if he’d just exposed his wounds and handed her a bucket of salt.

She retreated a step, staring at the ground as she wrapped her arms around her middle. “I’m ashamed of the way I’ve treated you the last few days, Levi.”

His heart gave an involuntary leap, but he quickly restrained it. Hope would only flay his wounds wider.

Eden’s chin lifted. “I’m sorry.”

Her eyes shimmered, but he hardened himself. He leaned back against the fence, giving no visual clues to whether he accepted or rejected her apology, though he’d forgiven her in his heart before she ever walked up the road. His control was too threadbare. He couldn't risk letting it slip completely. She'd told him he didn't have to talk, and he'd never been happier to keep his trap shut.

The expectation that had lit Eden's face dissipated at his continued silence, and a nearly imperceptible sigh slid from her lips. Then all at once, she dropped her hands to her sides and stiffened her spine.

"I was engaged to be married once," she blurted.

The change of topic caught him so by surprise he forgot to guard his reaction.

She must have caught a glimpse of the fevered curiosity he struggled to tamp down, for she plunged ahead with her explanation.

"Over five years ago. Before I left Austin." Roses bloomed in Eden's cheeks again, and she glanced down, kicking at the stump with the toe of her shoe. "He worked for my father," she said. "That's how we met."

Levi braced his elbows on the top

fence rail and propped a bootheel on the lowest. Acting indifferent was killing him. The very idea of Eden married to another man tore at his gut. He'd suspected there was a beau in Eden's past after Verna mentioned a fellow in Austin, but hearing that the two had planned to wed was torture. Another man holding her, touching her, kissing her . . .

"Stephen Hartshorn was handsome and refined and had a way about him that always put me at ease."

Levi hated him already.

"He took me to the finest restaurants and escorted me about town in a fancy carriage that all my friends envied. Everyone gushed about how fortunate I was to have such an eligible gentleman paying court to me. And I believed them. I was young and fancied myself in love, so when Stephen proposed, I begged Father to accept on my behalf.

"Everything progressed like a dream after that. Mother hired a team of seamstresses to create a sophisticated wedding gown fashioned after the latest Paris styles. She sent invitations to all the political and social elite Austin had to offer and spent days finalizing the menu while Stephen escorted me to events and showed me off to his friends and family. I was caught up in a delightful whirlwind. I had no control over where we spun but was too happy with the ride to care."

Eden gazed off toward the hills to the south, a rueful expression twisting her lips. "Stephen left a week before the wedding."

His casual stance forgotten, Levi jerked away from the fence. "What do you mean, he left?"

She shrugged. "He received a better offer."

A better offer? What could possibly entice a man to leave a gal like Eden? No better offer existed.

"From what my father told me later, he overheard Stephen bragging to some of his cohorts on the success of his coup. The eighteen months he'd invested in winning my hand was about to pay dividends. As Spencer's son-in-law, he'd no doubt be named partner within the year."

Levi angled his body back toward the corral and gripped the top rail in both hands, squeezing the wood so tightly, splinters dug into his palms. He wanted to hit something. Hard. Preferably something named Stephen Hartshorn, but he'd have to settle for strangling a fence rail instead.

"Unbeknownst to Mother or me, Father met with Stephen privately to determine for himself where the man's heart resided. He gave Stephen a choice—he could marry me and continue on as a clerk in Father's local land-development firm, or he could leave Austin a single man with a pocketful of earnest money to start his own business elsewhere. He chose the money. He didn't even care enough to tell me good-bye."

The wretch. Levi grimaced and forced himself to release the fence. As he slammed his back against the post and started pulling the splinters from his palms, he saw Eden reach for her water glass and take a drink. Her hand trembled slightly, as if the retelling of the tale had shaken her.

He wanted to go to her, comfort her. But before he could do more than lean forward, she set the glass down on the stump and cleared her throat. She finally looked him in the face, and the naked vulnerability in her eyes pinned him to the post.

"Stephen wasn't the man I thought him to be."

The quiet statement hit him like an uppercut to the chin. "I'm not either, am I?"

No wonder she'd pushed him away. To her, he was no better than that Hartshorn fellow.

"When I came to Spencer, I left all hope of marriage behind," she said, neatly avoiding his question. "I made peace with being a spinster and found purpose in operating the library and reaching out to the town's children. Then you came along and stirred feelings inside me I was afraid to explore."

Levi's heart thumped an uneven rhythm, and he couldn't seem to take in a full breath.

"As I came to know you better," Eden continued, "I started to believe that you represented everything I'd ever wanted—a man of faith who held fast to his convictions, a man of peace who despised violence as much as I did, a man who loved literature and could expound on philosophical ideas, a man with a tender heart who would go out of his way to help the unfortunate."

Eden stepped closer, and suddenly Levi was the one trembling.

"I put you on a pedestal. And when I read that letter, my image of you tumbled from its perch and shattered. How could I love a prizefighter, a felon, a man who had taken the life of another?"

"You couldn't." The words choked him, nearly tearing a hole in his throat.

"That's what I told myself. But I was wrong, Levi." She took another step and touched his arm. His bicep jumped at the feel of her fingers through the thin cotton of his sleeve, while his pulse jumped at the impact of her words. She was *wrong*?

"I've been hardhearted and selfish these last few days." Her lashes lowered over her eyes, as if she was too ashamed to hold his gaze. "You've been nothing but honest, honorable, and kind, yet I lashed out in the most hurtful ways."

Finally those lashes lifted to reveal shimmering pools of green. "God reminded me today that you are no longer the man you described in that letter. You are a man redeemed. I came here to beg your forgiveness."

She inhaled a tremulous breath, and he found himself holding his.

"I'm so sorry, Levi. So, so sorry." Her voice closed up and tears streamed down her cheeks.

Levi couldn't stop himself from reaching for her. His heart was too full. He clasped her face between both of his hands and tilted her head up to meet his kiss. His lips descended on hers. As if a dam had burst, all the feelings he'd worked so hard to restrain suddenly burst forth. He'd thought her lost to him, but here she stood, clutching his arm and returning his kiss with a sweetness he'd only dreamed existed. Levi stroked her damp cheeks with his thumbs and burrowed his fingers into the hair at her nape. He angled his face to deepen their connection, and when Eden made a tiny mewling noise in the back of her throat, exultation coursed through his veins.

She leaned into him. His left hand relinquished the softness of her face to caress her back and draw her closer to his heart. Her fingers twined in the short curls at his neck. He swallowed a moan as delicious shivers scampered over his skin. Kissing Eden was like tasting a miracle. He never wanted it to end.

Good sense and an increasingly adamant conscience prevailed, however. Levi gently pulled away, pressing his lips to her eyelids and forehead before completely letting go. He watched her breathe, her mouth slightly swollen. And when her lashes lifted, her dewy eyes looked up at him in a daze that filled him with masculine satisfaction.

A small sigh passed her lips. “Does this mean you forgive me?”

Laughter burst from Levi’s chest, and he tugged Eden back into his embrace, holding her close as giggles claimed her, as well. Loving this woman was either going to kill him or make his life richer than he'd ever imagined.

Chapter Thirty-Two

The following morning, while adding the finishing touches to her pressed flower design, Eden hummed a Stephen Foster tune about a cheery maiden frolicking in the fields. For the first time in days, the sight of the wedding bouquet brought a smile to her heart instead of a pang of bitterness.

Levi had forgiven her. Not only that, he had kissed her—kissed her like a man kisses a woman he intends to wed. At least she assumed that's how a man with strong feelings kissed. The only other man who had ever put his lips to hers was the one who'd jilted her, and while he'd initially had marrying intentions, his brief pecks had been too tame to stir more than a tepid reaction from her. Levi's kiss, on the other hand, had stolen her breath and set her heart to palpitating at such a rate she'd feared she'd succumb to a fit of the vapors. Thankfully, she'd remained conscious and blissfully aware of every delicious second of Levi's embrace.

Eden's cheeks grew warm at the memory, and she fanned herself with her hand. His lips had felt so wonderful against hers, soft and tender; yet they'd moved with an urgency that had her pulse fluttering more erratically than an autumn leaf caught in a whirlwind. And when she'd finally worked up the nerve to bury her fingers in those thick curls of his? Ah. Perfect was too poor a word to describe it.

Realizing she had stopped humming while her mind wandered, Eden cleared her throat and started the song again as she refocused on the task before her. Her toe tapped out the melody's jaunty beat while she applied a layer of glue across the gathered stems and pressed a strip of pink ribbon onto the surface. Eden held it in place, and while it dried, her humming gave way to singing.

> **"Fairy-Belle, gentle Fairy-Belle,**
> **The star of the night and the**
> **lily of the day.**
> **Fairy-Belle, the queen of all the**
> **dell,**
> **Long may she revel on her**
> **bright sunny way."**

Chloe danced into the room, dustcloth in hand, and joined in on the last line of the chorus. Embarrassed, Eden bit her lip and immediately stopped singing.

Chloe, however, moved right into the second verse without a hint of reticence.

" 'She sings to the meadows and she carols to the streams. . . .' Come on, Miss Eden. Sing with me."

Wrestling her self-consciousness, Eden tentatively added her voice to Chloe's squeaky yet enthusiastic soprano, unable to contain her grin when the girl twirled around on her toes, belling her skirt out around her ankles.

"She laughs in the sunlight and
smiles while in her dreams,
Her hair like the thistledown is
borne upon the air,
And her heart like the
hummingbird's is free from
ev'ry care."

Chloe tossed aside her cloth and grabbed Eden by the hands as they plunged back into the chorus. They giggled and danced and spun in circles until they were too winded to sing another note. They collapsed onto the rug and leaned against each other for support, struggling to catch their breath between residual bouts of laughter.

The kitchen door creaked, and Verna stuck her head into the room. "Harvey," she called over her shoulder, "bring me a broom. A couple of magpies got loose in the library."

Eden looked at Chloe and the two dissolved into another fit of giggles.

Verna left the kitchen doorway and strolled over to Eden, offering her a hand up. "At least the magpies chased away the gloom that's been hanging over this place the last few days."

She smiled and gave Eden's hand an affectionate pat before turning to help Chloe. The girl bounded to her feet unassisted and reclaimed her dustcloth, turning her attention to the bookshelves lining the outer wall.

"So, you and that handsome blacksmith work out your differences?"

Eden bit her lip at the older woman's knowing look, but she grinned and nodded, too happy to hide her pleasure.

"Well, it's about time. Poor fella looked like I done shot his dog every time you had me send him away. I was about ready to retire from door answerin' altogether."

Eden reached an arm around the housekeeper's shoulders and gave her a firm squeeze. "I appreciate your putting up with me, Verna. I know it was a trial."

"Bah." The woman brushed away

the words with a swipe of her hand like so much dust. "'Tweren't no hardship. You were hurting. Harvey and me, we can handle a little moping from you, just so long as it don't become a habit."

"You have my word." Eden laid a hand over her heart, and Verna winked.

"So I guess this means I can put the *Open* sign in the window?" Verna pulled away from Eden and wandered toward the hall.

"Is it time already?" Amazing how much faster the morning passed when her heart was light.

Verna nodded. "Fixin' to be. I'll go unlock the door and put out the sign."

A little tickle started in the pit of Eden's stomach after Verna left the room. Would Levi visit today? When he did, he usually came early. He could be on his way to see her right now. Eden pressed a hand to her quivering stomach and quickly set about straightening her desk. She carefully packed away her unused pressed flowers and scraps of ribbon and lace before placing the nearly completed picture into a hatbox for storage. A bow still needed to be added to the ribbon she'd placed today along with a few tiny blossoms near the bottom, but soon the bouquet would be ready for framing. She'd ordered a pretty oval one, finished in white and gilt with a shell-patterned molding.

Bittersweet sensations tugged at her as she placed the lid over her creation. It was too bad she'd committed it to the spring auction. She'd become more attached to this piece than any of her others. Every time she looked at it, she thought of Levi—the way he'd suggested the design, the memory of him holding her in the field where she'd collected the blossoms, the way his kiss made her think of weddings and bouquets and blacksmith husbands.

"Eden?" Masculine tones echoed behind her.

She spun around. "Levi!" Why could she think of nothing more intelligent to say?

"Found him out on the porch," Verna said with a pointed look at Eden as she strode past the desk. "Guess he was afraid to try knockin'."

The housekeeper chuckled quietly as she shooed Chloe out of the reading room to allow Eden some privacy with her beau, although she made a point to leave the kitchen door open for propriety's sake. Eden craned her neck, focusing solely on Verna's back until the woman disappeared around the corner.

Eden summoned a wobbly smile as she turned to face Levi again. He looked so handsome standing there, holding his hat in front of him, his wavy hair curling at the ends, where it was still damp from his wash. He looked from her face to the ceiling, and his mouth twitched as if he intended to say something, but no words came. She tried to come up with some innocuous tidbit of conversation to make things easier on him. Nothing. It was as if every social grace in her possession had taken flight.

Biting back a moan, Eden dropped her attention to her desk and fiddled with the handle on her hatbox. Levi's feet shuffled as he shifted his weight a couple times. Apparently neither of them was capable of breaking the stretching silence.

Where had this awkwardness between them originated? Her insides felt more tangled than the yarn in her scrap basket.

Levi finally cleared his throat. "I . . . uh . . . brought you . . ."

Lifting her chin, Eden met his eyes. Unable to finish his sentence, Levi shrugged and pulled his hand out from behind his hat. Clutched gently between his large workman's fingers were two delicate clusters of tiny purple flowers.

"Prairie verbena. These are lovely." She reached out to accept the gift, her smile no longer wobbling. As he loosened his grip on the stems, Eden slid her hand beneath his, loving the way his palm caressed the back of her hand with a light touch. Pleasant shivers danced up her arms as she slowly pulled away.

The leafy wildflowers didn't have much scent, so instead of lifting them to her nose, she stroked the petals with her fingertip. Most men would have pilfered some of the new rosebuds blooming on her bushes, but not Levi. He knew her partiality for wildflowers.

"Thank you. They're so bright and cheerful. And these press very well." Now she was babbling. But her mind was already making plans for how to preserve Levi's gift.

"I thought I remembered you . . . working with that kind of flower. Found . . . a bunch out behind the water trough near the livery corral. Hoped you might like them."

Eden held them up to her cheek, enjoying the softness of the petals against her skin. "I like them very much."

Levi stepped closer. "I'm glad." The intensity of his gaze held her captive until a dropped pan clanging in the kitchen jarred her free.

"Do you mind if I run upstairs and grab my field press?" Eden took a step back, inserting some distance between them to aid her concentration. "I'd like to preserve your flowers, but the color will fade if I don't press them while they're fresh. We can talk at my desk while I work, if you like."

Levi nodded. "I'll . . . uh . . . hang up my hat." He waved it at her as if shooing her up the stairs, then turned toward the hall.

Not wanting to miss a moment of whatever time they'd have alone together, Eden laid the verbena on the desktop and hustled to her room. She tucked the press under her arm, dug out a box of blotting paper from her trunk, and dashed back down to the reading room, where Levi stood perusing the fiction shelves.

He looked up as she entered and strode to her side, relieving her of the box and press. "Where do you want them?"

"Over on the desk, please." She led the way, plucking up the verbena stems to give him more space. "Would you like to help?"

Levi set the materials down and looked her way, his brows slightly raised.

Of course he wouldn't want to help. What a fool thing to suggest. Eden busied herself with opening the box and removing several sheets of blotting paper, willing herself not to blush. The man pounded iron all day. He was an ex-prizefighter, for pity's sake, not a slender-fingered dandy with lace at his cuffs. What had she been thinking?

"Forget I said that," she said, keeping her eyes on the desk. "I'm sure you have no desire to play with petals. It's not exactly a masculine pursuit." Her hands fluttered over the book strap she used to hold her press together, but the buckle refused to unfasten. The leather eluded her, as if someone had greased it with cooking lard.

Levi's palm settled over her fingers, forcing them to still. Slowly, Eden raised her face to his.

"I'll help." His lips curved, silently teasing her in a way that eased her embarrassment and made her want to laugh.

Grinning, Eden tugged her hands out from under Levi's palm and tilted her head in the direction of the far wall. "Why don't you bring your chair over here while I set the press up? Then I'll show you how it works."

As soon as Levi moved away, Eden's

capability returned and she found a way to unbuckle the strap without further difficulty. She opened the flower press like a book and set the top board on the floor, leaning it against the leg of the desk. Then she reached for the six or so pieces of blotting paper she'd laid aside earlier, glancing at Levi while she did so.

That was a mistake.

The paper shifted between her inattentive fingers as she watched her blacksmith lift the heavy leather wing chair before him as if it were made of nothing denser than *papier-mâché*. What would it feel like to have him pick *her* up? To carry her with those robust arms, toting her over a . . . a threshold, perhaps, as they entered their home for the first time as husband and wife. With his superior strength, would he set her down inside the door, or keep his hold on her, nestling her against that broad chest of his as he made his way to other rooms of the house?

Eden slammed the door on that thought before it led her into intimate territory and turned her attention back to pressing the verbena. She managed to get her paper properly stacked atop the bottom board by the time Levi returned with the chair.

"The blotting paper absorbs the moisture from the flowers as they dry, so we'll lay the blooms flat on the page and add another stack of paper on top. We should be able to get all of these in a single layer."

Levi nodded, his expression intent, as if pressing flowers was a skill he truly intended to learn. Perhaps he only acted interested because they were courting, but it seemed deeper than that. His focused attention conveyed respect—since pressing flowers was important to her, it was now important to him, as well. Eden couldn't help thinking of the curly-haired daughter he might have one day, and the daddy who would sip imaginary tea with her from a child-sized cup he'd barely be able to grasp with his thick fingers.

"How much of the flower do you want?" Levi's question brought Eden back on task.

"We can't press the entire cluster.

Each blossom will have to be removed individually. Just pinch the bloom off where it meets the stem and lay it on the paper." She demonstrated the procedure, then helped him with his first couple of attempts. His hands were large, but his fingers were amazingly adept. Soon they had the paper nearly covered with the small purple wildflowers. She added a few strips of the more interestingly shaped leaves around the edges, then covered their work with six more sheets of blotter paper and carefully lowered the top board into place.

"Why don't you fasten the straps?" Eden suggested. "Pull them tight so the flowers dry completely flat. They'll have to stay in the press for about two weeks before we can let any air hit them."

Levi complied and buckled the first strap. As he tugged the second into position, the front door burst open and heavy footfalls stomped down the hall.

Sheriff Pratt strode into the room.

Eden jumped to her feet, but the man barely spared her a glance as his eyes locked on Levi.

"Been lookin' for you, Grant." His razor-sharp eyes cut from him to Eden and back again. "Shoulda known you'd be here."

Levi finished latching the press before rising to greet the sheriff. "Morning, Pratt. What can I do for you?"

"Grab your hat is what you can do. You're coming with me."

Chapter Thirty-Three

Levi held his ground and his tongue, unwilling to give in to the sheriff's bullying. Even if Pratt had somehow discovered the details of his past, he'd done nothing since his release to warrant being hauled off to jail.

"What is the meaning of this intrusion, Sheriff?" Eden marched up to the man, bristling like a wet hen. "You can't just barge in here issuing orders."

"I can when men's lives are at stake."

Eden glanced back at Levi, confusion lining her face. Levi raised his brows in response, as much in the dark as she. Circling the desk, he squared off with the sheriff. "Get to the point, Pratt. What do you want with me?"

The man sighed and pushed his hat back on his head. "There's been an accident at the quarry. An explosion."

A gasp echoed from the vicinity of the kitchen, but Levi kept his focus on Pratt.

"Doc's headed out there now to tend the injured, but there's a handful of men pinned under a slide of limestone rubble. The faster we get them out, the greater their chance of survival." He stopped to clear his throat. "I ain't had much use for you up till now, Grant, but you've got the strongest back in the county. Borrow a horse from Barnes and hightail it out to that quarry. I'll meet you there after I round up a couple more men." Not waiting for an answer, Pratt dragged his hat back down over his forehead and spun toward the doorway.

Levi stood paralyzed. The quarry? He'd sworn he'd never willingly enter the nightmare of such a place again.

The sound of the front door banging

closed echoed through the room. And before Levi could do more than blink, Chloe rushed at him from the kitchen, tears coursing down her face.

"You gotta help them, Mr. Levi. You gotta." A sob choked off her words as she flung herself into his arms, grasping his waist as if he were the only anchor in her life. Levi patted her awkwardly on the back as he swallowed the bile that rose in his throat. The girl didn't know what she was asking. She couldn't.

Chloe pulled away slightly and tilted her face up. Reddened eyes pleaded with him. "Duncan drills for the blasters at the quarry. You gotta get him out. I can't explain it, but I *know* he's one of the men trapped out there."

Duncan—the Scotsman with the ready laugh and dancing feet. The kid was too young to have his life snuffed out. What about his dream of following in his father's footsteps to become a stonecutter? And his plans to woo that bonny lass of his?

As Levi stared at the distraught girl in his arms, the truth hit him between the eyes. Chloe was Duncan's bonny lass.

Levi clenched his jaw and hugged Chloe to his chest. He would go. Not just for Duncan, a man he liked and admired, but for Chloe, the girl he loved like a baby sister.

A soft touch on his arm drew Levi's gaze around to Eden. Compassion glowed in her eyes—compassion and a healthy dose of determination.

"Chloe and I will gather bandages and whatever other medical supplies we can find and come after you. We'll help Dr. Adams tend the wounded and support you however we can."

The promise inherent in those last words gave him the strength to separate himself from the women. "I'll get him out, Chloe. You have my word."

She nodded and sniffed, then brushed at her tears with the back of her hand.

Levi strode from the room, his growing sense of purpose crowding out his dread. God had made Samson strong for a reason, and it hadn't been to impress Delilah with his prowess. It had been to deliver his people. Levi had been blessed with strength, as well, and not for squandering on prizefights and selfish living. Perhaps he, too, had been given the gift to deliver people—people like Duncan McPherson and the other quarrymen trapped out in the pit.

Help me get them out, Lord. Whatever it takes.

Levi snatched his hat from its hook on the hall tree and turned for the door, nearly trampling Eden, who had come up behind him.

"God will help you, Levi. And so will I." She rose on her tiptoes and placed a kiss to his cheek. The simple touch drove away the last of his reservations. "I'll be there as soon as I can," she promised.

Not wanting to waste time searching for nonlisping words to convey his gratitude, he circled an arm around her waist, clutched her to his chest, and brought his mouth down on hers. She started to melt against him, but tempted as he was to continue, he pulled away. The trapped men couldn't afford a delay. The feel of her stayed with him, however, long after he left.

He stopped by the smithy to collect the largest of his sledgehammers, then hurried to the livery. The sheriff must have warned Claude to have a horse ready, for he stood in the yard holding the lead on a broad-chested sorrel gelding that was saddled and ready to ride.

It'd been years since he'd sat a horse, but some skills a man never forgot. Levi strapped the sledge to the back of the saddle, making sure it wouldn't bounce around, and then shoved the toe of his shoe into the stirrup and hoisted himself up.

"Head west," Claude said, pointing out of town. "When you get to the fork, turn north. It'll run along the rail route and lead directly to Fieldman's. You can't miss it. I'll head to the church and help Cranford rearrange the space for an infirmary."

Levi nodded and pressed his heels to the horse's flanks. As he rode, he tried to concentrate on Duncan and the others, but when the quarry came into view, his chest tightened. He could feel the whip cutting into his skin, hear the screams of grown men, taste the dust that hung heavy in the air. Past blurred with present, and nausea gripped Levi so fiercely it nearly bent him double.

Fighting for control, he closed his eyes for a moment and let the horse carry him to the base of the pit. When the animal slowed, Levi opened his eyes and took in the scene. The screams echoing in his mind dulled to a hum of concerned voices. Women clung to husbands who had avoided the blast, praising God for their safety. Others sat with the injured, holding a hand or cleaning a bloody face with a dampened handkerchief. The doctor, having just arrived, bustled from patient to patient, black bag in hand, assessing the damage.

Another group huddled near one of the cranes used for lowering blocks of limestone from the rim to the base of the pit. Recognizing the sheriff, Levi dismounted and led his horse to the corral that housed the draft animals used for transporting dressed stone to the waiting railcars. Levi looped his reins loosely around the tongue of an unused cart and gave his mount enough lead to reach the water trough. Then he unfastened his sledge from behind the cantle and headed toward the group of men arguing near the crane.

"We've got the manpower to move that rubble, Fieldman," Pratt ranted, gesturing to the half-dozen men he'd brought with him from town. "Why are you refusing our help? Your men are dying in there!"

"I'm well aware of the condition of my men, Sheriff." Fieldman enunciated each word as if he were flinging darts into a board. "I'm also aware that the stone is unstable. The explosion weakened several sections in the rock face above where the men are trapped. That stone is cracked and ready to throw down. Sending inexperienced men in there would be asking for more injuries. Besides, most of the fallen blocks are too large to remove. I've got a crew breaking them up now. It's slow going, but it's the safest procedure for all concerned."

The stocky man with graying temples turned to go, no doubt eager to rejoin the rescue effort. He'd given Levi every excuse to leave his nightmare behind, but something stronger than fear pushed Levi forward.

"I can help." Levi raised the sledge above his shoulder to catch the man's attention and edged past the others gathered around the sheriff.

Fieldman glanced back, his eyes widening slightly as he took in Levi's size. "Look, son," the man said, shaking his head in regret. "I could use a pair of arms like those, but even so, I ain't lettin' you in. If you don't know what you're doing, you could cause more problems than I already got."

Levi cleared his throat and took another step forward. "I broke rock at Granite Mountain. For more than a year and a half. I can help."

"Granite Mountain?" Alex Carson, the saddler, murmured. "Isn't that where the stone for the new capitol building came from?"

Levi could feel the sheriff's hot gaze burning into the side of his neck, but he kept his attention locked on Fieldman.

"Yep," Pratt said. "They used mostly convict labor, as I recall." Questions laced that statement. Questions Levi would rather not answer, although his gut told him his secrets wouldn't remain hidden much longer.

"What'll it be, Fieldman?" Levi asked, eager to escape the sheriff's scrutiny.

The owner waved him forward. "I ain't one to turn away what the Lord's providin'. I'll grab a chisel. You can be my striker."

Levi nodded, angling his shoulders to slide between Pratt and Carson in order to follow. Thankful to leave the townsmen and their probing glances behind, he stretched his stride to catch up to Fieldman.

"How many men you figure are trapped?"

The man's solemn face told Levi more than he wanted to know. "We're missin' four, from what I can tell. Dalton, Jones, McPherson, and Collier."

Duncan. Levi's heart sank. "You . . . think they got a chan—" He swallowed the end of the word and coughed to cover his inadequacy. The rising tide of emotion inside him was interfering with his ability to filter words. All he could think about was Chloe's face when she'd begged him to help and her certainty that Duncan was in danger.

"Chances are slim, but there's a hollow there on the right." He pointed to an area of the rockslide where four pairs of men were working in tandem to split and remove slabs of the fallen limestone. "If they managed to get into that space before the worst of it hit, they might still be alive."

Fieldman paused to grab a large chisel from where it leaned discarded against the rocks. He carefully picked his way atop the rubble, testing each section for stability before climbing farther. Levi followed precisely in his wake, stepping only where the other man had stepped. His fingers bit into the handle of his sledge as the sounds of quarry work drowned out all else. Iron clanged against iron as hammer met chisel or drill. Metal echoed against stone as the rock chipped away. A man shouted at a team of horses. Harness jangled and hooves thudded against the earth as the pair strained against the weight of the loosened limestone block their master had chained to them.

Lord, watch over Duncan and the other men. Help us get them out in time.

Levi's prayers continued as he settled into the familiar rhythm of swing and strike—swing and strike. Fieldman anticipated each hit, adeptly positioning the chisel along the rock's line of least resistance. With his expertise and Levi's strength, they cleared twice the stone of the other pairs.

The sun traveled across the sky and beat down on Levi's neck. His muscles screamed for rest, yet he couldn't stop—not while Duncan lay buried somewhere beneath. So he continued on, swing after swing. Someone handed him a canteen. He lifted it to his lips and washed the dust from his throat, then grasped the handle of the sledge once again. Fieldman offered to switch positions with him, but Levi refused. He didn't have the quarryman's skill in finding the weak spots in the rock. It would hurt their efficiency to change places. No, he'd keep the sledge and trust God to provide endurance.

"One more swing ought to get 'er," Fieldman said as he reset the chisel.

This slab was one of the largest they'd tackled so far, and the closest to the rock face. No one had verbalized the hope and dread they all held inside as they worked to clear away the stones. If the men had found a pocket of safety in the hollow, they should find evidence under this slab. If not? Levi clenched his jaw as he hoisted the sledge. Well, if not, they would probably find evidence of that, too.

The hammer came down on the head of the chisel, sending vibrations along Levi's arms and back. The slab cracked and split.

"Get the horses!" Fieldman ordered.

Levi stepped aside as a wiry fellow scrambled up to them, chain in hand. Fieldman used his long chisel like a lever to aid the crewman in getting the chain under the block. Then with a wave, the man signaled the horse driver. With a loud "Yah!" and a slap to the lead animal's hindquarters, the driver urged the horses forward.

As the team slowly dragged the oversized chunk of limestone away, Levi heard a faint sound. It wasn't clear, but something about it seemed out of place. He cocked his head and listened, mentally filtering out the scraping of stone and jangle of harness. His pulse skittered. Could it be?

He dropped to his knees and laid his ear to the newly cleared section, heart pounding.

"Hold the horses!" Fieldman yelled. "Hammers down!" After issuing the order, he fell to the ground beside Levi.

A muted call carried through the crevice. "We're here. We're here."

Levi looked up at Fieldman. Tears ran down the older man's face, leaving tracks in the limestone dust that coated all of them.

"Thank God," he whispered. Then all at once, he tore at the ground with his hands, pulling out the smaller rocks and debris.

"They're here!" Levi waved the other crewmen over. They all scrambled to the spot, digging with hands, picks, chisels, whatever they could find. Aches forgotten, Levi shoved stones aside, then braced his back against the rock face and used his legs to thrust the other half of the large limestone slab aside. A grunt tore from his lips as his knees slowly straightened.

"Look! A hand!" one of the crewmen shouted.

Beneath Levi's legs, a dust-encrusted gray hand reached up through a hole that had been uncovered by the removed slab.

A cheer rose from the men up top. Coughs echoed from the men below. Fieldman knelt on all fours and reached into the hole to clasp the man's hand. "We're gonna get you out. Just hang in there."

"I ain't goin' anywhere, boss," a raspy voice called back.

"Collier?"

"Yeah."

Fieldman smiled. "Shoulda known an old cuss like you'd be too stubborn to let a pile of rock do you in. The others there with you?"

The question was met with silence, and Levi's stomach soured.

"Collier?" Fieldman's smile fell.

"The others are here," the man said, "but only two of us are still breathin'."

Chapter Thirty-Four

"Are you still prayin', Miss Eden?" Chloe hopped down from the top rail of the corral fence, turning her harried countenance back toward the buggy. "'Cause it don't seem to be working."

Eden's heart ached for the girl. How would she feel if Levi were the one trapped under all that rubble? She'd no doubt be out of her mind with worry.

"I'm praying, Chloe. For all four of the trapped men, but especially for Mr. McPherson. And for you."

The girl's faith was just beginning to bud. If Duncan didn't survive, would it wither and die with him? As hard as Eden prayed for the young man's rescue, she prayed for Chloe's faith even more. Life was indeed precious, but a soul carried greater worth than a body. And right now, Chloe's soul stood on an eternal precipice.

"We have to try to be patient," Eden said, wishing she could offer more comfort.

Chloe stomped over to the shade of the buggy and plopped down on the slab of rock that served as a bench. "I don't want to be patient." She heaved a frustrated sigh. "They've been out there for hours. I want to *do* something. Something besides all this pointless waiting."

Eden reached between them and clasped the girl's hand. "Sometimes waiting is what God wants us to do. To give him time to work."

"It's just that—" Chloe choked back a sob. Eden scooted closer. "It's just that I never thought a decent man would look twice at a girl like me. Ma said I'd have to leave town and pretend to be someone else to have any hope of findin' a marrying type of man."

Chloe pulled her hand free. She picked at a loose thread on her sleeve, then looked out in the direction of the men. Yet Eden got the feeling she wasn't really seeing them.

A touch of a smile curved the girl's lips. "I met Duncan in the Hang Dog. Did I ever tell you that?"

Eden shook her head. "No. Though I suspected the two of you had met somewhere prior to the day we ran into him outside the dry goods store. He acted quite smitten."

Chloe shrugged, but her smile deepened. "He was different from most of the men who came to the saloon. Sometimes I'd watch him from behind the curtain that closed off the kitchen. He'd come in with a group of men from the quarry on a Saturday night, but while the others tossed away their pay on drink after drink, he'd sit at the bar sippin' a single beer. If one of the fellows started gettin' melancholy or if things got tense at the card table, he'd spin one of his fanciful yarns that would get the whole room laughing. I even saw him dance a jig when one of the quarrymen didn't like the song the piano player was thumpin'. No one could keep a straight face with all those knees and elbows flappin'.

"Never once did he go upstairs with one of the girls. Never once did he speak to anyone with disrespect. Never once did I see him get drunk. I think I started falling in love with him before he ever knew I existed."

Eden developed a whole new respect for Duncan McPherson as she saw him through Chloe's eyes. "How did the two of you finally meet?"

"Duncan always ordered one of Old Nell's pan-fried beefsteaks when he came in, but one night Roy was busy settlin' a dispute with one of my ma's customers when the food came up, and I was afraid the steak would get cold before the barkeep got back. So, after checkin' the big room to be sure no one was payin' me any mind, I slid out from behind the curtain and delivered the vittles."

Chloe sighed and finally glanced

over at Eden. "You shoulda seen the way he tugged off his cap when he saw me. That red hair of his stuck out at all angles, but it was the most beautiful thing I'd ever seen. He didn't look at me the way men looked at my ma and the other girls. His eyes held respect and appreciation and a touch of shyness that, coming from a man who'd dance an embarrassing jig just to keep the peace, made my heart skitter like a mouse dodging a barn cat.

"We didn't even say anything that first time." Chloe turned her attention back out to the quarry. "But after that, I made a point to deliver his beefsteak every Saturday night." A fond smile lit her face, although Eden could hear tears close to the surface. "Every time he came in, he tried to charm me into tellin' him my name, but I never did. I was too aware of who I was. And who I wasn't."

Eden rested her hand on Chloe's shoulder. "You've changed who you were."

Chloe bit her lip and nodded. "Thanks to you and Mr. Levi."

"You were the one who made the decision to leave. We just helped out a bit."

"More than a bit." Chloe fell silent for a moment, then took a deep breath and began again. "When Duncan and me met on the boardwalk that day outside Mrs. Fowler's store, it was like all the barriers between us crumbled away. For the first time in my life, I felt like a normal gal—one who was free to accept an honorable man's attention, one who could laugh and flirt, one who could reveal her name without shame." The tears she'd been holding back began spilling down her cheeks. "I can't lose him now. I just can't!"

A shout rose up from the men in the pit. Both Eden and Chloe jumped to their feet. Chloe scaled the corral fence again and shaded her face from the late afternoon sun with her hand.

"Can you make out what's happening?" Eden asked.

"It's hard to tell. The men seem to be workin' closer together now. Do you think . . ." Chloe sucked in a shaky breath and slowly exhaled it. “Do you think they mighta found them?”

“We can hope.” Eden stepped closer to the fence and shaded her eyes against the sun’s glare.

It was only a matter of seconds before she picked out Levi from the rest of the men, his bulky physique setting him apart. He seemed to swing that giant hammer of his twice as often as the other men. She could only imagine his exhaustion.

Keep him strong, Lord. And help him find Duncan. Alive.

The sound of an approaching wagon caused Eden to turn. Sheriff Pratt steered the team toward her and lifted a hand in greeting. Dr. Adams had enlisted him to cart the more seriously injured quarrymen back to Spencer after they’d been stabilized, to cots waiting at the church. The sheriff had made several runs since Eden and Chloe arrived, taking no more than two men at a time so the patients could lie flat on a pile of quilts in the wagon bed. Family members or friends had traveled with them, keeping the men still and as comfortable as possible.

"They still at it?" Sheriff Pratt thrust his chin in the direction of Levi and the quarry workers.

"Yes."

He set the brake and climbed down, pushing his hat back on his forehead. "We woulda had them out by now if Fieldman hadn't been so stubborn about only using experienced crew."

Eden shot him a quelling look. "Maybe. Or maybe someone else would have been injured. It's fruitless to speculate." The last thing Chloe needed was to start questioning whether enough was being done for Duncan and the others. "I'm sure Mr. Fieldman did what he thought best under these conditions."

Eden twisted her head to see if Chloe had overheard their conversation, only to find the girl gone.

Strange. She'd done the same thing when they'd first arrived. Dr. Adams had been discussing the transport of the patients with Pratt when Eden and Chloe walked up with their bandages and medical supplies. Once the doctor had finished instructing Sheriff Pratt on how to prepare the wagon bed, he'd motioned the women closer. Only, Eden had been alone. The small crate of rolled linen strips Chloe had been carrying was sitting on the ground a few steps behind her. Later, Chloe explained that she'd thought she'd seen Duncan among the crowd of worried family members and had taken off to search. Eden hadn't questioned the explanation at the time, but now doubt wiggled through her mind.

Conrad Pratt had been none too happy to have Chloe under her roof. Had he said something to frighten the girl? She stole a glance at the lawman as he kicked at a pebble with the toe of his boot, his attention focused on Fieldman's crew. Eden scanned her memory but failed to recover a single instance where she'd seen Chloe and the sheriff in the same area. Not here, not at the library, not at church.

"They're here!" Levi's distant shout tore through Eden, scattering to the wind all thoughts of Chloe's odd behavior.

"I don't care what Fieldman says." The sheriff stiffened like a hound dog catching a scent. "I'm going out there."

"Wait!" Eden grabbed hold of his arm. "If they've found them, they'll know the best way to get them out. Don't do something rash."

"Let go of me, woman." He snapped his arm out of her grasp, nearly wrenching her shoulder in the process. With pounding footfalls, he tromped off a few steps and then stopped and spun around.

"Do you think I'm stupid?" He advanced on her, and Eden leaned away from his dark scowl. "Just because you read all those fancy books don't mean you know more about the world than I do, Eden."

"I . . . I never said—"

"You didn't have to say it. It's written all over your face. You think more of that oversized iron-bender than you do of me."

Eden just stared at him, her stomach churning at the venom in his voice.

"Oh yeah. I know all about his visits to the library. And I seen how cozy the two of you were this morning. Shoot, if I'd known all it took to win your hand was to read a few novels, I woulda done that, too. But I thought you were too smart to fall for a ploy like that. I respected you too much. And now I learn that you think so little of me that you assume I'll march over to where those men are digging and cause a rockslide or something."

The man truly sounded hurt. She'd never meant to insult him; she just wanted to avoid an accident brought on by interfering with the rescue attempt. She opened her mouth to apologize, but the sheriff cut her off.

"Let me tell you something, Eden Spencer, of the high-and-mighty Spencers. I take my elected duties seriously. As sheriff, it's my job to protect the citizens of this town, and if there's a rescue to be made, ain't nobody gonna keep me from doing my part—you understand?"

She managed a nod.

"Good." His scorn melted away in

an instant, so swift it set her off balance. His frown curved upward in a one-sided grin. Then he raised a finger to her face and traced the edge of her hair from her temple to her chin.

An unpleasant shiver coursed down her neck.

"Something tells me you might soon be changin' your tune about that iron-bender. He ain't all he seems. Trust me, darlin'. You can do better."

For a moment she thought he might try to kiss her, and revulsion hit her so hard she had to fight the urge to flee. Instead, he winked and dropped his hand away from her face. "Yep, I got me a real good feeling."

As he turned and left, Eden rubbed the back of her arm along the side of her face where he'd touched her, trying to remove the feel of him from her skin. Unfortunately, it did little to ease her growing discomfort.

The sheriff's real good feeling gave her a real bad feeling.

Chapter Thirty-Five

Activity escalated in the quarry after the sheriff departed. He returned once to retrieve some long boards from a pile by one of the cranes, but that had been twenty minutes ago, and Eden hadn't seen him since. Which was probably for the best. At least for Chloe.

She'd found the girl amid the other huddled family groups that waited for news of their loved ones. Chloe had stood alone, her expression forlorn as her troubled eyes followed every move the workmen made. Aching for her, Eden had rushed to her side and clasped her hand. Together, they watched, waited, and prayed.

All at once, the dark cluster of men outlined against the gray stone shifted. Two crewmen separated themselves from the rest, something large wedged between them.

"They've got them out!" a woman cried as she pulled away from her teenage son and took a few tentative steps forward. "They're bringing them back. Look! They're bringing them back. And the first one's alive! Glory be!"

A murmur of anticipation swept through the group, and the separate huddles merged into one mass as everyone pressed forward to see who was being brought in. Dr. Adams sprinted out to meet the men, his black suit a stark contrast against the gray, dust-encrusted clothes and skin of the workers. The limping man suspended between them was even dirtier, nearly impossible to recognize.

"Is it Pa?" a tiny voice queried near Eden's elbow. Eden's heart broke as she looked at the cautious hope etched into the girl's face.

The child's mother folded her into a firm embrace. "I don't know, sugar. I can't tell from here."

"It looks a bit like my Joe," one woman offered. "He's about the right height."

"All of them are about that height," a masculine voice grumbled. "Could be my boy just as easy as any other feller."

Eden squeezed Chloe's hand, knowing that similar thoughts must be bouncing through her mind, as well—thoughts about how the gray dust could be disguising Duncan's fiery hair, or how the leg held stiffly out in front as the threesome hobbled along could be the same as the one that danced those jigs back in the Hang Dog.

Dr. Adams trotted back to the roped-off area he had set up for the injured. His eyes scanned the crowd until his gaze met Eden's. "Miss Spencer? Would you assist me, please?"

She gave a little start but complied with his request, slowly separating herself from the rest.

"Who is it, Doctor?" the mother of

the little girl called out. "Who are they bringing in?"

As Eden ducked under the rope to join him, Dr. Adams steadied his gaze on the young mother, swallowing three times before projecting any words. "It's Joe Collier."

The mother's shoulders sagged, but behind her, the older woman clapped her hands and folded them to her breast as a tremulous smile broke out across her face.

"I knew it was my Joe. I just *knew* it."

The man missing a son came up to the rope. His weathered hands gripped the strung boundary as if it were a lifeline. "How 'bout the rest of 'em, Doc?" He asked it quietly, but the others must have sensed the impact of the answer, for everyone hushed and pinned their attention to the physician.

Dr. Adams clenched his jaw. "They're coming" was all he said as he took hold of Eden's arm and steered her to the makeshift worktable that had been set up in the opposite corner.

Her limbs suddenly heavy, Eden

stumbled as she followed the doctor. He mumbled an apology and slowed his pace, but it didn't do anything to stop the growing numbness within her. When they reached the table, he released her arm and bent to retrieve a pail and a large speckled coffeepot.

Eden cast a glance back at Chloe before focusing again on the physician as he straightened. "Did the others not survive?" she whispered.

His mouth formed a tight line. "I don't know. From what I could see, the others were being laid out on boards. Could just mean that they're too busted up to walk, though." He didn't quite meet her eyes during that last statement, and that lack stole the reassurance from his words.

But then Dr. Adams lifted his chin and met her stare with his own unflinching one.

"Borrowing trouble won't help matters, Miss Spencer. Borrowing water will. Fetch some from the rain barrels by the corral." He held out the coffeepot and pail and waited for her to fit the handles over her fingers. "I won't know the extent of these men's injuries until we clean away that quarry dust. Looks like we'll be turning some of those bandages you brought into wash-rags."

By the time Eden returned from the corral, Mr. Collier had been deposited in the infirmary area on one of the saw-horse tables Dr. Adams had rigged with some pilfered boards. Mrs. Collier stood near her husband's head, stroking his filthy hair, her forehead bent toward his, the two of them talking softly.

Seeing the tenderness between the couple stirred her heart. Her eyes suddenly lifted to search for Levi's outline against the rocks.

"Miss Spencer? The water." The doctor's sharp voice ricocheted through her. Eden snapped her attention back to the situation at hand and bustled forward. She set the pail and water-filled coffeepot on the vacant sawhorse table to the doctor's left and turned to face the patient. A gasp lodged in her throat, causing her to choke.

Dr. Adams had slit the man's trouser

leg from cuff to lower thigh. A scandalous amount of male limb lay exposed. She immediately averted her eyes only to hear an exasperated sigh from the man beside her.

"This is no time for missish modesty. I need a nurse, not a debutante. Can you manage to assist me without fainting into a heap, or do I need to recruit one of the begrimed workmen who'd likely contaminate the wound the moment a breeze blows across his clothing?"

Years of social training kept Eden's lips closed against the flaming setdown that leapt to mind. Simply because she'd been caught off guard by a strange man's hairy limb by no means meant she was some namby-pamby who would faint at the sight of a little blood. Why, she was the one who'd bandaged Cook's finger when she'd nearly sliced the tip off preparing potatoes for one of Mother's dinner parties years ago.

She stiffened her spine and squared her shoulders. "I'll not faint, Doctor.

Just tell me what you want done, and I'll do it."

"Clean away the blood on his leg so I can see how bad the break is." Dr. Adams tossed her a rag and turned his back on her to question Mr. Collier.

Determined to prove her mettle, Eden gripped the pail's handle and pivoted to face the waiting limb. Her earlier glance had been of the healthy flesh above the man's knee, but now the sight of white bone protruding through bloody skin at the shin made her stomach convulse.

Give me strength, Lord.

She inhaled a deep breath and set the pail on the boards beside Mr. Collier's ankle. Then she dipped the cotton rag into the water and set to work. Each time she pressed the cloth to the man's leg, his muscles would clench, and she knew she was causing him pain. Tears pooled in her eyes, but she refused to let them fall. All her life she'd abhorred violence for the senseless pain it caused. She'd believed that education and enlightened minds would bring about a more peaceful society.

But now here she was, hurting a man who was already suffering. Where was the enlightenment in that?

As she completed her task, Dr. Adams motioned her around to the opposite side. “I need you to restrain his good leg while I set this bone. Mrs. Collier will hold his shoulders.”

Eden nodded stiffly and tentatively placed her hands near Mr. Collier’s right ankle. She met Mrs. Collier’s gaze, gaining courage from the other woman’s fortitude.

“Ready, Joe?”

“Get it done, Doc,” the man grunted.

Dr. Adams glanced meaningfully at both women, and Eden tightened her hold. She closed her eyes and leaned her full weight on the man’s good leg.

Suddenly, Mr. Collier cried out, and the leg Eden gripped rose up against her hand. She leaned more of her weight on it until her feet nearly left the ground. Then a gruesome pop sounded and some of the tension flowed out of the wounded man.

“All done,” Dr. Adams said, his voice enviously matter-of-fact. Eden opened her eyes and released her grip on Mr. Collier's leg, hiding her shaking hands behind her back as she fought to regain control.

The doctor went on to address the Colliers about the serious danger of blood poisoning and explaining how he would splint the leg in order to leave the open wound exposed so they could treat it with a carbolic-acid solution. Eden stepped back to allow them some privacy, only then recognizing the growing commotion from the crowd. Another pair of workers approached, this time carrying a plank with a disturbingly inert form upon it.

"Doctor." The word came as barely a whisper. Eden cleared her throat and tried again. "Dr. Adams."

He cast an impatient look over his shoulder.

"Another man is being brought in."

The physician straightened immediately, frown lines creasing his brow as he took in the sight. Without excusing himself from their presence, he dashed forward to intercept the quarrymen.

"Miss Eden?" Chloe's trembling voice

found Eden's ear. The girl had separated herself from the rest of the onlookers by moving several paces behind the others. Her face was an anxious mask, her cheeks pale, her eyes wide and a bit wild looking. Regretting that she had left her alone for so long, Eden hurried to rejoin her.

"All of 'em are coming in laid out across them boards. I'm scared, Miss Eden. What if Duncan's . . ."

Eden ducked beneath the rope and hugged the girl close to her chest. "No matter what happens, God will see us through, Chloe." She stepped back and clasped the hands of her friend. "Whether this day holds joy or grief, he will be here. And so will I. You're not alone."

"Will you stay with me while they bring 'em in?" Chloe sniffed and pulled one of her hands free to wipe at her eyes.

Eden squeezed her other hand. "Of course." And at that moment she vowed that if Dr. Adams requested her help again, she'd decline. Her place was with Chloe now.

The first trio straggled toward the waiting crowd. Eden and Chloe edged up along the rope barrier to a position where they could better see what was happening. Dr. Adams stopped the workmen several yards out, placed his ear to the prostrate man's chest, pressed his fingers to his wrist, then shook his head and straightened. Without a word to the families, he strode in the direction of the next litter.

Sheriff Pratt held the front of the plank that supported the fallen man the doctor had just checked, and as they neared the crowd, he signaled his partner to lower the board to the ground. He tugged his hat from his head and with slow steps, arrived to face the mother of the little girl. Two teen boys flanked her, each placing a hand on one of her shoulders as she clutched the young girl to her middle.

"Mrs. Dalton. Ma'am. I'm sorry, but your husband didn't make it."

The woman bowed her head, and if she wept, she did so quietly. Eden imagined her trying to stay strong for her children, but when the little girl twisted out of her grasp and asked why her papa was sleeping on that board, the woman crumpled. Her sons supported her elbows as the tight group crept forward to say their good-byes.

The next litter came in, and as the quarrymen called for Mr. Jones, Chloe let out a tiny moan that could have been sympathy or relief, Eden wasn't sure. The older man strode out to meet them as Levi and Mr. Fieldman approached with the final man. The doctor trailed behind.

"Duncan." Chloe released Eden's hand and ran out to meet them. Eden hiked up her skirt and followed, her heart sending a plea heavenward with every frantic beat that thumped in her chest.

Eden tried to catch Levi's eye as she ran, but he was focusing on the ground before him. The grim line of his mouth did nothing to lift her spirits.

When Chloe reached Duncan's side, she reached for him, but Dr. Adams stopped her by gently grasping her wrist and steering it away.

"Best not to touch him just yet, miss.

I suspect he's got several cracked ribs as well as a nasty blow to the head. The less we jar him the better."

Chloe spun to face the doctor, freeing her hand as she turned. "So he's . . . he's alive?"

"Yes. And I'm going to do everything I can to keep him that way." Dr. Adams stepped around her. "Now let's get him to the examination area, where I can tend him."

"He's alive, Miss Eden." The despair and fear that had been etched into Chloe's face for the last several hours gave way to a joyous smile. "He's alive!"

Levi glanced at Eden for a just a second, and a wealth of meaning passed between them. She read his exhaustion and his elation, his determination and his hope. But there was something else there, too. Something intimate and deep. Something meant for her alone. A promise. One that made her stomach tickle.

In a matter of minutes, Levi and Mr. Fieldman had Duncan laid across the second sawhorse table. His eyes were closed, but his chest rose and fell in a satisfying manner. After releasing the end of the litter, the quarry owner turned to face Chloe.

"McPherson's a good man, miss. And strong, too. He'll pull through. And when he does, you tell him I have a stonecutting job waiting for him."

Chloe smiled at the man. "Thank you, sir. He'll be happy to hear it."

Mr. Fieldman clapped Levi on the shoulder. "If you ever find yourself in need of work, Grant, you've got a position here for the asking."

Levi nodded. "I think I'll . . . keep on at the forge for now."

"I understand." Mr. Fieldman glanced past Levi to the families clustered around the bodies of the men who'd not been as fortunate. "I . . . ah . . . better go see what I can do for Mrs. Dalton and Ernest Jones. Take good care of our boy, Doc."

"I will." Dr. Adams already had Duncan's shirt cut open and was busy checking the young man's ribs.

Eden fetched the coffeepot of water she'd filled earlier and brought it to Chloe. "Why don't you bathe his face while the doctor is working. I'm sure it would be a comfort for him to be clean when he wakes."

Chloe accepted the task eagerly, but as she tipped the spout to dampen her cloth, she suddenly stopped. She dropped the washrag atop the coffeepot, then rushed over to Levi and wrapped her arms around his waist, much like she had in the library earlier.

"Thank you, Mr. Levi. You got him out, just like you said you would."

Eden smiled at the picture they made, her giant blacksmith giving Chloe an awkward pat while the girl burrowed into him.

"God got him out, Chloe," Levi said. "He merely borrowed my arms to do the heavy work."

"Do . . . do you think he'd accept my thank-you?" Eden heard lingering insecurity in Chloe's voice as she struggled to believe that God would listen to one such as her.

"Yep, I do, Chloe girl. I truly do."

"Chloe?" A rasping sound came from the man on the table, and everyone jumped. "That you, lass? I'm not seein' ye."

Chloe scurried to his side, taking the hand he lifted a couple of inches off the table. "I'm here, Duncan. I'm here."

Eden and Levi converged on the table, as well—Levi lightly fitting his hand to the curve of her back. She didn't realize how much she'd longed for that physical connection to him until that moment. His touch filled her with warmth and security, making it all the sweeter to see Chloe and Duncan share a similar bond.

"Ah, me darlin' Chloe." Duncan tried to smile, but a cough interrupted him. He grimaced and tried to curl in on himself, his broken ribs surely paining him as the cough worked its way free. Once it passed, though, his lips twitched, hinting at the charming grin that was so much a part of him.

"I dreamed o' ye, lass, down in that pit. I dreamed . . . and I promised meself that if the Almighty saw fit to spare me sorry hide, that I'd be asking a favor of ye the moment I saw yer bonny face."

Chloe lifted Duncan's filthy hand to her lips and pressed a kiss to his knuckles. "I'd do anything for you, Duncan. Anything."

"Are ye sure, lass?" He paused, staring up at her.

"I'm sure."

"Good. 'Cause I want ye to let me give ye a last name. . . . Mine."

Chapter Thirty-Six

Eden smiled to herself as the quiet banter of Chloe and Duncan filtered from the kitchen into the reading room. It had only been three days since the accident at the quarry, but Mr. McPherson was putting his convalescence to good use. Since he couldn't work, he devoted all his time to courting, and Eden had never seen Chloe happier.

Mr. Fieldman had paid to put Duncan up at the boardinghouse for his convalescence. It made it easier for the doctor to rewrap Duncan's ribs and check the stitches he'd sewn into his scalp. However, against the physician's advice, Duncan insisted on getting dressed and shuffling down the boardwalk and around the corner to the library in the afternoons. Not that he cared two figs for Eden's books, of course.

"I think I'm going to try this one." Pearl Lambert approached Eden's desk with her usual mincing steps. The elderly lady fumbled to catch the sliding edge of her shawl before it fell off her shoulder. Eden hurried around the edge of the desk to assist her.

Pearl had been one of the faithful few to continue visiting the library after Chloe's arrival, and thanks in part to her patronage, people were slowly trickling back in. Eden would be forever grateful to the retired schoolmarm for her steadfast example.

"Poems of Passion." Eden read the title of Pearl's selection aloud as she resituated the lady's shawl. "An excellent choice." Eden collected the slender book from the older woman's loosening grip and moved back to her chair. "This edition came out just a few years

ago, and I must admit that it is one of my favorites. I think you will find Mrs. Wilcox's work to your liking."

Eden marked down the patron's name, book title, and date in her ledger, then handed the volume back.

"I flipped through some of the pages," Pearl said as she tucked the book into her handbag, "and the start of one called 'Solitude' struck me as insightful."

"Ah, yes. 'Laugh, and the world laughs with you; weep, and you weep alone,' " Eden quoted. "Her observation proves true more often than it should."

Pearl murmured her agreement and turned to leave. Eden escorted her to the door, then meandered back to her desk, the words of Ella Wheeler Wilcox sitting heavily in her mind.

A muted laugh floated in from the next room, begging Eden to join in with Chloe and Duncan as the poem had suggested. They had all come so close to weeping, it made the joy of surviving that much sweeter. Yet not all were so fortunate. The Dalton and Jones families had just buried a husband and a son. Perhaps she should take the buggy out tomorrow morning and pay a call. She had no idea what she would say, but she couldn't leave them to weep alone.

Especially that precious little girl who'd stood next to Eden at the quarry. Maybe she could take a book with her, one with lots of beautiful illustrations. Perhaps they could find something to smile about amid the pages. Eden crossed to the children's shelves and began searching for one that might fit her needs. Her finger hopped from spine to spine until it landed on a collection of Hans Christian Andersen's fairy tales. But before she could do more than tip the corner forward, Harvey Sims walked in, snagging her attention.

Eden straightened. A little thrill of excitement hummed along her veins as she noticed the gilt object in his hands. "Oh! Did you finish it?"

"Yes'm. Got it mounted and framed just like you asked."

Eden scurried around behind him to

get a clear view, and Harvey held it up for her inspection like a proud papa showing off his latest babe.

"Turned out purty nice, I'd say."

"Harvey, you do splendid work. It's lovely!" Eden accepted the frame as he handed it over his shoulder. Her eyes caressed each bloom as she took in the full effect of the finished piece. The delicate pressed flowers were offset perfectly by the tiny shell patterns in the frame. An image of it hanging on the wall over her marriage bed filled her mind, making her smile.

"I bet it'll fetch an even better price at the auction than the one you did last year." He winked at her and patted her shoulder before heading toward the kitchen.

Her smile slipped a notch before she caught it and fastened it back into place. "The auction. Of course." She'd forgotten for a moment that she was supposed to turn the artwork over to the auction committee at the Ladies Aid meeting that evening. "I do hope it contributes well to the school fund."

She also hoped whoever bought it

lived far away. The bouquet reminded her too much of Levi for her to see it on a frequent basis without coveting it for herself.

As Harvey disappeared into the next room, Eden bent to collect the hatbox she'd been storing her project in and packed the framed bouquet on a bed of cotton batting.

Things had been so busy since the accident at the quarry that she'd barely had time to see Levi. She missed him. He still came by the library at noon every day, but he'd been cutting his visits short this week, explaining that he was working on a special project and needed all the spare time he could arrange in order to finish it. The odd thing was, whenever she asked him about what type of project it was or who it was for, he became elusive, changing the subject or giving vague answers that really told her nothing at all.

After all they'd shared with each other, it bothered her to know he was hiding something. Then again, she was probably just feeling put out because this mystery project was keeping him away from her more than she liked.

Maybe she would invite him to supper. He had to eat somewhere, and if he stayed in town instead of returning to the Barnes's homestead, it would save him some of that precious time he constantly sought, while giving them the chance to be together. Chloe could invite Duncan to stay, as well. And if all went as planned, the extra company would entice Levi to stay even longer.

Energized by her scheme, Eden rose from her seat, intending to warn Verna of the possible guests for dinner. Yet before she could do more than take a step or two, the front door opened. Biting back her impatience, Eden pasted a welcoming smile on her face and waited for the late-afternoon patron to enter the reading room.

A man in a tailored gray suit strolled through the doorway, a silver-topped cane in one hand, a leather satchel in the other.

Eden caught her breath. "Daddy?"

He bent to set his satchel on the

floor and held his arms wide. "How's my little bird of paradise?"

Shock gave way to delight, and reacting much like the child she used to be, Eden ran into her father's waiting embrace. She closed her eyes and breathed deeply as she burrowed her face in the hollow beneath his chin. The smell of shaving soap that clung to his skin evoked feelings of home and security and comfort—of love.

"Why didn't you wire ahead?" Eden asked as she stepped back. "I would have met you at the station and had Verna prepare your room."

Calvin Spencer grinned unrepentantly at his daughter. "You know as well as I that Verna always keeps my room ready. Besides, a father likes to surprise his daughter every now and then."

His gaze traveled about the library as if reacquainting himself with an old friend. However, his brows angled downward when his inspection reached the far corner.

"What is my chair doing out here?"

Eden couldn't help it—she laughed.

Which only made her father's brows angle more sharply. "Oh, Daddy. I have so much to tell you."

"And I want to hear it all," he assured her. Then he arched one of those expressive eyebrows that were just starting to streak with silver and gave her a look she knew all too well, one that made her squirm. "Especially about that blacksmith fellow you wrote to me about."

Levi examined the scrollwork he'd forged that afternoon, pleased with its vinelike appearance. It would frame the letters well, and once he shaped the roses and welded them in, he'd be ready to affix all the pieces to the arch itself.

Eden's Garden.

He prayed she'd like his gift, for if all went according to plan, he'd be proposing marriage under that arch. Levi traced the shape of a veined iron leaf, his blood pumping with nervous vigor as he contemplated the likelihood of a positive response. The first time he'd held Eden in his arms had been in that field, and his arms ached to hold her again—this time offering love instead of friendly comfort.

Levi lifted his hand away from the design lying atop his worktable and reached for the tarp, forcing his mind back to practical matters. Harvey and Verna Sims would have to be let in on the secret soon if he hoped to have the arched entry in place by the time the bluebonnets bloomed. He'd need Verna to keep Eden from running off to her field, and he'd need Harvey's help constructing the pillars and getting the heavy ironwork arch in place.

Fieldman had offered Levi free dressed limestone if he ever found himself in need of it as a gesture of gratitude for his help at the accident site. At first Levi had shrugged it off, but then he realized how sophisticated a pair of stone pillars would look and how much stronger their support would be than the iron rods he'd initially envisioned. When he mentioned the project to Fieldman, the man also offered him a cartload of smaller stones and even volunteered to throw in a pair of stone benches he had out by the cutting shed. The benches were old and weathered but were still as strong as the day they'd been chiseled. When Levi pictured himself sitting beside Eden—her hand in his as she gazed out over her flowers, his thumb stroking the skin at her wrist as he gazed at her—he'd been unable to refuse.

"Levi? Are you in here?"

Eden.

Levi jerked the tarp down over the worktable and hurried out to meet her before she could wander too deeply into the shop. The heavy leather of his apron slapped against his knees, filling him with a level of self-respect he'd never achieved by knocking men to the ground. With the Lord's help, he was becoming a man of honor, a man Eden could be proud of. Maybe even a man his father could be proud of someday.

So why was it when he caught sight of the dapper gentleman at Eden's side, he suddenly became conscious of the sweat stains and char marks on his apron and the disheveled state of his hair? The fellow was as shiny and fresh-looking as the gold watch chain that draped artistically across his vest. A keen reminder of the world Eden came from.

The man met Levi's eye with an assessing glance, one that bordered on disapproval. Levi clenched his jaw and stared back. He'd not slink away just because this dandy thought himself better. A man's character didn't reside in a bank account or fine coat. If it did, that idiot of a clerk who'd been engaged to Eden never would've traded her in for a pocketful of money.

From behind him, Levi heard the familiar rumble of Ornery's growl. The mutt snarled louder as he approached, taking his position beside Levi's knee. It gave Levi a perverse pleasure to see the man's eyes widen as they shifted uneasily to the dog.

His opinion of the man rose a notch as he shifted his stance to place himself between Ornery and Eden. The dog wouldn't harm a hair on Eden's head, but the stranger couldn't know that. Eden tried to step around him, but he held out his arm and refused to let her pass.

"No, darling. Stay back."

Darling? Levi's opinion of the man plummeted.

"Call off your dog," the stranger ordered.

Levi ignored him.

Eden tried to step around the man again, and again he pushed her behind him.

"Oh, for heaven's sake," she said. "This is no way to make a proper introduction. Ornery, hush."

Immediately the dog sat back on his haunches and started thumping his tail. He even whined a bit as if afraid he'd disappointed his mistress—the traitor.

On her third attempt, Eden maneuvered around the man successfully and crossed the dozen or so feet to where the dog sat. She patted Ornery's head with affection, then turned chiding eyes up to Levi.

"Why didn't you call him off?" she whispered. "I thought my father was going to have a fit."

A hole opened up in Levi's stomach. "Your . . . father?"

Eden nodded, her sympathetic smile offering little comfort. Her hand sliding around his bicep felt good, though, and the fact that she stayed by his side gave him the courage to meet the level gaze of the man before him.

Chapter Thirty-Seven

Levi was still meeting Mr. Spencer's gaze later that evening—this time over the dinner table. Eden had pleaded with him to come to supper, and he hadn't found the wherewithal to refuse. Not that he would have anyway. Playing the coward was no way to win her father's respect. And outside of his own father, Levi craved this man's respect more than any other.

"How long will you be staying, Mr. Spencer?" Harvey asked the question as he reached for the bowl of mashed potatoes and scooped a second helping onto his plate.

Calvin Spencer diverted his attention from Levi to smile warmly at the man to his right. “Only a few days, I’m afraid. You know how Marjorie gets when I’m away too long.”

The two shared a knowing look that seemed to eradicate any social barriers one would expect between employer and employee. Sharing a meal was unusual enough, but the two seemed as comfortable with each other as old friends. Eden’s father put on no airs around the Simses, and from the courtesy he showed to Chloe and Duncan, Levi sensed no criticism where they were concerned, either. The man’s censure appeared to be reserved solely for him.

The bread he was swallowing stuck in his throat as he made that observation. He grabbed his water glass and gulped enough liquid to dislodge the doughy bite, then stabbed his fork into the last piece of pan-fried ham on his plate in order to have an excuse not to add to the conversation. While he chewed, he surreptitiously wiped the sweat from his palms onto his trousers.

"I plan to call the town council together for a brief meeting tomorrow, and I'd like to stay for the auction on Saturday. After that, I'll head home to Austin."

Eden retrieved the napkin from her lap, dabbed her lips, then set it on the tablecloth beside her empty plate. "The ladies are organizing the auction items at the church tonight," she said, "but I'm sure they would understand if I cut my time short in order to spend the evening with you. I'll deliver my bouquet and help out for about thirty minutes, and then we can sit in the parlor and discuss whatever you've been reading lately. You know how I miss our chats."

"I'd like that." Calvin Spencer smiled at his daughter with such fondness that Levi's chest ached.

What he wouldn't give to share that kind of closeness with his father, to sit together after a long day, share stories about the odd repairs people brought in to the smithy or trade ideas about striking techniques or fire temperatures. Or maybe they'd talk about something completely unrelated to work—like the fine meal his mother had just cooked or the grandchildren who were chasing each other through the house. His kids and his brother's, playing together like cousins should. Eden reading a book to the youngest ones and glancing up to smile at him.

Much as she was doing now.

He blinked.

"Levi and I have been exchanging ideas on a couple of novels recently." Her face glowed as she looked at him, and then she shifted to address her father directly. "Jules Verne is one of Levi's favorite authors, and we had some spirited discussions on *A Journey to the Centre of the Earth* and *Around the World in Eighty Days*. He started working his way through *Ivanhoe* but hasn't had a chance to finish it yet."

"A reading man, huh?" Mr. Spencer leaned back in his chair, his eyes once again probing Levi. "You don't seem the type."

Levi shrugged. He knew the man was testing him, but he was afraid if he opened his mouth he'd stumble all over his words and end up looking the fool. So he held his tongue and prayed that the proverb about the man who shutteth his lips appearing wise proved true.

"Daddy, be nice," Eden chided.

She scooted her chair back and rose to her feet. Levi tossed his napkin aside and jumped up, as well. The other men stood at a more decorous pace, and for an instant, Levi thought for sure he'd seen Mr. Spencer's lips twitch as if to smile. But he must have been mistaken. The way the man stared at him left no room for levity.

There was no doubting Eden's smile, however. She obviously adored her father and couldn't wait to spend the evening with him. "If it's all right with Verna," she said, "I'll head to the church now so we can have plenty of time to visit."

"Of course it's all right, girlie," the housekeeper interjected. "Chloe and I will manage the dishes, and Harvey will see that Mr. McPherson makes it back to the boardinghouse in one piece. Won't you, Harv?"

"Yes'm." He nodded acquiescence, but his gaze roved to the rest of his potatoes as if he wondered if he'd get a chance to finish his supper before being pressed into service.

"Wonderful. I'll fetch the pressed bouquet and—"

"I'll walk you."

Eden turned startled eyes on him. He knew he'd interrupted, but he couldn't take the chance of her father offering to escort her before he could. After the constant scrutiny he'd endured, Levi craved a few private minutes with Eden. No, not craved—*required*. He was suffocating and needed a few moments alone with her like he needed air.

"Thank you, Levi."

His chest eased a little.

He followed her out through the reading room and to the base of the stairs. She touched his arm, and his lungs expanded a bit more. "I'll just be a minute. I'd like to change into a work dress."

Her silky, deep red skirts swished as she pivoted to climb the stairs. Black lace cascaded behind her. No, her formal dinner dress would not be suitable attire. It certainly made a handsome picture, though, bringing out the red in her hair and showing off the trimness of her waist. Levi feasted on the sight until she disappeared into the upper hall.

"She's a beautiful woman, isn't she?"

Levi nearly choked as his airway constricted again. Slowly he turned to face Calvin Spencer. The man stood leaning against the wall in a nonchalant pose, but his posture didn't fool Levi. Eden's father was poised to attack.

"She's been hurt before," he said in a low voice, pushing away from the wall. "I aim to see that it doesn't happen again."

No longer caring about his plan to remain silent, Levi stalked across the floor, indignation burning hot in his gut. "I would die before hurting her." He ground out the vow through a clenched jaw. He'd not allow this man to lump him in the same category as his idiot clerk.

Spencer didn't back down. "So your intentions are honorable, then?"

"They are."

The man stared him full in the face for several seconds, then, apparently having satisfied himself, nodded once and stepped back. "Very well. I'll be expecting your call in the morning, Mr. Grant. Eden informed me of her plans to visit one of the quarry families after breakfast, so you'll have ample time to convince me of your . . . *intentions* before she returns."

"I'll be here," Levi bit out.

"Be where?"

Levi spun around at the sound of Eden's voice and swallowed hard. "Here," he repeated, offering no further explanation.

She gave him an odd look but continued down the stairs, as lovely in dark blue calico as she had been in red silk. As he looked at her, some of the tension drained from his neck and shoulders. His mouth curved up in appreciation of her beauty, her heart, her spirit. This was a woman worth fighting for.

Eden glanced his way as she descended the final two stairs, and a smile broke out across her face. It beamed with joy and hinted at a future, a future he longed to share. Levi extended his arm and led her toward the hall. She stopped to kiss her father's cheek and assure him she wouldn't be gone long. As she collected her bonnet from the hall tree, Levi met eyes with Calvin Spencer one last time. But this time *he* was the one issuing the nonverbal challenge, making it clear that he would go to any lengths necessary to win Eden's heart. Even beard the lion in his den.

The next morning, Levi watched for Eden's buggy from the door of his shop, and once she passed on her way to the Dalton residence, he donned his Sunday coat and ran his fingers through his dampened hair. He stood in the doorway, staring down the street for a minute, and then inhaled a deep breath and let it out in a whoosh.

He'd debated for a long time last night whether or not to write out his intentions. It would be easier to present an eloquent argument, and he wouldn't have to constantly worry about lisping like a toddler in front of the man who had the power to deny him Eden's hand. But after praying and wrestling with the idea, he decided to forgo the paper. While he wanted to put his best foot forward, he also wanted to stand like a man.

Something nudged his leg. Levi reached down and patted Ornery's head, thankful for the support. He rubbed the fur around the dog's ears and patted his side. "If I'm not back by noon, boy, you might have to fetch the cavalry."

Ornery pulled away and gave his head a shake. Levi snorted. "No? Fine friend you are."

The dog barked a reprimand and padded off to the rear of the shop, leaving Levi with no excuse to dawdle.

As he made his way to the library,

several people nodded to him or called out a greeting when he passed, their cheerful demeanor lending him confidence. The people of Spencer were coming to accept him. Maybe it wasn't so implausible to think that Eden's father might, too.

Verna showed him in when he arrived and led him to a study at the back of the house that he'd never seen before. Mr. Spencer sat behind a large oak desk . . . in Levi's chair. The man had removed it from the reading room and placed it in his study. Of course, it was his chair to do with as he wished, but when he looked up from his papers and leaned back against the smooth leather with a satisfied grin curving his mouth, Levi had no doubt that Eden's father understood the significance of the chair and was using it to gain the upper hand.

The man was only being protective of his daughter. Yet Levi couldn't help wishing the fellow would cease toying with him.

Calvin Spencer stood and gestured toward the smaller chair in front of the desk, his smile warm, his eyes several degrees cooler. "Have a seat, Mr. Grant. I've been looking forward to this meeting."

Levi did as he was told, folding his sizable frame between the arms of a cushioned chair better suited to a woman like Eden than a man of his bulk. Verna excused herself and closed the door behind her, leaving him alone in the lion's den.

"My daughter speaks highly of you, Mr. Grant—as do many of the council members I paid calls on yesterday evening." Spencer returned to his seat, the leather creaking as he sat. He rested his left elbow on the upholstered arm and tapped a finger against his temple while his gaze bored into Levi's. "They tell me you run an honest shop and that your work is of admirable quality."

Levi blinked, the compliment catching him off guard. "Thank . . . thank you."

"Dave Cranford mentioned that you attend services regularly and that your heroic actions at the quarry this week helped save two lives."

"I . . . ah . . ."

Spencer's hand dropped away from his face, and his smile disappeared as he slanted forward in his chair. "You may be a decent blacksmith and handy to have around in an emergency, but what makes you think you are worthy of courting my daughter?"

"I'm not."

The man's eyes widened a bit at the simple statement, and Levi figured if he was ever going to take control of this interview, it would have to be now.

"Eden . . ." *is the finest* . . . Levi cleared his throat and searched for better words. "I've never admired a woman more than I admire your daughter. Her warm heart, her quick mind and love of literature, her nurturing nature, her devotion to the Lord. Even if my former life were irreproachable, I doubt I would be worthy of her."

"So, I take it your former life is *not* irreproachable?" Spencer rubbed his thumb along the edge of the desk in that deceptively casual way of his that Levi recognized for what it was—camouflage for an approaching strike. Nevertheless, Levi met his gaze straight on. He had no plans to hide anything from Eden's father.

"I aimed my life in a poor direction a while back. Turned away from the trade my father taught me and took up prizefighting. Liked the money and the . . . approval it afforded. Had an undefeated record. Then a fellow came up to the line one day, talking big. Looked drunk, but I took him on anyway. Another fellow, a brother, I think, tried to pull the man away, but when the bell rang, he came at me, and I fought. He took a hit or two on the chin and began wavering. I gave him the option to quit, but he came at me again. I walloped him hard, thinking to put a quick end to it. He went down and never got up.

"A judge found me guilty of man—" He swallowed the rest of the word. "I did time, a two-year term, much of that in a labor camp. While I broke rock there, though, God broke me. I realized how my rebellion had led to a man . . .

dying. And to the forfeit of everything that truly mattered in my life."

Levi paused and tried to gauge Calvin Spencer's expression, but the man was hard to read. He asked no questions, just sat there absorbing his words. Levi shifted in his chair, then continued.

"I repented and turned back to the faith my mother and father had brought me up on. Made a vow before the Lord to abandon fighting and to help people rather than hurt them. After being . . . granted my freedom, the Lord led me here. To a new life. An honorable life."

"And to Eden?" Her father threw down the question like a gauntlet, daring Levi to take it up.

Levi didn't hesitate. Holding Mr. Spencer's gaze, he nodded. "And to Eden."

The man's mouth did that nearly imperceptible lift again, but before Levi could decipher its meaning, Eden's father attacked from another angle.

"I've informed my daughter that her allowance will cease should she choose to wed. She will no longer have access to my financial accounts at the bank or at any of the local businesses. You will not be courting an heiress, Mr. Grant."

Levi had suspected the topic of money would come up, knowing Calvin Spencer's history with Eden's previous suitor. What he hadn't anticipated was the ferocity of his reaction to the man's insinuation. He clenched the arms of his chair until the wood bit painfully into his fingers.

"The man . . . lucky enough to marry Eden will be the rich . . . will be rich beyond imagination. And it will have nothing to do with her bank account." Rejecting the chair arms, Levi shot to his feet and planted his palms on the highly polished desktop. "I aim to provide for a wife like a man ought. I wouldn't take your money even if you offered it."

"So you say." The man's unflappable expression set Levi's teeth on edge. "I simply wished to make my position clear to avoid any miscommunication."

Levi turned away from the desk and strode toward the back wall. He stood staring at a painting of a bowl of fruit that probably cost more than he could earn in a year. Would Eden willingly sacrifice all the comforts she had known in order to be with him? He'd dreamed of the two of them as husband and wife, but until the reality of this moment, he hadn't really considered what all she'd be forced to sacrifice.

He could build her a little house out by her field of flowers, just like they'd talked about. They wouldn't have opulence, but they'd have the necessities. And love. They hadn't actually spoken the words, but he was sure he'd seen it in her eyes. That would be enough, wouldn't it?

As the apples and grapes blurred on the canvas before him, Levi replayed that conversation in his mind, the one when he and Eden had walked side by side through her field. She'd not wanted anything large, just a cozy cabin she'd said. With a plate-glass window. It might be a few years before he could afford that, but he'd manage it eventually.

However, there was one treasure he

couldn't manage, one that she'd be lost without. And the only way to save it would be to relinquish a good deal of his pride.

Chapter Thirty-Eight

Eden returned from the Dalton home tired but in good spirits. Helen Dalton had been in the midst of packing and was grateful to have someone to entertain her daughter while she worked. The family had decided to move in with an aunt who lived over in Travis County and they were busy consolidating their belongings.

Amelia, Helen's daughter, showed Eden the path to the creek and the two spent a full hour sitting in the shade of a sweet-gum tree, reading stories and looking at pictures. The girl had climbed right up into Eden's lap without a qualm, and Eden's heart had promptly melted.

After their story time, Eden had offered Amelia and her older brothers the cookies Verna had sent and volunteered to pack up Helen's dishes and kitchen supplies while the other woman helped her boys go through her late husband's tools.

It had felt good to be needed, useful. And spending time reading to a child again brought back precious memories that soothed her spirit with bittersweet warmth. Perhaps she could resume her story hours in the library one day. Or even have children of her own to read to. The thought made her catch her breath as she guided the buggy toward the shed behind her house. A month ago, she wouldn't have allowed herself to consider such a possibility. But now? Now she couldn't seem to stop hope from taking root. It sprouted like a defiant weed, tenacious and wild and beautiful as it blossomed.

When she pulled into her yard, Harvey met her at the shed and handed her down. She left him to see to the horse and crossed to the back porch, stripping off her driving gloves as she went. The savory aroma of Verna's vegetable soup met her at the kitchen door, sending a rumble through Eden's stomach.

"It smells delicious in here." Eden pulled her bonnet from her head and set it and her gloves on the table as she passed by on her way to the stove. She leaned over Verna's shoulder and peeked in the pot she was stirring. "Did you make corn muffins, too?"

"Nope," Verna said. "Chloe did." The woman's proud smile would rival that of any natural mother. "They're in the oven now. Need about ten more minutes, so you got time to freshen up."

Eden turned to collect her things, but Chloe reached them first. "I'll put those up for you, Miss Eden."

"How sweet, Chloe. Thank you." She moved to hold the door open. "I can't wait to try those muffins of yours. I'm sure they'll be wonderful."

The girl shyly lowered her lashes as she sidled past, but nothing could hide her grin.

"Maybe if there are some left over, you can walk them down to the boardinghouse to share with Duncan."

Chloe's face lit up at that, the eagerness in her eyes tempting Eden to laugh.

Her step and heart light, she traipsed through the library behind Chloe, then peeled off toward the stairs. Before she reached them, however, a movement to her left brought her to a halt.

Her father was lugging his leather chair *back* to the reading room. "I thought you told Harvey to put that in your study last night."

"I did," he huffed, straining under the load. "But I no longer require its use, so I thought I'd return it." With a loud exhalation, he dropped the chair into the corner where Eden had set it up for Levi. She certainly didn't begrudge her father the use of his own chair, but she'd come to associate it with Levi of late and had missed seeing it when she came down for breakfast.

Her father leaned against the chair frame, resting a bent arm across the top. "Mr. Grant came to see me while you were out."

Eden's pulse skittered. "Oh?"

"Wanted to gain my permission to court you."

Eden lunged toward her father and clutched his free hand. "You gave it, didn't you?"

"Eventually."

"Daddy." The word came out like a moan. Eden flopped into the chair and looked up at the man who had always been her champion. "Please tell me you did not try to bribe him to leave." Hurt, embarrassment, and not a little fear twined together in her midsection.

"Until you marry, it's my job to protect you, Eden." He chucked her under the chin, like he had when she'd been a girl, and some of her irritation dissipated. "Every day I deal with men who want something from me—political advancement, financial backing, information, social advantage. I've learned how to mine a man for the truth. And when it comes to the future of my only daughter, I use sharper methods and dig twice as deep before I'm satisfied."

"Did . . ." Eden squirmed in her seat. "Did Levi satisfy you?"

"For now." His mouth didn't curve, but his eyes twinkled the way they did when he surprised her at Christmas with an unexpected gift.

Eden grinned and clutched her father's hand, suddenly feeling gossamer light, as if she would float to the ceiling if she didn't hang on to something. "Oh, Daddy. I just knew the two of you would get on well together!"

"Well, I wouldn't go that far," he said with a quiet chuckle. "Right now he probably thinks I'm a devil sent to torture him. You should have seen how incensed he became when I made it clear that he would have to provide for you without the benefit of my money. He gripped the chair arms so hard I thought they were going to snap. It's no wonder the man was undefeated as a fighter. He's fierce."

"But always under control." A vivid image of Levi's restraint when the drunkard had attacked him played in Eden's mind. "He's vowed never to fight again, and I believe him, Daddy.

I've seen him provoked and not defend himself. It's a promise unto the Lord, and he won't break it."

"I think you're right," her father said. "When you told me about his past last night and all the violence that had surrounded him, I didn't understand how you could love such a man. But now I'm starting to see. Your blacksmith was completely forthright about his past, giving me all the details without my having to ask. He spoke of you with admiration and respect, and I sensed deep feelings behind his faltering words. He even swallowed his pride and asked that I allow you to keep operating the library, knowing how much you love it. Offered to rent the reading room from me—and knowing what I do about his bank account, that was no paltry offer.

"Levi Grant is an honorable man. You've chosen well, daughter."

Eden couldn't help agreeing with her father's assessment as she stole glances at Levi from across the churchyard the following afternoon at the auction. Dozens of townspeople and area ranchers milled about, looking over the items that would be up for bid later, but Eden had eyes only for her blacksmith. He stood chatting with Claude Barnes near the side of the church. She was supposed to be cutting the cakes the Aid ladies had brought to sell for a penny a slice, but her hand hovered uselessly above Bertha Springer's chocolate one as her gaze strayed.

How was it that he seemed to grow more handsome the longer she knew him? Did love actually alter one's perception? It must, for where she once saw a hulking brute, she now saw a gentle warrior—one whose arms could bend iron yet hold her with such tenderness she never wanted to leave his embrace.

She hadn't felt that embrace in far too long. Eden bit her bottom lip as she surveyed the breadth of his chest. What she wouldn't give to lay her head in that spot beneath his chin, to close her eyes as his strong arms drew her close, to tangle her fingers in the hair at his nape, to . . .

Her gaze lifted to find his lips but instead collided with gray eyes that were looking directly at her. Levi's jaw lolled open a bit, as if he'd been in the middle of a sentence when he caught her ogling him. Heat climbed up Eden's neck and into her cheeks, but she couldn't look away, not when he was staring at her with such intimate intensity. Then the edges of his mouth bent up, and a different kind of warmth spread through her. She ducked her head and returned her attention to the cake, but her pulse beat so erratically, her hand shook as she pressed the knife into the icing.

Eden had successfully cut three slices and had nearly banished her unsteadiness when a loud thump reverberated across the table, causing the planks to wobble and her body to flinch. Heart skittering, she glanced toward the sound and found a man's hand, tan and long fingered, slapped flat against the wood. The hand slid back to reveal a copper coin.

"I'll take a piece of that."

The familiar voice brought Eden's head up, a forced smile locked into place. "Sheriff Pratt. Enjoying the festivities?"

He stroked his mustache and stared at her in a way she couldn't quite decipher. Then he dropped his hand and gave her one of those grins she supposed others found charming. Unfortunately, all it made her feel was impatience.

"I imagine I'll enjoy myself a lot more now that you're looking at me instead of that ox of a blacksmith."

A retort sprang to Eden's lips, but she bit it back, not wanting to invite a scene. Instead, she slid her knife under the last piece of cake she'd cut and carefully maneuvered it onto a plate. As she handed it to him, she tried to inject as much sugar into her voice as Bertha had into her dessert. "Well, I *know* you'll enjoy this cake. No one in the county can outdo Mrs. Springer's chocolate icing. It'll leave you smiling for a week."

"Well, I don't know about that, but I

can think of something else that would make me smile for a week."

Eden wasn't about to ask him what that was, certain she wouldn't care for his answer.

"Have you seen any auction items that interest you?" she asked when he gave no indication that her silence would successfully drive him away. "I think there's a meal at the café up for bid, and the Fowlers are offering several items from the general store, including a pearl-handled pocket knife and a fishing set with rod, reel, and tackle box. We're hoping it fetches a good price."

"A lawman don't have time to fish, darlin'."

Not when you spend your off hours in the saloon.

Eden busied herself by cutting the rest of the cake, hoping her opinions didn't show on her face. "I plan to bid on Emma Cranford's quilt. She does such beautiful work." Every year Eden picked one item to overbid on so she'd have an excuse to give a sizable donation without excluding others from the bidding. But when she'd seen Emma's quilt last night, she knew no price would be too high. The minister's wife had pieced a wedding-ring pattern out of deep red, brown, and cream-colored fabric, creating a design that emanated a rich, mature appearance that Eden found incredibly appealing. She could think of no better coverlet for her trousseau now that she was being actively courted again.

The sheriff finished his cake and held out the dirty plate and fork to Eden. Eager to send him on his way, she stepped around the end of the table to collect the dish from him. Only he didn't release it. Instead, he captured her elbow and drew her to his side.

"You go ahead and buy that blanket you got your eye on," he whispered into her ear, his mouth so close she could feel his breath. "It'll look good on our bed."

Eden tried to step away, but his grip only tightened on her elbow. Incensed, she stared daggers at him. "When are you going to get it through that thick skull of yours that I'm not going to marry you? Not now. Not ever."

"You'll change your mind after you see the surprise I been working on for you." His cocky tone grated like sandpaper on her skin.

"I have no interest in your surprise. Now, let . . . me . . . go." She kept her voice hushed but imbued it with the command of a shout.

He released her elbow but continued to clasp the plate. She was about to drop her end, no longer caring if it broke upon the ground, when he spoke a final time.

"Just wait a week, Eden. You'll see things a whole lot clearer. Trust me."

She trusted him about as much as she trusted a coiled rattler.

He let go of the plate, tipped his hat, and swaggered away toward the spot where her father and the councilmen were gathered.

Eden retreated to her serving position behind the table and took several deep breaths to cool her temper. She bent to place the dirty dishes in the washtub near her feet, and as she straightened, she glimpsed Levi cutting through the crowd to get to her. Smoothing her hair and finding a smile, she greeted him as if nothing out of the ordinary had happened.

"Would you like a piece of cake?"

Levi peered down at her, concern lining his face. "Are you all right?"

"Yes, of course. I'm fine." She tugged on her sleeve as if it could conceal the evidence of the sheriff's touch and reached for a clean plate. "You should try some of Chloe's lemon pound cake. It's delicious."

Levi stroked her arm, his caress a soothing balm after the sheriff's manhandling. "Eden, look at me."

She did, and all pretense fell away.

"Did he hurt you?"

"No." Eden sighed. What could she say? That the stubborn fool kept insisting he was going to marry her? Such a confession would only increase the already simmering animosity between the two men. "He just became a tad highhanded with me when I tried to hurry him along. When I made it clear I didn't care to listen to the nonsense he was spouting, though, he got the hint and left. The fellow's dense, you know," she said, a teasing lilt in her voice. "It takes longer for him to catch on to things than most."

Levi grinned, but his gaze left hers to seek out the sheriff. When he finally turned his attention back to her, his eyes were glowing with purpose. "Maybe I'll have a piece of that cake after all."

He dug a penny from his pocket, and Eden cut him a wide slice of Chloe's lemon cake. She knew he was only buying a piece to stay close to her until the auction started, but she didn't mind. She liked having him close.

The sheriff posed no real threat to her. She was sure of it. But his intent toward Levi was another matter. Pratt wanted his rival gone and wasn't above using questionable methods to achieve his goal. Eden frowned. Perhaps she ought to be more concerned about that surprise of his.

Chapter Thirty-Nine

It had been nearly a week since the auction, and now that Calvin Spencer was no longer around to scrutinize his every move, Levi couldn't wait to declare his feelings, and his intentions, to Eden. But before he could do that, he had to finish her gift.

So he'd arrived at the smithy by dawn every morning to labor over the remainder of the lettering and floral detailing before tackling his normal workload. He finished off each evening the same way. He hadn't shaved for five days and barely managed to wash out his shirt each night before crashing unconscious upon his bed. Yet as he surveyed the finished product, a new energy surged through him.

"'Tis a fine gift, Levi. Your lady will nae be able to help herself from fallin' into your arms when ye show it to her." Duncan waggled his brows from his bench seat just inside the newly installed arch.

Harvey Sims lifted his elbow from the handle of the shovel he'd been resting on. "If she does, you better set her right back up on her feet where she belongs or I'll come after you with this spade. Don't think I won't." He yanked the tool from the ground and waved the steel end at Levi in a manner that would have been threatening had the man not been fighting a losing battle with his grin.

Levi held up his hands and laughed. "Point taken." Harvey lowered the spade, and Levi strode over to him and gripped his shoulder in a companionable fashion. "Thank you for helping me today." He twisted his head to include the Scotsman in his gaze. "You, too, Duncan."

"Ach, Levi. The only duty I be fit for is running me mouth." Duncan cradled his ribcage with one arm as he pushed himself upright from the bench with his other. "The two o' ye did all the work."

"But you provided the . . . know-how."

Duncan shrugged, then winced. "Well," he said as he hobbled under the arch, glancing up at the ironwork sign suspended between two limestone pillars, "me da always said that knowledge unshared dies. Seemed only fittin' to pass on to you some of what he passed on to me. Keeps that part o' him alive."

"I'm grateful for it."

Not wanting to bruise the young man's ego, Levi didn't offer to help him back to the wagon, but he did position himself at Duncan's side should his assistance suddenly be required. A tortoise could've outrun them, but Levi was in no hurry.

Metal thumped against wood as Harvey tossed the tools into the wagon bed next to the pieces of leftover stone. Birds twittered from the branches of the sister oaks, and Levi's heart sang along as he thought about bringing Eden out there.

Once Duncan was settled on the wagon seat and Harvey took up the reins, Levi thanked his friends a final time and waved them off. The sorrel gelding Claude had loaned him raised its head and stamped the ground with a hoof, obviously expecting to accompany the wagon team back to town, but Levi made no move to fetch him. Instead, he turned to survey Eden's field one last time, trying to see it through her eyes.

The two stone columns stood eight feet tall, centered between the sister oaks that formed a natural entrance to the wildflower field. The whitish-gray stone formed a vivid contrast to the black wrought-iron arch stretching between them, both in color and decoration. Where the stone was flat and square, the ironwork was scrolled and ornamental. Blooming rose branches wove in and out of the frame, serving as a backdrop for the lettering—*Eden's Garden*.

And what a garden it was. Bluebonnets were just beginning to bloom—not yet in their full glory, but the hints of color splashed across the field promised a feast for the soul, one that Levi was eager to share with the only woman he wanted playing Eve to his Adam. To maximize the effect of the spring flowers, he should probably wait a week or two to bring Eden out, but he couldn't imagine waiting that long. No, he'd be asking her to take a drive with him tomorrow.

"Won't you tell me where we're going?" Eden nestled closer to Levi on the carriage seat, anticipation fluttering in her stomach.

Levi grinned at her. "Nope."

She tried to pout like the society girls she remembered from school in hopes of prompting a more informative answer, but Levi's grin only grew wider as he shook his head. Unable to hold the petulant expression in place, Eden bailed out of the attempt with a giggle and leaned into his side. If she couldn't get any information out of him, at least she could enjoy being alone with him.

"All right." She sighed, rubbing her cheek against the edge of his shoulder like a kitten searching for affection. "I'll be patient."

"Keep that up," he said, his voice a little gravelly, "and I might have to pull off the road to ki . . . to get even. Then you'd have to wait even longer."

Eden tipped her chin back to meet his gaze. The heat emanating from his storm-gray eyes left little doubt in her mind as to what form his retribution would take, and her lips tingled in response. Perhaps a slight delay wouldn't be so bad. Levi's gaze dipped from her eyes to her mouth. She leaned toward him, her eyelids growing strangely heavy. A sound that was half-growl, half-moan rumbled in Levi's throat.

Yes. A brief stop might be exactly what she needed.

Clearing his throat, Levi tore his gaze

from hers and once again stared at the road.

Then again . . . maybe not.

Eden sighed at the opportunity lost, but consoled herself with the fact that something special lay ahead. Despite the fact that she had offered him the use of her buggy for their drive, Levi had shown up outside her home with a rig rented from the livery. He wore his Sunday coat and had even found time to have his hair trimmed since she'd seen him the day before.

The man was definitely up to something, and Eden prayed that *something* involved a particular question.

Levi turned the team off the schoolhouse road and onto the thin path she would take when she wanted to visit her field. Lone Oak Hill rose in the distance, and Eden pressed her lips together to keep her excitement from bubbling out in juvenile giggles.

Her field. Could there be a more perfect place for a private stroll, a stolen kiss, and—dare she voice the thought even to herself—a proposal?

Eden wanted to snatch the reins

from Levi and urge the horses into a trot, but she didn't want her blacksmith to know that she had guessed their destination, so she eased back against the cushioned seat instead and scanned the passing landscape for new flowers. She'd spotted yellow mustard flowers and some tiny white fleabane, and was squinting into the distance to determine if the red dots at the base of a rock several yards to her right were Indian paintbrush or Drummond's phlox when the sound of hurried hoofbeats pounding up behind them rendered the question moot.

Craning her neck, Eden spotted a familiar brown quarter horse with white stockings gaining on the carriage, its rider sporting a black hat and a tin star. She groaned. Could the man not simply let her be? She'd told him flat out that she'd not marry him, so why must he continue pestering her? And today of all days.

Sheriff Pratt drew abreast of the buggy on her side and slowed his mount to match pace with the carriage horses. He winked at her, and she bristled. She inched closer to Levi, hoping Conrad Pratt wouldn't be too dense to recognize the significance of the action. But when he shook his head at her as if she were a child who didn't know her own mind, she decided his arrogance must have made him too thickheaded to process such simple concepts.

"Hold up there, Grant. I need to talk to you."

"Now ain't a good time." Levi made no move to slow the team. "I'll come find you in town later."

"I'm not askin'. I'm tellin'. Pull up." All amiability vanished from the sheriff's voice.

Eden's chest tightened. She laid a hand on Levi's arm. "Maybe we should stop and hear him out. Then we can be back on our way."

"I'd listen to the lady, Grant."

A muscle ticked in Levi's jaw, but his gaze never strayed from Eden's. Tension radiated down his arm, making it rock hard beneath her fingers. She hated giving in to the sheriff's bullying as much as he did, but what choice did they have?

With a sigh, Levi faced forward and tugged on the reins. "Whoa there."

The sheriff halted his mount, as well, and flashed an oily smile. "Now, I need you to turn the rig around and follow me. I've got something waiting for you up by the schoolhouse."

The surprise.

The skin on Eden's arm prickled. "We have other plans, Conrad. You understand, don't you?" She simpered at him in the same placating manner she'd witnessed her mother use with great success whenever a recalcitrant guest at one of her parties needed soothing. She even called him by his given name in an effort to melt his resistance. But judging by the chips of ice in his cool blue eyes, the thaw was far from coming.

"You don't understand, my dear," he explained in the condescending tone she despised. "The council members have already gathered, as have many other key citizens. All we need now is our two guests of honor—you and Mr. Grant, here."

Dread swelled inside Eden as her mind scrambled for some way to extricate Levi from a situation that smelled as strongly of trouble as a skunk smelled of stink. "If it was so important that we attend your little gathering," she said, "you should have informed us of your plans ahead of time. It's a little late to be issuing invitations."

"Well, I'm issuing one now." He reached to his hip and pulled his gun free of its holster. He pointed the barrel—not at her, but directly at Levi. "I recommend you quit your squawkin' and accept before things get ugly."

Chapter Forty

Levi's hands fisted around the reins in his palms. Pugilism had always been a sport for him, never personal. But right now, he itched to smash his fist into Pratt's face for the sheer pleasure of feeling the man's nose break under his knuckles.

"Put . . . the gun . . . away."

Pratt pointed the barrel of his pistol upward and used the muzzle to tip the brim of his hat back on his forehead. "Not until you agree to follow me up to the schoolyard." He crossed his wrists over his saddle horn, casually re-aiming the weapon at Levi.

Only it wasn't a clear shot. Eden sat between them. And wedged as he was into the carriage seat, Levi had no way of shielding her. The sheriff might have faith in his ability to hit the correct target, but Levi wouldn't take that risk.

His jaw clenching so tightly his teeth hurt, Levi managed a stilted nod. "Lead the way, Pratt."

The sheriff holstered his weapon and adjusted his hat. "Wise choice."

Pratt circled the buggy, and Levi clicked to his team, encouraging them to follow the lawman's horse. Once the rig was straightened out and the sheriff had pulled a short distance ahead, Levi turned to Eden.

"When we get there, keep out of the way. Whatever trouble he cooked up, I'll handle it. You hear me?"

She nodded, but her eyes held a glazed look that worried him.

"Eden?"

"I can't believe he drew his gun on us." The buggy hit a rut in the road, and the jarring thud seemed to shake her out of her daze. She blinked a couple of times, then focused more clearly on his face. “We’re unarmed, Levi. Why would he draw his weapon?”

“To get what he wants.” And looking at Eden, Levi knew exactly what the sheriff wanted. But he wasn’t about to relinquish his claim. Not for anything.

As they closed in on the schoolyard, some of the tension coiling within Levi unwound. A crowd awaited them, just as Pratt had said. Levi recognized Norman Draper and several other councilmen. Chester Fowler from the dry goods store was there, too, and had even brought his wife. Surely, Eden would be safe in their company. Sheriff Pratt wouldn’t dare pull his weapon in front of Spencer’s elite.

However, as he brought the carriage to a halt and handed Eden down, he scanned the rest of the crowd. They were a more scraggly bunch—out-of-work cowhands, rowdy teen boys likely playing hooky from farm chores, and even a few fellows he thought he remembered from the quarry—men who'd look more at home in the Hang Dog than a schoolyard. As if in confirmation of his assessment, he spotted a couple women from the saloon mingling with the rough set.

Chloe's mother, Violet, clung to Roy's arm. When the barkeep noticed Levi's attention, he bent his mouth to her ear and her head came around immediately. The look in her eyes shouted a warning that went straight to Levi's gut.

"Go wait by Hattie." He put his hand in the small of Eden's back and pushed her toward the council members.

"What's happening?"

He said nothing, his eyes locked on Pratt, who was strutting toward the two groups as if he were an actor taking the stage.

Levi took his eyes off the sheriff long enough to stare Eden down. "Go. Now."

She bit her lip, indecision furrowing her brow.

"Pleasthe," he whispered, the word hissing through his teeth.

A dewy mist shimmered over her mossy eyes a second before she spun away and scurried over to Hattie.

Feeling more in control with Eden out of harm's way, Levi braced his legs apart and waited for the ax to fall.

Having reached center stage, Pratt raised his hand to silence the crowd. "Gentlemen . . . and ladies," he added, dipping his chin in Eden's direction, "you are well aware that I have sworn to protect our fair town from criminals and those of unsavory influence."

He knows.

Levi steeled himself for what was to come. He could feel Eden's eyes on him, but he forced himself not to look. He wouldn't drag her down with him.

"And I honor that oath even when it means turning against one of our own." The sheriff pivoted, gesturing to Levi. "The man you see before you would have you believe that he is a mild-mannered, church-going man. An honest laborer. A hero. But in truth, he's a brawler, a man with no conscience, one who wouldn't hesitate to end a man's life with his fists if there was money to be had.

"You know him as Levi Grant, the

blacksmith. But the prizefighting world knows him as the *Anvil*."

Murmurs worked their way through the crowd.

He used to hunger for those sounds of excitement, for the satisfaction that came from boys looking at him in awe, and men eying him with respect or even envy. Today he wanted nothing more than to be left alone.

Suddenly a woman's shrill gasp cut through the low hum. "Chester! I want that man out of our town. It's not safe to have that kind of brute around our children."

"Hattie, you don't understand." Eden's voice. "The sheriff is twisting things around."

"Be quiet, child," the older woman snapped. "You're not exactly the best judge of a man's character, now, are you?"

The sly insinuation was too much for Levi. He turned and glared at Hattie Fowler until she cringed and latched on to her husband's arm.

"See, Chester!" she screeched. "He's a beast. Do something!"

Norman Draper, head of the council, stepped forward. "Is it true, Grant? Are you this Anvil character?"

Levi stood straight, unflinching, as he met the banker's eye. "Not anymore."

"But you were."

He nodded.

"The Anvil. I hearda him." The awe in the young cowhand's voice made Levi sick to his stomach. "My uncle saw him fight. Said he'd pummel a feller till he was a bloody mess and then drop 'im with a single punch. Stopped fightin' a couple years back, though. Kilt a feller, or something, I think."

Levi closed his eyes against the old shame for a moment, then focused on the clouds above Draper's head.

"A killer?" Hattie squawked.

"I'm afraid so." The sheriff took control of his little play once again. "Killed a man with his bare hands. Did two years in Huntsville for his crime."

"It was an accident!" Eden lunged out of the group and advanced on Pratt, obliterating Levi's hard-won stoicism. He jumped to intercept her, not wanting her anywhere near the sheriff. But before he could reach her, Pratt's buddy, Salazar, drew his weapon.

"Back off, Grant. Your time will come." The Hang Dog owner twitched his gun to the side to get Levi to step away from the sheriff, then aimed it back at his chest.

Eden, however, made no move to back off. She threw herself directly into Pratt's path, and Levi was helpless to do anything but watch.

"Stop this, Conrad. Please. Levi *is* a good man. The fighting is just part of his past. He's changed."

"You knew?" The sheriff's eyes widened for a brief moment, then narrowed into slits. "Why, you little hypocrite." He towered over her.

Levi surged toward them, intent on protecting Eden. Until Salazar shouldered him in the chest and dug the barrel of his gun into his abdomen.

"Let's give them a minute, shall we?"

Levi scowled at the saloon owner but yielded. As he stepped back, he told himself that Pratt wouldn't hurt Eden, not with council members looking on. But the reassurance did little to calm the fever building inside him.

Sheriff Pratt grabbed Eden's arm and hauled her back toward the buggy. "All this time you kept telling me you could never be with a man who made his living with a gun, and now you throw yourself at a man who passes the time by pummeling people? He killed a man, Eden!"

"He's paid for his crime. Leave him be."

The sheriff stared at her long and hard, then shoved her aside and addressed the crowd. "Miss Spencer thinks I should leave the poor blacksmith alone. Says he's paid for his crime. But I stay he still owes a debt. A debt to this town for his deception, but more importantly, a debt to *that* man." He pointed behind the roughs from the saloon, to someone lurking in the shadow of the schoolhouse.

"The man who lost a brother at the Anvil's hands."

Chapter Forty-One

If hate could put on a body and walk around, it would look exactly like the stranger who pushed through the crowd and planted himself in front of Levi. The coldness of the man's gaze sent a shiver through Eden. He slanted his head to the side. The sound of cracking vertebrae echoed in the sudden stillness. He repeated the action in the other direction and slowly circled his shoulders.

"In the interest of justice," the sheriff announced, "I arranged a sparring contest mimicking that fatal bout from two years ago. Tom Goodwin deserves the chance to avenge his brother, and the town of Spencer deserves to see the true nature of the man they welcomed into their midst."

The saloon crowd buzzed.

"The Anvil's gonna fight! Did ya hear?"

"My money's on Goodwin. Look at his eyes. He's gonna settle that score or die tryin'."

"I'll take that bet. You didn't see Grant swing that hammer out at the quarry. The man's tireless and strong as an ox."

Money changed hands, voices rose, and panic seized Eden by the throat. She had to do something—but what? Conrad Pratt was so bent on discrediting Levi that he refused to listen to anything rational. Eden focused on Levi, willing him to look at her, to somehow communicate to her what she should do. But he had eyes only for his opponent.

She knew the toll fighting had taken on his soul. He couldn't do this. They were backing him into a corner. It wasn't fair. Why didn't somebody stop it?

Eden searched the crowd for help, only now realizing the lack of sympathetic faces. Sheriff Pratt had rigged the game in his favor. Dave Cranford, Harvey Sims, Claude Barnes—none of Levi's friends were among the throng. The only person who met her gaze with a hint of compassion was Violet, but she made no move to interfere.

Someone came up behind Eden and cupped her shoulders. "Come, Miss Spencer. You don't want to get caught up in the middle of this mess." Alex Carson drew her back to where the council members stood.

She turned to him and grabbed his hand. "Please, Alex. You must stop this."

"I don't think I can." He shook his head. "The townsfolk feel betrayed. Mr. Grant played them for fools."

"No, he hasn't. The past is just that—the past. What matters is the man he is now." Eden tightened her grip, squeezing the man's hand as if she could force the truth under his skin and into his heart. "Levi's been nothing but good for this town."

"He killed a man, Eden. That can't be forgiven."

"Yes it can!" She was living proof. But before she could argue further, Hattie Fowler let out another gasp.

"Merciful heavens, Chester." She fanned herself with her hand as she sputtered. "They're . . . they're disrobing!"

Eden spun around. Mr. Goodwin had stripped out of his shirt and snapped his suspenders over bare shoulders—shoulders that were nearly as wide as Levi's. Unlike the drunkard who had accosted Levi outside the smithy, this man would inflict serious damage if he were set loose.

Her heart thudded painfully in her chest. *What can I do?* Her mind screamed the question but offered no answer.

Levi hadn't moved. He stood ramrod straight, eying Goodwin but making no move to follow his example.

"Time to show us what you're made

of, Grant," the sheriff prodded. "Make ready."

"I'm not fighting."

He said it loud and clear. With conviction. Silencing the crowd. Hope soared in Eden's breast. Maybe now reason would finally penetrate the thick skulls of the onlookers. It took two to fight, and Levi would have no part in their bloodthirsty game.

"He *has* to fight," one man called out. "We already laid wagers."

A roar of agreement escalated.

"Salazar. Help him with his coat." The sheriff motioned for the spectators to move back and then used his bootheel to draw a line in the packed dirt of the schoolyard. "I promised the men a fight, and a fight there will be. If Grant wants to bleed all over his shirt, that's his choice."

Eden felt reason drain away from the group once again, taking her hope with it. She turned once again to plead with the councilmen. "Mr. Draper, please. Call Pratt off. Don't you see how pointless this is? Levi has admitted his wrongs. What does forcing him to fight achieve? Nothing!"

"It gives Goodwin a chance to right the wrong done to his family."

Eden blinked at him, incredulous that he made such an absurd statement with a straight face. "Pounding fists into a man's flesh doesn't make anything *right*. All it does is make an old wrong worse."

The banker pushed her gently aside. "You're a woman, Miss Spencer. You wouldn't understand."

She stared at each of the council members in turn. "Levi's a man of his word. If he says he won't fight, he won't. Forcing him to face Goodwin will be inviting a massacre. And the blood will be on your hands."

"Your man is built like a mountain," Chester Fowler said. "He won't let Goodwin take him down without defending himself." He patted her arm with such placation, Eden wanted to scream. "He might not want to fight, but his survival instinct will surge and he'll protect himself. Don't worry, dear."

Dear? Of all the condescending, addlepated . . . The man was acting as if she were some hysterical, irrational creature in need of soothing. Didn't they realize *they* were the ones being irrational?

Disgusted, she stepped away. She'd receive no help from that corner. Eden walked toward the carriage, her eyes once again on Levi. Salazar was working to strip the coat from his back, with little success. Levi didn't struggle but neither did he help. He was a picture of dignity. Eden was so proud of him, she ached with it.

The saloon owner finally managed to get the coat off and tossed it onto the ground a few inches away from the rear buggy wheel. Her focus still on her blacksmith, she bent to retrieve the coat. She dusted it off, smoothed out the wrinkles, and held it close to her heart, just as she longed to do with the man who'd worn it.

"Toe the line, gentlemen." The sheriff's call speared through Eden like a dart. She tossed the coat onto the buggy seat and grabbed onto one of the spokes that supported the bonnet, her grip so tight the slender rod dug painfully into her palm.

Without hesitation, Goodwin moved to the far side of the dirt line.

Levi, however, held fast. "I made a vow, Pratt. A vow before God that I would never again fight for man or money. I will not break that vow."

"Is that so?" The sheriff walked a slow circle around Levi, his skepticism palpable. He halted directly behind him and clasped the blacksmith's shoulders. "Well, now's your chance to prove to the good people of Spencer exactly how much you've changed."

In a blur of motion, Pratt brought his boot up and shoved. Levi staggered forward, tripping across the fight line as he grappled to regain his balance. Tom Goodwin's fist immediately pounded into the side of Levi's head.

Eden gasped. She squeezed her eyes shut and turned her face away, the violence making her ill. But her heart wouldn't let her hide. Not when the man she loved was under attack.

She opened her eyes in time to see Levi throw up a hand to ward off another blow. He pushed Goodwin back and somehow managed to get his feet under him.

Sheriff Pratt's laughter rang in Eden's ears. "Now we'll see the kind of man you truly are, Grant."

Shouts thundered from the saloon crowd, the noise increasing with each punch Goodwin landed.

"Get him, Anvil. My money's on you!"

"Rip his head off!"

"Don't just stand there, fool. Fight!"

But Levi refused. He blocked what shots he could and dodged others, yet he never struck back.

The longer the one-sided fight went on, the more unruly the crowd became. The cheers for Levi dissipated, replaced by boos and insults. Those who had wagered shouted out angry threats each time Levi took a hit. Which happened with growing frequency.

Tears ran down Eden's cheeks as minute after minute passed and Levi visibly weakened. His blocking slowed, and Goodwin connected blow after blow. Each time Levi took a direct hit, Eden's agony intensified. Then as she watched, Goodwin's fist smashed into Levi's side. It collided with such force, the resulting thud echoed in Eden's chest. Before Levi could recover, his opponent struck his jaw hard enough to snap his head back on his neck like a boneless rag doll. Her blacksmith, in all his powerful glory, crumpled.

"Levi!" Eden ran to him as he labored to his knees and then his feet. But before she could touch him, a pair of hard arms banded around her middle.

"Stay out of this, Eden," the sheriff growled in her ear as he dragged her away.

She kicked and twisted and contorted her body until she slipped beneath his grasp. She lunged forward and grasped Levi's arm. He wobbled and had to step back to steady himself. Blood stained his face from a cut above his right eye and another from his lip. Red abrasions marked his jaw, and his torso bent protectively to the left. He wasn't going to survive this unhampered brutality much longer.

"Fight back. I can't bear to watch him kill you. Please, fight back!"

Soul-deep sadness radiated from Levi's eyes. Eden knew what his answer was going to be before he uttered a word, but when he spoke, the finality of it cleaved her in two.

"I won't break my vow, Eden. Not even for you."

This time when the sheriff's arms closed around her, Eden didn't fight. As he pulled her away, she smiled through her tears at her brave warrior, lending him the only support she could. "I love you."

"I—" A fist to his face cut off his reply.

Sheriff Pratt tossed Eden back into the crowd. He glared and pointed a finger at the man who caught her. "Talk some sense into the little she-devil, will you, Alex? She's liable to get herself hurt with another stunt like that. Fighting's a man's business."

Eden leapt to her feet, her own hands balled into fists. "But Levi's not fighting! Surely you can see that. He's proven to be a man of his word. Call it off."

"Not a chance, sweetheart. I'm a

man of my word, too. I promised Goodwin a chance to avenge his brother, and I'll see that he gets it."

Just then a groan vibrated through the crowd. Eden swiveled back to the fight. Levi had gone down. Goodwin grabbed him by the hair and slammed his fist into his face. Levi's body flopped to the ground and didn't move. That did nothing to deter Goodwin, though. He reached for his hair a second time.

"He's killing him! You've got to stop this. Please!" She broke away from Alex Carson and grabbed the sheriff by his shirt, but he pushed her aside.

"It's gone far enough," she heard Norman Draper say. "The man's beaten, Conrad. Call a stop to the fight."

"Not yet. Grant's just playing possum." The sheriff crossed his arms over his chest, and no one made a move to do anything. Meanwhile Goodwin continued his beating. Levi's battered body lay limp upon the ground, moving only when his opponent rammed a fist or foot into him.

Eden eased away from the men, her mind suddenly calm and clear. She circled past the carriage, then over to the schoolhouse. No one paid her any mind. They were too busy drinking in the gore of the one-sided match.

A homemade baseball bat and ball lay forgotten against the side of the building, waiting for the boys who had left them there after yesterday's recess. Taking the bat in her hands, Eden gripped the handle and crept forward.

Levi might have promised the Lord not to fight, but she'd made no such vow.

Chapter Forty-Two

Not wanting to think about what she was about to do, or worse, give someone the chance to stop her, Eden rushed at Goodwin from behind, bat raised. The man had Levi by the hair, his arm poised for another blow. But Eden beat him to the punch. She swung the bat with all her might, crashing it across his wide shoulders.

The man roared and turned on her, his eyes glazed with rage. He swatted the stick out of her hand and shoved her to the ground. Eden collided with the unforgiving earth, her grunt echoing loudly through the stunned silence that gripped the crowd.

"Stay out of this, woman," Goodwin seethed.

Eden braced her arms beneath her and met the man's glare. "Where is the honor in brutalizing a man who doesn't fight back? It's no better than gunning down an unarmed man in the street. You're not honoring your brother by your deeds today, Mr. Goodwin. You're dishonoring yourself."

"Don't talk to me of my brother. He had a wife, children. His family deserves justice!"

"This isn't justice!" Eden yelled.

Goodwin growled and drew back his arm. His open palm barreled toward her face. Eden cringed and cried out. A gray blur sprang across her body and latched on to Goodwin's arm. Eden scurried backward on her hands and heels. Ornery!

The dog's throat rumbled guttural threats as he dug his teeth into the man's flesh. Goodwin cursed and tried to shake him loose, but Ornery held firm.

Eden scrambled to her feet as Goodwin leaned down and closed his left hand on the handle of the discarded bat. He swung an awkward arc and glanced a blow off Ornery's head. The dog yelped and fell away, thudding onto the ground. But he wasn't done battling. Ornery shook himself and rolled to his feet. He eyed his opponent, growled, and bared his teeth. Goodwin waved the bat in the air, shouting at the dog to back off. Ornery lowered his head and held his ground. The fighter heaved the bat over his shoulder. Eden jumped forward, thinking to grab the weapon from behind, but the percussive crack of a shotgun pulled her up short.

"Drop the bat, mister, or I'll fill you so full of lead the undertaker will charge double to bury you!"

Chloe? Eden spun toward her friend's voice. Sure enough, Chloe stood in the driver's box of a wagon, a shotgun wedged against her shoulder and a scowling Duncan holding a tight rein on the horses.

The bat fell to the dirt, and Goodwin

raised his hands in the air. Ornery retreated until he straddled Levi, then snapped and snarled at the surrounding crowd.

"Ooooh, Chester . . ." Hattie's voice died off, halting in a thump.

Eden felt no sympathy for the fainting woman, but her heart cheered as she saw Levi's hand reach out to pat Ornery's side. *He's alive! Thank you, God. Thank you!*

"I warned you about that dog, Grant. He's a menace." Sheriff Pratt pulled his revolver.

"No!" Eden cried.

"I'd hate to be putting a bullet in a lawman, so I'd appreciate ye lowerin' yer weapon, sir." Duncan now stood beside Chloe in the wagon, a rifle braced against his hip, the reins tied off around the brake lever. The Scotsman's middle must have been on fire from all the jostling of the wagon ride and the sudden lurch to his feet, but his face betrayed not a hint of it. He looked as steely as a hired gun. "In fact," he said, "why don't ye toss it on the ground and kick it back toward that tree, there. Roy, if ye'd collect it, please?"

The bartender stepped away from Violet and strode purposefully toward the sheriff. He retrieved the gun and promptly pointed it at his boss. "You ain't plannin' on causing any trouble, are you, Salazar?"

The owner of the Hang Dog moved his right hand away from his hip and shook his head. "No. But you can count yourself out of a job after this."

Roy shrugged. "I've been savin' up to buy my own place anyway."

With all the immediate threats to Levi neutralized, Eden rushed past Goodwin and knelt by her blacksmith. She rubbed Ornery's neck. "Good boy. Easy now. The danger's over."

The dog stepped aside and sat down as she instructed, but he remained between Goodwin and Levi, continuing to protect his master.

Eden gently stroked Levi's cheek, afraid to do anything that would cause him more pain. His thick hair was matted with blood and dirt, one eye had swelled shut, and his lip was twice the size it should have been, but he was breathing, and right now that's all she cared about.

"Levi? Can you hear me?"

He groaned and tried to lift his head. Eden uncurled her legs from beneath her and carefully steered his battered head into her lap. He sighed. Not caring who saw, she bent forward and pressed her lips to his temple.

"How fares he, lass?" Duncan's question brought her head up.

"He could use a doctor."

"Jamison," he called to one of the quarry workers in the crowd. "Would ye be so kind as to fetch Dr. Adams?"

The man tugged at his collar and tried to duck behind the man at his side.

Duncan cleared his throat and added a layer of steel to his voice. "It'd be a shame for Mr. Fieldman to learn of yer part in these goings-on, Jamison. I'm thinkin' he might be a tad displeased to learn ye did nothing to help the man who worked beside him to save the lives of yer fellow quarrymen."

The young man backed away, holding his hands out in front of him as if to ward off the guilt Duncan was dishing out. But he made it to his horse and kicked up a cloud of dust in his hurry to get to town.

"And Reed. Find something to bind our friend's wrists." Duncan cocked his head at Goodwin and another quarry worker jumped to do his bidding. "The circuit judge will be deciding his fate."

"Now hold on," the sheriff sputtered. "You can't go around arresting people. I'm the law in this town, not you."

"That may not be the case much longer." Eden cleared her throat, choking down the anger and resentment that rose within her as she stared down the cocky sheriff. "I'll be writing my father this afternoon with the recommendation that the council begin impeachment proceedings immediately. Not only did you fail to protect one of Spencer's citizens, you forced him into harm's way."

Pratt glowered down at her. "I committed no crime here, Miss Spencer. You can't impeach me."

Eden's mind spun, searching for a

logical argument to throw in his face. But nothing came. She glared at him, hating the impotence of such a gesture. The harder she frowned, the wider he smiled, the smugness of it eating away at her.

"What about trying to force himself on a woman?" Chloe interjected into the quiet. "That's a crime, ain't it, Miss Eden?"

Having Levi's head in her lap was the only thing that kept Eden from leaping to her feet as outrage sluiced through her veins. "Are you saying that Sheriff Pratt was the man who attacked you that night, Chloe?"

The girl nodded, her cheeks flaming.

Duncan vaulted off the wagon and charged the sheriff, his rifle held like a club.

"No, Duncan! Don't!" Chloe scrambled after him.

As Duncan barreled past, Eden pleaded with the Lord to intervene. The young man's ribs would never stand up to Pratt's fists, no matter how brave his heart. Thankfully, Norman Draper stepped between Duncan and the sheriff at the last minute and wrested the rifle from the Scotsman's hands.

"Easy, son."

Duncan reached over the banker's shoulder to point an accusing finger at the sheriff. "He attacked an innocent young woman. He deserves to rot in that jail o' his."

"Innocent?" Pratt laughed. "She's the daughter of a whore, boy-o. There's nothing innocent about her."

Duncan bellowed and launched himself over Draper to get at the sheriff. He punched the lawman square in the mouth before two council members pulled him off.

Pratt worked his jaw and spat out a stream of bloody spittle. "Thanks, fellas. It's good to know the council has my back."

"I wouldn't count on that." Norman Draper turned to meet Eden's eye. "Miss Spencer, in that letter, you may tell your father that I fully support the impeachment proceedings."

"What?" Pratt yanked his hat from his head and beat it hard enough against his thigh to mangle the brim. "The girl is lying. She's got no proof."

"I got a chamber pot with a dent in the bottom that'll match your head," Chloe quipped.

Nervous laughter tittered through what was left of the crowd.

Roy stepped forward. "I heard him rake Salazar over the coals for letting the girl escape. Demanded his money back and threatened to close the saloon down if Sal didn't make it right."

"And Levi told me that he overhead a man's voice and a scuffle before Chloe climbed out the alley window," Eden added. "I'm sure when he recovers, he'd be glad to testify."

"Hand over your badge, Conrad." Draper held out his palm, his face stern. "You're hereby suspended of duties pending a full investigation."

Pratt slammed his hat onto his head and tore the badge from his vest. Ignoring the councilman's hand, he hurled the piece of metal into the dirt at his feet and stormed off.

Eden sagged in relief and turned her full attention back to the man stretched out beside her. His breathing was steady, if a bit labored. He looked terrible and no doubt hurt everywhere, but he would mend. Her hand moved to resume its stroking motion over his hair when the less swollen of his two eyes opened and met her gaze. Her fingers froze.

Pounding hoofbeats forecasted the doctor's arrival, but Eden's focus never strayed from Levi. "It's over," she said.

"I know." He tried to smile, but his bloodied lip wouldn't do more than twitch. "Want to tell you . . . got interrupted . . . ." His eyelid drooped, and his words drifted away.

Eden's chest throbbed. "You can tell me later," she assured him, stuffing down her disappointment while her fingers brushed the hair at the top of his head. "It's all right to rest."

"No . . . tell you . . . now." His words were so low they were hard to make out.

Eden leaned closer.

Levi's languid eyelid slowly rolled upward. "Love . . . you."

Chapter Forty-Three

It took a full week for Levi to recover the strength and stamina necessary to walk erect and drive a wagon, but he was determined not to postpone his outing with Eden again. So, the following Saturday he had her in the same buggy, on the same road, headed for the same location—with the same nerves churning in his stomach.

"You're sure you're up for this drive?" Eden's hand lay in the crook of his arm, and she gave his bicep a squeeze. Warmth radiated through him, making him long for more of her touch, for the right to claim her fully as his.

He glanced her way and smiled, the corner of his mouth still tender where the scab tightened the skin. “Yep.”

She smiled back, and the quivers inside him accelerated.

Who would have thought a fine lady like Eden Spencer would ever look twice at a coarse ironmonger like him? Yet even now with his face a patchwork of green, yellow, and deep purple, her beautiful mossy eyes glowed with an inner light that exuded love. For him. A convicted felon. A man with neither wealth nor reputation. A man who couldn’t even properly enunciate her entire name.

A man who returned her love a hundredfold.

He’d be forever thankful for the quarry worker who had seen Duncan and Chloe sitting on the boardinghouse porch last week and casually mentioned the fracas going on at the schoolyard. Had that conversation not taken place, Eden could have been seriously injured trying to defend him, and he'd most likely be dead. Made a man appreciate his aches and pains, when he considered the alternative.

It also made the time he had to spend with the incredible woman at his side that much more precious. Who would have guessed that his little pacifist would become such a fierce warrior when pushed to her limit? Spencer had been abuzz all week with gossip about how Eden had faced down a Goliath with nothing but a baseball bat. It even seemed to overshadow the news about his time spent in Huntsville.

Levi shook his head, a small chortle reverberating in his throat.

"What?" Eden gave him a quizzical look.

"Nothing." Levi couldn't hold back his grin, though, and Eden started looking perturbed. "I . . . uh . . . thinking about the time you got mad at me for . . . trampling that cockroach. Then remembered how you lit into Goodwin with that bat. I found it funny."

The stiffness drained out of her, but she didn't seem to share his amusement. Instead, she sighed and stared out at the landscape, although he sensed that she wasn't really seeing it.

"I feel guilty."

Levi sobered, mentally kicking himself for bringing up the stupid cockroach.

"I'm not sorry for intervening," she said. "In fact, I'd do it again. But it seems like in choosing to do so, I surrendered my pacifist principles. Am I a hypocrite?"

He laid a hand on her knee. "No, Eden. Not a hypocrite. You are a brave, beautiful woman, a guardian of pea . . . of life. You fought only when you had no other option. Truly honorable."

Her eyes searched his gaze, and he looked at her with all the admiration that swelled in his heart. She turned away, unconvinced. So he reached across his body and cupped her cheek, drawing her lips to his. It was a light kiss, intended to reassure, but as they swayed with the rhythm of the carriage, the caress deepened. And when Eden splayed her palm across his chest, desire surged so hard and strong, Levi had a hard time pulling away.

Neither spoke as they separated. Eden's lashes lowered shyly as she dipped her chin, but her arm, hip, and thigh remained pressed snugly against his. A most welcome distraction as he returned his faltering attention to the road.

They crested the final hill, and a sea of blue spread across the field below them.

Eden's indrawn breath coaxed another smile to his face. "Oh, Levi. How glorious! Look at all the bluebonnets. Have you ever seen anything more stunning?"

"Only you."

She tipped her head toward his shoulder, a lovely pink blush stealing across her cheeks.

As the buggy rolled closer to the field, Eden sat straighter and leaned forward in the seat. "Levi? Do you see that over there?" She pointed toward the arch. "It looks like some kind of structure. You don't think squatters have intruded on my field, do you?"

"No." His heart started thumping

and second thoughts started nagging. "I . . . uh . . . built it."

"You . . . ?"

He nodded.

A smile lit her face. Then, without warning, she lunged back against the seat and held her hands over her eyes. "Tell me when we get there."

Levi's brow puckered as he looked from her to the road and back again. What was she doing?

"I want to see the whole thing all at once. Get the full effect," she answered, as if privy to his unasked question.

She looked like a little girl on Christmas morning, obediently hiding her eyes while her parents fetched her present. Levi chuckled.

When the wagon reached the front of the arch, Levi stopped the horses and set the brake. "Don't look yet," he whispered in her ear. He came around to her side of the carriage and lifted her into his arms. She squealed and reached out to steady herself but managed to keep her eyes closed through the process. He set her feet on the ground and led her by the hand until she stood in position. When he released her, she lifted her hands back over her eyes as if afraid she'd give in to the temptation to peek without them in place. He smiled and moved around behind her, tugging her toward him until her back rested against his chest.

Levi ran his palms slowly up her arms, from elbows, to wrists, to fingers. She trembled and leaned more fully into him. He savored the feel of her for a moment, then gently slid her hands from her eyes. "Now."

Eden gazed at the pillars and arch without a word. As the silent seconds ticked by, Levi found it harder and harder to stand still.

Finally, she turned. Tears shimmered in her eyes. "It is the most beautiful thing I've ever seen."

Taking her hand again, he led her through the arch to one of the benches on the other side. As they sat, he kept her fingers clasped in his.

"Eden," he said, staring at their joined hands. "I built the arch to reveal my heart. Your name will forever be the focal point, uplifted by love. And if you would permit me, I'd like to build more with you—a family and a life." Levi raised his gaze to her face, surprised to see wetness glistening on her cheeks. "Eden, will you marry me?"

Her lips curled in a smile that rivaled the beauty of any wildflowers. "Yes. Oh, Levi. Yes!"

She pulled her hand from his and threw her arms around his neck. Joy erupted inside him. He brushed her upturned lips and pressed her body close to his. She sighed against his mouth and tangled her fingers in his hair. Levi's blood heated. He moved in for another kiss, and another—each meeting of their lips making him hungry for more.

God had granted him a second chance at life, and this second life was far sweeter than anything he could have imagined for himself while in the first.

Epilogue

Spring had retreated under summer's advance, taking with it the bluebonnets Eden so loved. But as Levi leaned against the arch's pillar and sipped his too-strong coffee, he had to admit that the yellow flowers that had sprung up in their place had a beauty all their own. Sunflowers and smaller black-eyed Susans dotted the field, waving a cheery hello to him as the wind ruffled the prairie grass.

Tomorrow was his wedding day.

Levi grinned as a second thought followed on the heels of the first. Tonight was the last night he would sleep alone.

He pushed away from the pillar and strode up the trail to the cabin he'd built for his bride. Not yet able to afford window glass for the front room, he'd fashioned a large porch facing the wildflower field, where the two of them could sit together and share the happenings of their day.

Emma Cranford had rounded up the Ladies Aid group and organized a furniture drive. They'd collected enough spare pieces to fill a wagon bed and brought them out to the house. Most needed significant repairs, but he and Harvey Sims had managed to make them serviceable. Two mismatched rockers sat on the front porch; a table, two chairs, and a bench graced the kitchen; and a small bedstead and chest of drawers resided in the room that would hopefully become a nursery one day.

Yet, not all their furnishings were secondhand. Eden kept her parlor set, and her pressed-flower art decorated their walls. She also brought in her chiffonier, bureau, and washstand, but after taking one look at the spindly doll-furniture legs on her bed, Levi had insisted on making a new one for them to share. A man needed a bed that would support his weight and not have his feet hanging off the end. So now, in the center of their room, sat a sturdy, oversized, somewhat crudely fashioned bed surrounded by pieces of more refined craftsmanship.

Eden's mother had been horrified when she'd first seen it, but Eden had argued that the room harmonized perfectly in her opinion. And when she'd looked at him and smiled, he'd seen it, too—a room that reflected the couple who would live and love within its walls.

Levi stood in the bedroom doorway, imagining what it would be like to come in after morning chores to find Eden making their bed. The wedding ring quilt she'd bought at the auction would be rumpled and tossed aside. She'd reach for a corner, and he would sneak up behind her, wrapping his arms about her waist. She'd try to shoo him away, but he'd ignore her and kiss her neck until she stopped resisting. The quilt would fall from her hands and the two of them would—

"Levi? Are you in here?"

He jerked away from the doorframe, nearly spilling the last bit of coffee from his cup. "In the back," he called.

Eden rounded the corner into the narrow hall, her face beaming when she saw him. "After Mother and Father bought us the new cookstove for the house, I didn't expect any other wedding gifts, but last night they surprised me. Look, Levi." She held up the basket that swung on her arm and gestured for him to follow her to the bed. "Look what they gave me."

Thankfully, when she sat, she placed the basket between them. After the direction his thoughts had been running, he needed the barrier. At least for one more day.

She reached into the basket and extracted a cloth-wrapped bundle, her excitement palpable. Eden laid it on her lap and folded back the edges of fabric to reveal a familiar oval frame. "Our bouquet! Isn't it wonderful? When

I was making it, I used to imagine it hanging above our . . . well . . . our . . . um . . . marriage bed."

Eden suddenly dropped her gaze to her lap, and Levi grinned. So he hadn't been the only one thinking such thoughts.

"When Father bought it in the auction, I was happy to know that it would stay in the family. But I never dreamed Mother would guess how much it meant to me, how it reminded me of you and our courtship, nor that she would actually present it to me as a wedding gift. Is it not marvelous?"

"Very thoughtful." Did she know how adorable she was when she was excited? "If you leave it here, I can hang it tonight."

"Would you? That would make everything perfect!"

Yep. Definitely adorable . . . and delectable.

"Oh, and you must see what Daddy gave me." She pushed a folded sheet of paper at him. "Read it."

Levi took the paper from her and

scanned the contents. Gratitude welled in him as he read.

"I don't know if it is even legal to deed over a single room of a house, but Daddy did it anyway. The library and all its contents are mine to do with as I please for as long as he owns the house."

Her father had lived up to his agreement, and Levi would forever be in his debt. Although all Mr. Spencer had asked in return was that Levi make his daughter happy—a debt Levi was glad to make payments on for the rest of his life.

"Your father knows how much the library means to you."

"Yes. Even more now, because it is where I fell in love with the man who is to be my husband." She looked at him, her lips parted in invitation.

Kissable lunged to the top of his adjective list. Levi bent toward Eden. His mouth covered hers. His hand lifted from his lap, aiming for her nape, when a masculine voice boomed from the front of the house.

"Eden! What's taking you so long?

Your mother's growing warm out in the carriage. Hurry along."

Levi sprang to his feet. "You didn't tell me your father was waiting out there," he accused in a hoarse whisper.

"Sorry," she whispered back, fidgeting with one of her hairpins. "I . . . um . . . forgot."

The way she looked at him from the corner of her eye and bit her lip gave him the impression that he was responsible for her forgetful state, an idea that filled him with such satisfaction, he couldn't possibly be upset with her about it.

"Grant?" The man's voice sounded decidedly less pleasant. "Best get out here, man."

Eden rolled her eyes. "We're coming, Daddy." She grabbed Levi by the hand and tugged him out to the parlor.

Mr. Spencer's gaze raked his daughter as if verifying that every button was done up, and then glared at Levi. "Took you long enough."

"I was showing him the gifts you and Mother gave me. I haven't even had a chance to tell him about our outing yet."

Levi squeezed her hand. "Where are you going?"

"Not just me," she said. "You're coming with us."

"But I have work to do here to get ready for—"

Eden shook her head, interrupting him. "It'll have to wait. The train will be arriving in an hour, and we can't be late."

"Why do we have to meet the train?" It seemed like a waste of time to him. Everything was in place for the ceremony tomorrow. All he had to do was add a few finishing touches to the cabin—hang some curtains Georgia Barnes had sewn for him, pick some flowers for the jars Chloe had spread throughout the house—little things to surprise his bride. He didn't want to go wait on a train.

"Please, Levi. You have to come." Those big eyes of hers got all dewy, and Levi's resistance wavered. "I sent away for something special, and it is to arrive today on the train. It is my wedding gift to you. You have to be there. Please say you'll come."

"All right." As if there were ever really any question. "Let me get my hat."

The train rolled in twenty minutes late. Levi had watched Eden pace the platform for the last ten, her parents having left them in order to lunch at the café. But when the whistle blew and the brakes squealed, she ran back to him and pulled him up off the bench.

"Levi, I have to tell you something."

He scrunched his brows. What was going on in that beautiful head of hers? She'd had twenty minutes to tell him something. Why would she wait for the train to actually arrive before bringing it up?

"All right," he said.

Eden gripped his hand between both of hers and gazed up at him, her fidgeting having finally stopped. "Since the day I met you, you have challenged my assumptions and pushed me beyond boundaries in my thinking that I didn't even realize existed. I am a better person because of you."

Humbled and overcome with pride in this woman who was about to be his wife, Levi struggled to find words to express what he felt. "Eden, you are . . . everything to me."

In the background, people had started to disembark the train, and porters dashed to and fro, but Levi kept his gaze on the woman before him. She glanced over her shoulder once, then turned back and squeezed his hand.

"You encouraged me to expand my life in new directions and step out in greater faith. I want to do the same for you."

Prickles of unease skated across the back of his neck.

"No matter what happens," she said, "remember that I love you and believe in you with all my heart." And with that cryptic pronouncement, Eden swiveled around to his side and faced the handful of passengers making their way toward the depot.

Passengers who looked strangely familiar.

Tension immobilized his muscles—all except his heart, which beat an increasingly rapid staccato rhythm against his ribs.

"Levi?" a feminine voice called—a voice he hadn't heard in years.

"Mama?" he choked out, his voice broken.

She separated herself from the wide-shouldered man at her side and ran—yes, ran—to him and threw her arms around him, pinning his elbows to his sides when he failed to release Eden's hand fast enough.

"Oh, my boy. How I've missed you."

Levi absorbed the affection like the ground absorbed water after a drought. "I'm thorry, Mama."

His mother let go and stepped back, wiping tears from her cheeks yet smiling as wide as he'd ever seen. She patted his face like she had when he'd been a boy, and that simple gesture seemed to erase all the poor choices he had made since then and offered him a place back in her good graces. She looked him up and down, then apparently satisfied that he hadn't wasted away while they'd been apart, she turned her attention to Eden.

Leaning forward, she hugged Eden with the same enthusiasm with which she'd hugged him. "Thank you, dear girl. Thank you for giving me back my son."

Levi didn't catch the rest of what she said, for a shadow fell across his face, and he sensed another's presence. His father. The man stood before him, his face more haggard than Levi remembered, his hair grayer around the temples, his eyes full of regret.

This was what he'd feared, why he'd never gone home, never even sent a letter. His father's disappointment cut through him like a blade.

"I don't warrant it, Pop, but I beg you to forgive me."

His father just stood there, not saying a word. He pulled his hat from his head, and stared at the ground for a moment. When he finally looked up, his eyes were suspiciously bright.

"I . . . uh . . . hear you got a shop of your own, nowadays." He coughed as if something had lodged in his throat. "Care to show your old man around?"

His eyes dampening, Levi nodded. "I'd like that, Pop." Holding his breath, he reached out and clasped his father's shoulder. Not only did the man not flinch, he clasped Levi's arm in return. The grip of acceptance.

His father stepped close, his low murmur vibrating in Levi's ear. "If your choice in bride is any indication, son, you've gained a great deal of wisdom in the last few years. I'm proud of you."

Levi swallowed hard, the words he feared never to hear again falling like a healing balm upon his soul. His gaze sought out the woman who'd made it all possible and found the mossy green eyes he loved so well.

He mouthed the words *thank you.* She replied with a silent *I love you.* And Levi's heart shouted his joy to the heavens.

About the Author

KAREN WITEMEYER holds a master's degree in Psychology from Abilene Christian University and is a member of ACFW, RWA, and her local writers' guild. She is the author of *A Tailor-Made Bride*, which was honored as one of the Best Western Romances of 2010 by the Love Western Romances Web site. *To Win Her Heart* is her third novel. Karen lives in Abilene, Texas, with her husband and three children.